D1490846

Laws
of
Migration

J. SUZANNE FRANK

**TYRUS
BOOKS**

F+W Media, Inc.

Published by
TYRUS BOOKS
an imprint of F+W Media, Inc.
10151 Carver Road, Suite 200
Blue Ash, Ohio 45242
www.tyrusbooks.com

ISBN 10: 1-4405-5773-X
ISBN 13: 978-1-4405-5773-6
eISBN 10: 1-4405-5774-8
eISBN 13: 978-1-4405-5774-3

Printed in the United States of America.

10   9   8   7   6   5   4   3   2   1

This book is available at quantity discounts for bulk purchases.
For information, please call 1-800-289-0963.

To Hanne and Sydney:
For sharing your magic attic, hosting milestone celebrations, asking
"what is your kidnapping talent?" and so much more. Much love
and many thanks!

❖

To Scott . . . our first

Acknowledgments

There are a lot of thanks surrounding this book: Scott Henry, for taking this adventure with me and opening doors I didn't even see; Mathias Dubilier, as a first line reader and compassionate advocate for Elize; Kate Defrise, for endless encouragement; Melanie Wilson, who always adds heart; Peter Larsen, for highlighting my best; Amanda Lynn Swanson for beauty, especially in the map; Jenny Timberlake-Bellamy, for cheering so loud; Ben LeRoy and the team at Tyrus Books, for the chance, the support, and the beautiful book; Ashley Myers, my editor, who understood and improved Elize; and underscoring it all, Daniel J. Hale—who believed without ceasing. Thank you!

A list of the people who encouraged, stimulated, and refined this story, these characters, and their creator could fill another chapter. To the ladies in my writers group in Port Aransas, the volunteers at the Rockport-Fulton HummerBird Celebration, all the birdwatchers who offered insight, experience, and stories along the way, the lovely Moroccans who graciously opened their homes, the fellow travelers who provided expertise and inspiration, my students at The Writer's Path at SMU whose trust and faith is humbling and inspiring, and my parents who always pray for me, I say thank you.

Though writing itself is a solo act, because of you all I was never alone. Thank you all for being a part of my flock/covey/bazaar of support!

If you would like to know more about how to support the ongoing efforts to save the Northern Bald Ibis, visit: *www.iagnbi.org*.

Prologue

Somewhere in the Gulf of Mexico yet another tropical storm brewed, undecided which path it would spin its destruction. But on this Friday the thirteenth, in the Texas coastal town of Port Rockton, the sky was clear and the waves gentle.

Three women sat dockside at a waterfront café, lunching under a September sun.

The tall blonde, Elize, was deeply tanned and fit. The lines around her eyes hinted she'd spent her life watching, staring, waiting, and squinting while doing it.

She wore a dark, fitted suit, but had shucked the jacket the moment they stepped outside, revealing that her businesslike blouse was, in fact, a halter top. Moving with an athlete's grace, she slipped off her shoes the moment she sat down.

She ordered without opening the menu or looking at the waiter, her bare hand resting on expensive binoculars—bins—her Oakley-shielded gaze scanning the nearby trees.

Her pedicure was zebra-striped.

A punk fantasy of a pre-Raphaelite Madonna, tall and big-boned with opalescent white skin and a web of red-gold curls—Zephyr—sat down next to the blonde. A skull medallion hung from a black velvet ribbon around her neck. Red ruffles cascaded down the front of her denim skirt, and a hint of tulle brushed the tattoo climbing up the back of her leg. She carried two bags: a utilitarian Gore-Tex rucksack with Eastern, Western, and Caribbean field guides and two pairs of binoculars in it; and a 1960s doctor's bag stuffed with the latest phone, SPF 100 sunscreen, and Chanel red lipstick.

She flipped through the menu before ordering, and smiled at the waiter, all the while exchanging waves with many of the other patrons.

The third woman—Frankie—was the youngest, and conventionally, the prettiest. Her suit was delicate, expensive, and tailored; her shoes and bag were the latest style, even if the spindly heels were incongruous with the dirt trails and stony paths she frequented. Her bag couldn't fit even one pair of binoculars.

She had perfect teeth, perfect skin, and a perfect nose. Where the others were tall, with muscles that moved just beneath their skin, she was petite and curvy, boasting the hip-to-waist ratio statistically guaranteed to drive men mad—a number that she both knew and worked hard to maintain.

She contemplated the menu, queried the waiter, pondered some more, and finally ordered soup with a tinge of regret in an accent that came from the around the Great Lakes.

The redhead raised her glass of tea in a proposed toast, and the other two joined her. "To today's life-changing potential," she said, her accent vacillating between deep southern drawl and Brooklyn growl, the accent of native New Orleans.

The three clinked glasses.

This is the scene you would look down on if you were watching from a bird's-eye view.

As a bird you would know that who they were, where they worked, what they did, was all about you. They counted your movements, they protected your habitats, they observed your birth, life, and death, and then recorded it.

All three were ornithologists.
All three were single.
All three had expectations, ambitions, and wounded hearts.
And this was their last moment of peace. Storms were coming.

Elize

The Surprise

"So what *is* your kidnapping talent?" Zephyr asked, twisting her hair up and away. I counted silently as it uncoiled, *Ten, nine, eight* . . . She's been my assistant for years and I've never seen her hair hold.

It sprang free.

"I didn't know at lunch," I said, waiting in the foyer, flipping through the *Audubon* magazine I'd read at least a dozen times, "and I don't know now." Why was she keeping on about this? Where was her adult ADD when I needed it? I resisted the urge to look at my watch. Instead, I counted: five *b*'s in the title of the article, three *c*'s. I already knew there were nine windowpanes, and fourteen ceiling tiles. I'd sat in this room many times before.

The board would buzz me in when they were ready.

This interview was just a formality. I was the natural for the job. I'd been here the longest. I was a native Texan, and had gone to school locally. I knew these birds. I'd managed this place when it was just some windows, some pathways, and a bird-loving old man.

Director of the Woodrow Wilkerson Institute for the Study of Ornithology. I saw the words in my mind—noticing all the *o*'s—seven. Actually, I saw them embossed on a door in a lovely gilt script. But I was careful to keep my expression blank. *Never let them know what you want. Then they can take it away.* Pop's voice was never too far from my mind.

I glanced up at Zephyr, seated at her desk opposite. "Be useful," I teased. "Check your Magic Eight Ball."

"To see if you're going to be kidnapped?"

I sighed and tossed the magazine on the coffee table. "I'm going to Morocco to see migration season. Birds, not people. Not the Moroccans and certainly not the, the carpet people you talked about earlier."

"Berbers are not carpet people," she said, picking up the black plastic ball she had more faith in than she did insurance agencies. "Berbers are one of the tribes. They're incredibly hospitable, but have a rigid social structure. If you take one cup, then you have to take three cups of tea with them." She looked at me over the edge of her rhinestone-rimmed glasses. "Elize, you really should read about the place and the people. It's a whole other, wonderful, fascinating, world of—"

"I'm not going to see tribes. I'm going to see—"

"Doctor San Diego," she muttered beneath her breath.

"Just shake the damn ball," I said with a chuckle, and picked up the magazine again. "Ask it how the interview will go. Not about kidnapping." I tried to ignore the image of the tall, blond, and essentially perfect Dr. Sam Donaldson, AKA Dr. San Diego, from my mind. He smiled and waved before vanishing.

"Will Elize get what she wants?" Zephyr asked, then shook the ball.

The buzzer on the intercom went off. My hands suddenly seemed sticky. My skirt looked wrinkled. I'd waited so long for this moment, and now I felt unprepared.

Zephyr stared at the ball, then looked over at me with wide eyes. "You're on."

I stood, smoothed my skirt, straightened my jacket, and strode forward. This was it: a decade and a half of working and sweating and waiting, about to pay off. The opportunities I'd bypassed, the deadlines I'd let fade, all in favor of staying here, of waiting for my chance, my reward.

It had arrived, at last. I was going to be director, at forty.

My heels sank in the plush carpet and I missed my Birkenstocks. I opened the doors and stepped inside the Library.

No, really, it was a capitalized *L*.

Three men with bad suits, bad hair, bad bodies, sat behind a carved table, before the ceiling-to-floor ornithological library that I'd helped catalog. My chair, a fold-up no less, faced them. Adversarial positioning at its finest. These men were all idiots, but, I acknowledged, they were the idiots in charge.

For the moment.

We went through the motions of greeting, with its competitive handshaking and teeth baring, and only then was I invited to sit down.

They didn't even mention the one detail in this process that worried me. Instead they praised my accomplishments, they applauded my dedication. Then, as if in the hush of a secret, they apprised me of the new situation: was I aware the Institute had just received new funding?

I nodded. Who did they think had written the grant proposal?

Well, they continued, since I was obviously aware that the new funding allowed for a position of full-time director, was I also aware that the Institute would be open full-time to the public? Much of the director's responsibility would be dealing with the public and educating them about our "avian friends."

Mrs. Darnells, I thought with a grimace, that species of birder who never passed the beginning stage. They couldn't remember a detail for five minutes or understand how to look at a bird. Age, gender, and nationality didn't matter; they were a slow menace. The Institute would host hundreds of Mrs. Darnells. Thousands, even. That was the plan.

But I smiled. Delegating is the key to good leadership, right? The job of carting around a bunch of birding newbies and Mrs. Darnells would be delegated, and fast. Once she learned her birds, Frankie would be great at dealing with them. I'd hired her because, despite her Easter-egg-colored wardrobe, I had faith in her ability to be a useful staff member. I had faith she'd do all of the stuff I hated, like dealing with people.

So far, so good. She'd gone to the dinners, been on local radio, started the Internet stuff, left me time to research and watch the birds, which was what the Institute—what Mr. Woodrow Wilkerson —had been about.

The Woodrow Wilkerson Institute, the Dubya, was a rarity on so many fronts. First, for our habitats. Because we were an island, we had shore birds: pelicans, seagulls, terns, plovers . . . the list was enormous. Because we had marsh, too, we got herons and cranes, gallinules and egrets. As a barrier island, we were the first landing spot for a lot of migrants, which made spring and fall a joy of surprises like brightly colored buntings and warblers. We also had a palm forest and a freshwater creek, and were *the* place in the U.S. where the White-faced and Glossy Ibises crossed habitat.

The ibises—my area of expertise and my great love, which Mr. Woodrow had shared. I smiled at the memory.

"Which is one of the reasons why—" Wilkerson Jr., Mr. Woodrow's rich playboy son, said.

Here it comes, I thought. *Finally! Finally!* I bit the inside of my cheek to restrain my welcoming smile.

"—we're offering you the position of assistant director."

I started to smile, but my face froze.

Junior was still talking. His mouth was moving, but I didn't hear anything.

"Assistant?" I said. Croaked. Surely . . . surely I hadn't heard correctly? Fifteen years in this place, and I was offered *assistant*? I'd been Mr. Woodrow's right hand. *No. Not right. Impossible.*

He swallowed, and I watched his Adam's apple moving above his shirt collar. "We feel that Doctor Stein—"

"Doctor Stein? Frankie, that Doctor Stein?" No wonder she hated her mother.

"She has a wonderful way with the public," one of them said.

"Yeah," I said, using my most modulated, reasonable tone, "but she's fresh out of school, and—"

"*She* received her PhD," Wilkerson said, simpering.

Dammit, they had taken that into consideration. I had *two* master's degrees in the field of biology. Shouldn't that equal a doctorate? I exploded to my feet. "She's twenty-five, she's from Michigan and she . . . she's a taxonomist! The only birds she knows are dead ones!"

Wilkerson was standing now, too.

Assistant director? Under her? Subservient to my *hire*?

I had to get away. The door slammed behind me, and my heels punched holes in the pile as I walked down the hall.

"No!" Zephyr, already standing at her desk, called after me. "Elize, wait!"

"What, your Magic Eight Ball didn't clue you in that I was getting the shaft?" I shouted. I spun around and we stood almost nose to nose. My sense of betrayal choked me as I realized she'd been waiting. "You knew? You had to know! You little . . . "

I turned my back on her and threw open Frankie's door.

The flowers were the first thing I saw. An enormous bouquet, with "Congratulations" sticking out of it in some nonrecyclable plastic. The bouquet was all *my* favorite flowers: hydrangeas and iris and eucalyptus. Did this girl have nothing of her own?

Frankie jumped to her feet, fortressed behind her desk. Scared. Good.

Times like this, it helped to have a reputation for a temper.

"I hired you," I said, almost too angry, too hurt, to look into her big blue eyes. They were wide, still playing the innocent. "I picked you out of all the applicants because you were female, and I was supporting the limited sisterhood available in this field. And you do this?"

"Elize, I . . . I didn't know." She moved her hands in protest, but still graceful, still . . . acting.

I glanced at the bouquet. "You expect me to believe that when you have proof that you did in fact know, sitting on your desk! How stupid do you think I am?" My voice sounded loud. "Was this the reason for the short skirts and heels, even when walking through the habitat?" My gaze moved beyond her for a moment, out into the sky and the sea where autumn sunlight washed everything clean.

The gilt, scripted word "Director" was erased from the door of the office in my mind, and "Assistant" was scrawled in its place. By a four-year-old. With chalk.

I'd lost. All the waiting, for nothing. Nothing to show for it. Forty years old, and fucked over. The phone call this morning was just another bridge forever burned to me, another door slammed shut, and now this? I felt Zephyr holding on to my arm as Frankie talked.

Outside, behind the little betrayer, a line of brown pelicans swooped down over the palms, flying toward the shore. As always, the introduction to Wagner's *Ride of the Valkyries* swelled in my mind as the birds dropped, one by one in a line, low over today's bright blue water. I interrupted Frankie. "You know what you are?" I said, sick of her words, her posturing, her protesting.

"What?"

"A thieving, deceiving, manipulative misogynist," I said. "In heels!" It wasn't enough. "You're nothing but a blue jay!" Not the best fit with misogynist, but God, how embarrassing this was.

Never let them see they got you. Never back down.

I'd been beat out by a pastel-suited socialite who probably couldn't identify a Laughing Gull if it still had a heartbeat and guts. I had to get out of here.

Once in my own office, I saw the white ibises eating. The creek they preferred ran right by my window. A few egrets and herons had joined them, and they were all pleasantly occupied, searching for lunch. I laid my forehead against the glass. My skin was burning hot and my lunch of fish tacos simmered in my stomach, seasoned with the bile of anger and humiliation.

How was I going to face this down? Port Rockton was a small, incestuous town. Everyone would know, everyone would comment. No matter where I went, they would be talking about me. Feeling sorry for me. Laughing at me.

And then, when the news about . . . him . . . got out, when some enterprising reporter connected the pieces, the name, the estranged daughter . . . that gossip would be worse than anything they could say about losing the directorship. It would also probably be true.

In a quick glance I counted the pieces of posterboard on my wall: seven.

The number of *o*'s on the pages of the tabloid about an international artist's surprising death: seventeen. Three chairs in the office. Four windowpanes. Nine shelves, each holding twenty-two books. Six books on my desk. Four pairs of shoes in my desk drawer— though counting what I couldn't see was cheating.

I leaned against the window, looking at the birds again.

Fly away.

Leave early.

It was the answer. To all the problems. Hell, even Mama was finally getting out of the country before the reporters descended. Taking one of her Lutheran ladies' group friends and flying the coop on a trip she'd always dreamed of, but had never taken. I could do the same.

I had the vacation days. I could drive out of here right now and not have to deal with anything until after my Morocco trip. A whole three weeks.

Then, if I still wasn't ready to come back, I could take another week or two of vacation. Because the needs of the Institute came first, I hadn't taken vacation. For years. I'd waited, knowing that my time would come and my persistence would pay off. Mr. Woodrow had picked me, straight out of school. I was his choice. It would all pay off.

Yeah, well, no good deed goes unpunished. This was loyalty for you. I looked down to see a magazine cover of an icy-eyed man in artist-black crumpled in my fist. I dropped it in the trash, trying not to look.

My brain felt like a fishing lure was lodged inside, with an insistent pro on the other end, tugging.

I grabbed a bag and threw things in: stuff for the trip, stuff I might need just in case: field guides, my kit of sunscreen/lip balm/bug spray.

"Elize?" Zephyr cracked open my door. "Doctor San Diego on line one."

I nodded without turning around, and waited until she closed the door. Smoothing my skirt, I sat down in my chair and watched the flashing red light. I'd rather be dead than admit what had just happened.

Dead. I shook my head, dislodging the thought.

Six *f*'s on the second page of a different celebrity rag.

I pressed the button, pleased to see my finger was steady. "Sam," I said. My voice even sounded normal.

"How is the Birdiest City?" he asked, his tone chagrined. Nearby Corpus Christi had just swiped the national title back from San Diego. The honor of "Birdiest City" bounced between them, and was a reliable conversation starter among birders. A certified polarization point.

Of course, Sam and I were more than birders. We were professionals.

Assistant. After fifteen years. The fisherman tugged harder, drawing a headache toward my ear with a whine.

"Are you ready?" Sam asked. Coming from Sam, it could mean several things.

"Born ready," I said. Any breathiness in my voice was intentional. Sam and I were more than colleagues. Morocco would be a steamy conclusion to what had begun in Miami three years ago.

He waited a beat. "Well, I've got the last little bit of ticket info. We're meeting in New York, right?"

Did I tempt Fate and agree, with the ways things had gone today? Zephyr might love Friday the 13th, but now I hated it. I'd certainly remember it as one of the worst days in my life.

"You *are* going to show, aren't you?" he asked. "Stay?"

My last attempt to get away for a birding trip had ended disastrously with the beginning of the end for Pop. But this time Mama was on a cruise. Safe. We were rats, all leaving the sinking ship.

H.M.S. *Fischer* had gone down alone.

Yeah, and H.M.S. *Elize* was sinking, too.

If Sam knew I'd lost the position of director, which everyone had assumed I'd get, he'd think I was a loser. Know I was a loser.

My stomach fell: I *was* a loser. As quickly as gossip flew around our small professional community, the news was probably already posted. Why make out, or do anything else, with someone who was incompetent enough to be demoted below a *taxonomist* who specialized in DNA and blood types? For an institution that dealt with live birds!

"Of course," I said. A thought occurred to me. "I was thinking about going a few days earlier. Get a chance to catch up on my jet lag before getting to Morocco." I'd never been to Europe. I'd always waited for an invitation, waited for an escort. But I couldn't stay here now. "Maybe spend two extra days in Paris?"

Since I wasn't getting the job, I wouldn't be getting the pay raise that went with the new job. I'd hoped for that money. I'd counted on it.

I was apparently not going to inherit anything, either.

"Paris, hmm?" Sam said, his voice taking on an edge that reminded me that Paris was allegedly for lovers. "Sounds very appealing."

A cough. I turned to see Zephyr standing in my doorway. I couldn't say she was ashen—she's the whitest thing I've seen this side of an egret—but something was up. Oh. Frankie stood behind her. I spoke quickly into the phone. "Sam, we'll talk later."

I hung up.

They waited on the threshold. "Yes? What do you and the thieving blue jay, who steals other people's jobs and runs them out of their nests, have to say?"

Frankie stepped forward. Despite my comment, she wore a smile. The kind of smile customer service wears when they're not going to help you. "Elize," Frankie said, "I think I have some news that might change your plans."

"You don't appear to be struck by lightning," I said, "so I guess not."

"It's about Morocco."

My glance dashed to Zephyr. *Never let them see they got you.* She looked sick. "Yes?" I said, walking around to the front of my desk and leaning back on it, crossing my arms.

Frankie gestured, indicating helplessness, loss of control, or possibly doom. "Since you didn't make director, you don't have the budget or the authority to travel under the auspices of the Wilkerson Institute."

I held very still, so that the pieces of my falling world wouldn't stab me further as they crashed around me.

"The Morocco trip," Frankie pontificated, "was chosen specifically for building networking relationships between this institute and various other similar organizations throughout the world."

"The trip was for migration season," I said through my teeth. "Observing birds, not networking with people. You might not recall, but the birds are what *ornithology* is about."

"Well," Frankie said, "I won't be going in your stead, so the ticket will be refunded to us, although the nonrefundable deposit will, I guess, be a wash." Then she said, with a killing smile, "We won't make you reimburse us."

Frankie had been here for all of five months.

She came the day the witch moth showed up, a detail that Zephyr of signs-and-wonders had noticed. In Jamaica, where Zee had done her internship, the witch moth was associated with death and destruction. Witch moths only rarely invade Texas, and the Mexicans feel they are harbingers of evil. When it, and she, arrived on our island, I guess I should have paid more attention.

Frankie had been "director" for less than fifteen minutes, yet already she was "us" and I was alone. Waiting for nothing. No one waiting with me. Or for me. I swallowed hard.

Frankie's suit had six buttons in the front, a double row of trim on each lapel. Each shoe had six dips in the design of one color atop another. Her Tiffany necklace had fourteen links on each side of the silver heart.

I didn't move.

"I know you wanted to take this trip, Elize. Perhaps another year?" She slipped out and Zephyr closed the door behind her.

"I'm so sorry," Zephyr said, stepping forward.

I warded her off. No directorship, no trip. No future? My mind reeled, and my limbs screamed for a run, for the stretch and the freedom of it. Out of here.

No family. No past that could be healed. No tomorrows.

I forced my arms to unbend, my body to lean forward and off the desk.

"Maybe there's another way," Zephyr said. "Though . . . it would be your money."

I glanced at her. Wilkerson Jr. and his cronies knew I wouldn't stay on as an *assistant* director. This had all been deliberate, planned. Yes, a conspiracy theory against me was so much better than thinking I wasn't capable as a twenty-five-year-old who had never even seen a Roseate Spoonbill, the resident bird of Port Rockton, before this past May.

I turned toward the ibises, watching their sewing-machine feeding motions as I blinked furiously. All other birds might lounge about and preen or sun, but ibises always worked. I loved ibises. I understood them.

No Morocco. No trip. No job. Which would mean no house, no beach, no . . . I would have to tell Mama I'd failed. I would have to endure her pity, her shame. With a demotion like this, what other job could I get in ornithology?

I turned back and sank into my desk chair. Zephyr's skirt had five flounces. Her belt, low-slung, was made of nineteen interwoven strips of leather. Twelve feathers on one flip-flop, ten on the other. I wasn't close enough to count the teeth in her skull choker, but I knew there were four. *Not fair to count what you can't see.*

Zephyr's rhinestones flashed at me as she looked up from her fancy phone. "What if you didn't fly from here to Houston to New York to Paris to Agadir, but took alternative passage?"

"Yeah? What alternative passage is there between Texas and Africa? Shall I dig a tunnel? Hire an air balloon? Kiteboard?"

My stillness was overtaken by shaking, shaking that I had to hide. I leaned forward and interlaced my fingers. "What I want to know is why everyone wants me gone. What have I done except embrace the Institute's vision of growth? Why . . . " I trailed off and looked back out the window. The ibises now fed peaceably alongside the herons and egrets, and even a few spoonbills. A glossy ibis walked along the edge, dark iridescence in the sunlight.

"I have an idea," Zephyr said, "but I need some time to check it out. I'll bring it tomorrow."

Tomorrow. Saturday. The weather had promised to be perfect. I'd planned it as my last day in the water before I started on my way to Morocco. But I wasn't going to Morocco.

The birds outside took wing, and though I couldn't actually hear the wind through their feathers, I'd heard it so often that my imagination supplied the sound. *Fly away, just fly away.*

"Elize?" Zephyr said. "Breakfast? The Lodge? Hello?"

To what end? I wanted to say. Yes it was something we did every week, but it would be spending money that I wasn't going to have. I was effectively unemployed. How was I going to tell anyone? How was I going to live?

The reporters, when they did descend, were going to love this. Talk about fodder!

Why did this all have to happen now? A week ago I could have handled it. I swallowed. Typical selfishness of Fischer to think of no one else. Now I was unemployed—maybe not technically, maybe not yet—and broke.

"How much money do you have?"

I turned. Zephyr's near-mind-reading skills always creeped me out. "What did you say?"

"What resources do you have, if I can find you an alternate route to Morocco? Obviously, the Dubya isn't going to help out."

Yeah, obviously. The Woodrow Wilkerson Institute, the Dubya. My home. My dream. I'd never cared about money. Here I had the birds and the outdoors, and enough cash to buy my kayaks and surfboards and Coronas and condo and weekly pedicure. But now money was important. I recalled my last bank statement—only one *o* in the bank's name. "A couple thousand," I said, deliberately vague. *$8,016.42.*

"Cash?" she asked.

I nodded.

"Credit cards?"

"I have some, but I don't use them." Pop had always insisted I keep some open, in case of emergency.

She grinned, impish. Well, as impish as a six-foot-tall female surfer can be. Her eyes gleamed. "You'll get to Morocco. Maybe not comfortably or rested, but you'll get there."

Something in the way Zephyr said it, almost brought me a breath of hope, of calm. "Tomorrow, huh?" I asked.

"Yes. Go for a run, go get a pedicure, forget about this, pack."

A feather tickled my spine. She was making me believe. Leaving would solve all of my problems, for a while. Everything would have died down by the time I returned. *And if this isn't an emergency,* Crazy-Elize whispered in my head, *what could one possibly be?*

Zephyr twisted her skull medallion ring. "How many weeks will you be gone?" she asked.

"Three." Suddenly the pages in the calendar in my mind blew away like in an old movie. I had nothing else scheduled for the rest of my life. I swallowed my panic and glanced back at the ibises. *The Bald Ibis lives in Morocco,* Crazy-Elize said. *Endangered. Only a few colonies. You could see it.*

"You could lease your place," Zephyr said.

Port Rockton was part of the Redneck Riviera, and this was the best season on the beach. I shuddered to think of hooligan tourists in my house. But I'd be in Morocco. *The Bald Ibis, the Waldrapp* Crazy-Elize whispered, just in case I didn't remember its other name.

"Leave your Lalique here at the Dubya, for safekeeping," Zephyr said. "I'll keep an eye on it."

My Lalique falcon, the one thing I owned, that was valuable, other than equipment. But did I care about protecting it? Who needed to protect a raptor, with its false tear mark, even if it was glass? Okay, crystal. One of a kind, custom-made crystal. The only glimmer that ever indicated Fischer knew who I was; a belated-everything present I'd gotten sometime around my third year here.

"All you need are cheap sheets and towels. I have a friend at the real estate office who could lease it for you."

My gaze moved across the books on my desk. *African Wildlife, Morocco, Lonely Planet Guide, Fodor's Morocco.* Parrot-colored jackets, a pandemonium of parrots. Reds and greens and blues.

I'd always hated the thought of someone living in my home, having sex in my bed, luxuriating in my shower. However, it would be a source of income. Leverage against unemployment, if it came to that. "Okay," I said, because there was no choice. I couldn't stay here. Whatever it took, I had to get out of here. Shame, on all sides, was coming for me. "Usual time?"

Zephyr nodded and smiled, then bounced out the door. After sending my telephone line to voicemail, I resumed packing my office.

Morocco. I was going to Morocco. I pitched the other celebrity magazines in the trash and avoided the picture of the man with the icy blue eyes.

I had my father's eyes.

The Lodge has a reputation: great breakfasts and the cutest bartenders on the beach. The new guy was a natural flirt, with long blond hair and piercings. As we sipped our first cups of coffee Zephyr said, "He's totally your style."

I liked my men young, hot, and easy to push out of bed at 3 a.m., my personal witching hour. That gave me just enough of a nap before the birds woke at dawn.

"What happened to Chad?" she asked.

"Brad."

Zephyr frowned. "You sure?"

I shrugged. Conversation hadn't been my latest lover's strong point. Stamina and fantastic abs were, however. "He was great. Fine. But he wanted a hit after—"

"Ah, so he fell through Elize's Trap Door."

"That cop lives two doors down. I'd be the one he'd bust. I don't need the grief." Or any of the other grief that comes with a user.

Like an overdose. Or had it been suicide?

Zephyr raised her brows above today's round frame glasses. They went with today's missed-Woodstock-by-decades hippie ensemble. "So you're not tense."

I grinned. "Not too much."

"Your bags packed?"

I nodded. My toes were freshly painted, my hair trimmed, and I'd even picked up an all-weather trench, because it was zebra-patterned on one side.

"Glad to hear it," she said. "Your flight for Houston leaves at one."

My coffee sloshed as I set my cup down. "Today?" It was already 8:30.

"Today," Zephyr said, then smiled and pushed me a folder with a thousand colored notes stuck to it. "Or, I could e-mail it to you," she said, waving her phone in the air.

I shook my head. Phones were leashes. I'd resisted being leashed. I didn't need one in the habitat of the Dubya or on the island. Why would I get one now?

She tapped the page. "So, Houston's the start of a long journey, but one that will get you there for under eight hundred dollars." I stared at the page, but I couldn't see it. I blinked rapidly, trying to keep the telltale drops from falling.

I was going to Morocco.

Zephyr flirted her way through placing our orders as I sifted through the notes, the confirmation numbers, the directions.

Days of traveling, a half dozen connections that had to actually connect, but I'd be in Larache, Morocco, by the time Sam and the rest of the group arrived. I'd be there affordably. I'd be there without having to admit I wasn't, essentially, me.

And such a convoluted trail that no one, even the most intrepid reporter, should they choose to waste their time, could follow.

"You have got to write a paper," Zephyr said as she poured sugar into her coffee. "Get published. Nothing else can save you, Elize."

I shrugged. Fine. I'd write a brilliant paper. I'd get it published. I'd . . . *I was going.* I blinked back those damned tears again, looking over the dunes to the placid Gulf waters. Was all my waiting finally paying off?

"Stop waiting," Zephyr whispered with her weird mind-reading. "Live," she said, and patted my hand.

Our food was served, and as Zephyr attacked her breakfast, she spoke to me around a mouthful of syrup-soaked pancake. "Just don't get kidnapped; it would take a lot more than a carwash to raise a ransom."

"I told you, I'm going to see the birds, not the country."

"Elize, those birds live beside the people, *in* the country."

The Country

Morocco.

The coastline edged the horizon, but despite squinting through bleary eyes, I couldn't make out details. Just an edge to the sea, a southern frame for the Strait of Gibraltar.

Everything was colorless mist, like the indeterminate grays of immature gulls, the air dense, but soft, like feathers.

The ferry was the penultimate leg. It was good to stand, despite the rough waters and the cold spray. Days, it had taken. Houston to Miami to Madrid. Bus after bus after bus to Algeciras, and after this ferry to Tangier I'd catch another bus to Larache. My passport wasn't virgin anymore.

I looked at my watch. The schedule I'd engraved on my brain said we had an hour to land, disembark, and go through Customs before the bus to Larache left. Zephyr had e-mailed me to take the early ferry, a note I'd gotten at the last Internet café in Spain. Which meant another night of limited sleep. When was the last time I'd really slept?

Slept without being haunted, anyway. Dreams of Frankie wearing a suit covered in the word *LOSER!!* with each *o* neon red and bleeding. Then *him*, sitting up in his coffin shouting, "Why did you come? I didn't *invite* you!" the words pouring from his mouth in cartoon bubbles, the *i*'s like daggers. Birds seeing me and flying away, in the thousands.

Café con leche sloshed in my stomach and acid burned into my throat as I returned to my seat inside the ferry.

Almost there. I was almost there.

❖

Instinct woke me seconds before my forehead cracked against the porthole. White waves surrounded the ship as it rose up and crashed down rhythmically. I closed my eyes to will away the nausea.

Cool water, I thought, standing up, grabbing hold of the plush headrest in front of me. A splash of cool water on my pressure points and I'd be fine. Should I take my suitcase? I could have left the rolling bag somewhere, in some locker in Spain, except I didn't have a plan to get back to the States. Zephyr had said she would figure out those details while I concentrated on the African sky.

At this point I wished all I had was my bird bag, a toothbrush, and Birkenstocks. Maybe someone would steal this albatross?

I crawled over the rolling bag, grabbed my duffel—which had grown exponentially heavier at every airport, taxi stand, and bus station—tossed it over my shoulder, and staggered off in search of the restroom, ping-ponging from wall to wall as the boat bounced across the strait.

Whatever restorative the water could have offered was immediately negated by the sounds and smells of the bathroom.

Outside, that's what I needed. I stumbled to the deck and opened the door, only to have it ripped from my hands. I didn't hear the metal slam against the side of the ship; the wind was too loud, howling and shrieking. My hair flapped free around my face, the ends like little whips.

If this was normal, I'd hate to see a storm!

I clasped the metal railing as the nausea passed and reality flooded in. A flicker of excitement burned in me.

I'm on the Mediterranean. The end of the Greek world, beyond the Pillars of Hercules. Flamingoes migrated through here; the Moroccan Cormorant, with its white throat and chest, nested here. Even though I couldn't see them, they were here.

I opened my eyes when I felt the sunshine warm through my trench.

Africa, shapely now, stretched along the horizon. I knew if I followed that coastline south, I would find the Souss-Massa lagoon, and in it the bald ibis, also known as the Waldrapp, one of the world's rarest birds. Six hundred in all the world, and most of them roosted there. For an ibis lover, they were the pinnacle.

But, the Souss-Massa extended about six hundred miles out of my way, and even farther outside my budget.

I'd have to wait for next time. Which meant that somehow, there had to *be* a next time.

Zephyr was right. Even though I hated writing papers, I was going to have to apply myself to this trip and write something, preferably brilliant, in order to . . . to what, get a new job? The thought made me a little sick. I didn't want a new job. I didn't want to leave my coastal paradise, which was a paradise even with Frankie and Wilkerson clotting up my days. Would I let the blue jay win?

I'd rather be dead than bested.

Dead . . .

I turned my thoughts to the tumbled blocks of white as they became distinguishable along the shoreline, defining themselves into flat-roofed buildings, sheltered by palm trees.

Just one more hurdle, the bus to Larache. Then I could collapse for a day or two. The rest of the birders wouldn't arrive until tomorrow or Sunday.

I imagined sitting in the rented boat beside the North African isthmus, counting and observing the birds as they landed, gasping, from their flight across the strait. I felt another beat of excitement.

I couldn't get the deck door open again; the wind pressed it shut. I braced all my weight, and the weight of my duffel, and pulled.

It banged open. Banged into me. Banged me over. Nose, knees, hands, butt. *Never let them see they hurt you.*

I shook off the helping hands, ignored the comforting words, and stepped into the cabin. A careful exploration indicated my nose wasn't broken, but it was hard to tell since it was a block of ice set into my face. It contrasted with my ears, which felt on fire; apparently they'd gotten banged too. I crawled over my bag—which no one had stolen, ingrates—and slumped into the seat. Abraded palms. A tear in my pants. The polish on my big left toe was gone, chipped off in one piece.

As my eyelids slid shut I realized the announcer was rattling on and on in French. If it was important he'd say it in English or Spanish, right?

He fell silent, and I fell asleep.

A ship's blast startled me. That didn't make sense . . . but then I awoke with my heart racing.

Ferry. Gibraltar. I looked at my watch; we were late. If I were the very first person off the ship, I could make the bus to Larache. Provided the station was nearby. Why had Zephyr made my connections so close?

The crowd was just now filling out the embarkation form we'd gotten in Spain. I checked. Mine, already filled out, was in my passport.

I was the first by the door. I'd said I was going to Morocco, and here I was! I felt a triumphant smile hover on my chapped lips as I counted the nails in the door, the windows in the cabin, the number of "watch your step" signs, and waited.

Maybe I could repair my toe on the way to Larache? Nothing made you feel as undone and unpolished as a chipped pedicure. I'd have to chip the rest of it off.

As we docked, the Europeans and the tiny, scarf-wearing Moroccan women jostled around me. I broadened my stance, like a grackle ruffling its wings to intimidate. I had waited in line while they had dawdled. Though to call the shifting swirl of people behind me anything linear was a joke.

A Spanish mannequin opened the doors, spoke through perfectly painted lips into her walkie-talkie held by perfectly painted fingertips, then told me to follow.

Down the stairs, across the now-empty car hold, over the gang-plank, I race-walked with my duffel over my shoulder, bird bag across me and suitcase screaming on its wheels.

I could still make my bus.

Three men in uniforms waited on the pier as I stepped onto the African continent.

"Welcome to Morocco," one of the officials said, while another took my passport. He flipped it forward and back. Then he looked at me, his gaze accusing. "Where are your papers?"

What? Was this a World War II movie? What was he talking about?

"Where are your papers?"

Oh! The piece from Spain. I pointed to the document tucked into my passport. Officials. Couldn't they see it, right before their eyes?

"No," he said, tapping the form. "This is to leave Spain. You cannot enter Morocco without a proper Customs form."

"*You cannot enter Morocco . . .*" the words echoed horribly, joined by other horrible echoes.

"*Assistant director.*"

"*Fischer died this morning under suspicious circumstances. An overdose of some sort. Expect the press.*"

I stared at the official, feeling the swollenness of my hands, the sweat that stuck my jacket to my back. No. No!

"You must go back," he said, and pointed . . . to Spain.

The Town

Of course he didn't mean *Spain*, just the Spanish ship. I raced past the clump of other travelers, all of whom had flapping pieces of yellow paper in their possession. Why hadn't anyone told me, or was it just funny to watch the dumb American go in circles? I walked faster, the official's words, "You should hurry. The ferry makes a quick turnaround," beating in my brain.

The hold was empty, no people, no cars.

I needed the captain, who would be on deck, as would the blank, ready, forms.

The staircase was barricaded by suitcases and baskets, baby carriages and shrink-wrapped boxes. Sweaty, swarthy, jovial men in full-length shapeless dresses all stopped moving to watch me, a sweating, wind-whipped blonde in a zebra trench coat. Muttering excuses, I clambered my way up, yanking my bags behind me and ignoring their comments. French? Arabic? Something else?

I ran to the snack shop. I'd spoken to the girl there, maybe she would know where the form was? But then I stopped. There, on the counter's edge, sat a stack of maybe a hundred yellow forms.

How incompetent was I?

Just tired, a voice like Zephyr's said.

Or blind, one like Frankie's amended.

I pulled out my pen, ignoring the whistles of the ship as I tried to guess what information went where in the French/Arabic directed blanks. Did I need the captain now that I had the form?

The maid was seated, taking a cigarette break before she emptied another ashtray. "*El capitán?*" I asked. She pointed and I followed, around a corner, to see a man seated at a booth, a mass of papers in front of him, a cigarette in his hand.

I slapped my paper in front of him, explaining in a torrent that I'd missed the form and I couldn't get into Morocco. Only after he perused the form and asked for my passport did I realize I'd spoken to this Spaniard in English, though I speak Spanish.

He flipped through the pages. "Where is your Spanish form? This is no good to me," he said in accented English.

Dammit. Where had I put that other form? Had I left it with the Moroccan official? I tore through my bag, but found it at last, tucked in an outside pocket. Exactly where I'd put it for easy access. I handed it to him, resisted the urge to check the time, and took a breath.

Men with little power tend to like big power trips. *Let him take his time.* I counted the five cigarettes stubbed out in the ashtray. Twenty-four studs decorated the tabletop. He had nine tassel fringes on one loafer, and eleven on the other.

I waited as the captain took another slow drag of his cigarette and exhaled. Then he stamped my Spanish document and my passport, and scribbled something on the Moroccan paper. In freeze-frame, he handed everything back.

I shouted a thank you as I fled down the almost-cleared stairs, across the hold and over the gangplank. Workers sat on the dock, talking, laughing, and smoking. They watched me dash by.

Where was everyone? The other passengers, the customs officials, everyone else had vanished. *They're just ahead*, I thought, but as I walked faster, then half ran, fighting my rolling bag every few feet as it went off-center and tried to flip over, I realized they must be way, way ahead.

I was sweating in my trench coat. The papers in my hand were damp. I hoped the ink wouldn't run.

The dock behind me was empty. The lanes before me were also empty. A still silence, broken by the occasional birdcall. Where had everyone gone?

The ferry terminal building was a likely spot.

The Mediterranean wind had died, but I couldn't take the time to shed my coat even though I was burning up. The bus and train station was adjacent to the ferry station, about an eighth of a mile up the concrete driveway. I could just see it, a huddle of concrete.

No time to look at my watch.

No train whistles, no honking cars, no rumble of conversations. The shadow of a portico loomed before me, and I raced into it, running smack into the two officials.

I thrust my yellow form at them. They spoke between themselves. I handed them my passport, too, lips pressed tight in order to not shout *Hurry!*

One signed my form, the other grunted at my passport and returned it. "Have a nice day," he said. Automatic words, followed by a formulaic smile.

"The only guides to accept have this pin," the other said, pointing to a Wild West sheriff star on his dark lapel. "All others, they are not approved by the government."

I hadn't even asked.

"They are dishonest," the other man said, before breaking into a smile. "Welcome to Morocco."

I didn't have time to change money. I'd do it when I got to Larache. Surely the drivers made exceptions for people just arriving from Europe?

I stuffed my papers in my bag and took off at a jog toward the terminal, a death grip on the bag rattling behind me.

"Lady—need a guide?"

"Lady—welcome to Morocco."

"Lady—my name is Abdul—"

"Lady—"

They descended on me like gulls. A screech of gulls. Five thin males, ranging from late teens to mid-forties, all of them talking, reaching for me, getting in my face, slowing me down.

"Need money changed, lady?"

They kept pace with me. No one else, not a car in the lanes, not a pedestrian, not even a pigeon, was around. One woman against five men. Three wore long dresses, the other two jeans. *I could take them one at a time,* I thought as adrenaline cleared my head. *I'm taller and certainly more muscled.* Not the best odds, but I could handle it.

"Guide to the Old City?"

"A place to stay?"

"Cheap, very cheap—"

No one was seated at the booths we passed. No one waited in line for anything, anywhere. Now we, me and my wheedling flock, stepped into the sunlight.

I caught my first glimpse of Tangier.

To my right a hotel perched on a hill, its weathered lettering announcing it as the Continental, its wide veranda filled with tables and chairs. White houses clustered around and above it, and the hill was crowned with a tall, delicate tower. Ramshackle buildings also covered the adjacent hills, everything baking in the sun, palm trees like shards of green against the white.

"You want a taxi?"

"Need a hotel?"

"Best price, lady, best price—"

I looked from the empty ferry building across empty traffic lanes, to a strip of tourist and travel shops on the road below the hotel.

"Is that the bus station?" Against my better judgment, I interacted, pointing to a building in the distance.

"No, lady," the oldest looking man in the group, said. The others melted away at his words. "The station is on the other side."

"Of the terminal?" I asked, looking over my shoulder where the ferry terminal abutted the docks.

"No. They built a new station for the king. Where are you going?"

"Larache."

"The bus is gone."

I looked at my watch. "I still have five minutes!"

"No, lady. Is two-hour difference."

I marched away from him and his obvious lie, toward the strip of shops.

"Need a hotel, lady?" he called after me.

"No."

Despite being shorter than me he could move quickly. "The next bus for Larache is not until tomorrow at thirteen-fifteen. You know this time, lady? One hour fifteen minutes in the afternoon. Come, I show you hotel, give you tour of the Old City—"

My head throbbed from the blinding sun. My nose throbbed from its encounter with the door. My hands throbbed from fighting my damn bag. "I want to go to Larache," I said. It was only sixty miles away.

"You can't go today, only tomorrow."

"I'll take a taxi," I said, walking faster, trying to lose him.

"Oh, lady, is not possible. Very expensive."

"I have to be in Larache!" *I have to prove I can get there. I have to do whatever professional damage control I can. I have to have some sort of sanctuary, and the birds give me that. I have to have a chance at Sam, before he loses interest. I have to get to Larache.*

I have nothing else in my life.

I swallowed the panic, the tears, the tiredness in my throat.

"We go here," he said, indicating the strip of shops ahead of us. "Buy your ticket for tomorrow, then I'll show you nice hotel in the Old City. Have couscous for dinner—"

"Fine. I'll buy a ticket." He was screwing himself. I would just ask the ticket seller the time, and where the station was, and be done with it. I'd take a taxi to the station. Maybe not get this exact bus to Larache, but I'd get the next. God, I just wanted to sleep. To get out of these clothes and sleep.

"My name is Abdul," the man said. "I am the best guide. People from all over your country think much of me. But you pay only what you think it's worth. Where are you from?"

I settled on "Texas" and tried not to think about having to move away from the Birdiest City in the nation. Where could I be happy after that?

The shell of a train terminal stretched out beside us and gave me pause. The station *had* moved? I tuned Abdul out. It couldn't really be two hours later. Spain and Africa weren't that far apart. Surely I would have heard something about it?

"Here! Here, we go here," Abdul said, stepping up into a shop. "Let me carry your bags."

"I've got them," I said, avoiding his hands. He pulled, I pulled, and tugging the bag between us, we entered the shop. The storefront was hung with faded posters of Moroccan destinations and a brilliantly tinted, gold-framed painting of a man, labeled in English, "The King."

Abdul greeted the old man behind the counter with hugs and kisses, and waved at a young man who was perched on a stool, smoking. Abdul spoke rapidly and the older man's expression grew grim as his wide dark eyes came to rest on me.

"I want to take the next bus or train to Larache," I said, enunciating. He looked grandfatherly, trustworthy.

"Tomorrow, one-fifteen o'clock," the old man answered, quickly and in English. They were in cahoots.

There was just one bus? Ridiculous. "What time is it now?" I asked, trying to trick him into the truth.

"Just past three o'clock."

I felt my face burn. It was a scam! Get the tourists to miss their connections, then they would stay and dine and shop. It appeared I wasn't going to escape this old boy's club of misinformation.

"Buy your ticket now?" the old man said. He pointed to a weathered and stained piece of paper beneath the glass on his counter. "See," he said. "*Tanger à Larache. Une heure et quart.*"

It was there, written down, in French, on what looked to be a genuine printed schedule. I rubbed my eyes. What I wouldn't give for a pot of coffee. And a woman to talk to, someone who would tell me the truth.

I couldn't believe I'd missed the bus.

Plan B. I needed Moroccan money, and then I could take a taxi to Larache.

"A hotel, lady?" Abdul asked.

I picked up my bags.

"Buy ticket?" the older man asked.

"Hotel, lady?"

The calls followed me out of the shop and down the stairs. Abdul shouted his farewells to the old man and ran to catch up with me. "Hotel, lady? Tour of the Old City? Money change?"

Money change. Something to get me out of this predicament. "Moneychanger," I said. I'd try to find it on my own, but I understood none of the signs. Even the numbers looked weird.

He beckoned. Defeated and resentful, I followed.

We approached a small dark shop next to a broken ATM. After my eyes adjusted, I saw that a portly man in a three-piece suit watched television and sipped tea behind one of three teller windows. A black and white program played; there might even have been a puppet involved.

It was quiet enough to hear the whir of the air conditioning. Minty air. Fresh.

I dropped my luggage and sank into an upholstered armchair, noting another painting of the king, this time wearing traditional dress, but still in a gaudy gold painted frame. I sighed. Money.

According to the chart by the windows, the exchange rate for dollars to euros was terrible. But the dollar compared to the Moroccan dirham looked reasonable.

Maybe Morocco would be affordable?

The whole trip is a deduction, I heard Zephyr say. *You're a professional.*

An assistant *professional,* I railed.

I countersigned some of my traveler's checks, and while the teller consulted my assorted colored pieces of paper and official documents, I shed my striped coat and tied my self-abusive hair in a scarf. Maybe Abdul wouldn't recognize me when I stepped back out? But he had the instincts of a vulture, and I was little better than a prone side of beef.

The teller counted out dozens and dozens of bills, then bid me adieu before returning to his TV and tea.

What would he do if I just stayed here? I didn't want to face my self-elected guide. Of course, I never would have found a moneychanger—at least not this moneychanger—without him.

The hotel on the hill probably had a restaurant, a proper bathroom, maybe even a cheap room. Larache just wasn't going to happen today. I ignored the voice that said it could have happened if I'd been more competent. I especially ignored that it sounded like Frankie.

Waiting would give me a good chance to catch up on my sleep. Maybe a chance to speak to the hotel's concierge and get some honest answers. Catch tomorrow's bus? That seemed a reasonable plan.

Abdul, I thought with a tremor of glee, probably wouldn't even be allowed in the hotel.

Carrying my wheeled bag, I stepped into the blazing sunshine.

Not only was Abdul allowed inside, in fact, he escorted me to the front desk, babbled at the young, bareheaded female receptionist, then waited—and eavesdropped—while I checked in. Which took twenty minutes, it was so thorough.

"Now, Miz Elise," he said, putting his information to use before I made it to the staircase, "you have a good sleep, then I will take you tour the Old City and for tea, later."

Anything to get rid of him. I nodded.

He dropped his voice, leaned closer to me. "I don't want to scare you, but the Old City can be dangerous for a woman, very dangerous. First, the tour guides will bite at you, they are like wild dogs. They are my brothers," he said, pressing his hand to his heart, "but they scramble for work, for a little money to take to their wives and children. They are my brothers, but they do not know as much as Abdul, a worthy guide for a bird-lady."

He'd overheard I was an ornithologist.

Abdul stared at me with green eyes, not dark. Well, he stared with one eye, and the other wandered. Altogether, he looked clean, pressed and trimmed. Unlike the few other men I'd seen, he was clean-shaven. "So, do not go into the city alone. Be very careful of anyone, not here in the hotel, it is a very fine hotel, but other places. Once, two American girls came to Morocco, they went walking in the souk, and boom! they vanish like wind in the desert."

His hand was on my arm, insistent, and I was sure he didn't care about my safety that much. Why wouldn't he let me go? The girl at the desk ostentatiously ignored us.

Abdul started in on another topic and it dawned on me: money! He was a guide and worked for tips. Pay him and he would leave! He knew I had money, too.

Because the hotel's credit card machine was broken, I had had to pay for my room in cash. I slipped the few remaining dirhams out of my pocket and handed them to Abdul. The money vanished somewhere on his person, then he was all smiles and bows, wishes for good rest and promises for a good tour. And, blessedly, gone.

I dragged my body up the stairwell, over a mismatched, off-center Oriental rug, my bag bumping up each step behind me. Seventeen steps. My door was the fourth down. Twenty-five tiles between each door.

The first thing I saw when I stepped into my room was the clock: 4:33.

Dammit.

The Culture

The turtledoves drew me in. I watched a pair while I enjoyed my post-nap coffee on the hotel's terrace, noted that they winged their way between their palm tree nests that flanked the harbor and the tower at the top of the hill. Back and forth, back and forth, like suburbanites on their commute.

The hotel itself was old and seedy, but with a certain style. The cushion I sat on had lost most of its cush, just like the once-enameled gold had all but worn off my tea cup. But I felt better.

Caffeine was a good drug, though twenty years after quitting I still missed the ritual of smoking.

Ferries moved in and out of the port, and further down other vessels set off on a sea as blue as an indigo bunting's wing. In the cloudless sky, I fancied I could see the faintest black dots of migrants. I patted my lips, applied some more balm, and harnessed myself with bags and bins.

As soon as I walked through the front garden and out the hotel's wrought iron gate, the line of boys and men I'd thought were sipping tea or lounging in the shade attacked like something from Hitchcock. They were all guides.

"Abdul's my guide," I half shouted in self-defense. They stood down, muttered as I walked by, my gaze fixed on the hilltop tower that pierced the sky like a heron's bill. No one followed.

Was that professional courtesy, or honor among thieves?

Tangier had sounded romantic, flavorful, exotic. However, as I walked the streets I saw it was narrow and twisty and sort of grubby. I needed to get cash again, but I was sure, now that I was rested and calm, I could find someplace on my own. The girl at the front desk had told me to go to the casbah. When I'd asked where it was, she'd pointed up here.

She'd also confirmed the bus station's move: they'd built a new one for the king's use. And she'd said that there *was* only one bus to Larache per day. Because she was female and already had a job, I trusted her.

Ornate buildings towered over the streets, crumbling in some places, tinted a dozen shades of yellow, pink, blue, and green. I could hear sounds of life, of cats and children, of radios and tinkling fountains, but there was no direction to the noise. Doorways just melted into the walls. Sounds came from nowhere and everywhere at once.

Every step pulled me uphill, the direction the turtledoves flew. I passed through sections that smelled like mint, others like urine or spices that I couldn't name. The rare times I cooked, it was traditional German food, which was noted more for weight and heaviness than subtlety of flavor or a mix of spices. Though I had to say that my venison wiener schnitzel was both heavy *and* flavorful.

Zephyr had claimed her crawfish étouffée was one of her "kidnapping talents." Étouffée, and chess. Frankie's claim to a kidnapping talent was her skill in plumbing. The visual of petite Frankie in one of her pink or green or aqua skirt suits, wielding a plunger, had stunned both me and Zephyr into silence until dessert had arrived.

Lunch. Just a few days ago. Before my whole life had turned over, like a nuthatch on a tree, pecking at the bark upside down.

What would my kidnapping talent be, if not wiener schnitzel? Did I have anything else? I used to be a famous man's daughter . . . ? Though that oversold our connection by a lot.

As I walked down wider, more populated streets, men in dresses and skullcaps moved around me. They sat at open-air cafés; they squatted on low stools in shops. I felt extremely aware of my blondeness. Even though I wore shapeless drawstring pants, the men in the streets watched me like I was a stripper.

The birds, I told myself, and looked up, where the deepening blue sky was framed by the frosted buildings. The gentle purring of the doves guided me. I breathed through my mouth as the stench became powerful.

A market area, humming with buyers around bins of herbs, leather stools, embroidered robes and beaten-up jewelry, spilled out on one of the streets. Dozens of men called to me, with offers to buy, to sell, to save. They all shouted in English. I ducked back into a narrow twisty street.

Some young boys ran past, kicking a can. Boys not so different than boys on the beach at home, kicking a ball. For the first time, I felt my shoulders relax. I kept to my upward path, following the boys, then sea air blew through my hair and I heard the shushing I knew so well.

Waves.

I walked toward the breeze, drawn to the sound of the water. I followed the boys around a corner. A path edged the sea, winding up the outside of the hill toward the tower.

Below me, the Mediterranean dashed itself against a sandy shoreline, then rushed off into myriad blues, greens, and purples in the late afternoon light, like a glossy ibis's wings. I didn't see any migrant birds, but among the many shrubs, bushes, and plants, empty plastic garbage bags struggled as if yearning for flight.

I took the path, climbing past hovels and lean-tos so broken down I wouldn't store a kayak there. Women and children watched me from open casements. The smell of soiled diapers and spoiled milk mixed with the sounds of bleating goats and the cries of gulls. Plastic trash, bottles, bags, forks, and cartons clung to the ground like nestlings. On the other side of the path, the sky soared up into a heavenly blue, and the Mediterranean frothed at my feet.

In one turn, the sight and sound of the sea vanished. Once more I was inside the Old City of Tangier, all familiar touchpoints gone.

People walked through the ancient tower building, not even seeing it. How wild it would be to live surrounded by history like this? Walking through a fortress to pick up some eggs and bread at market? The shadows lengthened around me, reminding me that I needed to get more cash, find a Net café, send e-mail, and get back to the hotel before dark. Wandering the streets alone at night would be stupid. Like inviting a kidnapping.

"Kidnapping talent." Where did Zephyr come up with that stuff?

Somehow, I made a wrong turn. After twenty minutes of wandering, ensnared in a loop of streets, I was relieved to hear my name called. Yes, by Abdul. But at least he could get me out of this maze.

I didn't even care that he'd shouted my name so that half of Tangier heard it.

"Miz Elisse," he said, hissing the z into an s. "I thought you were taking a big sleep?"

"I did."

"Didn't I warn you about these streets? Very dangerous. Two American girls—"

"Yes, yes, you told me. But," I said, getting into this game a little, "you told me you would guide me. I need an ATM and a Net café."

"It is closed."

Of course it was, and the ATM was broken as well. But Abdul had a "perfect place" for my dinner, after I took a tour of the casbah and the warren of streets and markets called the Petit Socco.

But my coffee energy had evaporated somewhere in the street loop. I agreed that an early dinner would be good. For five streets I declined the tour, and then Abdul delivered me to an empty restaurant.

Four different waiters, none of whom spoke English, tripped over themselves to assist me, pulling out chairs, opening my napkin, holding the menu, and removing the painted placeholder plate before me.

I was surprised when Abdul excused himself; I thought he'd invite himself to dinner, that it would be part of his "payment," but he said he would eat later with his wife and son, then vanished outside.

I stared at the menu, too tired to even breathe.

"*Prix fixe, Madame?*" one of the waiters said.

I nodded. Deciding what to drink was challenge enough. From the range of three soft drinks, I ordered an Orangina.

The soup was lemon and mint, and as I ate it, I became aware of the gaggle of waiters standing and watching me in the open but empty restaurant. They whisked away my empty bowl and set a clay pot, its top domed like a tea kettle, before me. When the waiter removed the top and the steam cleared, I expected him to say abracadabra.

The ordinary looking chicken was surprising in its sweetness. "What is this?" I said, pointing to the pot.

"*Poulet,*" the waiter said.

"Not the chicken, the pot."

He frowned. "Yes, shick-hen."

I tapped the clay thing with my finger. "*Qué es eso?*"

Another waiter intervened. "Tagine," he said. "For Moroccan cooking. You like?"

I nodded. Sure, fruity chicken.

The noise level outside had increased and more and more people passed the window, looking in at me.

A zoo exhibit: *Tourista north americanus.*

Nothing like being stared at to put you off your meal. The waiters brought the last part of my feeding: tiny, brittle, teeth-achingly sweet pastries, decorated with nuts.

A group of young natives leaned against the wall opposite my window and smoked, laughing and staring at me. As the meal passed, the group grew bigger. I looked around for my waiter, for any waiter, now desperate to get the check and get out of there.

They'd vanished. All four.

I fiddled with my napkin and debated taking out my bird book, but didn't want to flash the contents of my bag, so I got to my feet. That brought a waiter around, who went in search of the bill.

He brought back numbers higher than I expected. More than the menu had said. "See, is in euros," one of the supporting waiters said. "I gave you in dirham."

"Yeah, well, your exchange rate is rather inaccurate," I said, looking at the contrasting numbers, comparing them to what I'd seen earlier in the day.

Like a genie, Abdul appeared. When I explained the difference to him, the shouting between him and the waiter began. People stared in through the window; the other waiters and cook gathered. The bill was passed back and forth with great heat. The audience grew.

Why hadn't I just paid it? I could be asleep in bed by now. Instead, I looked like an idiot who had to fall back on her guide in order just to buy a meal.

The men huddled together, passing a calculator back and forth, then Abdul delivered a piece of paper to me. "You pay this price," he said, tapping the numbers.

In giant capitals, in English, underlined, the bill stated: No Gratuity Added.

All four waiters had served me. All four watched me.

I counted out my last dirhams—they sure spent fast—realizing the current bill was the same sum as I'd been given before, only now it was on different paper, and I had a headache.

Abdul and the waiters, who'd been shouting at each other five minutes earlier, embraced and kissed as we left, like it was a far journey and they'd be parted a long time.

I was pretty sure I'd been set up, but at least having Abdul kept the other dozens of guides who lurked in doorways and congregated at tea shops away from me. Kind of like smearing yourself with mud and excrement so that the wildlife would accept you as one of their own.

Abdul was my . . . mud.

❖

Once in the shelter of my room, I watched darkness dust onto the Old City. "Tangier here since the time of the Phoenician!" Abdul had said.

The white-stacked buildings bristled with antennas, an incongruous note of modernity. Calls between friends and neighbors rose up from the street, and in the distance a man sang, his voice embodying the exotica around me.

The doves continued purring. A pitying of doves, the collective noun was a poetic term to describe the plural. Or a prettying of doves, or a piteousness. I wasn't sure who had started it, but Pop and me had collected all the crazy names you could call a group of birds. In the end, it was all he remembered.

The darker it got, the louder the outdoors grew. The exact opposite of tomorrow in Larache, when the darkness would signify the birds going to sleep and the ornithologists crashing out as well. The gathering was small, and was the first time the Dubya had been invited to such an elite group. *Birds*, I thought to Frankie, *not people!*

I lay down at an angle, the only way I fit on the bed. The way things had turned out was probably for the best. This way I'd be caught up on sleep. I'd be ready for the activities of Larache as soon as I arrived.

My earlier exhaustion was the reason why everything had seemed so menacing. I laughed out loud when I remembered that I'd thought the official was returning me to Spain. Tangier wasn't a bad place, you just needed a bit of money and guile in order to manage. And lots of time.

Even Abdul hadn't been bad. I'd kept expecting him to drag me into a carpet store, or something like that, try to get me to buy his cousin's wares. He hadn't even asked me about shopping.

Though why didn't he wear the star of the government-approved guide? I checked my alarm and turned off the light.

Just as I was drifting off, someone turned on a recording.

I could have gone downstairs and complained, because it was sudden and it was loud. But also glorious. A male chorus.

To me, men's choruses are the epitome of sailing history, hearkening back to when sailors on the open sea carved and sewed and sang and sang and sang. I'd cried at the men's chorus scene in *The Hunt for Red October*. Something so poignant, so strong and masculine, and lost.

So beautiful.

My culture seemed to destroy beautiful things. I wouldn't think of the habitats encroached upon, the golf courses built in breeding grounds, the trampling of native grasses and the nests they shielded.

Maybe Morocco still kept beautiful things alive.

The bald ibis *had* been brought back from the edge of extinction.

Six hundred miles away, a once-in-a-lifetime sighting.

The evening breeze blew over me, carrying scents of flowers and notes of music. What group could it be? What recording? It sounded like several hundred men. Was that Arabic?

The music lasted from nine until midnight. In that time, twenty-eight birds flew past my window; "Hassan" was called for fourteen times. A donkey brayed nine times. I dozed as I listened. When it was over, there was laughing, clapping. It sounded close.

Applauding a recording at a party, odd, but nice. Civilized, in a way.

Tomorrow, Larache, was on my lips as I fell asleep. But I was glad I'd waited, stayed the night.

The singing men had made it worthwhile. Something beautiful, preserved.

❖

The breakfast room dazzled me. Intricate carvings lined the perimeter of the room and covered the ceiling. Colorful tiles, mismatched and interwoven, layered the floor and went halfway up the walls.

It was like being inside a Fabergé egg.

Granted, inside this egg the tiles were cracked, the chairs were scratched. and the rugs threadbare, but it confirmed the aura of genteel neglect. Like maybe Jim Morrison had stayed here.

A waiter, looking as worn out as the decor, slung coffee, juice and a basket of bread on my table, then muttered in French. I shook my head. "What?"

As though it caused him great pain, he spoke in English, indicating the other chair and plate and cup. "To join you? Anyone?"

I shook my head. He removed the setting, wincing every time he clanged a dish. The other, empty, chair faced me. Obvious.

Nature tends toward pairing; it's a biological imperative. Mating is proof of thriving. Different species, when they reach a certain low population, just stopped mating. The principle of quorum sensing. At too small a group they dwindled, waiting to die. One of the pathways to extinction.

I shook my head to clear it. The other tables were filled with paired Europeans.

A French man and woman, both older and fit, tanned and stylish.

Two men in their fifties, paunchy and grayed, dressed alike down to their black sport sandals.

A young Scandinavian couple in matching round glasses, with knobby knees and thigh-length shorts.

I stirred milk into my coffee, feeling conspicuous. I didn't feel alone often, but the details—the French couple both reading at the table, their shoulders brushing; the Scandinavians hunched over a guidebook, and feeding each other bread; the gay couple flipping through a magazine together, pointing to pieces of furniture—smarted.

The patio was empty, waiting in the yellow morning sun. I picked up my cup of coffee and moved outside. The terrace hadn't been swept, and my waiter, holding his head as though it ached, sent a girl scurrying for seat cushions and an umbrella.

After a refill of my coffee they left me in peace. Birdsong and the distant whistle of the ferries filled the morning air. I scanned the area with my bins, but didn't note anything else. Time enough in Larache.

Yesterday's receptionist hurried up the stairs, smoothing her hair and adjusting the jacket of her suit.

"Excuse me," I called, then dashed down to meet her when she didn't acknowledge me. "The bus to Larache?"

"No Larache today," the girl said, pleasant enough.

I'd already checked out of the hotel. "Yesterday, you said—"

"Today, no Larache," the girl repeated. Then she held up her hands and shrugged her shoulders, international for it's-out-of-my-hands-what-can-you-do? and walked into the hotel.

I sat down and looked at my watch. Funny thing was, I believed her. Morocco operated on caprice, no doubt. Or secret rules. What could I do, except wait?

"Greetings, birdlady," Abdul said the second I stepped out of the hotel's gate. I couldn't help but feel it was a starting gate, and the whistle had just blown and we were ooooooff to the races! "How are you today?" he said. "Did you get enough rest with the wedding?"

What was he talking about?

"You didn't go?" he said, his nontracking eye bulging. "Why is it you didn't go to a proper Moroccan wedding? The parties! The food!" He kissed his fingers. "*C'est magnifique!*"

"That was a wedding?" Those voices, that singing, *was* singing?

"It lasted until dawn. Two very prominent families from the Old City. You should have gone."

"No one came and got me."

He shrugged. "All the hotel guests were invited. You must have been the only one missing."

I could have seen that chorus, *live*? "I need to go buy my ticket for Larache," I said. Again.

"Ah, there is no bus for Larache today. Buy ticket for tomorrow."

"How can that be?" I asked, trying to keep my voice even, but wanting to shriek. Was I the only person in Tangier trying to get there?

Abdul shrugged. "It is canceled until tomorrow."

"It's public transportation! You can't just cancel public transportation!"

"No bus to Larache today. Instead, I will give you great tour of the fortress, the Old City—"

"I'll take a taxi."

Abdul pursed his lips and shook his head. "Is not so easy, and very expensive. And today, tonight, is Friday, Muslim holy day, so no good taxis."

I took a deep breath. Thank God the hotel wasn't too expensive. "I'll need an ATM." I was sick of that refrain.

"I can take you."

"And a Net café."

"It should be open, about eleven, twelve thirty—"

"And I want to buy my ticket for Larache, for tomorrow." I said it through gritted teeth.

Abdul wasn't fazed. "No problem. You want, I will take you by taxi to the station and you can get it there."

That seemed accommodating. I felt suspicious. "If I can take a taxi to the station, why can't I take a taxi to Larache?"

Abdul sighed and stroked his chin like it should have a beard. "Is very complicated—"

I held up a hand. I didn't want to tax his powers of fabrication, or my patience, much more. Just for comparison I asked, "How much would a taxi to Larache cost?" If it was cheaper than the hotel, I'd have to go. Regardless of the supposed complexity.

"*Tres cher*," Abdul said, blanching. "Maybe for you, two hundred euros."

Even if he was exaggerating an exaggeration, staying here still made more sense. "I need to check back into the hotel," I said.

He shrugged. "After lunch. They are holding your bags, *non?*"

Did I answer yes or no to that "non?" "Uhh . . . yes."

"No problem. They will give you a room."

Dammit. What else could I do? Might as well enjoy it, I reasoned, as I followed Abdul into the busy, noisy, sun-streaked streets of the Old City.

In the course of a day, as defined by two meals, five tea shop stops, one Net café stop (closed), two ATMs (both working) and six hours, Tangier became my city.

Yeah, it was a little disturbing that Abdul exchanged plastic bags with every third man on the street, but kif, whose effect was like marijuana, I had learned, was okay for Moroccans "so we will stay quiet about injustice and corruption."

That same kif would land a tourist in prison for a long time.

Because of that, Abdul would sit at a different table in the tea shops, in order to smoke, while I would sit beside a window and sip. He might have been high on whatever weed kif was, but I was flying from the sugar in all the tea. They might not drink alcohol, but religious Muslims did have their vices.

Walking with Abdul was a cross between being with a grandfather and the mayor. Everyone knew him, from the kids who played in the streets and ran by in their long robes and knitted caps, to the shopkeepers with windows full of stuffed leather camels and cheap T-shirts.

People smiled as they passed us; children danced—no really, danced!—around him, laughing and teasing with him. Abdul laid his hand on their heads like some kind of blessing, everyone shouting. The little boys watched me with big brown eyes, smiling, and

I couldn't help but smile back. Mothers trailing girls, like waterfowl herding chicks, wove in and out of the masses of people, and everyone talked, everyone laughed.

People stopped in the center of the street to greet each other and, I guess, gossip. No one, anywhere, seemed to be in a rush. No one seemed short-tempered. The tension along my back and my shoulders eased. My grip on my bag loosened and I found myself meeting people's curious gazes and smiling back at the bright, white smiles around me.

I was accepted as part of the human flow. I liked it.

Some little girl had handed me flowers with a shy smile and a flash of bright eyes, as inquisitive as a warbler's. I followed Abdul, flowers in hand, smiling at the men closing their shops for the siesta, at the women hurrying home for their naps.

As I followed Abdul down another street, I saw him.

He stood out because he was tall and handsome. Some Mediterranean blend of genetics had given him light eyes and a black beard. He wore a native shirt and blue jeans, and I watched him walk toward me, his strangely beatific expression fixed on my face.

I couldn't look away from his savage beauty, his mesmerizing gaze. My heart was racing and I felt a smile on my lips. Abdul, high from our last tea shop, was around the bend ahead of me. Pedestrians moved around me, between me and the gorgeous man.

Sunlight striped the street, cut off by the blackness of the opposite alleyway. It was like stepping into a black and white photo, except for his eyes.

We approached each other, passing within inches, his gaze fixed on me, mine, hidden behind Oakleys, watching him. When he was close enough to smell, I felt a vise around my wrist, tugging me sideways. Hard.

Dragging me into another twist of this maze-like street.

Toward the maw of the dark alley.

What had been sexy suddenly became scary.

"Missing women in Morocco." "Kidnapping talent." "It's dangerous."
Everyone would be right, I thought as I felt my shoes sliding across the cobbles like they'd been greased.

Junior and Frankie would shake their heads, confirmed in their belief that I couldn't have managed the Dubya. I couldn't even take care of myself for one day in a foreign city!

The man dragged me deeper into darkness, further into the recesses of the alley. I would vanish, leaving this final incompetence as my gravestone. *No!*

How dare he? I wrenched away and ran the opposite direction. My breath echoed in my ears, I felt icy sweat over my body, the racing of my heart as I slipped and skidded down the alleyway, into the street.

It was broad daylight. This was a wide, fairly busy thoroughfare. He'd grabbed me in daylight! Without a glance behind me, I chased after Abdul. Only when I caught up to him in front of a shop did I realize I still clutched the flowers the little girl had given me, some bedraggled, some beheaded. I tossed them away, overtaken with shaking. He'd grabbed me in broad daylight!

"Please, bird-lady," Abdul said to me, his disconcerting gaze innocent, not noticing my fear, my panic, "Mustafa is the finest carpet sellers in all of Tangier. Please to enjoy."

Safety, inside. I nodded at the questions that peppered me. Patterns on top of patterns, colors on colors, a headache-inducing flurry of images hanging from the walls, stacked on the floor, surrounded me. Rugs everywhere.

An older man with a large mustache approached, and a young boy offered me tea.

Hadn't Abdul wondered what had happened to me? Didn't he see my clothes were grubby, that I was breathless? Shaking? But outrage was overtaking fear, and mounting. My suspicion was growing.

Abdul had known every thing I had done and not done since I'd stepped off the ship. He seemed to know every conversation I'd had, what I'd eaten. He'd chosen the road we'd walked down. He'd gotten ahead of me as we had gone around the turn.

Had he known about the grabber?

Had he planned it?

To what end? He hadn't appeared surprised to see me appear again.

"What kind of rug do you want, *madame?*" the older man asked, twisting his mustache like a silent screen villain.

I looked around, registering my surroundings for the first time. A rug store! In the end Abdul *had* taken me to a rug store. I hissed, "I don't want a rug."

"Please to sit," he said, indicating a chair against the wall. "Mint tea while you look at rugs?"

"I don't want to sit," I said.

They'd set me up.

The man started to talk about the rugs, the number of knots, the quality of the wool. "Please, mint tea?" he offered.

"How do I make this clear?" I said, standing up. "I don't want tea and I don't want to buy a rug." I hadn't paid attention coming in, but I remembered stairs had been involved. I stalked around and found the door, but was reluctant to step into the street, darkening now, filled with greedy hands and jeering dark gazes. I stayed inside as the gatekeeper held a one-sided conversation with me about Texas and cowboys while someone chased down Abdul.

He was probably off paying the grabber, or berating him. Or getting stoned. I heard the hissing and throat clearing of Arabic, but I ignored it. Served 'em right for tricking me!

How dare that man touch me? How dare he! My shaking was gone, but I was livid.

"You did not buy a beautiful rug?" Abdul asked, stepping into the store.

"I do not want a rug," I said. Shouted. I didn't want a guide either, but every glance seemed malicious.

"Rugs are very good investment," Abdul said, his voice sad.

"I want to leave," I said, and managed an icy smile for the carpet sellers before marching out to join the multitudes doing their shopping, their gossiping, their errands, their plotting.

Abdul had to run to catch up.

I felt watched. A creepy feeling that ran right up my spine and bored into my head. Was this how a bird felt before it was snatched by a raptor? The hazy awareness that danger was out there? But no certain knowledge of what it meant, exactly, until a shadow fell across you, and you, too, became a statistic.

"Shall we go for dinner?" Abdul said, in front of me again. "Perhaps—"

"The hotel," I said, tripping into him as he slowed and turned to me.

"The hotel doesn't have a good dinner, they—"

"Take me to my hotel. Now." It was the tone that got sixth graders to shut up while visiting the habitat, and it also worked on Abdul. He shrugged and set off at double his normal pace. With one arm over my bag, and a glare around the street in general, I followed him, up and down the rough pavement. Some junctures looked familiar, but I didn't feel like striking out on my own.

We exited the souk, onto the street that ran above my hotel. Taxis lined the sunset-stained road. I waved one down. Abdul turned to me, confused. "Your hotel is right there. You don't need a taxi."

My hotel was in the souk. Right here. Not far enough away. I wanted out. Never in my life had someone laid hands on me, or taken any kind of advantage of me. I'd tried to embrace this city, but it had tricked and fooled and lied to me at every step. I felt violated. "I'm going to the station."

"But the bus for Larache isn't until tomorrow, one-fifteen o'clock," Abdul said, frowning and puzzled. I glared into each eye. The taxi driver watched everything with crossed arms, the trunk of his Mercedes already popped.

In my euphoria of belonging this afternoon, I'd opted not to buy my Larache ticket. Which was good, because while the bus to Larache might not be until tomorrow, something was going somewhere tonight, and I was going to be on it. I couldn't stay here another night. I was shaking. I was horrified to be so weak, but it didn't matter.

Out. Away. Gone. "I'm going to the train station."

The Train

We boarded in full darkness. The overnight express to Marrakesh was scheduled to leave at 10:15, but we were still loading at 10:45. I was hungry, but the station was so new—literally built so the king could visit the city—that despite signs advertising a cafeteria, one hadn't been built yet. Same with the Left Luggage office, though again, there was a sign.

If I had known how late our actual departure was going to be, I would have walked across the darkened fields toward the place where the magic word "pizza" flashed in pink and green, like the taunting glimpses of a rare bird one hears, but never fully sights. Why hadn't I banked on the train being late and gotten food? It's not like anything else ran on time!

Then again, would I willingly step into darkness alone in Tangier? Better to be hungry.

How dare that man touch me? Why me? Had it been a set up? What if . . . but better anger than fear. Better to be outraged than consider that if something had happened, no one would know, I'd just be another statistic. *"An American woman walked into the souk . . . vanished."*

Two bunk beds equaling four couchettes filled the room. Stomach growling, I climbed into mine, as narrow as a cot at a cheap sleepaway camp. But my sheets were ironed, and my blanket hadn't pilled. I wadded up my jacket for a pillow and tied my bags to a wall rack at my feet. I adjusted my stupid money belt, worn at Zephyr's insistence, so that I could lie down comfortably. With a groan I slipped off my shoes. The noises and voices in the corridor lulled me. I might have the cabin to myself.

Wrong.

In quick succession two young Frenchmen took the lower berths. Both stripped off jackets and shirts and shoes, made their beds and lay down after mumbling, "*Bonne nuit.*"

I dozed until the purser came by to check and clip our tickets. The two Frenchmen turned off their reading lamps as the train rolled out of the station.

Tangier was almost behind me.

The tension of the past few days evaporated. I had the grim recollection of skinning a bird and watching it fold in on itself when the skeleton was removed.

I felt like that, but in a good way.

After all, no matter what Marrakesh was like, it had to be better than Tangier. And I cared less about getting to Larache than getting out of Tangier.

Patterns of light shifted through the window. The train slowed and stopped several times. I heard doors and low voices, but I felt safe.

The door jolted open. I heard Arabic whispers.

A man stepped into my cabin.

Through slitted eyes I saw that he was tall and black haired. He tossed a single backpack on the bed opposite, then pulled off his shirt in one movement, revealing strong, broad shoulders. When he turned toward the window I saw his black beard.

The man from the souk!

It couldn't be the man from the souk, I thought, wide awake and pulse throbbing.

Yeah, how many tall, broad Arabs have you seen? Crazy-Elize asked. Just a coincidence, I reasoned.

I should have bought both berths. My peace of mind was worth the extra fifteen dollars. *How did he get in here? How did he know?* Was the purser in on it? Ignoring the three-step ladder, the man lifted himself onto the bunk.

Proving himself strong enough to yank me into an alley.

The zip, or rather, unzip, of his pants made me start shaking again, but the sound was followed almost immediately by snoring. Didn't sound like he was faking it, either.

After he'd been snoring for a while I turned my head and peered at him through my eyelashes.

He had the height and a beard, just like the grabber.

But his hands crossed on his chest, almost in prayer, glittered. I couldn't make out exact details, but every finger had a silver ring. One leg hung out from his blanket, and his skin wasn't dusky, just tanned. Of course, I was making these decisions based on the occasional streak of light from the window as we hurtled south.

My glance returned to the rings. I didn't recall rings. Wouldn't I have felt them with how hard and tight he'd grabbed me? I ran my fingers over my wrist, but found no marks, and I didn't remember any sensation of being pinched or cut. He continued to snore, and breath by breath, I unkinked.

Even if he was my would-be kidnapper, we were both on a train now. I opened the edge of the curtain with my toe. Blackness. No villages, no towns. Just brilliant stars in a raven-dark sky. Nine screws on each side of the windows. Twenty-eight curtain rings.

Everyone was pretty much stuck with the status quo, until Marrakesh.

The rhythm of the rails soothed me. In the end, the grabber hadn't gotten me. No one ever had to know that I'd let my guard down, that I had been so gullible, so stupid. I wouldn't be again.

As I drifted off to sleep, I wondered: what *are* my kidnapping talents?

❖

Zephyr's notes, done in her loopy handwriting when I know she'd rather have e-mailed them, made me cringe. She'd noted details like the time difference, the new location of the train station, the gull-like guides in Tangier. My ears burned with embarrassment. I could have saved myself so much grief. At least I'd followed her final piece of Tangier advice: "Get out at any cost!" Her next suggestion was to buy antibiotics; they were OTC here, but I never got sick, so I wouldn't worry. To be safe, though, I wouldn't drink the water.

I'd slept through all three men leaving their berths. Disembarking had been disorganized and I hadn't seen them or the maybe-grabber. The passengers had scattered, leaving me sipping my coffee in the Marrakesh train station, looking out on cloudless blue skies and pots overflowing with scarlet flowers—nine pots by the benches, four flower beds built around trees on the platform. Maybe I was catching up to what this trip was supposed to be.

Getting from here to Larache was going to take effort and multiple stops. For reasons I didn't understand a direct taxi wasn't possible, but I could at least leave my cursed rolling bag here in the Left Luggage office while I spent the day in town. Then I'd take the evening train to Casablanca, then buses and buses and buses to Larache. I'd gone south to go west and then far north. I shook my head.

ETA 3 P.M. tomorrow, 5 P.M. at the latest. Plenty of time to shower before going out to the site, or before seeing Sam. Sam. He seemed so removed from the squalor and confusion and randomness of this place and these past few days. He was order and precision, Teutonic, like my folks.

Well, like the grandparents who raised me like parents. I didn't think of Fischer, and was grateful that all the periodicals I'd seen had been in Arabic.

I finished my coffee, and swiped on lip balm. Marrakesh, even this early, felt warm and dry. I pocketed the receipt. Zephyr would be so proud, since she'd reminded me this trip was tax deductible. I picked up my bags, and strolled through the doors.

After checking my luggage (which could be left for up to six months, I was told), I walked past orange juice sellers ("Do *not* drink because it's made with tap water," Zephyr's notes said), nut sellers, what looked like milkshake vendors, and a man hawking bread rings stacked on a six-foot pole on the way to the taxi stand.

A place, I gathered after glancing around, also known as the curb.

A taxi pulled up and I took a deep breath, ready to butcher some French. "Place Dj—"

"Place Djemaa El-Fna," said a man, appearing from nowhere and cutting in front of me, leaning into the passenger window to speak to the driver.

The taxi driver hopped out to open the trunk. "How much?" I asked, ignoring the interloper. I was calm. Reasonable. I'd been here first. Waiting. I even knew what the charge was supposed to be, thanks to Zephyr's notes.

"Ten," the driver said, reaching for my bag and dropping it in the trunk.

"Ten! It's supposed to be five!" I said.

"I'll split it with you," the line-cutter said to me in accented English as he opened the passenger door for me. He threw his backpack in the back seat, then crawled in after it. A shared ride. Okay. A common practice, Zephyr's notes had said.

I was still closing the door as the taxi driver squealed out of the station. I held on as the driver pulled a U-turn, then screeched to a halt behind a row of camels and some bicyclists.

I stared. Camels. On the roadway?

One looked over its shoulder like it heard my thoughts. It seemed to say to me: *Shut the hell up. Of course camels. It's Morocco.*

Fourteen pompoms hung off each side of the camel's saddle, swaying in time.

"*Bonjour*," I heard from the interloper in the taxi's back seat.

I turned around and came face to face with the bearded man from the train, seeing him properly for the first time. The one whose many rings had suggested, but had not confirmed, that he wasn't the grabber from the Tangier souk.

He grinned at me, white teeth framed between a black beard and dark shades. "*Ça va?*"

I controlled my flinch, grateful for the Oakleys that hid my gaze.

Was he the guy, or not? He looked like him, but he didn't seem to smell like the grabber, and did I even remember what that guy had actually looked like? Could I just ask the man in the back seat to remove his glasses? I grimaced at him and turned back to the front. Was he following me?

He couldn't be the grabber, I was sure of it. The rings. I would have felt the rings.

My pulse slowed again.

Traffic idled, then raced. Businesspeople on bikes; pairs of boys on all manner of two-wheeled, motorized conveyances; donkeys and their robed owners; camels, sleepy eyed and chewing; and a dozen different small, featureless cars zipped in and out and around assorted lumbering Mercedes. Choking dust and the smell of donkey droppings floated through the window. I breathed through my nose, eyes watering.

"That's the McDonald's," he said from the backseat as we passed an affluent-looking building. How could he tell? I didn't see golden arches. All the buildings on the road were the same reddish color, the same squarish shape. Then as we passed, I saw the familiar logo on the wall. Discreet. "All the local girls go there to meet their American Prince Charmings."

I couldn't place his accent.

"McDonald's," the taxi driver said with sudden animation. "You like McDonald's?" He smiled. "All Americans like McDonald's." He turned to me, "You are American."

It wasn't a question. He knew. "How . . . ?"

"Your money belt," the voice from the backseat said, in a birder's whisper. "Only Americans wear money belts. You might as well flash the stars and stripes."

We entered a newly constructed traffic circle. An official-looking building spread on one side, flanked by formal gardens and a fountain. Opposite it empty lots collected trapped plastic bags and construction debris.

Reddish walls rose three stories on either side of us, closing in. Too fast to see detail, too many details to count. More people. More action. The taxi screeched left and we entered an enormous plaza. I braced for impact as we raced through the middle. The driver braked before we funneled into a narrow street. "La Place."

I opened the door and a roar surrounded me. Submerged me. More crowded than ten Spring Breaks and more clustered than a dozen Christmas Bird Counts. Movement everywhere. Color on everything. Chaos. My eye couldn't settle. My ear couldn't distinguish. My esophagus felt constricted, my feet rooted to the ground.

I found myself holding my bag, the money I'd had out to pay the driver gone, as the taxi zoomed halfway across the market place—backward.

"C'mon," the bearded, possibly dangerous, but English-speaking guy said. "I'll buy you breakfast. Pay you back for the ride." My gaze fell to his silvery fingers. *He spoke English.*

Other voices, other languages, beat off my eardrums. Wailing, whispering, laughing, talking. I couldn't hear the wind or birdsong. I couldn't understand a word around me. Red dust already coated my feet, but I was terrified to take a step.

Some people complain that when they're in the midst of a group of birds—any birds: grackles, seagulls, even sparrows if there are enough—the noise is disorienting, the confusion of the flapping and flying makes them almost uncertain which way is up. I'd never felt that way in avian culture, but I felt it now.

A screech of gulls; a ubiquity of sparrows. I swallowed hard.

Had I ever been in such a large space? Maybe the size of six, eight football fields? And my eye didn't know where to focus. It wasn't like there was some activity I was trying to narrow in on, it was nothing but panoramic fluttering, flitting, cawing, crying . . . and these were people.

I heard a horn, and before I could ascertain where it was coming from I was yanked backward as a car zipped by my legs, with barely an inch to spare. "Not good to stand in the street," the English speaker said. "Where are you going?"

Never explain yourself. Zephyr hadn't said that. Zephyr wouldn't even agree with that, but I'd heard it before, all my life, from Pop. *People are out to get you. Never tell where you're going or what you're doing, or why.* A lifetime of fighting nature, the government, and his community had taught him those lessons.

I couldn't think of a response.

"I repeat: how about I buy you breakfast to pay you back for the ride?"

Never accept offers from strangers. I opened my mouth to decline, but his words were the only ones I understood in all this babble. If he left me here, alone . . . I swallowed again and tried to corral my thoughts. Breakfast with him would give me a moment to get acclimated. All I needed was time to adjust, to sit a little while, like a migrant who catches its breath and needs to feed when it finally reaches its destination. My racing heart was coming under control.

"We'll go right over there," he said. "Café de France."

I followed his pointing finger, past the man selling water from a contraption on his back, past the group of men in long white robes playing instruments—the same five or so notes, up and down the scale—and past the women, swathed to their eyebrows, or wearing jeans with merest excuse of a dress over them, walking back and forth, talking on phones, wrangling children, balancing enormous loads of mint or clothes, to the awning of the café. The Roman English words made me sigh with relief. Perched on the edge of the Place, the café looked almost empty. Calming. "Okay," I said.

He walked away.

Not four steps in front of me, he was halted with shouts, hugs, back slaps. A man queried him in staccato Arabic (I assumed), and the bearded guy responded with ease. So English wasn't his native tongue? He moved on, waved goodbye, but another four steps and it happened again. Shouts, hugs, but this time I noticed he had exchanged plastic grocery bags, opaque and brightly colored, just like Abdul had done in Tangier. Was this whole country into drugs? I didn't think this guy was Moroccan, so he was tempting prison. But he was my only link to this world, at the moment.

I followed his stop and start progress, watched the people as they passed by me. We were a channel meeting a sea. Young men in open-necked shirts and jeans; older men in robes and turbans; kids in soccer shorts or dresses or any combination thereof. Some with satchels, some with earphones.

We arrived at the shade of the Café de France. The waiter greeted the guy in French, like a lost relative. Was the guy European? The English speaker pulled out a chair for me and another for my bag, waited until I was seated, then sat beside me, facing the Place, dropping his bag on the ground.

He ordered, and soon I had frothy coffee, a pastry, bread, jam, and butter before me. I couldn't look away from the Place, but I couldn't actually see it either. My eye jumped from movement to movement. I scanned the sky for something feathered, something familiar, but it remained an empty blue bowl.

The café's other patrons were older men. They read papers and chatted on phones and drank coffee. Normal, except one was in a suit and one in the dress I'd come to realize was typical for Moroccan men. Neither of them gave us a second look.

The guy turned to me. "First time in Marrakesh? You don't have to answer. The Place is pretty intense, at first go."

I'd kept my Oakleys on, but as I looked at him, I realized how impersonal it was to converse with someone who was wearing dark wraparound sunglasses. Questions that could be harmless on the surface, without being able to see this guy's eyes took on an ominous tinge. He definitely wasn't the guy from the souk. He was shorter, and he moved differently. Last night I'd been too scared to realize that. But who was he? And why did he want to know about me?

"What are those dresses the men wear?"

"Djellabas," he said. "More properly termed as 'robes.'"

"Of course," I said, and felt stupid for allowing myself to speak without caution, appearing more ignorant, than, admittedly, I already was. It had been in Zephyr's notes; I just hadn't known how to pronounce a *d* and a *j* next to each other. (A sort of silent *d*, apparently.)

He watched me for a minute. "You're going to get a headache, looking around like that."

I already had a headache. "Can you ever not be bowled over?" I said, admitting my weakness as my eyes darted from one movement to another. "I don't even—can't even—see it all."

"Ah, it's always overwhelming, but you learn to take it in little pieces. In vignettes. Like over there," he said, pointing with his chin. "See the orange seller in the turban?"

An old man, his wrinkled body wrapped in a dirty sheet with a bright orange turban on his head and a metal container strapped to his back, limped through the Place. I realized now that the center section of the plaza was striped with salesmen laying out their goods, the space bordered with restaurants and shops. Not a tree in sight.

Behind the orange seller, a little boy, not much bigger than a toddler, imitated the old man, his walk, his hunch—he even wore half a juiced orange as a "turban."

I laughed.

"Drink your coffee," the guy beside me said. "Fifty years of French occupation has made Morocco one of the best places in the world for *café au lait* and pâtisserie."

"You're right, the coffee is delicious," I said, looking at the cup for the first time, tasting it for the first time, despite having consumed half the cup. "What is that noise?" I asked, watching the hordes of people moving on all sides of the restaurant.

He chuckled. "Which one? By the way, I'm Erik. You are . . . ?"

I tore my gaze away from the Place and turned toward the man. His hair was dark and curly, his beard fairly new, his cheeks rough with stubble. He did look a little bit dangerous. I saw evidence of multiple ear piercings, though he wore no earrings. "Do you have a name?" he asked. His lips were a little thin, his left incisor chipped. He also looked amused.

"Elize," I said, extending my hand automatically.

"*Bienvenue à Marrakesh*, Elize," he said, taking my hand. Shock rocketed through my body at his touch. Definitely not the grabber—if it had been this Erik, I might not have minded.

Though I couldn't see through his dark lenses, I felt his gaze. He'd received that shock, too. Slowly, he smiled.

The din of the Place faded. I felt that smile all the way to my core. It was a tempting revelation, like when a tree's branches moved in the wind and gave you a glimpse of that rare bird. It made everything else . . . still. It stopped the moment. It brought silence, beauty, and wonder all together.

The world seemed to widen around us, until it seemed as though we sat at a table outside of time. No pressure, no rush, no impatience, no waiting. Everything existed for our pleasure, at our whim. How could I help but smile back at such an irrational, comic, delicious thought?

He pushed his sunglasses up, and I stared into the darkest blue eyes I'd ever seen. Dark as those last minutes of dusk, dark like the shadowed feathers of a white-faced ibis, so darkly blue that you needed light to tell they weren't black. His lashes were short and spiky, and his nose had been broken once, then reset badly. I felt my responding smile.

He was waiting; there was anticipation in that smile. I pushed my Oakleys up to meet his gaze.

His expression flooded with surprise. "You," he breathed. That word felt like another kind of shock and I saw his pupils widen as we leaned toward each other.

A policeman's whistle brought back the reality of the square. Noise and smell and movement crashed in, and I looked away, chiding myself. What was wrong with me? What was that weird hypnotic feeling about? "Excuse me?" I said to Erik, turning back to face him.

Where had been the line of experience versus imagination at his response? I felt breathless, excited and bare. I dropped my Oakleys back down. Protective coloring.

In the center of the Place, a man dressed like a cop out of a Pink Panther movie stood on a podium and seemed to be directing the donkey-drawn carts and the bicycles, motorized bikes, mopeds, and other things that had engines and wheels but didn't strictly fit into any category of conveyance I'd seen before.

Erik smiled again, just an ordinary guy, and shook his head. "This is the Place Djemaa El-Fna."

"I've read about it. I guess you spend a lot of time here?" I said, fumbling for a topic even though I could barely focus. Six orange juice stands, that I could see. Were there more? *Can't count what you can't see—that's cheating.*

He shrugged. "I know some good men here," he said, then looked out at the center and nodded, directing my attention. "I'm always amazed at how much the women can carry," he said.

I saw the little old lady he indicated. She wore black veils, and balanced a wrapped parcel as long as she was tall on her head.

"Do you think she can make it?" Erik asked me, a dark brow lifted in query.

"Without ever touching it?" I said, watching her cross the Place at an angle. The thing wobbled on her head, but didn't fall. This time. That was incredible. Also impossible. "No," I said. "It's not attached?"

He shook his head. "She'll drop it?" Erik asked.

"No, but she'll definitely have to touch it," I said. "It's inevitable. It's too busy out there." A case-in-point bike screamed across the Place, dodging people and donkeys. The cop in the tower shrilled his whistle, but the biker just squealed into the narrow street at the opposite side of the Place, lost. Invisible.

"Betcha she doesn't," Erik said.

"You're on," I said, my eyes on the old woman, willing her to misstep. Wouldn't it be cool if she didn't, though?

Erik sipped his coffee and ate a piece of bread. He might have been dressed in ratty shorts and sandals, with a backpack that looked like it had been carried up Kilimanjaro and thrown back down, but he ate with grace. No crumbs, no dribbles, no open-mouthed chewing. A pleasant surprise. He appeared to have complete confidence in the old lady.

I kept trying to count the buildings surrounding the Place, but I couldn't discern where one began and another ended. Too far away. Too much obstruction.

Instead I counted the café. Thirty tables. Thirty bud vases, ten filled with three flowers each, the others with two. I let out a deep breath as my headache eased.

"What brings you to Marrakesh?" Erik asked. "You don't appear to be a tea-in-the-Sahara-beneath-the-sheltering-sky type."

Tea in the Sahara? What was he talking about? "Birds," I said, opting for honesty, and because I couldn't think of anything else. I opened my third bottle water of the day.

"Always get carbonated water."

"What? Why?"

"Because they can refill and reseal a plain spring water bottle, and you'll never know it, won't know why you get sick. But if your gassy water has no gas, you'll know not to drink it."

Gassy water . . . it took me a minute. Carbonated. "Does the water make you sick?" I asked.

He shook his head. "Carry my own. So, birds? Pretty serious about them, I see. Business or pleasure?"

He *was* following me! How did he know—? I felt my throat constrict.

"Calm down," he said. "You're carrying expensive binoculars and you have a pretty dark tan. Plus . . . " he gestured at my clothes.

Zip-off cargo pants in khaki. Darker khaki shirt, the kind that has sunscreen and bug repellant built in. Compared to the other tourists in brightly colored togs, tennis shoes and hats, I did look more serious. Severe. "So you're Sherlock Holmes? Putting all the pieces together and making your deduction?"

He laughed. "And you're an ornithologist?"

I chuckled, always surprised when someone got it right, didn't call me an orthodontist, or an ornerythologist, or a urologist. Blue eyes, nice manners, *and* he knew some Latin. "Yes, I am."

"Here to see the bald ibis, then?" he said. He'd put his glasses back on. "Or are you going farther into the desert?"

"You know about the bald ibis?"

His gaze on the Place, he said, "One of the—" He shook his head. "Unlucky me. She touched."

I looked back to the hunched figure, now almost undistinguishable in the confusion of the Place. She'd stopped, and had a hand up to balance the bundle before stepping into the narrow street.

I felt a little disappointed.

Erik turned to me, pushed his glasses up. His blue gaze was unearthly. "The bald ibis is one of the rarest birds in the world, and Souss-Massa is their confirmed nesting place. Everyone here knows that. You're an ornithologist from . . . somewhere in the southern U.S.? . . . so it makes sense that's why you're here. If you didn't fly into Caza, then stopping in M'kesh makes sense, *n'est-ce pas*?"

Logic. Reasoning. "Actually, migrations."

A frown flickered across his face. "Across the strait? You're a little south, aren't you?"

"A little," I bit off, finishing my coffee. *About 250 miles.*

He sat back and folded his arms over his chest. His shirt was like most Moroccan men's, open-necked, collarless, and long. I tried not to notice how it tightened over his chest. For a druggie, if he was one, he was rather well-muscled and healthy. Was kif a steroid? "I'm sorry if I woke you up last night," he said. "I'd been at a wedding in Tangier, and it lasted until, well," he chuckled, flashing his chipped incisor, "noon the next day."

"The wedding at the Hotel Continental?" I blurted. He'd recognized me from the train?

"Yes," he said, leaning forward. "You weren't there." It was a statement.

"No, I wasn't, but I heard the music."

"Yeah, we sang until we were hoarse. Then we drank tea and sang some more."

I almost came out of my seat. "*You* were singing!"

He nodded, half-grinning. "It happens."

"I thought it was a recording! You were so perfect."

"Words I've rarely heard," he said.

I still stared at him, trying to put it all together. "What were the songs?"

"Traditional pieces," he said. "You should have come down, it was a great wedding. The daughter of the mayor and the son of one of the city's carpet merchants. Both old *familles tangéroises*."

"You sing?" I asked, feeling my face redden. "Obviously, I mean, but . . . professionally? What group are you in?"

"No group, it's family," he said.

"Yours?"

"No," he chuckled. "No, but I blend and I can be loud and," he shrugged, "I've been lucky to know them." He chuckled again. "You came from Tangier to Marrakesh, to go north?"

Was it a change of topic because he was embarrassed, or something else? His rings flashed in the sun.

I shrugged.

"Same hotel, same train, same taxi," he murmured. "Interesting." He took a sip of coffee as I stared at the Place, inhaling the fumes, the underlying stink of sewage beneath the aroma of croissants and coffee.

Interesting how? I wanted to ask.

"The souk's open, if you wanted to get anything," he said.

I smiled. "I don't really shop." I heard the primness in my tone. "I mean, there's other things to do with one's time, and who needs all that stuff anyway?" Erik stared at me as I recited the speech I'd heard a hundred-dozen times from Mama. "Women don't need trinkets to prove their femininity."

He looked down at his hands, all the rings. "Always the male bird that's flashier, right?"

"Yeah, the female is always drab."

He laughed.

"Part of keeping themselves and their progeny safe from predators." I imagined he was looking at my bare throat and arms and ears. I was a scientist, a serious female. Frankie was the one who paraded makeup and jewelry and elaborate plumage.

"That was a bad thought," he said, and I realized he'd been watching my expressions.

"I'm just not a big fan of blue jays," I said.

He glanced the direction I stared. "Aren't they pretty blue birds?"

I stared blindly at the Place. "Yeah, that's what they want you to think."

Awkward silence.

"Speaking of blue, do you like gardens? The Majorelle is stunning. Yves Saint-Laurent refurbished it, and it has a thousand kinds of cactus—"

"Cacti," I corrected automatically.

He fell silent.

"I'm sorry," I said. "That was rude. It's a plurals thing."

He stared at me, and I had the sense he was debating whether or not talking to me was worth it. Suddenly I wanted very much for him to decide yes. "Where are you from?" I asked.

"Everywhere."

A slap down. I watched the covered women in brightly colored, glittering scarves pass in front of us. The men, slight, bearded. My gaze shifted back to the women. I didn't shop, but I did give gifts. Zephyr would love this place, would love the colors, the vibrancy of it all. "What do they sell in the souk?" I asked, trying again.

Erik turned an eye on me. "Anything. Everything. What do you want?"

"I have a colleague," I said. "Maybe a scarf?"

He stared at me, and I was aware of time ticking by. He hadn't actually offered to show me around the souk, he'd just mentioned it. I'd presumed too much. Twenty Moroccan robes hung in the store exactly opposite. Five brass pots glittered out front.

"I could show you a place," he said. "If you want."

"I'd appreciate it," I said, stifling a yawn.

"You've got a room, right?" he said.

"I'm meeting friends," I said, seizing on my protective coloring again. *Always pretend to be waiting for friends. Waiting for a call. Never let someone know you're alone.*

"I don't doubt it. Here or there?"

"They'll call," I said.

He sighed. "Because if you are going to need a place to stay tonight—"

I cut him off before this became embarrassing. "No, but thank you. It's a kind offer."

He half-grinned. "I offer nothing except advice. If you're staying the night, get that booked first. Rooms in Marrakesh, especially now, are hard to find. By one P.M. most everything will be booked."

"You're kidding!" I said. My train was tonight, but I couldn't forget that transportation hadn't been particularly trustworthy.

"It's high season," he said, looking at me with surprise. I hadn't known that. He slipped his glasses back on, becoming a slightly menacing stranger. "You could go to Caza or something this afternoon, but . . . " He smiled again. Fortunately, it was a normal smile, "But then you would miss the storks."

"*Storks, Ibises and Spoonbills*," I said. "One of my favorite books."

"So you've heard about Marrakesh's famous storks? Don't you want to see them?"

I did want to see them. "Used to be a stork hospital here, right?"

He nodded. "There's a great little *riad* around the corner. Are you game? It's nice, it might be a bit dear, but the view is stunning." He spoke with his hands, reflections of his rings dashing all over the place. "Rooftop garden, a view of the Atlas when the peaks are out. You can just look at it if you want."

"Ree-ahd?" I repeated. I'd seen that word, but hadn't known how to pronounce it.

"A townhouse in the medina, though most of them are hotels these days," he said.

I rose, picked up my duffel, and tossed it over my shoulder. "Sure," I said. As we walked to the edge of the Place I saw the signs of lunchtime approaching. Tables and chairs spilled into the street and vendors doubled their cries. I felt aware again.

I hadn't seen Erik pay, but no one tried to stop us, so I figured it was okay. We walked to the corner where the taxi had stopped, and crowded into the narrow street.

Almost instantly the dull roar of the Place disappeared. I heard a panicked *krok,* the call of a cattle egret. Relief flooded me. There were birds here. Above a shop in the Place, one perched on the flat roof. The same species I saw in the pasture on Mustang Island, feeding off the flies that bothered cattle, here, in Morocco. Something familiar. Something I knew.

I'd be all right.

The street was wide enough for four people to stand shoulder to shoulder. Every door was full of men, women, children: buying, talking, smoking. Though I tried to note the landmarks, the feeling of being stared at distracted me. I kept looking back at the white plumed bird, adapted to its environment, content here.

The stones were slimy and I felt myself slide once or twice. Urine. Mint. Leather. Roasting chicken. We passed several signs in English, with directions toward Riad This or That, but Erik continued walking.

Tagines cooked in the open air. Cured meat hung from hooks. Windows filled with Nikes (in colors that I doubted Corporate had ever imagined) lured the eye. The street felt informal, filled with conversations, calls, laughter. I relaxed. People, going about their day.

People like me. Differently dressed than those in Port Rockton or Corpus, but the same. Late employees, hungry kids, tired moms. Dads going to and from work.

"It's here," Erik said, and turned into a narrower, darker alley. I pushed my Oakleys up on my head, and glanced after him. No people, no signs, nothing except an opening halfway down. It seemed to be a dead end. I gripped my duffel tighter. He stepped into the opening, a doorway. I followed, three cautious steps behind.

The foyer of the hotel—the riad—was claustrophobically tiny and hallucinatingly tiled. Erik chatted with the beautiful dark-haired girl behind the desk. "They don't have any of the rooftop rooms available," he said to me, "but they do have a room with a bath."

The girl said the price, but the words "with a bath" had already sold me. I nodded and she asked for my passport. "To register," she said to me.

"It's the law," Erik said at my hesitation. Right. The same as in Tangier.

I pulled out the document and handed it to her, and she handed me a sheet to fill out, as lengthy and comprehensive as a health insurance application. "Did you want to go to the souk now?" Erik asked as I scrawled my signature, twenty minutes later.

The girl looked at my last name, raised her brows in disbelief. "*Merci, mademoiselle*," she said, and handed my passport and key to me. It would be great just to have a place to drop my stuff.

"Yes," I said to him.

"I'll wait for you."

The City

The sun blazed down now that it was full noon. Sweat speckled my shirt as we crossed the Place, joining the insanity. But once in it, the Place seemed less congested. No one walked too close, or stared too hard. Everyone was occupied with his or her own task. Erik walked slower than I preferred and I found myself adjusting to his pace.

Something in my focus changed, and the blur of images became pieces, parts. Shops with leather ottomans and leather camels the color of goldfinches. T-shirts with rude sayings and poor translations, hung between generic "I (heart) Morocco" ones.

"Scarves, hmm?" Erik said, pushing his glasses up and looking at me.

"Yeah, I think so," I said.

We were swallowed alive by another world.

The street was covered now, narrow and jostling with people. Underwear, sports shirts, and djellabas swung from hangers above us. Gold-embroidered sashes and veils and hats were pinned to the walls, like exhibits of butterflies. Display windows filled with dull silver jewelry set with reddish and bluish stones dangled with chains and bells, heavy pieces that would weigh down a camel. Earrings, dozens of pairs, were displayed on bulletin boards, prices handwritten on tiny pieces of paper resembling carrier pigeon messages. Shoes, pairs on top of pairs, ranging from smaller than my palm to the size of large ducks, all backless, all bright or embroidered or appliquéd, or all three.

"Would she like some babouches?" Erik said, noting my gaze.

I'd seen these shoes on everyone. Before we could move on, an old man started in on his spiel, his voice leaden, his smile chipper. I had no resistance. "What shoe, *madame*? What shoe you want? What shoe, *madame*? Which shoe you like?" I pointed to a pair, just to stop the questions.

He cleared the top off a stool and told me to "Sit, sit" while he found them in my size. I didn't tell him what it was, he just guessed. "Tea?" he said to Erik. "Like tea?"

Erik glanced at me and I shook my head. The man waited while I ripped open the Velcro on my sandals. I slipped into the babouche and noticed it was slick as ice, the sole thin as felt. I shook my head, putting my sandal back on, as the man brought out another style and another color.

"*La shukran*," Erik whispered, "It means 'no, thank you.'"

On my feet again, I *la shukran*ed the man until we were out of sight. We passed shop after shop displaying leather and brass and jewelry, the hawkers knowing what we wanted, jumping in front of us.

But somehow, it wasn't annoying. Not like the midges of Tangier who clung and surrounded and harassed, block after block. "Expensive scarves, or cheap?" Erik asked me. A whiff of scented air caught me, stopped me. I turned toward it, and Erik glanced back at me and laughed.

"Time for the spice market? Come on," he said, and I followed him down an even narrower, busier alleyway.

Both sides were lined with tables and bins, all the colors of Morocco heaped in them. "Paprika," Erik said, pointing to a mound of red. "Called *fefla hlouwa*. And saffron," he said, pointing to a jar filled with red-gold tendrils. "Expensive, but essential to Moroccan cooking."

"I know that one," I said, indicating a mound of warm brown, "it's cinnamon."

He nodded, then held some seeds beneath my nose. They smelled almost Mexican to me. "Cumin," he said, "and of course, hot red pepper."

I inhaled too much and turned away to bury my sneeze. My eyes watered.

"Are you okay?"

I nodded.

"And my favorite, *ras al hanout.*"

"What is it?" I said, sniffing the sweet-spicy mixture made of seeds and powders and flakes.

"Means "top of the shop." Each merchant makes a little different combination. Generally though, it's thirteen spices, a magic number," he said with a flash of a smile, "and if you mix it with minced garlic and chopped fresh herbs to spread on fish or poultry, it is a taste of heaven."

It smelled exotic, flowery, and a little decadent.

"And all of these aid in digestion, help the body, do all the things that Western medicine is looking for right now."

"Spices are the new medicines?" I teased.

"For some things."

The next stand was sweets, thin pastry sheets wrapped in a dozen different ways, with honeyed nuts peeking through the leaves or layers or strands. Naked nuts were mountained beside them, cashews and pepitas and almonds and pistachios. The pastels of sugared almonds contrasted with the Spanish red pistachios and the bleached husks of pumpkin seeds.

"Through here," he said, stepping into a narrow space. One other person was in the alley, an old woman selling mint, gorgeous handfuls of the stuff. The bright smell won against the stink of urine as we passed. We stepped forward onto a main thoroughfare and joined in with the masses, remnants of a flock joining the main body again.

"This is the area for most textiles," he said. "If you want something to treasure, you'll probably find it here."

The shop we entered was more enclosed than the others, and the keeper spoke to Erik as I looked through stacks of color.

The scarves were large. Cardinal red, oriole yellow, peacock blue, and jay green, spanning Audubon's palette. Silver and gold threads picked out secondary patterns on the weave. Zephyr would love one. She wore scarves in her hair, around her hips, she tied them as bandeau tops and wrapped them into belts. But which one?

The shopkeeper left for a moment, and Erik joined me as I plowed through the collection.

"What's she like, your friend?" he said. I glanced at him, for the emphasis on "friend" made it sound like he thought I was using her as an excuse. Like maybe she didn't exist.

"My colleague is dramatic," I said. "Dynamic."

"What colors does she like?"

"Bright ones. She's a redhead, but despite that she wears red and orange and pink. She also likes blue."

"What color are her eyes?" His tone was serious, and he watched me flip through the scarves, laid flat, like miniature rugs. "Are they blue, like yours?"

I opened my mouth, Zephyr's eyes were brown, but . . . "What do you mean, 'like mine'?"

"Icy," he said, staring into me. "Cool. Almost gray, maybe silver. Scandinavian eyes."

I wasn't sure if I'd been complimented or insulted. Icy silver eyes?

Erik watched me until I looked back at him. "Do they smolder?" he asked.

"Her eyes?"

"No," he said, stepping closer. "In the right situation, do yours?" The look he gave me melted my kneecaps, and I clenched the scarves in my hand. I couldn't look away from him. Then it dawned on me . . . he was flirting.

Flirting wasn't a skill I'd acquired. Oh sure, I could seduce, but my success had more to do with my aggression and long legs than any perceived style. I tended toward the forthright: your place or mine?

Talking about eyes was out of my league. Not up or down, just out.

"I bet yours do," I gambled, staring into his almost black gaze.

"My friends, do you need any help?" the shopkeeper, who introduced himself as Oman, said.

"You have to have these," Erik said, holding up a tiny pair of filigreed hand earrings, each with a dark blue stone in the center of its palm. "It's the Hand of Fatima, which will bring you good luck."

"I don't know about Fatima, but I could sure use the luck."

"We make our own luck. But Fatima," Erik said, stepping toward me, earrings in hand, "was the daughter of the prophet Muhammad. You do know who Muhammad is?"

"The god of Muslims? I mean, the prophet?"

"The prophet," Erik said. "There is no God but Allah."

"Allah," I repeated, pulling the hair back from my ear. He slipped the earring in and stepped back. "It looks beautiful."

Oman thrust a mirror at me. "To see. Very beautiful."

I looked into the mirror, and was surprised at how different I looked. I wear my hair in a braid most of the time. Today I'd unwound it so it swirled over my shoulders, blonde, streaked with near white. My eyes did look gray in this light, but also light-filled. The earring—small, delicate—looked . . . sexy.

"Do you like?" the shopkeeper asked.

Erik didn't say anything, just watched me.

I nodded, surprised my earholes were still open. It had been years, I guessed, since I'd worn earrings. I put the other earring in and swung my head, feeling the gentle shift of weight. I liked them.

I chose three scarves, two pair of earrings, and a bangle bracelet, and pulled out my card. The sign proclaimed all plastic was welcome.

"Oh, *madame*, we are so sorry, but the machine," the shopkeeper shrugged. "It is broke! Cash only."

Exhaustion rolled over me like a ten-foot wave. Another ATM, then I'd have to come back, find my way through those winding streets to this shop.

Erik took the stuff out of my hand and set it down. "We don't have cash," he said. "Thank you." He took my hand and led me away.

"Wait! Wait! I will try once more, but the machine, it is—"

Erik looked at me. "Honey, do you want to wait?"

We were playing some game, because "honey" seemed a fast progression from strangers at breakfast, without sex in between. "Not one of their machines has worked since I landed," I whispered, glancing at the shopkeeper, who watched us like prey.

"You'll be amazed how fast it can be fixed," Erik said. He turned around. "Thank you, but we'll just go. We don't want to trouble you—"

I noticed he wasn't speaking in French or Arabic. He was acting like an American tourist.

"No, no! I try my brother's shop! You wait here!" Oman motioned to us as he shouted at a young boy across the way, then dashed out.

Erik and I stood, watched by the boy, awkward with each other. Our hands fell apart and I wandered to look at leather camels, aware of Erik's presence like I was a radar, and he was a flock of banded piping plovers.

The shopkeeper ran back in, with a handheld card reader. "My brother! He loaned me! Now, you wanted?" he said, and began to ring me up. I looked at Erik, who grinned. As we walked out, still playing the parts of "honeys," I linked my arm in his. "What was that about?"

"Credit card machines are always broken, but they can be fixed with just the threat of lost business."

"At the Hotel Continental—" I said.

"Their machine actually was broken. Their phone lines were down, too. The technician came to the wedding, but he had to fix the machine before the dancing began."

I laughed.

"It was rude, for Moroccans, to make him work like that," he said. "Proof of how much they needed it to work."

We made our way back to the Place, back to the sunshine. But the shops were closing, the square was emptying, and the sun kept growing stronger.

"If your colleagues aren't occupying your evening, perhaps you'd like to see the storks. With me?"

I turned to him, feeling the earrings shift with my movements. He handed me my Oakleys and put his sunglasses on, but I'd learned to read his face better. "I'll stop by for you, say six-thirty?" We stared at each other, and the square faded away from my awareness again. He bit his lip for just a moment, the chipped incisor making a quick appearance. "Meet you on the roof of your riad?" His tone made it sound like a proposition.

I glanced at my watch. It was almost three. A shower. A nap. And storks before my train. When I looked back at him, the spell was broken. I nodded my agreement.

The Night

At first I thought it was a bird—a weird squawk that sounded like a crow being choked—but then the feedback of a speaker jumped in and I sat up, sweat-soaked and confused. The noise continued. It seemed to be about to burst through the wall. Was someone being killed? After a few minutes it ended with another squawk and . . . feedback. Some kind of siren?

Then I heard a repetition of the noise in the distance, minus the squawk and the feedback. It was almost a song, joined by another somewhere else in the city.

What the hell? I crawled across the bed to my duffel—I hadn't gotten it into the armoire yet—and flipped through the pages of Zephyr's notes. Something in here . . . ah yes, call to prayer. Five times a day good Muslims prayed, facing Mecca. I must be right next to a minaret where the muezzin called the faithful. Had I slept through it before? How had I missed this? Or had I just not been beside the guy?

You would have thought that someone who made his living through public speaking would not have so wobbly a voice.

I rolled onto my back. The bed fit me. My room was narrow and long, the bed at one end by a window that looked into the courtyard with a splashing fountain open to the sky. A banquette seat with a table faced the door, just past the foot of the bed. Beyond that, the armoire faced another set of windows. The bathroom door was on the short wall. I'd scored my own shower and commode.

Everything was tiled: across the floor and up the walls—yellows, blues, reds. The doors were painted yellow. The heavy fringed wool bed covering was a different pattern of red and yellow. The ceiling was high, hung with pierced metal and stained glass lamps. The room felt cool and large. Nothing fussy or extraneous. You could decorate a beach house like this.

I thought of my beach condo. It would be a good rental. Sand colored, with everything nubby, which went well with wet bathing suits. Or just wet, in general. The balcony overlooked the Gulf. I'd painted the walls a dark robin's egg blue. Then I'd converted two old surfboards into a bench for the bar.

The shower was what had sold me on my condo: a place to sit, and a drink holder. It was a lazy shower, and I had great water pressure and one of those multiuse showerheads that provided hours of entertainment.

I'd have to hose my shower down with bleach before I stepped into it again, having rented it out. But as I looked around the hotel room, it occurred to me that my condo, where I'd lived for over ten years, was as impersonal as this room. Anything that indicated who I was, was in the storage area: bikes, kayaks, shoes, jackets, skis, and fins.

Beyond all that gear, did I have anything? I played with one of my new earrings, feeling the bead against my finger. I didn't have jewelry. Not one ring.

Erik sure did. What would make a man wear rings on every finger? Did they mean something?

Doctor San Diego—I couldn't keep calling him that in my head or I'd say it aloud one day—didn't wear jewelry. His clothing, from what I remembered in Miami, had been expensive and simple. I guessed his house was very spare, very expensive, too.

Erik most likely lived in a tent. He was a gypsy. With that scraggly beard he probably shouldn't try to get through U.S. Customs for a while, but there was something about him. An aura.

I pulled a pillow over my head, laughing. *Dear God, I sound like Zephyr, talking about auras.* She'd be so pleased, would regard it as "personal growth." Of course, the hotel–train–taxi coincidence she would take as a sign, as well. I sat up. What did getting shut out of my promotion indicate? What kind of sign was that? I jumped up, filled with nervous energy.

For all that Erik seemed hippie-cool, he had said 6:30. After checking the time, I hurried to the shower, stripping as I turned on the water. It was stupid that I was glomming onto some stranger because I didn't know . . . well, anything.

Stranded in this place, ignorant, because nothing had turned out right. I'd waited so long for that promotion. It would have made everything perfect. I still didn't understand what had happened, how Frankie—I spit, standing in the shower—could have done so much damage to me, so fast.

Sneaky. Tricking me, like Abdul.

Like Erik would? Like Erik was? Mr. Mysterious?

Sam, at least, was direct. In our clinch in the elevator, on my single trip out of Texas, he'd told me he was going to want me the next time he saw me. I'd asked, *Not till then?* And he'd said, *Out of sight, out of mind.*

No problem. It was true for me, too. My last serious relationship . . . I shrugged away the memories of Alan, of those dreams, of that heartbreak. Sam would be different.

However, my pulse didn't race at the thought of Sam. It had raced plenty at the touch of Sam, but—

Erik? Now we're talking a heartbeat.

He had an energy.

I got out, toweling briskly.

Erik had a vitality. Not rushed, or goal-oriented, but he hummed with intensity, with action. It was the way he watched the plaza, picking out dramas. Fitting into the scene, but with ease and leisure. Not even put off by the shopkeeper's intention to . . . what? Not swindle; just make it easier, cheaper, for himself. Couldn't fault him for that.

On the island the shopkeepers had a policy of cash only. Most of them conveniently had ATMs in their lobbies, but still.

I attacked my hair.

Frankie Stein wouldn't be in this position, a day's drive from the Waldrapp but incapable of getting there. She probably spoke French. She had probably done her dissertation on the Waldrapp ibis

The dead and dissected Waldrapp ibis

Frankie, I thought as I combed out my tangles, would take advantage of a guide. Handsome in his own way and knowledgeable, who knew a place she'd never been. Why not do the same? What was the point of having an enemy if you couldn't learn from her? Boy, did that sound like I was channeling Zephyr!

I threw the offensive money belt into the bottom of my rucksack and stuck my ID and money into a string purse I slung across my chest. I crossed my bins the other way.

Storks—and Erik—awaited me.

"Good evening," he said as I walked onto the roof. The sky was already streaked with color. Flowers wound through trellises, and potted plants in vibrant pinks, purples, reds, and terracotta dotted the scattered sitting areas of tables and chairs, lounges, and cassocks. Five sitting areas. Eleven tables. Fifteen lit candles. A tent pitched at one end was missing only a belly dancer and a camel.

The sounds of the Place were here, but distilled to the never-ending up and down of the flute, the chatter of voices, the clash and clatter of people and things. In the distance, it glowed as the city came alive for the evening. "How was your sleep?" Erik asked. Hadn't Abdul asked me exactly the same thing? I'd never had so much curiosity expressed about my napping. Of course, I didn't usually nap.

Erik's shorts had morphed into pants, his Moroccan shirt was a now dark green instead of dubious white. His cheeks were smooth above a trimmed beard. No sunglasses in sight.

A neater version of himself. He seemed expectant.

And knee-weakening sexy-raw.

"It was nice, thank you," I said, grateful I'd changed at the last minute, exchanging cargo pants for a long skirt, and a tunic top over my T-shirt. Zephyr had loaned me her low-slung belt—"It's not jewelry, Elize"—a new project by one of her artsy roommates. It did look great with the shirt and skirt. She'd be pleased to know she was right about that.

"What kind are those?" he asked, pointing to a line of birds in the distance.

"Sun's in the wrong place," I said, without a glance to the west. "Not even bins can help."

"Bins?"

"Binoculars," I said, tapping mine.

He nodded. "Ready?"

I followed him down the four flights of squared stairs, through the ornamental courtyard, and into the street. We got swept along with a flood of men wearing crocheted caps. I felt Erik take my hand, the shock of this morning somehow deeper and quieter, but still very noticeable. He glanced over his shoulder and smiled at me. He felt it, too. His collection of rings felt warm against my fingers. I kept my other hand on my string bag.

His hand was callused. What kind of backpacker had a callused hand?

"I guess the minaret is up the street?" I said to him as we stepped into the larger thoroughfare and could walk side by side.

"The mosque, you mean?" he said.

"Mosque," I said, corrected. That's what I got for knowing nothing and trying to show it off.

"The minaret is the tower," he said, "associated with the mosque."

"My mosque-man," I said, unwilling to try to pronounce "muezzin," "needed some lessons in using a mic." We walked away from the Place. The streets were filling up; I saw more women than before, women with lists and children and lots of shopping bags, plastic ones, doomed to end up with their kindred, trapped and empty along the roadside. Something the U.S. and Morocco had in common.

"Mew-ehz-zin," Erik supplied. "Yes, technology makes it a new world. Used to be the muezzin climbed to the top of the minaret and called out, but now it's a digital recording and he's at the bottom. I miss the old way."

"Mine sounded less than enthusiastic," I said.

"Each mosque, each muezzin, has its own character."

"Are you Muslim? How do you know so much?"

He laughed and glanced at me. "No, no, but I've traveled a lot in these countries."

"'These' meaning Muslim, or 'these' meaning African, or what?" I said.

He smiled at me, then pushed me forward, releasing my hand. "Glad to see the nap revived you," he said. "Step carefully here."

The man hated answering questions. I hated not getting answers.

I'd seen cow paths wider than this street. Above me the buildings all but blocked out the sky, now dotted with the silhouettes of birds. Pigeons and doves and swallows, but no storks. The walkway stones were dry, but I still had the sense of stepping on them in bare feet. I could feel every curve beneath my sandals. Erik walked with confidence behind me, but I felt like I picked my way. Wrenching my ankle would be stupid, if just a moment of caution could prevent it.

Frankie, in her initial birding enthusiasm, had halted a whole group's progress by doing just that. On a day, as irony would have it, that she wasn't wearing heels. Zephyr and I had taken turns getting her food while she worked from her motel room, one leg elevated to help with swelling.

We'd laughed a lot together, then.

"Here," Erik said, and darted into an even narrower alley. I felt a moment of trepidation: if he was going to do anything grim, it would be here, now. Braced, I hurried after him. A moment later we stepped into another street, jostled by people. I relaxed. Again he took my hand and led me.

Led me. Had I been drugged? Was this Stockholm Syndrome? I didn't respond well to being led. I either led, or forged my own path.

Yet I trailed him like some kind of entranced, hopeful peahen after a peacock.

I was following a total stranger alone, in a city where I wasn't altogether certain I could find a taxi or a cop or anything else, especially my way back to my hotel.

I could almost hear Zephyr's conspiratorial giggle. Conspiring against me.

Erik halted, facing a stone wall across a narrow, mostly empty street. "The storks of Marrakesh," he said.

The sound of hissing, how storks communicate.

Ciconia ciconia. The birds nested on the roof, the sunlight perfectly revealing them.

"A muster of storks," I whispered.

"What did you say?"

"Each bird group—well, a lot of them—have a poetic plural. Like a muster of storks."

He stared at me. "Like 'a wake of vultures'?"

I nodded.

"So what kind are they?" he asked, looking at the storks. "What kind of muster?"

"White."

"I see that, but—"

"It's their common name. It differentiates them from the black stork, which is all black, except for its belly and breast," I explained as I took out my notebook and opened it.

"They look like they have eye makeup on."

I glanced at him with a grin. "That's a field mark called an eye ring." We had wood storks at the Institute sometimes, but not like these beauties. The black and white of their feathers, the red of their beaks and legs against the rosy wall, the backdrop of the setting sun—all of it took my breath away.

"They stand out well against the *pisé*," he said. "Those are their nests?"

Piles of big sticks lined the top of the wall, like a street in an avian suburbia. "Four nests, and what appear to be six pairs," I said, noting it. "Do you want to see?" I took the leash from around my neck and handed him my bins.

He peered through them. "Oh, wow," he said. "It's like being up there."

I fought the urge to put the leash around his neck. First rule: Hang them in case you drop them. "What do you see when you see birds?" he asked.

His question was innocuous enough, but just the sort of thing to panic me. "Incredible evolutionary architecture," I said, my answer well rehearsed, not sounding defensive at all.

"Thank you," he said, and handed the bins back to me. I put the leash back around my neck.

"Are those families? Is that what you mean when you say pairs?"

"Yes," I said. "In breeding season, each of those nests would contain about four eggs. But these are migrants, flying between—" I summoned the numbers from my memory. "—twelve hundred and sixty-five hundred miles for the winter."

Erik whistled low. "How many birds do that?"

I continued to watch the birds, noting that it's numbers that make up ornithology: how often a bird eats, grooms, interacts. "Storks fly on thermals, so they have to use daylight hours and rise high to make it across the sea. I think they've counted three hundred fifty thousand at the Bosporus, and probably another hundred and fifty thousand at Gibraltar."

"You can see them?" he asked. "I mean, flying in the sky?"

"Sometimes in flocks of five hundred or more," I said. Or so I'd read. I looked at him. "However, since these birds are already here, I guess they came early."

"Is there a difference between the male and female? They look the same to me."

"The female wears heels, can't you see?"

Erik looked at me, then looked at the birds. "Is that some kind of scientific term?"

I laughed. "No, I'm teasing. There's not much difference."

"When you first start looking at birds, what do you look for?" he said, watching the storks walk around on long legs, hissing greetings and warnings to each other. "I don't know anything about birding, birds. I mean they're all around, but—" he shrugged.

"Umm," I stalled, thinking back to the most basic point of recognition. The bird moving above us gave it to me, a black shape against the evening sun. "Silhouette. General families of birds have specific silhouettes." I glanced at my watch and noted the number of bill clatterings we'd heard in the last ten minutes. "What do you see when you look at it?"

"Look at the bird?"

"What else?"

"Uhh . . . long legs," Erik said, "a heavy body, a long beak, and a slight curve to the neck."

"Now," I said, "starting at the head, pick out its most distinguishing characteristics." As he spoke, I counted.

The bird fluttered its wings, walking back and forth on the ledge.

"Red beak. Its back is white and its wings are two-tone."

"The wing," I said, as the stork considerately flapped its wings in the dying sun, "is divided into sections. You've noticed the secondary coverts on the upper wing are white, while the median and greater primary coverts and flight feathers are black."

"It does look like an imam," he said.

"A what?" I said, looking away from the stork to Erik.

"Legend has it that these storks are transformed humans."

"Transformed, like reincarnated?" I said, making my notations for the second ten minutes.

"Yeah. Story is that an imam, in his white djellaba and black robe, got drunk and climbed to the top of the minaret. He blasphemed and so Allah struck him down, turning him into a stork."

"That accounts for one," I said.

Erik watched the storks scatter some curious pigeons, before one sat on a nest, leaning forward and back, settling its long legs. "Huh," he said. "It does look like the faithful at prayer." He glanced at me.

"It's an offense in Marrakesh to disturb a stork. Like, three months in jail."

I kept my eyes on the birds.

"In case you felt inspired."

"No, but I do like the idea of fining for disturbances." That's how Junior could make his money, yet leave the Dubya untouched. The storks did look like they were wearing the black cloaks and white robes I had seen on the Moroccan men. Erik didn't seem disturbed by thinking the bird was like an imam, by the anthropomorphism. Then again, I reminded myself, he was just a guy. Not a scientist.

If I were true to my calling, I would have reminded him that the stork was a stork and nothing more. It bred here and then flew elsewhere; its habitat was grasslands and savannas, maybe lakesides; and that the numbers of storks, both white and black, had decreased since 1900, probably due largely to loss of habitat and an increase of pesticides.

But I liked the idea of the struck-down imam. I'd keep it to myself. "What did you call the wall?"

"Pisé," he said. "It's a mixture of straw and limestone, mixed with local dirt. In Tangier, the rule is that every building has to be white. In Marrakesh, the law is that every building be built of pisé. You haven't seen the walls at sunset, but they glow," he said, glancing at the sky. "And it's too late for a calèche ride. Pity."

That was fine. I had no interest in riding some strange animal to see the city.

I noted the time—twenty minutes—and closed my notebook, snapping the elastic band around it before putting it back in my bag.

"Do you believe in reincarnation?" Erik asked

I glanced at him through the gathering dusk. It would be an odd question for a stranger to ask, except we were talking about the imam. "No. Life's a one-shot deal. You do, then you're done."

Erik watched me, not quizzical or condemning, but just . . . watching. I had that weird sense of time ceasing again. Earlier, I'd put it down to exhaustion and maybe carb overload. Now, I wasn't sure. "You're very certain," he said.

"I am certain. I grew up a conservative Lutheran. We're told that everyone else will burn in Hell, so we'd better be certain." My tone was flippant, but I shied away from thoughts of Fischer, from the final despair in Mama's voice that her son *had* gone to burn in Hell.

Erik chuckled. "You hungry?"

An innocent, logical question, so why did my breath catch? Why did I suddenly feel too warm? *He's asking about food, you dolt.* But his eyes were so dark, and I knew his hands were strong and that spell he cast . . . weird and great. I looked up. As it grew darker, the city grew louder.

"I mean, if you don't have other plans, I would love to show you the Place at night." He extended his hand.

The train to Casablanca was another all-nighter. Or I could take the morning train and be there by 10 A.M., which would get me there at the same time the all-nighter arrived, but without all the stops, and I'd catch the same buses to Larache. I could have dinner tonight, in this city of transformed imams. The Place couldn't be much more public, which would make it safer. And I wouldn't be alone with my thoughts. I nodded and followed.

The Place had transformed in the intervening hours. The population had doubled and the throughway for traffic had been all but swallowed up by merchants and orange juice sellers. One whole side had become an open-air buffet, with food stalls and picnic-style tables set out in avenues lit with hissing flame torches. Groups gathered around entertainers, dancers, storytellers, and lecturers.

Our arms linked, Erik led me from group to group, giving me a glimpse of each. The area felt magical, but the tawdry side of magic, like carnivals and street performers and the adrenalin hit of wonder. Was anything real, or safe? Or was it all just smoke and mirrors?

A man played a flute, drawing a snake out of the basket. Was its mouth sewed shut? Was it defanged? But in the hissing lantern light under a dark sky with stars scattered like shells, it didn't matter. It was magic. Dangerous magic.

A twelve-year-old raconteur entranced a group of men, his body and voice rising and falling, his flashlight and oil fire casting shadows that helped convey his tale.

Acrobats and dancers entertained alone and in groups of twos or threes.

"You'll like this," Erik said, drawing me toward a group of male singers performing to the rhythm of a drum. A hundred or so watchers swayed and stomped with them.

I listened, dropped a few dirham in the passed hat, and we moved on.

"So do you want to eat Moroccan food, or do you want to eat like a Moroccan?"

All around the Place above us, rooftop cafés glittered with lights. Up there, they'd speak some English, and maybe serve hamburgers and fries. But I had a personal guide down here. "Like a Moroccan," I said.

We moved into the streets of food sellers. Each purveyor had its own table and hawker. "Anything you don't want? Like sheep's head or offal?"

"No offal," I said, wary. "No head."

"Well, damn," I thought I heard him murmur, but when I turned to him, his expression was bland. Just my own dirty mind.

Before each cook's station, a chalk-written menu posted the specials. As we passed, the hawkers first spoke in Arabic to him, German to me, then they switched to English and French. They quit when we moved beyond their range and into the territory of another vendor.

Erik steered me, by a hand on the small of my back, to a picnic table. Antiquated, sure, but strangely intimate. "This is good food," he said, pulling out a pen and making a few marks on the butcher paper covering the table. The waiter put down two pieces of bread. "Reasonable, too."

The waiter greeted him in French, and me in English.

"How do they know what I speak?" I asked him, irritated.

"Teeth are too perfect to be your age and European," he said.

After a childhood in braces, I should be proud someone noticed, I guessed. His weren't. He wasn't American?

"What do you want?" he said.

I looked up at the scribbling on the board and could make out a few words, but then I saw something Zephyr had written in my notes. "Pastilla," I said.

"You do want to eat like a Moroccan," he said. "Anything else, or should I just order a variety of plates and we'll share?"

I looked at him. He didn't appear malnourished, but maybe this was a technique to avoid paying for his meal? "Sure," I said, at ease. "I'll just need a receipt."

"A receipt," he repeated, lips twitching as he tried not to smile.

We had chosen the corner of the table, less than a foot away from another vendor. A veiled woman and her companion finished their meal and stood to leave.

It happened as quick as a crane catching a fish: a bony arm grabbed the picked chicken carcass off the couple's plate. Shouts. A chase. One of the hawkers shouted imprecations at the felon, who crouched at the edge of the lamp light, picking at the bone as fast as he? she? could. The hawker didn't pursue; the thief didn't approach. I got the feeling this wasn't an unusual occurrence.

We all returned to our meals.

Olives, fried fish, a paste, and something with tomatoes appeared before us. Erik tore his piece of bread into pieces and pinched some of the paste as he wished me *bon appétit*. I saw his list on the paper had grown; I appreciated him keeping track, but I also wasn't going to begrudge a guide who'd showed me the storks. I pinched some paste, too. Spicy, chewy stuff filled my mouth.

"Thank you for showing me the storks," he said, with a related-to-Zephyr, almost-mind-reading thing.

"You're the one who got us there," I said. "What is this?" It was good.

"Eggplant."

Did I like eggplant? I guess so.

"You told me what I was seeing," he said.

"Teamwork," I said.

He smiled. "I haven't heard that phrase in a while." He took a sip of his Orangina. "I'm glad to see you've relaxed."

I smiled into his dark eyes. I knew when and where my train was. Either late tonight or early tomorrow, but the hard part was done. I *could* relax. All I had to figure out was how to proposition this man, because, face it, that's why I'd stayed here. If a touch on the hand was almost orgasmic, then what about other touches? Other places? I shivered.

"How did you become an ornithologist?" he asked.

People surrounded us on every side, walking by, cooking before us, wedging in to sit. Convocations, coveys, broods, bevies, and colonies of people. Still, amidst it all, it felt intimate to sit beside Erik, close enough to see his spiky eyelashes. I felt his thigh next to mine; I could see the few fine hairs on the backs of his fingers.

"I went to school," I said.

"Sorry," he said. "I didn't mean to intrude. Perhaps my question is 'why.'" He thought I was brushing him off? "It just seems something so intense and focused would require a lot of devotion and dedication. Forethought. Not just waking up as a junior and going, well, I like the outdoors so I'll become an ornithologist." He popped a piece of fish in his mouth and chewed.

"It had been my plan for a while."

"What was the initial attraction?"

"What do you do," I countered, "aside from making educated guesses about the women you meet in your travels?"

Was it my imagination or did he stiffen a little? "I have some business interests," he said. "In Morocco and elsewhere. Keeps me on the road."

"How often do you make it to Marrakesh?" I said, discovering that roasted meat on skewers had arrived.

"Those are beef," he said, pointing to some of the reddish brown glazed pieces, "and those are liver." He pointed to some other reddish brown glazed pieces.

"Do you sit out here often?" I asked.

He shrugged, and dedicated himself to eating.

I followed suit for a few minutes. Apparently Erik liked to ask questions, not answer them. He had secrets. The server set down a pastry stack before me. Spices formed lines across it, making it look grilled. "*B'stilla, madmoiselle.*" I stared at it.

"Have you had it before?" Erik asked.

"No," I said. "It was just a suggestion from a friend. Is it good?"

"It's a taste, texture thing," he said. "I guess I'm just surprised to see an ornithologist eat pigeon."

He'd be horrified to know how field ornithologists stayed alive on expedition: they ate birds. A little secret kept from the general bird watching population, who'd liken it to Walt chowing down on Bambi.

As I cut into it, the flaky pastry layers crumbled onto the cinnamon-flavored ground meat. I took the first bite. "Tastes like peanut butter and jelly," I said as the flavors hit me.

"Not like chicken?" he said, and we chuckled.

Okay, that was American.

We ate in silence, though it wasn't quiet. The singing, the wailing, the players and hawkers vied for attention. Erik waited for me to answer. *What's the harm?* "My attraction to birds," I said, thinking, trying to recall that initial moment, that first sense of rightness and belonging. Bird watching still gave it to me. A sympathy, somehow.

I wouldn't order pastilla again, but it was nutrition. "My birding began when I was in trouble," I said. "Grounded. I think I was in third or fourth grade."

Erik ate with one-handed grace.

"I was in my bedroom, which looked out on the backyard. I don't know if it was the fact that we were studying ancient Egypt or what, but all of a sudden I saw this bird, white, with this long red beak land in the yard. My Pop was working out there, but he didn't turn and look. The beak was sharply decurved—"

"Decurved?" Erik interrupted.

"Bent downward. I was looking at a white ibis, but I didn't know it. I just knew it matched the picture of a bird that I'd seen the ancient Egyptians had."

"You like ancient Egypt?"

My eye drifted to one of the rings he wore. An ancient Egyptian symbol, but I didn't know for what. "No, though studying Egypt did make me look at the bird. No, it was how the bird, this one lone ibis, worked and worked and worked, while all the other birds in the backyard, songbirds, a few waders, a duck or two, preened and rested. The ibis was nonstop. I guess I felt some solidarity with that."

Erik frowned. "You were a workaholic, even in third grade?"

I laughed. "No. Well, yes—but no. I was grounded, and thus working. I felt somehow the ibis was being made to work, too. It understood me. There was room for me, with it." I scooped up some eggplant and added fish. The bird had invited me to share its life. With it, I belonged, not an experience I'd had many times before or since. Yet how could I explain that, without seeming twelve cats away from crazy? "Anyway, the white ibis was my spark bird."

"Spark bird?"

"It's a birdy term for the bird that turned you on to birding."

He chewed thoughtfully. "I don't think I have a spark bird."

"You're not a birder."

"What is a birder, anyway?"

"A lunatic who spends her life, or his, chasing down birds. Whether in their own backyard or yours. It's an experience thing."

"You say lunatic, but you're here."

"It's like any pejorative: if you are one, the insult doesn't stick. I am a birder. Of sorts."

He stared like he was trying to see through me. "What does that mean?"

"There are different kinds."

"Levels?" he asked, his dark eyes dancing.

In levels, I'd be close to the top. A professional. "Not exactly, more like . . . species. There are birders who know their home turf perfectly. I'm one of those."

"Birder domesticus?"

I nodded as I chewed my pastilla. "There're birders who go all over the world to catch a glimpse of some rare, exotic bird."

"Like the bald ibis?"

"Exactly. I'm sure they have bald ibis tours."

He nodded. "Morocco is trying to increase tourism, so if they don't have them yet, they will soon. Birder touristicus?"

The PB&J, North African style, lumped in my stomach. Awareness could spare an animal, a bird, from extinction. It could also eliminate any hope of natural continuance. So far, it had done nothing but help the bald ibis. "Then there are professionals, who watch specific birds, study them. Birder professionalis, to go with your example."

"That's you?"

"I'm a local expert, but also here to see what Morocco has."

"What part of the south are you from?" he asked.

"Are you American?" I fired back.

The waiter interrupted, speaking something that wasn't Arabic or French, and Erik and he spoke at some length. Erik tapped his list several times and finally dug in his pockets for money. I reached for mine, but he stilled my hand. "Always keep track," he said, "they lose count easily."

"Let me pay you back," I said.

"Not here, where every pickpocket in the Place can see which pocket you reach into," he said. "I ordered us some tea."

My concern at the idea that the evening was almost over subsided. "Great," I said.

"You have a thing for ibises, but missing the bald ibis isn't going to hurt you?" he said, after a pot of steaming tea and two glasses appeared before us.

"It will hurt me more than you can know," I said, "but there's nothing I can do about it."

"You're not here to check out the new flock in the mountains?"

"What new flock? For a nonbirder, you know a lot." Suddenly I was suspicious. Of what, I didn't know. Being set up? If Zephyr had found this guy and somehow arranged for him to be here, then it would be more to convince me to relax and enjoy rather than work more.

And Frankie, well, she didn't have supernatural powers, despite the control she'd managed to wrest from Wilkerson. Or had it been wrested? Had he given it to her? Was she just going to be his puppet? His slave?

I hated seeing any woman, even Frankie, subjugated to a jerk. Mr. Woodrow, I'm sorry, but Junior is a jerk. Maybe that was it: Frankie had gotten personal with Wilkerson? No, she had a definite weakness for medical doctors, with their prison tans, baggy eyes, and methamphetamine habits. She wouldn't look at Wilkerson.

How could Erik know so much about birds, have so much time to spend with me, and it not be suspicious? Was he going to take advantage of me somehow? "How do you know?" I asked, and I heard the suspicion in my tone.

"I told you. People know. I hear things. I know it's an important bird. Eco-tourism is the trend of the future. Hence, the birds."

"The bald ibis," I said.

"Did the white ibis stay your spark bird?" Erik asked, then proceeded to pour a cup of tea into his glass. Before I answered, he poured the tea back into the pot, then poured a second glass. He poured it back into the pot too, then poured a third. I felt like I was in a fairy tale, waiting for the right sized bear.

"What are you doing?" I asked when he left the tea alone, still in the pot, and our glasses empty.

"Dusting it," he said with a glance. It was full night, and in the glow of the lamps, his eyes looked almost black rather than blue. "Who did you forsake the white ibis for?"

"The glossy and the white-faced," I said. "Where I live is one of the few overlaps in habitat for them. It's rare, seeing them both at the same time and place, but it happens. I do comparison studies."

He nodded as I spoke, then poured our teas. The steamed mint was perhaps the cleanest, most refreshing smell I'd ever experienced, but the sweetness of the tea made my eyes bulge. It was sweeter than what I'd had in Tangier. Of course, I'd been paranoid in Tangier, and had added my own tablespoon of sugar. Not the fourteen cups they'd used here.

"First mint tea?" Erik said.

"They like a few leaves with their sugar?"

"Caffeine, kif, and sugar," he said. "Makes the world go round."

I wondered if he was speaking personally, but decided if he wouldn't tell me where he was from, he probably wouldn't tell me his drug of choice either.

"Earrings look good on you," he said.

I touched them; I did like the way they felt. I needed to remove them before I left for Larache.

His gaze dropped to my mouth. "Ready to leave?"

Somewhere in all that sugar, I'd become very aroused. I got up in response.

❖

Smoke hazed the Place, which gleamed with a thousand lamps. Circuses of salesmen, performers, storytellers, and thieves minced in and out of the pressed masses. Australians fearlessly downed orange juice beside American students who ate their liver brochettes with pita, their eyes darting, their money belts hidden. Now, like a Moroccan, I could see those thin belts. Yeah, obvious the second you moved.

Men grouped around makeshift classrooms, learning what benefits certain tinctures and concoctions could have on them, if only they'd buy. We walked by an herbalist with wares spread on the blanket-covered ground: anatomy charts, a miniaturized plastic human skeleton, and jars of pickled mice on display. Jars of powders, open to smell. He pounded some concoction as we wandered. "It's to please an angry wife," Erik whispered in my ear, sending clichéd shivers up my spine.

"With a patent, he could be a millionaire," I said.

"Not everyone seeks the magnification that money brings," Erik said, his sweet breath warm on my earlobe. I had no idea what he was talking about, but he could read his laundry list to me, if he'd do it this close, this . . . intently.

Erik took my hand, pulled me close so that we walked hip to hip, shoulder to shoulder. My bag and bins were twisted to the safety zone between our bodies. I wasn't doing anything, planning anything, just . . . being. How wild. How extravagant. How I wished it could last. I'd only ever felt this before while birding: belonging and being a part, without being the center. Like every element mattered, every minute counted.

"Just a minute," Erik said, "I need to speak to this *marabout*." He glanced at me, then explained, "The healer, a holy man."

We stood by some display laid on the ground, bones and herbs and powders and placards at my feet. Erik knelt beside a man and greeted him, then they squatted together, close, talking. He looked more like a witch doctor, but that seemed to fit here.

I looked across the Place filled with its . . . Mews? confusion? charm?—what poetic plural fit?—of people, up to the rising moon, floating in the magic. The wind shifted, the sounds of the ever-present snake charmer's flute advancing and retreating with the smoke. A young girl appeared, about chest-height, and asked to henna my hands.

Before the words "another time" were out of my mouth, my palm sprouted a flower. I couldn't pull away; the girl's grip rivaled a hawk's talons. I watched as an otherworldly vision of a vine grew up each of my fingers.

"I am Berber, from the mountains," the girl said. "I paint your hands for good luck. For marriage, for babies." She smiled up at me. "Is pretty, yes? Very bootiful."

"I didn't want my hand painted," I said. At least not until after Larache.

"Is very cheap. Only twenty dirham."

"I don't have twenty dirham."

"I am Berber," she said, and fixed me with her pale eyes. A scarf was twisted around her hair and throat. "Is good. Very bootiful. Twenty dirham."

"No."

"Okiy, okiy, fifteen. A special present for marriage, for children." She was holding my hand and blowing on the paste on it. "Will dry in maybe twenty minutes."

"How long will it last?" I asked. Could I get it off by tomorrow?

"Two, three weeks."

Dammit. I could be rude and pull away, but the Berber girl wasn't stealing, she was trying to work. She also appeared to be about fifteen years old, with a gold wedding band and a substantial bump.

"Okiy. Ten dirham," the Berber said.

I'd spent more than that on ice cream this afternoon. But the point was, "I told you no."

"Is very good," the girl said. "Bring you good luck."

I nodded, worn down. "Okay, but all I have is seven."

"I am Berber!" the girl shouted. "From the mountains! I give you good job!"

I slipped the change out of my pocket. "It's all I have." It was the truth. I needed to get to another ATM. I used it more often than the bathroom, here.

The girl dropped my hand, snatched the money, then spat at my feet.

I saw red. "Would you like me to take it back?" I shouted, following her. "I didn't ask for you to do it. I said the opposite!"

But the girl had vanished into the mob. Despite my shouting, no one looked concerned. Probably not a local Better Business Bureau around. I stood there, fuming. My palm began to sting.

"What have you got there?" Erik asked from behind me. "That's pretty. Just the one hand?"

"One hand more than I wanted," I said. "She just . . . did it!"

He chuckled. "You have to walk away. Conversation is consent."

"She threw a fit when I paid her seven."

He shrugged. "Part of her job. She can't be happy with her pay or she would never make more."

I held up my hand. "It burns a little."

"It's probably just the staining process," he said. "Very few people are allergic."

"So I'm a science experiment?"

"In the service of botany, would be my guess."

We walked toward the street of my hotel. Now that I was calmer, I saw the advertisement for the riad, painted in letters two feet high. Easy to find. Set tables edged the Place. I needed to make my move. "Another tea?" I asked.

We sat down and Erik held up two fingers. Within a minute, fragrant mint tea steeped before us. The lull in the conversation came from my alarm: beyond sex, why did I want this evening to continue? He was cute, and knowledgeable, but he must be a loser. Young, healthy, but wandering around the world instead of working?

At least he wasn't an artist. I'd just walk away.

Zephyr, of course, would consider him the perfect man. For whom? She specialized in lying losers; I courted those too young to know their minds.

"So are you a doctor?" Erik asked.

In that moment, the square and every part of the mystical, magical day, vanished. "No. I opted for master's degrees and actual experience on the Gulf Coast."

"So you *are* from Texas?"

Dammit, he was still searching for information? Why? What would it hurt to admit it? "Born and bred," I said, slowly.

"You didn't want to leave, go study somewhere else?"

God, how badly I'd wanted to go away. East Coast, West Coast, anywhere. But . . . "My . . . folks . . . are older. I was sort of a miracle baby." His penetrating stare disconcerted me. He knew the bones of the story were true, he just wasn't sure about the skins. As well he shouldn't be. This was my long-told cover story because the truth was too messy. A thought struck me: was he a reporter? My gaze dropped to his hands, but I just didn't envision those silver-ringed fingers doing a lot of typing. I continued. "I didn't want to be too far away, in case. Anyway, by the time I was going to grad school, Pop already had signs of Alzheimer's."

"That sucks."

I looked away from him, stunned by how compassionate and how true that simple statement was. "Yeah."

A mechanical beep pierced the air, utterly at odds with the laughter, the rush of languages, the smells of tea and spices.

Erik lifted his shirt, revealing a dark-skinned waist so trim that the skin folded on itself—and a phone. He clicked it, stared at it for a long moment. "Business," he said.

Drug deal, I amended, disappointed beyond all reason.

You were just going to use him, Frankie-in-my-head said. *To mutual delicious satisfaction,* Zephyr-peacemaker countered.

"I'm sorry," Erik said. "I have to go."

Just like that. "Of course." I was within shouting distance of my hotel. Hell, it was early enough to make the Casablanca train.

But he made no move to leave, kept his gaze on mine. "I've enjoyed it, Elize," he said and refused to let me look away. He stared so intently that I got the feeling he might mean it. "May I give you a number where I can be reached?"

For drugs or a booty call? "I . . ." I said, falling into the façade, "my colleagues—"

"Of course, of course, but just in case . . . " He trailed off. In case I got lonely? Lost? Just in case of anything, his look seemed to say, but that couldn't be. We were strangers, after all. *Don't depend on anyone.*

He scribbled on the back of a piece of butcher paper from dinner. "Your receipt, such as it is, is on the other side," he said, pointing to the list of food we'd eaten.

"Thank you." I'd forgotten all about it.

"And . . . " he handed me a card. "It's a Telecard. If you need to use a public phone, they don't take money."

"Thank you," I said again, touched.

He stood, and the light limned his body through the thin Moroccan shirt. He held out his hand, and I gave him mine. Instead of shaking it, he kissed it, his gaze intent on me.

"Enjoy your journey, *ma petite,*" he said. "*Bonne nuit.*"

Halfway across the Place, he was stopped and embraced by a man in a robe and skullcap. Together, they walked on. *I've been beaten out by an old man*, I thought, as I poured my tea, "dusting" it three times. It was overpoweringly sweet on every taste, but at least I looked like I knew what I was doing. Protective coloring to the rescue.

A crescent moon hung above the Place. I swore I could feel all the curves sketched on my hand, all the swirls and patterns. The pastilla and eggplant and lamb sat in my stomach, coated by the sweetest, strongest mint tea I'd tasted.

No one looked at me. No one bothered me. I drank cup after cup, feeling the breeze in my hair as the henna dried and began to flake off, leaving the pattern stained on my palm. The magic of the night, of the Place, reasserted itself. It was in *my* hand, *my* stomach, *my* ears and *my* mind.

I'm in Morocco, I thought.

I'm in *it*.

❖

I was still *in* it when I arrived at the train station the next morning. But I was the only one there. No cabs pulled up out front. No rings of bread for sale, no vendors to push orange juice or anything else. Left Luggage was locked. So was the café, and the newsstand.

Deserted would be the term I'd use.

Marrakesh's station was old-school, with flip-style destination boards and windows through which you spoke to actual people. Except the boards were blank and the windows closed.

"Dammit!" I hissed, with only the pigeons and the bougainvillea to hear me. No wonder I'd had to argue with the taxi driver to get here; why hadn't he told me the station was closed?

Would I have believed him?

I sat on a bench, alone, with the wind moving across the empty tracks, out into the empty streets. I'd noticed the cafés were shut. I'd seen no buses and few cars. Dammit! I put my head in my hands, almost laughing. What else could I do? No Larache today.

It was after eleven. The café au lait I'd counted on wasn't available.

What a bewildering, back-assed country.

I walked outside, but the taxi curb was empty. I knew where McDonald's was from here, but I didn't even eat there in the States. Couldn't start now.

Hotel, I thought. *I need a hotel. Again.* I sat down and rummaged through the papers in my bag. The receipt, and consequently the telephone number, for the hotel should be in here. Instead, I found another set of numbers. Erik's numbers and e-mail address, wrapped around the Telecard.

The phone booth was to my right. I stared at the card. Erik hadn't meant that I could call him, he was just being polite. *No good deed goes unpunished*, I thought, then took a deep breath and walked to the phone booth. After a few false tries, the phone rang.

A woman answered.

His girlfriend? His wife? God knew. I'd hang up, but I refused to be that infantile. This would teach him to be more discreet, at least.

"Erik, s'il vous plaît?"

"Ah-rik? *Ah, oui. Un moment.*"

"*Oui?*" Erik said a minute later. He sounded sleepy.

"Hi. It's Elize. From yesterday?" Too pleading. "Uhh . . . how are you?"

"Elize. I'm fine," he said, then yawned. "How are you?"

"Well," I said, "I'm not going anywhere." There was a moment of silence.

"The colleagues you mentioned, they weren't already in town," he said, as though just now figuring it out.

"Not really," I choked out.

"I'm sorry. If I'd known you were trying to get somewhere, I would have told you of the coming holiday."

"Holiday?" I repeated as my stomach dropped.

"Two days for Moulay—" some name I'd never heard and wouldn't be able to repeat.

"For two days, nothing will run?" I said, hearing the pitch of my voice.

"Are you at the station?" he asked.

"Yes." I sighed.

"Where are you trying to go?"

"Larache," I said. Why hadn't I just told him yesterday, and saved myself so much effort and loss!

"Larache? On the coast?" His tone was amused; I was not.

"Migration," I said.

"Tangier to Marrakesh to Larache," he said. "Tangier must have freaked you out. Uh . . . wait there."

"For two days?"

He chuckled. "No, now. I'll come get you."

The rush of relief at those words dizzied me. Yeah, sure I wasn't waiting for a knight in shining armor. *Tell yourself another one*, Crazy-Elize whispered.

"Should I call your hotel and get your room back?"

"Yes, please," I said, disgusted with myself, but so, so thankful.

❖

He stepped out of the cab and embraced me, a hug intended as a quick greeting, I think, but . . . I clung.

I clung?

One-way hugs usually consist of a clinger and a clingee, who pats the clinger's back as a cue to let go. I know; I'm usually the clingee.

He enveloped me, his scent, his space, the security and stability and competence of him. I felt immersed and calm, suddenly . . . free. We were pressed together and I felt his heart beat, the curve of his abdomen against mine. His smooth cheek touched me and I was surprised by how soft his beard was, how citrusy and yet masculine he smelled, surprised by the warmth of his body.

I didn't want to let go.

He didn't let go.

He held me, his hands gentle on my back, his pulse sure, as though time didn't exist. Like we were immortal and things like needing to get it all done before we died just didn't apply. No more waiting, just being. He brushed his lips over my temple, and the feeling of security plunged somewhere interior and core in me, underlining my aware-ness of his hard, hot body.

I dropped my hands and stepped back.

"Good morning," he said, stepping back too, but maintaining the intensity of our connection by the expression in his gaze. This man was not afraid of excessive emotion, even if it was uncalled for and inappropriate.

I looked over his shoulder at the cabbie. Was I nuts? "Thanks for picking me up," I said.

"Of course," Erik said, in a tone that indicated it was the mini-mum he could do. "The hotel had your room still. They're holding it for you."

"Thank you," I said, picking up my duffel. He took it from me.

"Have you eaten?" he said, helping me into the back seat.

I shook my head. He turned around in the passenger seat. "The reason I ask is, being a holiday, everything is closed. I am on my way to see friends. You could come with me, if you like."

Yes, I wanted to shout, because I didn't want to be away from him, out of the range of the hypnotic calm he cast. "If it won't be an inconvenience," I murmured, my good manners automatic, but lies all the same. If I had to displace the King of Morocco to sit beside Erik all afternoon, I would.

My hands trembled. What was my problem?

He smiled at me, revealing that chipped incisor. "It will be a plea-sure," he said, then turned and gave the cabbie directions.

I sat back and watched the pisé walls zip by. There was no getting to Larache today, no sense in fighting what appeared to be fate. I glanced down and saw Erik's silver beringed hand reaching back for mine. I laced my fingers in his, feeling the liquid heat of my body rise another degree. My breath felt short, and I hoped lunch wouldn't be too long of an affair.

I had a hotel room *and* an excuse, now.

The Lunch

After the low tables and tiled walls of my hotel, I wasn't sure if I liked or hated the very Western space of this white, bright, bare-walled room; the sheer blowing curtains, the couches upholstered in very new, very pristine yellow, gold, and white damask. The couches bristled with a thousand stiff pillows. A heavy dark wood table sat before one of them. Abdullah, our host, indicated we should sit on one of the couches.

It was oddly familiar. In the formal room of the house where I grew up, a Victorian horsehair couch ruled. It had a high curved back and cushions that were comfortable, but only if you didn't move, didn't breathe, didn't adjust. If you did, one of the pieces of stuffing would poke you and not in a place that, in the formal living room of an orthodox Lutheran home, you could tug or scratch or shift. So you'd move to get away, and another piece would poke you.

As a child, I had the mental image of the couch being full of claws, like crabs beneath the sand. When you sat, you disturbed the crabs and they grabbed at you. Needless to say, I wasn't fond of the couch at home, and I eyed Abdullah's with suspicion, even as Erik stood aside for me to slip in first.

The couch stuffing was soft, like pillows. I relaxed.

"My friends, thank you so much for gracing my humble home with your presence," Abdullah said. I'd met him in the courtyard, so obviously the "friends" title didn't belong to me, although he included me in his smile.

"It's lovely," I murmured. The house was immaculate, with scrubbed tile floors, and clean painted walls. But there was nothing else in it. Not a photo, a tapestry, or a knickknack. It was cheerful though, all the yellow and white. "Thank you very much for including me."

"Beautiful lady," Abdullah said, bowing, "it is the pleasure of mine to have you here. Erik has talked of nothing but you."

I glanced at Erik, who shrugged, leaving me to guess whether this was a practice of the Arab art of overstatement, or if Abdullah was just teasing a good friend, or revealing the truth.

"How is your family?" Erik asked him.

Abdullah inclined his head, and a shout from the next room heralded a small boy dressed like a miniature rap star, complete with gold chain and sideways ball cap. Abdullah scooped up the boy and tossed him in the air. He laughed all the while, a very secure child.

I looked away.

"Erik, Miss Elize, this is my son Mohammed. Mohammed, meet my friends, meet the friends of your papa."

Mohammed was fair skinned, with shiny dark hair and bright, dark eyes. He smiled and waved, not at all shy, and babbled away. I gathered that his mother owned the genes for smooth hair and pale skin, because Abdullah was wooly-headed, with murky skin and opaque, dark eyes. He seemed cloudy, next to the shine of his son. The boy squirmed and was let down, then ran out of the room back to his mother, who must be cooking.

I guessed she'd join us at lunch.

Two other men came in with hugs and back slaps for Erik and Abdullah. Both wore robes, and one wore a fez, the hat of organ-grinder fame. The other had closely cropped hair. Both men were in their forties. Fifties? I'm terrible at guessing ages.

They'd left their shoes at the door, and I was tickled to notice that one of them, Gregor, wore white pants and metallic threaded white socks beneath his robe. Gorgeous tassels hung from the hood of his djellaba, and fancy cording worked up the front of it. No surprise, he was the owner of a clothing shop in the souk.

"Come to my store, I give you very special price! Presents for your home? Your father, your mother," he said to me. I tried to picture Mama in Moroccan dress, and fought back a smile. "Ah, for yourself," he said. "Pretty things to take home to America." He frowned. "You need pretty things! No jewelry, no scarf!" He turned to Erik and fired off several comments.

Erik held up his hands, shrugged.

"Not to be rude, dear lady," Gregor said, "But Erik is a bad friend to not give you pretty things!"

I was puzzled; why didn't Erik tell Gregor we'd been shopping yesterday?

"I told him you were an independent woman," Erik said. Erik, for some reason, didn't want to tell Gregor; he'd rather take the ribbing.

"And this independence means you have nothing to sparkle, no color for yourself?" Gregor asked.

Again I was dressed head-to-toe in drab. Without the belt, without yesterday's earrings. I'd blend in beautifully with the trees at the bird site, but in this room where everyone, even Erik, glimmered and glistened, I was a wren.

"Pah," Gregor continued, committed to his speech. "I have seen independent women. They have big rocks, yes?" he said, laughing. "Rings to prove they need no man!"

"It's beautiful workmanship," I said to distract him, indicating his robe with its elaborate braids and tassels.

"*Passementerie*, a specialty of Fez that I bring here, to the souk of Marrakesh."

"Maybe next time," I muttered as a fourth man joined us.

"Ali live in America," Abdullah said, pointing to the man with the hat. His robe was striped, and simple. He stood taller, wider than the others, with enormous feet in black socks. Erik, I'd noted, had worn socks too. I curled my bare toes under the table. "In New York?" Abdullah said.

"In Boston," Ali corrected. "I am musician."

"He plays trumpet," Erik said.

Abdullah left the room as the rest of us adjusted the table and couches.

"Where did you play?" I asked, useless, because I'd never been to Boston and all I know about it I learned on *M*A*S*H* reruns, through Charles Winchester the Third.

This kind of small talk is what Frankie excelled at. *Which is why you made her attend all the social functions. You, essentially, forced her into relationships with those people. No surprise they chose their friend instead of the usually silent, always condemning stranger.* I hid my grimace at hearing the truth. Especially from myself. Was it actually from me, or had Zephyr cast some sort of hoodoo on me?

"Clubs, the street. No matter. It is very beautiful there," Ali said. "To play by the sea, is very nice."

"Now Ali owns a club in 'Saouira," Erik said to me. When he saw how blank I was, he explained. "Essaouira, on the southern Moroccan coast. A little fishing village, all blue and white."

"The club is on the water, just like in Boston," Ali said. "Only is Morocco, so is better."

"Come to the shop," Gregor said to him. "A man of business like yourself needs fine clothes! New djellaba!"

Abdullah entered with a plate of steaming food, and set it before us. Eggs nestled between cooked grains and among meatballs with no known pedigree. "To God," he said, and reached for a meatball.

I asked, "Isn't your wife going to join us?"

Silence.

Abdullah set down his meatball. "I love my friends, very much," he said, looking at them, looking at me. "They are my brothers. But if they were to see my wife, I would have to kill them."

Ali and Gregor and even Erik chuckled. None of them had been expecting her. This was normal? I saw women on the streets, all the time. Veiled, unveiled, his wife had to eat, didn't she? It was her home! Ali, sitting adjacent to me, passed me some bread. Each of the men tore a piece, and used it to scoop from the plate before us, dribbling oil on the piece of bread like it was a plate.

I sat between Erik and Ali, a piece of bread in my hand, aware that I didn't belong here, on so many levels.

"In Islam, many ways to live," Abdullah said to me. "Eat, eat. Some men, they do not care if their friends see their wife." He shrugged, while conducting a meatball to his mouth. He chewed while he talked. "Me, I am conservative. I protect my family. I protect my friends. I would not want to inspire my friends to be unholy, by letting them see my wife. A wise man cherishes his treasure, ah?"

Ali and Gregor, grease running down their elbows, murmured agreement. Erik passed me a bottle of Coke. No ice in the glass. I poured some and took a small bite of the food. All I had to do was taste it, just to be polite. But it was good, if a bit gamey.

"A wife is a possession, then?" I said. I wasn't trying to pick a fight, *exactly*.

"A possession that possesses," Ali said with a laugh. "The wife rules the house!"

Gregor met my glance, and I noticed his eyes were gray, almost blue. "In Berber, is not different," he said. "Wives, mothers, sisters, they are queens in their home. But when a man comes, poof—" He tossed his hand. "—they are gone to not shame the man."

I felt Erik's gaze on me. I looked at the platter before us, studded with fried eggs. The metallic threads of the fabric of the couch felt rough against the fingers of my left hand. I was not in my world at all.

But they weren't asking me to conform. I was sitting here with my hair uncovered, conversing with them, wearing pants and a shirt. If I believed a person could behave however he or she wanted in his own home, didn't that extend to dining, entertaining? Regardless of race or religious inclination? Didn't it extend to being more conservative than me? "Tell your wife, please," I said, "that it is very good."

The men, who all ate like they were starving, nodded in agreement. Then, by some unspoken agreement, they all sat back. Finished, though the platter was still half-full. I swallowed my second bite and took a sip of warm Coke. Before I got another pinch of food, Abdullah cleared it away.

With finger bowls and heavy napkins we washed our hands and then sat back, waiting for Abdullah's return.

He came back with a tray of steaming mint tea, tiny glasses, and a plate of five cookies. One per person.

I might end up at McDonald's today, out of desperation. Or was McDonald's closed for the celebration of . . . Moulay Whoever?

"May we?" Abdullah asked me and Erik, holding up a baggie of kif.

"Of course," Erik said. "We'll sit by the window."

Was he not partaking because of me? But Erik didn't glance at me, just made sure the windows were open on both sides of our couch. The men seated themselves opposite us, lounging on the sofa and floor.

"How do you like Morocco?" Ali asked me from the floor.

"It's quite striking. The tiles, and the market, the souk—"

"Where has she been?" Gregor asked Erik, puffing to start his . . . joint? What did one call a kif cigarette?

"Tangier," I answered for myself.

"Ah, we are lucky you didn't get back on the boat and leave!" Ali said. "Tangier is the worst of Morocco!" He imitated spitting. "Everywhere, people to steal from you." He huffed for a moment, then exhaled. "Of course, there are good people, people with golden hearts, everywhere. And bad people, people with no love, who just want the money. Everywhere."

"Most of them in Tangier," Ali said.

"We saw the storks yesterday," I said.

Abdullah looked confused. "Storks?" he repeated, and I was reminded that as easily as they all spoke and seemed to comprehend English, it was probably their fifth language.

Erik explained to them in French, and they all nodded. "You are here to see the bald ibis, then?" Ali said. "It is south of 'Saouira, very beautiful."

I shook my head.

"Eleonora Falcon, then? The island is just off the coast. Very fine hotel. I will tell you," Gregor said.

"Migration," I said, again surprised that so many people seemed to know the birds. Did even one out of four Texans know the mockingbird was the state bird? Or that brown pelicans had made a comeback from extinction, all along the Gulf Coast? Doubtful. "I'm here for migration."

The men looked at Erik for translation. He spoke in French, and then in Arabic. They all nodded.

"It is easy for the birds, to just fly back and forth," Abdullah said, his motions growing more fluid the smaller his cigarette became. "Not so easy for Moroccans. We have to pay, we have to leave our families, we go and only hope we come back."

"In Morocco is eight-five percent unemployment," Ali said to me. "University degree, no university degree, to clean the streets or to judge the peoples, nothing matter except . . . " He rubbed his fingers together. "Baksheesh."

"Very corrupt," Gregor agreed. "Is all about who you know, who is your family, how much you can pay. Families who have their home for centuries, since the Reconquest, their families now go from their homes, to be sold to rich Europeans who bribe in Rabat, or Caza." He shrugged. "They have big houses in Paris, in Spain, but they want Morocco, too."

"The Reconquest was 1492," Erik whispered to me. "Ferdinand and Isabella of Spain reclaimed Andalusia from the Moors."

"In 1492, Columbus sailed the ocean blue," I said, my sole connection to that date.

He grinned. "Didn't you ever see *El Cid*? Charlton Heston? Sophia Loren?"

"*Beautiful Andalusia*," Ali sang. "*The best of Morocco is you.*" The three Moroccans were getting bombed.

"This is why we are allowed the kif," Abdullah said. "To keep us shh." He put his finger to his lips. "We are quiet, we are happy, we don't fight and riot and scream about our jobs, or no jobs. Not like the French."

"We don't strike," Gregor said.

"Opium is for the masses," Ali said, startling me with his quote. "To keep them quiet and docile." He inhaled and shrugged, his gaze growing soft. "What can you do? Have a golden heart, so when you enter paradise, the virgins wait for you." He shrugged again. Erik leaned back, his eyes half-closed, and I realized that despite the windows being open and the breeze blowing through, we were all stoned. My stomach growled, and Erik poured me more mint tea.

Sun streamed onto the damask couch, sparkling in a thousand points.

"You have been to Andalusia?" Ali asked me. "Most beautiful of Morocco."

"Seville. Cordoba. Cadiz. And, and . . . " Gregor sighed. "Granada, the jewel on the crown of Morocco." He opened sleepy gray eyes with dilated pupils and looked at me. "You have seen this places?"

I shook my head. "Only their bus stations."

"Ah, you must see it! You must see! Erik, my friend, you must take her to see the beautiful Alhambra, the Medersa, the—" He shook his head, disappointed, despairing. "We, we don't even get to see it. If we go to Andalusia, it is *cher. Trop cher.*"

"Too expensive," Erik whispered to me.

"I have never seen," Ali said, "but I have seen pictures!"

They were talking about land that they hadn't owned in five hundred years! Was that what the kif did? Make them focus on the Reconquest of 1492, rather than complain they had no jobs and no healthcare and that their women were confined to the kitchen? But though I had the thoughts, there was no ire behind them. The embroidery on Gregor's djellaba glittered, and Ali's fez had slid to the side. Abdullah was lost in a haze of smoke and the tea had settled, silencing my stomach.

Something brushed my fingertip. I looked down and saw Erik's silver-covered hand, stretched along the couch, one finger touching me. My gaze followed his arm, the veins wrapped around it like power cords, to the deep vee of the collar of his shirt showing his brown skin, the pulse in his throat. I looked into his eyes and felt a shock of pure lust. He felt it, too; his eyes darkened, and he pressed that finger against mine. It felt like he touched a far deeper and more intimate nerve than just in my hand.

One by one, the men stubbed out their smokes and staggered to their feet. Erik and I stood, joining in the chorus of gratitude and compliments, and Ali and Gregor stumbled into their babouches and down the narrow steps. Abdullah waved goodbye to us all, and Erik and I took the steps one at a time, watching the blue-white shadows on the wall, hearing the bird song and the occasional distant baby's cry. He carried my duffel.

"Does the unseen wife do the dishes, too?" I muttered. Erik stopped, and I stopped, too, a step above him.

He turned and looked up at me, his eyes shot with blue. "It is the afternoon rest. They're making love."

I felt the breath catch in my throat. "So grandma is doing the dishes?"

Erik grinned and continued walking downstairs.

The tiled courtyard was so peaceful I felt I had to whisper. "Lunch was de-luscious." Something was wrong with that statement, but I didn't know what. "I've never eaten with men in dresses—oops, robes—before."

Bougainvillea struggled up the walls and a tiny fountain tinkled in the corner. Erik's navy gaze dropped to my mouth. I heard an intake of breath. His? Mine? His dark fingers, sparkling with silver rings, touched my neck. His other hand touched my cheek and I met his gaze, letting it anchor me in the blue and yellow sunlit space.

Erik leaned toward me, his mouth just above mine. I smelled mint from the tea, and felt the warmth of his breath on my lips.

With our eyes still locked, he placed his mouth over mine. I felt my eyes close as I sank into his kiss. His touch was gentle, but sure. His kiss was so slow, moving over my mouth in microscopic nibbles. I felt the sun on my forehead, smelled baking bread and a waft of roses. Each tiny kiss turned on another part of my body until I felt my skin humming with activity.

He tucked a strand of hair behind my ear, stepped closer, and put his other hand on my neck, drawing me in. He traced my lips with his tongue. I was shaking, dizzy from the blood racing straight to my mouth, my breasts.

Erik stepped back, smiled at me, then kissed my brow. "Luscious Elize, I do believe you're stoned, we're stoned, despite the open windows."

I giggled, clamping my hand over my mouth at the sacrilege of sound in this space. Furthermore, I don't giggle.

"I'll walk you back," he said, taking hold of my hand.

The sun was high. Hot. My hand clasped Erik's as we wove up and down residential streets until we reached the main souk area. I wouldn't have recognized it. Today, all the shops were closed. As we drew closer to the Place, we saw more westerners wandering, hot, confused, and aimless. We walked by, hands linked, with knowledge and a destination. I tried not to feel superior.

"Would you like to come in?" I asked Erik as we turned onto my street.

"Very much," he answered, glancing at me out of the corner of his eye.

I smiled at the girl behind the desk as I checked in again, and then I had Erik in my room. He captured my hand and brought it to his mouth, kissing the back of it, then the palm.

He looked over his fingers at me. Without taking his gaze from mine, he kissed the inside of my wrist, the inside of my forearm. My linen shirtsleeve kept him from going any further. He put his arms around me, like we were going to dance, then bent his mouth to mine.

His kiss was hungry. I grinned against his mouth: now we were talking.

I opened my mouth to him, but Erik just smiled and began a career of kissing my face, my neck, my ears, my throat. He guided me to the banquette, and slipped me onto the woven seat cushion. He slid pillows beneath my head and feet, and every time I opened my eyes I saw a dark head, a strong throat, silver-streaked hands and dark eyes.

"Pretty feet," he said, running his hands under my insteps.

He licked my neck. I grabbed for him. Our kiss was open-mouthed, tongues entangled. *How do I get his shirt off*, I thought, feeling his pecs through the linen. It lacked snaps or buttons; I yanked at the tail and we stopped kissing long enough to pull it over his head and send it flying.

Erik's skin was dark, not brown, not copper, but something between. A smattering of dark hair sprinkled his chest, a touch on his navel, and a trail disappeared into the waist of his pants.

He had a hard body, like a surfer's or a kayaker's, with strong shoulders, a sunken belly, and arms veined with blue. I reached for him, pulling him to me. I felt him hard against my legs, spicy-scented and silky everywhere else. We kissed again.

I slid my hands down his back, my fingers in the groove of his spine, to cup his butt. He groaned as I caressed those perfect curves of solid muscle. But when my fingers slipped into his waistband, he caught them and pulled them up over my head. "What?" I said. We were adults. We wanted each other. What—

"Time, luscious Elize, we have all the time in the world," Erik whispered, then kissed my cheek, my neck, my throat. "No goals. Just be." His lips migrated down the collar of my shirt, keeping to my skin. They reached the buttons—progress!—and he breathed through the shirt onto my nipple.

Without touching me, or it, he heated and cooled, blew on and teased my nipple to an awareness so sharp I wasn't sure it wasn't pain. The different textures mesmerized me. I felt his beard, a subtle roughness; his nose, as he drew circles around my breast; the heat of his breath, the suction of his mouth; the near nip of his teeth. He took the placket of my shirt between his teeth and pulled it forward, then back, arousing me with my own shirt, still on my body.

The courtyard fountain covered up the sounds I made.

Erik licked my nipple through the fabric, his tongue a long swathe of heat and moisture. He tugged the shirt back and forth.

There is such a thing as a nipple orgasm.

He turned his attention to my other breast, and I closed my eyes, letting the sensations wash over me. He kissed my mouth again, tasting my lips, my tongue, running his tongue over my teeth. My wet shirt cooled as Erik sat up, straddling me. When I opened my eyes, he blew on my breasts. I arched my back, fire shooting down my stomach, through my veins.

With the tail of my shirt, he teased my navel. "No piercings, no tattoos?" he asked.

"Too long to heal," I murmured. "Couldn't bear to be out of the water that long."

"Lady Impatience," he said, tracing a circle around my navel. Every tiny hair stood on end.

In one move he slipped down my thighs and breathed between my legs. Dry-wick pants, cotton underwear; neither was a barrier to his breath, his heat. I groaned as he untied the drawstring and pulled my pants down. I lifted my hips, already wet, beyond ready for the main event, but Erik slid my pants to mid-thigh. Only. He picked up the end of the drawstring and sucked on it.

I watched him through a haze of want. I could smell myself, my breasts felt electrified and I couldn't wait to see where that tease of dark hair on his belly led. What I felt seemed fantastic, but he wasn't very speedy in getting his pants off. I sat up on my elbows. "What are you doing?"

He lifted a brow and twisted the string with his tongue. A very talented tongue, one I could put to better use than just a drawstring.

"Did you have plans?" he teased. "Am I keeping you?" He drew the drawstring around my navel, down to the edge of my panties. Holding the wet string in his teeth, watching me with his navy-blue eyes, he followed the waistband of my underwear, so slowly, so precisely, that I felt branded.

I writhed beneath him, then cried out when he followed the path with his tongue. He nuzzled me—through the damp cotton—with his nose. Then with the string. He held it taut between his fingers and strummed me, stroke after sliding stroke. I wasn't one to resist, especially when he whispered, "Let go, luscious."

He swallowed my shouts with his kiss. I shuddered and shook in his arms, throbbing inside. Erik kissed my brow.

To think, we weren't even naked.

The Walk

"Ahhhhhhahahhhhhhhhahahahhh . . . "

I snapped upright.

"Sssh. It's just the muezzin," Erik said. We were crammed on the banquette, his arm beneath my head, holding onto the back of the cushion.

He kissed me. I expected a quick kiss, torn between embarrassment and vulnerability.

But Erik's kiss wasn't quick. He held my lips, breathing slowly. I felt myself sink, breathing in tune with him. Breathing him. He manipulated time again, and all my instinctive behaviors—get out; get away; go cold; go demanding—melted away. It was only him, his breath, his scent, his touch, his heat. "How are you?" he whispered, a breath away from my lips.

Outside the speakers crackled and the muezzin's tone went flat.

I chuckled. "Sorry," I said, "it's just—"

"Yeah, Barney needs some help," Erik said.

"Barney? He has a name?"

"He just sounds like a Barney. Listen to that prayer. It's less of a proclamation of the glory of God, and more like he's seeking affirmation. God is great? There is no God but Allah?"

I listened, heard the uncertainty in the muezzin's voice. "You're right, he does."

"Does what?"

"Both," I said. "Sounds like he's a Barney. and like he's asking for confirmation."

With a last crackle of the speaker, Barney was gone. But in the other parts of the city the prayers continued. *Allahu Akbar*, I could understand it now. God is great.

Erik kissed my forehead. "Things should start opening, for a few hours. Did you say wanted to check your e-mail?"

No. "I need to." I didn't move. He was an inch away, spiky lashes framing eyes that looked black. "Before we leave, however," I said, tracing my finger down his chest in an attempt at playing a femme fatale, "is there anything I can do for you?"

He frowned at me, then gave a smile I couldn't interpret. "I'm perfectly satisfied," he said.

I nodded, remembering he was a total stranger with some nice manners, but no history to speak of. "Are you infectious in any way? Anything I should know about?" Why else would a guy refuse sex?

"I'm clean," he said, then grinned, "but my arm has gone to sleep."

"Oh, I'm sorry," I said, sitting up. Erik, freed, turned on the banquette. "May I—" He pointed toward the bathroom.

"Of course." I stared at the closed door for a moment. I had to admit, I felt deliciously relaxed. So he didn't want sex. That didn't have to mean anything bad. Hadn't he said "we have all the time in the world"?

Of course, any fool knew that wasn't true.

I stood up, tying my pants and looking down at the puckers on my shirt. What did he mean by that, anyway? He'd been aroused. As Zen as he seemed to be, I realized, he was probably into that long-delayed sex. Tantric. I'd be game.

Shy, or embarrassed by my neediness, I turned my back to the bathroom door just as Erik opened it. "So the Net shop and then . . . ?" I said, looking through my limited wardrobe, striving for the unconcern I usually felt at this juncture.

Erik put his arms around me, holding me against his very nice chest. "I'm open. Do you want to see the newer city?"

I closed my eyes. I wanted to stay here, in his arms, forever. Why? What was it about him? What he could do to me? "Sounds good," I said, trying to regain some balance, some control, some customary Elize-ness. "But I think I should change shirts." My linen was noticeably puckered.

He chuckled and kissed my neck, then sat down.

I grabbed the first shirt I saw, originally a beach cover up, and tossed it on.

"Migration season, then?" Erik asked, glancing through the books I'd brought.

"It's supposed to be spectacular."

"What makes it spectacular?" he said.

"Same things that make anything spectacular," I said. "Wonder, beauty, and surprise." I was unwilling to meet his gaze, aware of my vulnerability. "I'm ready."

This Net café was more like an attic bedroom, stuffed head to tail with aged machines. As far as I could see, all forty computers were using the same dinosaur-slow modem. But at least it was open. When at long last my e-mail account screen came up, I realized the keyboard was different: some letters were swapped, and others just didn't exist. I wasn't using the alphabet I knew.

When I opened my e-mail, I was surprised at the lack of messages. I would have expected twenty from Zephyr alone. Sometimes she sent me that many when we were in the same office. Instead, I had five, and as I read them I wondered if she was mad at me. Her tone was so . . . formal. Or was the new "director" monitoring e-mail now?

I opened the most recent one and felt my ears burn.

Elize: It's been days since your scheduled arrival, yet SD reports you have neither appeared nor communicated. Please remedy this irresponsible (not to mention discourteous!) conduct, immediately. Unless you have been kidnapped, in which case, we have no ransom. Sorry. :) ZH

Irresponsible. It seemed to glow on my monitor. Irresponsible! Had Frankie already rubbed off on her that much? How could Zephyr ever judge me—judge anyone—as irresponsible? I was shaking as I typed.

Morocco, as a country, can be blamed for my late arrival. I will arrive in Larache . . .

When?

Playtime was over. I had a paper to write, a career to save. A man—both employed and bird savvy—to seduce. As I touched the *e* I thought of the man at the café outside. My lips were still puffy from our kisses.

My head had begun to ache from my second-hand kif hangover.

One of the keys had a swirly line on it. An Arabic letter? It didn't matter. What I'd experienced wasn't real. Erik couldn't stop time, or bend it, or do anything else. I looked up at the blinking cursor and typed my response, picking over the keyboard in search of the correct letter, like a starling looking for just the right seed.

I walked back into the dirty street. Mismatched café tables were filled with youths wearing jeans and T-shirts, all of whom stared at me as they smoked.

Erik, his glossy curls dark as a raven's wing, looked up from his book. He rose to pull out my chair, but I shook my head. "You don't want some tea," he said. "A pastry? French pastries?"

My stomach growled, disagreeing, but I shook my head.

"Bad news?" he asked, his sunglasses-shielded face studying mine.

In the sunlight he wasn't as young as I'd thought. He had some lines around his mouth, a few silver hairs mixed in with the russet and black. I felt his questions, but I didn't answer them or look into his face. With one glance, he could freeze the world. I couldn't be lost like that again. This wasn't my world. "Tomorrow, Larache," I said.

He was why I was late, why I'd been called irresponsible. Erik! The reason I'd gotten stuck in Marrakesh and worried my assistant, embarrassed myself—

"That's tomorrow," he said, picking his words.

I crossed my arms, eyes darting around the broken-down street with its dingy signs. "Weren't you the one who told me that in Islam, in Morocco, tomorrow begins tonight?"

He sat and stared at me for a moment. "I'll just pay for my tea," he said, then turned and counted out change. Coin by coin, like he was paying in pennies for something that cost three dollars. I waited, my teeth gritted. Methodically he stowed his book, zipped his bag, rose and gestured for me to go before him. I ignored his half-full glass.

I was halfway across the Place before I realized he wasn't with me. I waited, toes tapping. Nineteen lines in the asphalt. Seven open cafés; one with nine tables, one with twenty, one with four—Erik caught up. "Why are you so slow?" I snapped.

"Why are you in such a rush?" he asked. "It's a holiday."

"I'm already late."

"Yeah, I understand. But you can't get there before tomorrow. Why not enjoy today?"

Enjoyment. That was what he was about. I guess accomplishment meant nothing. "I have things to do."

"Okay."

Despite this exchange, he still walked slowly. I wanted to scream, but then I asked myself why. Erik had no reason to speed up. He had nowhere to go, nothing to do. His friends were druggies, and for all I knew, he was a gigolo in search of a good napping spot. We reached the doorway of my hotel.

We stared at each other for an awkward moment. I refused to invite him in. Erik didn't reach for me, didn't suggest we spend a last evening together.

"Enjoy the birds, Elize," he said, not even taking off his glasses. He shot a half smile at me, the barest glimpse of his incisor, then he turned and ambled away.

I looked up at the slice of blue sky. This time yesterday I'd seen the storks.

Yesterday.

With a list running through my head, I stepped into my room, which looked assaulted: pillows on the floor, my crumpled shirt. As if on cue, Barney started to rumble next door. Erik's scent.

"It was an interlude," I said out loud. "A tall dark stranger I met on the midnight express to Marrakesh." He was probably a drug dealer, or just a jack-of-all-trades, incompetent, a drifter, a grifter. He wasn't even that tall or dark. I picked up my shirt; it smelled like him.

I allowed myself the moment of honesty: whoever he was, he was the hottest thing I'd ever touched. And the way he made me feel—

Think about Sam. He was attractive, employed, and we had a whole world in common. "Still, I'm never washing that shirt," I argued aloud as I threw it in my bag.

The Trip

They all stared at me. Young, old, male, female. I met the gaze of a wizened old man in a turban and dusty black suit, but he didn't flinch, just kept staring. I looked away, uncomfortable. A fat blonde woman spoke English to a young couple, complaining about how the Moroccan men wouldn't stop hassling her. She enumerated her dozens of marriage proposals, her hundreds of propositions. She was going to Casablanca—"Caza." She'd already bought her ticket for the afternoon train. Train, not bus. I breathed a sigh of relief.

Right on schedule, a bus pulled up. Those waiting stirred. I was already on my feet. Twenty-five windows on the bus, eighteen in the strip shopping center where we waited. Five palms, each surrounded by eight pots of flowers.

A self-important uniformed man stepped off the transport and began accepting tickets. It was assigned seating, so I took my time getting in line and checking my luggage.

The bus was new, plush, with a/c and onboard toilets. Still clean, too. I checked my ticket, matched my number with the seat number, and sat down, tucking my bird bag and bins beneath my seat.

I'd change buses in Sale, and then hop a local to Larache. From the proud-to-speak-English ticket seller, I'd gotten the skinny. I didn't need French to get around.

Or Erik.

Outside, the line grew. Did they oversell buses here, like airlines did seats in the States? Bags were parked in the underbelly, and a whole assortment of Moroccans boarded. Through the window I watched the driver walk back to the main office. The young couple devoured croissants and sat so close to each other that no light showed between their shoulders.

I became aware of talking. The "Hey you!" got my attention. I turned.

"My," a gold-chain wearing man said to me. He pointed to my seat. "My."

"No," I said, pulling out my ticket. It was the right seat, wasn't it? The numbers at least, were recognizable. He held out his hand for my ticket.

Hell, no.

"My!" he said, turning and speaking to another man. His voice rose, he gestured, he stuck his ticket in my face.

It wasn't a ticket, it was a letter. I could piece together the French. Some official had given the man my seat! I squinted at the writing: it was fill-in-the-blank a few places, one of them being the seat number. The seven looked like a four had been squashed in front of it.

Had he been given some sort of governmental preference? I stayed calm, but wanted to scream, *You can't do that! Are there* no *rules in this country?*

Six people were involved now, talking back and forth, staring at me. I handed his letter back. He passed it around the tribunal crowd, who had about thirty teeth between them. The man frowned when I shook my head. I showed him my ticket, matched it to the number on the seat, and stared at him. *Don't mess with me, buddy, I'm a pissed-off blonde.*

Suddenly, everyone looked at their seats. It took me a minute to realize it, but they didn't know the numbers had meaning. They didn't even know where they were posted, until now. When the driver returned twenty minutes later, people were still shuffling seats. The man who'd claimed my seat wedged himself in the aisle. I pretended

I didn't feel his gaze. I was also glad I didn't understand the things he muttered.

The bus driver pulled the doors closed. Everyone fluttered, like disturbed pigeons redistributing themselves on a statue. At the fifth stop before leaving Marrakesh proper, I got a seatmate, a woman in her late thirties or early forties wearing a sequin-studded black scarf and full length, long-sleeved, transparent robe. It revealed more than it hid. Did it follow the letter of the law, or the spirit of it? She settled next to me, and I started counting the sequins on her dress.

Halfway through the ride, we stopped at a rest stop in the middle of nowhere. Nowhere in Morocco was truly *no where*. After all my sparkling water, I needed a bathroom, and the one on board had been broken. I followed the general exodus.

The rest stop was part deli, part auto shop, and looked like the lobby of a 1960s hotel. There was nothing else around, as far as the eye could see, other than road, sky, and dirt.

And empty plastic trash bags. It seemed that any above-ground projection in Morocco, be it natural or manmade, had trapped those bags. The noise was a rattle or a whistle, depending on the wind.

A boy sold pomegranates and melons at a covered stand beside the parking lot. Single-serving tagines filled the counters of two of the outside vendors. I followed the group of women around to a garden in the back and access to the facilities.

The teals of North Africa, a duck that had been painted on the tomb walls in ancient Egypt, strutted around behind the pomegranate trees. Not enough to qualify as a flush, but still, a family or two. Graylag geese waded in the rivulet, protected on both sides by papyrus plants. Another family of graylags strode around the yard, a formidable mother trailed by her chicks. The goose looked like she had knee socks on, rolled at the knees. Everyone knew the term gaggle, but geese could also be a skein, or a nide or a wedge, depending on what they were doing.

The mother goose squawked at her young, especially the last gosling, who seemed awed by everything. He stopped to gaze at a butterfly on a blade of grass as his siblings marched away.

Apparently even goose mothers had eyes in the back of their heads, because the goose halted and squawked until Junior snapped out of it and rejoined the lineup. Not four paces further he was daydreaming again, watching the flowers sway in the breeze.

After parking the attentive goslings in the shade of a shrub, Mother Goose came after Junior, nipping him this time. I smiled. I could almost hear the threat: "Don't make me come after you, young man!"

An automotive honk startled us all.

I stood alone in the garden. Panicked, I raced through the empty rest stop. The bus was full, the lights on, and the driver in place. A few smokers stubbed out their cigarettes and moseyed toward the bus.

I was just like that damned duck, I thought as I got back on—still with a full bladder, still thirsty and hungry. Easily distracted.

That's why I didn't get the job.

No, I didn't get the job because I wasn't a PhD. Though Frankie knew more about dead birds than live ones, the prestige of those three letters was what the board really cared about. Experience meant nothing; my relationship with the Institute, with Mr. Woodrow, counted for less. I sighed.

No, you didn't get the job because you didn't want the job. You wanted the money, the prestige, the approval, the confirmation. Not the actual job.

After telling mind-Zephyr to shut the hell up, I reached for my Larache migration list. I shouldn't waste valuable study time.

❖

The signs for Rabat were, thankfully, recognizable. We drove in winding streets that turned into cement house additions, and at last, lined boulevards.

I gathered my things, ready to jump. The woman next to me spoke in Arabic, or something. I smiled, but shook my head politely.

The driver pulled to a stop before a hotel-restaurant-café-tour strip that looked just like the bus stop in Algeciras, Spain, if you subbed Arabic for Spanish. This was it?

The woman spoke to me again, but I shrugged and shook my head again. Didn't she understand that I couldn't comprehend her? Then I crawled over her into the aisle. Outside the driver handed me my bags and I turned toward the restaurant. Someone here would speak English, tell me which bus to take to Larache.

That woman, I thought, remembering her 3,286 black sequins, sequins I counted when I wasn't learning birds, had probably been trying to tell me I was getting off at the wrong stop.

Why hadn't I thought it odd that I was the only one who had disembarked? I held onto the strap as the local Sale-Rabat bus took a corner, from the stop where I'd gotten off. Taking me to the stop where I needed to go *in order* to catch the bus to what-better-be-the-experience-of-my-lifetime Larache. The palm trees moved so slowly by the window that I had a chance to count them, seventeen before we stopped and I got off. Again.

Signs in English, or at least the alphabet I knew. Hurrah.

Today, Larache.

Four hours later, the final bus stopped. Everyone on it, the old women in headscarves, the young men who smoked and slept, the old men who snored and glared, turned to look at me.

"Larache?" the bus driver said. "*Les aves?*" He opened the door, and made shooing motions.

As best I could figure, I was being dropped in a ditch. But *aves* was the root of the Latin word for bird. "Larache?" I asked, as I stood, trying not to bump my head.

"Larache!" the driver said, now facing forward, done with me. *Larache*, the other travelers muttered, smiling and gesturing, and at last I walked forward, grabbed my luggage and stepped down onto the narrow edge of gravel.

The bus roared away, moving faster now than it had the whole trip. The passengers waved and I wondered if they laughed at the stupid American stranded on the roadside.

In a few moments, the wake of dust had settled. I looked around. We'd passed a smaller village, and in the far distance ahead of me I could make out some buildings. Larache? Was this was the spot?

I'd known that some walking would be involved, but I just wasn't sure how much or in which direction. The accommodations were on the beach. But where was the beach from here? A few scraggly trees provided shade and a comforting whisper as the wind blew through them. I ignored the ever-present rattling bags.

It seemed that the road we'd been on had run parallel to the coast, so if I walked straight out, perpendicular to the road, I should hit the sea. I checked my methodology by looking up. Birds would be flying toward the shore.

After a few minutes of walking, the bushes and trees were supplanted by buildings, and I found myself walking down a narrow street, empty. Part of the town? Larache, I knew from Sam's statements, was a summer resort, and it was late on a fall afternoon. Still, I didn't see anything that could qualify as "town."

I crested a hill and saw it: the beach, the sea. The Atlantic.

The wind blew harder here, unimpeded and delicious. The cries of the gulls sounded so familiar and so welcome—who would have ever thought I would welcome a gull?—that my eyes filled with tears.

I must still be exhausted. Jet-lagged. Bus-lagged.

The waves were crashing, not surfable but not flat, and I feasted on the shades of blue, ignoring the dark patches. Dark blue water meant danger of the deep, tricky kind. Dark blue eyes should carry the same warning. I closed my eyes and felt the salt air melt away my tension. Birds, sea. Almost there.

Almost wasn't quite enough.

Following the remembered directions, I turned north. My hands were blistering from my damn bags. I lumbered along, stopping and starting as my bag's rolling wheels got stuck in the sand every two feet.

"Elize! My God, is that you?"

I looked up from where I was cursing and wrestling with my bag, my heart pounding in my throat both from surprise and, well . . . surprise.

They streamed over from the beach, in birding khaki and green. They wore more zippers and Velcro between the six of them than I had seen since I arrived in Morocco. Sam led the charge, his beach-boy-blond good looks enhanced by camo cargo shorts, khaki shirt, and bush hat. "How are you?" he said, then paused when he reached me.

Colleagues generally didn't hug. The question remained: were we more or less? I rubbed my hand on my pants and extended it to shake.

"Elize." Janice, a colleague from Oregon, touched me on the shoulder. "We were so concerned when you didn't arrive, and then we couldn't get hold of your assistant—" Janice's wide blue eyes flickered from me to the sky. "Oh look," she said, lifting her bins. "Did you see that?"

"Caught nothing but a flash of blue," someone else said.

"Flying like a roller, though," another added.

"It's been pretty dry," someone explained to me, without dropping their bins.

"Wind through the straits, dropping 'em in Spain," another said.

"Of course," I said, too tired to even pick up my bins.

"We're just headed out, but if you want, the cottages are right through there," Sam said, pointing down another path. "Dinner will be about nine."

"Take any empty bed," Janice said, scanning the trees opposite.

"Thanks," I said, and watched them trek off. I picked up my bins and scanned the sky, but it was pretty still. Promising myself a shower, I walked on, but the adrenaline was there. I was listening for the squawks and coos, the flutter of wings. It might have been a disaster to get here, but this was my world. The birds wouldn't be alienating and challenging, even if everything else had been.

❖

The dining room wasn't designed for a group of twenty-five, so there was some sort of popularity shuffle going on. Clive and Lettice, whom I knew by name only—they were great supporters of Sam—had seated themselves beside his chair. A phalanx of bird ladies, with hummingbird earrings, flamingo-painted safari hats, and gull-embroidered jackets, wearing Columbia's finest trek wear, had picked a table in the corner. Janice seated herself across from Sam.

First come, first served, and it was protocol that any late arrival just take what she could find. Zephyr had told me this, since I'd never been on a foreign birding excursion with other pros.

"Shall you join us?" a bespectacled, rumpled, mid-fortyish man asked me with an English accent. "Name's Spenser, and you must be Elize. Heard all about you."

I waited a moment. Heard about me *how*?

"Difficult trip?" he said, "Yes, well, some couscous will fix you right up. Have a seat."

Two other men joined us, a slender, pale one, who introduced himself as Jackson, and his boyfriend, John.

"John," I said, shaking his hand. "Sam's friend from—?"

"Yeah, we were at Cornell together."

A pang of jealousy. Not for going to school there, but for having access to the Cornell Lab for Ornithology.

A stunningly beautiful black girl with ringlets in her hair and glasses joined us. "Oh, good," she said, touching me on the arm. "So glad you're here. Thought you were going to . . . "

"To what?" I said, trying not to sound defensive.

"Bail," she said, but without malice.

I muttered some apology about her concern, but she waved it away. "Unless you fly directly to Casablanca, it's just hard to get here." "And you are . . . " I started.

"I'm Dr. Donaldson's assistant," she said, tapping the pen tucked behind her ear. "Now that everyone has arrived, I can start worrying about other things."

"Arabella, there is no need to worry," Spenser said, with his plummy accent. "It's the Mideast, and everything will happen, Inshallah. As God wills. Isn't fatalism beautiful?"

I couldn't tell if he was being serious or sarcastic. Or if he was sober. Any of it would work with his indulged ennui persona.

Sam burst into the room, apologizing. "I've been online with the Institute."

In my exhaustion it took a moment to realize he was referring to his institute, not mine. Then the other part dawned on me: "We have our own Net service?" I said, thinking of who I'd e-mail. Zephyr?

Erik.

"Slow, but yes," Arabella said. "There's a queue for it, if you want to sign up."

"Good to know." No. I didn't want to talk to Zephyr, after that last note. There was nothing to say to Erik. No need to go into the computer room.

"Since we're all here, a few announcements," Sam said. "The Color-ringed Great White Egret has been noted, but it will be a few days before we know if it's a first or not."

"Who sighted that?" I asked.

"I did," Clive said, smiling back at me. "Good eyes, even if they are old." His gaze had a twinkle in it and he looked familiar. Maybe a former movie star? A politician? I grinned back.

Sam continued. "The boats leave tomorrow morning at five. Coffee will be available here, and if you want to fill a carafe, you need to turn that request in tonight. Arabella, anything else?"

"The wind is still ripping through the Straits," she said, "so it may continue to be slow, but there are still the wetlands residents to see."

There was a general groaning, but not too much complaint. Birds and birders are subject to the caprice of nature. I knew people who had been to South Texas four, six times, and had never seen a green jay.

I also knew people who had seen so many, especially around their picnic tables, that they considered the green jay as big a pest as a grackle. You can't plan on birds.

I'd never seen a color-ringed great white egret before, though, and the thought excited me.

Western-dressed Moroccan men served dinner: several chickens, a side of couscous, and vegetable salad. None of the aromas I'd come to associate with Moroccan food, or the flavors, but it was fine.

The sightings of the day, to hear tell, had been extraordinary. Unless you already knew wetland birds. Spoonbills, smaller than flamingoes, with bills that look, well, like large wooden spoons, had been sighted in the hundreds.

Not to be blasé, but where I live, we have roseate spoonbills as residents.

They recited the ducks and the waders, and it read like a list I'd get from walking around the pond at work. I smiled and ate my couscous. I'd counted on getting some passerines, the songbirds flying between Africa and Europe, resting on the greenery by the sea.

There's always the bald ibis, if you're not satisfied with migration season, my wicked, greedy, Crazy-Elize brain, whispered.

Dinner was done, and with no ceremony everyone headed off to bed. Arabella, Janice, Lettice and I roomed together. I'd taken the bed that looked unoccupied, and discovered I was sleeping next to Lettice.

Discovered also that she snored.

Five A.M. seemed to come earlier than usual. I hadn't brought a thermos, so I made do by slamming back two cups of coffee. We huddled in the boat, and the men in djellabas called to each other through the predawn fog as they rowed us into the Loukkos river. Wonderful citrusy smells blew over us from the orange and tangerine groves to the south.

Janice spotted the first bird, and we were off.

❖

"Nice day, huh," Sam said, sitting down opposite me. Tonight someone had sprung for wine, so dinner had been more relaxed, and we weren't dispersing for bed quite yet. Someone had set up a spotting scope, focused on the moon.

I nodded at Sam. The day had been nice, but nothing so extraordinary that I couldn't have seen it at home, or South Padre or Sabal Palms.

Not like seeing the bald ibis, Crazy-Elize in my brain singsonged. I'd gotten six different Life List birds; I told her to shut her up.

"Do you know how to play shesh besh?" he asked me, gesturing to the game board on the table between us.

I'd seen it played in Tangier cafés. "It's backgammon, right?" I shrugged. "No, I'm good, thanks." I sat back and sipped my wine.

Sam chuckled and stretched back. It was the first moment we'd had alone since I got here and I felt his gaze on me. Shouldn't my blood be racing? "It's been a while, Elize," he said, his voice an unaccented rumble in the darkness. "Glad you're here."

I raised my glass in a mock toast. "As am I."

"You're looking good."

So was he. Sam was the quintessential surfer boy, with the buff, blond good looks you'd find on an anatomically correct Ken doll. But he was also a birder, which made him perfect for me. *Perfect,* I reminded myself. Easy. I understood him.

"How long has it been?" I asked, leaning forward, forcing myself into a posture of interest. Zephyr said that some things, if faked, could be summoned. My interest wasn't faked, just kind of buried. It needed resuscitation.

"Two years and something since that conference in Florida." He glanced over his shoulder at Flamingo Hat, who was waiting for migrants to fly across the face of the moon so she could count them, and dropped his voice. "Better accommodations there, for sure."

Sam and I had made out in the elevator, one of those glass-fronted kind that looked out on the Atlantic, for four hours one morning. "The rooms here at least assure that we get sleep," I teased.

"I'm wide awake now," he said. "It's morning in San Diego."

We stared at each other for a moment. I couldn't see him in the dusk, but I knew his eyes were light blue and edged with golden lashes, his skin tanned, his body firm and fit. Best yet, he was tall. He made me feel petite, like we were a set.

Sam and I fit together; we look good in pictures together; we have worlds in common. Yeah, so my blood wasn't singing. Maybe my blood was tired.

"How's the Dubya, Elize?"

Dammit. *We'll fit, until he finds out what a loser I am.* I shrugged and finished my wine in one gulp. "We've gotten new funding. Opening to the public now." Grants I'd written, that I'd assumed I'd administer. The thought made me grind my teeth.

"How's Wilkerson Junior?"

I shrugged. "He's definitely not his parents."

"I wish more people would follow their example," Sam said, "and donate everything for ornithological research."

The Institute, the island, buildings, everything, had been the Wilkersons' home. Private property. They'd built it in the heyday of sixties architecture, and refurnished it in the seventies after Hurricane Celia raked the coast. My office had been a stately bedroom with a stunning view of the creek—but a room also stunning in its abuse of orange and brown. And the stuff the Wilkersons had bought was of such high quality that it would *not* die. It was so old, it was almost in fashion again.

I didn't care, but one of Zephyr's many roommates had studied interior design and treated the Dubya like a museum.

One of the boons to the directorship would have been to move to the master bedroom-cum-office. White and Plexiglas, yes, but one whole wall was windows. "That would be especially impressive in La Jolla," I responded.

"There are some amazing homes there," he said.

"You didn't strike me as interested in architecture."

"I do live in La Jolla," he said. "Not that you've been there. You've certainly never visited me." Was there accusation in that?

"Work, you know." I shrugged it off.

"That's feeble, Elize. You never leave Texas."

"I went to Miami!" And look what happened; the words went unspoken.

"Yeah, and you left, too."

Flamingo Hat wandered away from the scope; apparently she wasn't seeing much. I jerked my attention back to Sam, forced to recall Miami.

Mama had called me at the hotel, a rare and terrifying thing, because she hates the telephone and isn't any kind of conversationalist. Rocks chat more. Pop, she had informed me in terse sentences, had collapsed.

I'd raced home, fearing this was It.

"He ended up okay, right?" Sam asked. "Your Pop?"

"Yeah." Pop had fallen out of the tree he'd been pruning; he didn't die till a year later. Unrelated causes. "We're tough stock," I said. In my German family you worked until you died, or until work killed you. That was the motto. *For most of us*, my mind whispered. Had being an artist been what killed Fischer?

Sam said nothing in response. The uncomfortable silence grew, deepened. I moved over to the scope, adjusting the focus, then turned to him. "How are your birds?" Sam studied ibis, too.

He looked straight at me, even in the dark I felt it. "What happened to you? Delayed you?"

So we were going to get personal. I declined to name Erik. I shrugged, peering through the lens, seeing nothing but the white of the moon. "I had to change my travel plans—"

"Yeah," he said, drawing the word out. "I kind of got that impression after two days in Paris. Waiting."

Waiting! I felt the blood leave my cheeks. I'd completely forgotten Paris when I'd changed all my travel plans! I turned to look at him as bile rose in my throat. I counted fourteen buttons on his shirt, two on each breast pocket. Nothing could make me feel worse, more contrite, than to hear that he'd waited. My voice was raspy, defenseless. "I'm so sorry, Sam."

"Anyway," he said, looking away, his tone casual, "you're going to hate working with the public. People are always asking questions, interrupting your research. How are your ibis?"

He'd waited.

Sam had waited for me. I couldn't imagine anything worse. How could I have done that to someone else? I knew how it felt! How could I be so heartless? I seized on the rope he'd thrown me and cleared my throat. "The glossy are rare visitors, and the white-faced are doing well. Mortality rate was about fifteen percent, including everything from eggs to juveniles."

"Nice numbers. How's the race for director going?"

Now the blood rushed back into my cheeks. I took over counting through the scope. Flamingo Hat had marked only two birds in ten minutes. Obviously the migrants were still held down on the other side of the straits. I fiddled with the focus and stared at the surface of the moon while I tried to think of what to say. I'm not a liar—at least I'd never thought myself one—but here, and now? Lutherans didn't believe in white lies. Any shade of untruth was as black as pitch, regardless of trying to spare someone's feelings—in this case, mine—or ease someone into an unpleasant reality.

"Elize," Sam said, standing behind me. "Can I get you some more wine?"

"Please," I said, staring at the moon. I turned to watch him walk back to the dining cabin.

Hiding behind the scope, I stared at the man in the moon, undisturbed by flying silhouettes. What was I going to tell Sam? How was I not supposed to writhe in embarrassment? Had he talked to anyone? Did he know anything? How much could I say, but still keep the horrible truth from getting out and poisoning all these people against me? Ruining any chance I had of getting another job?

Easier to get one when you had one. The same was true of cars and boyfriends and colds.

One lone bird, a duck trying to either catch up with its flock or an outrider for its flock, came spearing across the white orb. One duck in eight minutes. I twisted my braid and closed my eyes, listening to the gentle hush of waves a moment away.

What was I going to do about my life? Could I live without the sea?

Sure I could. I'd been landlocked most of my young life, until I saw the Gulf. I recalled my first walk down to the Corpus Christi beach, a short but deep stretch of sand. The smell of the sea, the feel of sand in my shoes, the liveliness of the waves, the birds, how everything interacted, and every minute it was all new. I'd never lost that feeling of fascination for the shore. Could I get Sam to hire me in San Diego? Then I definitely couldn't sleep with him, not even as an apology.

He'd waited.

"Shall we go sit on the beach?" he said as he walked up behind me a moment later. "Talk. Catch up." He held up a new bottle of wine with a smile. "Unless of course, you're tired?"

Gull Jacket was ten steps behind him. If we wanted any privacy . . .

He'd *waited* for me. Waited in Paris. "Lead the way," I said. My guilt made me want to throw up.

Sam started a fire in a pre-dug pit as we each wrapped up in blankets. The breeze was cool. "I spoke to someone down there, a few days ago," he said as he poked at the branches, fanned the flames.

I tucked the blanket around me, and then it dawned on me he was talking about the Wilkerson Institute. He'd talked to someone. "Zephyr," I said, picking up my refilled glass.

"No, not Zephyr. She's got that great, husky voice. No, this was someone else. A strong accent, from Wisconsin or somewhere. A Frankie, maybe?"

Frankie was answering the phones? I almost laughed. "Yeah," I said, downing my glass of wine. "Could be." Alcoholic calm raced into my bloodstream, took away my nausea. "She's new. Taxonomist from Michigan."

"Michigan, yeah, that fits with the accent."

I leaned back and looked up at the stars, ignoring the silence, the questions that hovered there like night herons, a rookery of herons just waiting for the right moment to scream and fly away. A zillion stars scattered across the blackness.

"Don't get to see the Milky Way too often," Sam said.

I got to see it almost every night. One of the many benefits of not living in a metropolitan area with its attendant light pollution. How many other places were by the water that weren't major cities with airports and sky scrapers and well-lit streets and homes?

A place that would have my birds?

"How is your research going?" I asked him. A dull throb worked its way from my spinal column to between my eyes. *He'd waited.* He'd waited and he'd talked to someone at the Institute. I poured another glass.

"Like yours," he said, firelight catching the few white hairs amidst the blonde, muting some of the lines that fanned out from his eyes. He stared into the fire as he spoke. "The numbers on the white-faced held steady from last year. Less predation on the eggs, we saw to that, but the numbers stayed the same."

"We're losing more wetlands," I said, looking back up at the sky. This was why I didn't drink wine, I realized. I got maudlin. Then angry.

"Designated ones?"

"No, just the ditches and fields alongside the public road. They're widening it, to provide for more traffic, and in the process—"

"There go the ditches."

"Herons and egrets feed there all the time," I said, sighing. "Between that and drilling allowed on Padre Island National Seashore, it just seems like it's all going to hell."

"That's why Wilkerson is opening the doors to the public, right?" Sam asked.

"I'm pretty sure he's doing that because of money," I said. "Tickets cost, and even the low price of a something like a national wildlife refuge ticket, compared to charging nothing, adds up."

"How'd you ever wind up there?"

"The Wilkersons had all those wetlands to observe."

"You studied wetlands biology, right?"

"Yeah. Mr. Woodrow would sit out with me, day after day, just watching the birds as I took notes, kept records. After Mrs. W. passed away and he decided to make the site available to a select group of other birders, I was offered a position."

"One that you actually took," he said.

I let it pass. With maudlin also came a clarity regarding how much I'd screwed up along the way. "Life," I said, "sometimes gets in the way of plans."

"So you don't approve of Wilkerson Junior's decision to open the gates? Elize, you can't halt progress."

"Ha!" I said. I hated that statement, hated that progress was popularly defined by nature being replaced by concrete. "I want what's best for my birds. If the habitats can be maintained undisturbed, with visitors watching from blinds or distant paths, that's one thing. But school kids? By the hundreds, just running around? Especially during breeding and brooding seasons? We might as well just shoot the birds—" Wouldn't Frankie love that? "—it will have the same long-term effect."

Irritation crept into my voice as I realized I had just finished another glass of wine. Third? Fourth? "Junior is a multimillionaire. He's not married, he has no kids, he's got houses and boats and planes and cars. Why can't he just leave the Dubya alone?"

"I didn't realize you were so anti-public," Sam said, refilling his glass. "How else do people learn what wetlands are, unless they go there?"

"I'm not anti-public," I said, though I wondered. "I agree. People need to see wetlands and the birds, so they know what they are protecting. But isn't that what public parks are for? National Wildlife Refuges? Zoos?"

I stared through the darkness at him and I wondered which one of us was the devil and which one was his advocate. "The Dubya is so rare and so valuable because it *is* untouched. It's a haven for everything, not just wetland birds. We have the northernmost standing forest of native palms left in Texas; we have riparian edge; we have cypress and live oak and Spanish moss. Not many places have so many options."

"All the more reason for it to be open to the public. It's walking trails, right?" He came around to my side, sitting close enough that I could feel the warmth from his body.

"So far," I said. "Give Wilkerson enough time and he'll probably build a highway with TollTags."

Sam chuckled, and I felt my hand covered by his. "Does Wilkerson know he's nursing a serpent?" His tone was gentle, so it took a moment for the barb to settle.

I jerked back. "I'm not a serpent." That was uncalled for.

"You're at total odds with his vision, and yet you're working for him."

"Nothing's sacred anymore," I said, catching his eye for a moment. "We forget beauty, we forget wonder. We just use everything up and don't care." I heard the petulance in my voice, but how could I get rid of it?

"That Padre Island thing really has upset you, hasn't it?"

"We're locusts, but there's no place to move on to."

"Elize," Sam said, reaching out for me, resting his hands on my blanketed hips, "it's not our job to try and save the world."

I stared up at him. He was healthy, comfortable, nice, and I felt choked by hopelessness. He was one of the good guys, and he didn't feel a need to save the world? If not him, then who?

"I'm drunk," I said, picking my words as carefully as my rubber lips would allow. "I'll see you in the morning."

He pulled me close, wrapping his strong arms around me. "I'll save you a place in my boat," he said, and pressed his mouth against mine.

Sam wanted me; his kiss, his body, said so. My kiss back was stimulus reaction. I wanted my bed. Alone. Me and my secrets and my disappointments. "I'm sorry for making you wait," I mumbled.

"Oh, Lettice and Clive joined me. We had fun."

Mollified, and a little snubbed, I went in search of my bed.

Once in it, just before I closed my eyes and surrendered to sleep, I touched my mouth.

But it wasn't Sam's kiss that caused a sudden craving in my belly, a flooding warmth. It was the mere memory of Erik's. I rolled over and buried my face in the pillow.

❖

Winds largely determine migration patterns. A strong northern wind moves over Europe in the autumn, and the birds, aware that it's their final warning, their boarding call, ride it south to their winter nesting grounds, be they Morocco, along the equator, or further south. Birds from as far east as Russia and as far north as Scandinavia fly over that juncture where the warm Mediterranean meets the cold Atlantic: the Strait of Gibraltar. That narrowing serves as a type of funnel. Interestingly enough, the two actual bodies of water don't mix; the warm flows on top, the cold stays below.

We were on the North Atlantic, and as I focused my bins I saw dozens of barn swallows swoop and dive as they made their way from sea to land. A gulp of swallows. Sam sat beside me, Lettice and Clive on either side of us. We were in the estuary, so the migrants moved past us to the beach at our backs. From here one could see the town of Larache, blue and white like a postcard, with an old Spanish citadel commanding the area.

"Is that a Squacco Heron?" I asked, spotting a longer whitish body among the mass of blue-black birds. I kept my bins on it as it landed, tucking its neck, heron style. Though it looked white at first glance, it was really a golden brown with a beak of teal.

The older couple, experienced birders, sat entranced, too.

The heron was tired, wiped out. Its wings drooped as it stood on the ground. It had flown at least 2,500 miles, most of it alone, since the squaccos were more solitary than a lot of migrants.

"Here's another," Sam said, as the next squacco landed on a ledge above the beach.

The second was less tired, immediately staring down at a tidal pool, looking for breakfast.

"Look up," Sam said, and I saw a mass of ducks with white wing-bars overhead.

They lighted on the fresher part of the estuary and I laughed in delight. "Red-crested Pochards?" The males' red beaks were brilliant. Almost immediately the ducks upended themselves, diving, searching for food.

I scanned the group for a female. Male pochards leave the north first and stake out the easiest and best grounds. Gender segregation, for what reason I didn't know, required that the females, who arrived later, fly farther south. A female in this group would be a rarity. There wasn't one.

Sam reached over and tucked my blowing hair behind my ear. "First ones?"

I nodded.

Birding is like Christmas should be—every day. You never knew what surprises would land. Rarities occurred far more often than anyone would suspect. A bird blown off course, a wanderer, an outcast. No matter where you were, it was possible to see almost any bird.

During migration, that possibility became a probability. I thought with a pang of my beachfront condo. The bushes seaside provided first stops for warblers and buntings in the spring. A fantastic flash of color, or the treble of an uncommon voice—always a surprise.

Sam smiled at me, and I smiled back.

The day was wonderful, large numbers, a few rarities; everything was perfect.

Until dinner.

Later I wondered, had they set it up? Planned it? Discussed among themselves how exactly to humiliate me? I'd thought they were nice people.

I'd thought I was camouflaged.

❖

The soup had been served family style, and I'd found myself at Sam's table, though Sam wasn't there. The smell that filled the room was chicken, but spicy, and my last thought before the night fell apart, was that maybe we would get true Moroccan-spiced food tonight.

Janice was serving, each person handing her a bowl. She held my bowl and dipped into the soup tureen. "I understand Doctor Francesca Stein is the new director at the Wilkerson Institute."

I froze, prey under a predator's eyes. "Yes," I said, maintaining my calm in the suddenly static-filled, silent room.

"Well," Clive said with a sigh and a glance at me, "another one got away from you, didn't it? Too bad."

"Another one?" Arabella asked.

Dear God, please don't explain. But Clive jumped right in. Who the hell he was and how he knew so much about me left me baffled.

Four pieces of white meat floated among the thirty-two visible pods of garbanzo in my bowl. One lone sprig of herb. I dipped my spoon as Clive explained.

"Elize was the wunderkind in school," he said. "Invited to do graduate work at LSU and Cornell, and with Doc Sutton at OU. Invited for expeditions—O'Neill wanted her."

"Wow!" Arabella said, looking at me. "I'm sorry, but I don't know any of your work."

All I felt was the metal of the spoon in my fingers.

She smiled, interested in me now. "Where have you been published?"

Ornithology was all about numbers, counting, in the field.

But for success out of the field, it was about writing. "I haven't," I said, my tongue stuck to my mouth, my teeth dry as chalk.

Movie stars, whose lives are dissected in the weekly tabloids, at least get a chance to rebut. But in that moment I realized that everyone seated at this table had an opinion of me and the choices I'd made. How could I refute their opinions? My spoon clattered against the bowl and I put both hands in my lap.

Lettice smiled at me, a pitying smile. I saw her exchange a glance with Clive. Everyone else ate, focused on their soup, as Arabella said, "Oh. I see."

"I've never submitted anything," I said, lest she compound the mental strikes against me by deciding I couldn't communicate, either. "It's like the lottery; you have to play to win." Not even a chuckle from the condemning audience.

Each window had four panes. Five archways led out of this room. Arabella looked at me, puzzled.

How could I explain? Invitations were useless. If someone wanted you, they came and got you. Anything else was just good manners. Yeah, I'd gotten letters and phone calls. My professors had said this and that, but it . . . it wasn't real. It was just waiting. I swallowed. It was all a game, until they came and got you. Then you *knew*.

Zephyr had taken me to Miami. She said she wanted to go, she said she wanted me to go with her. She came and got me. It was real.

"Not everyone is ambitious," Lettice said. "No shame there." Her tone suggested the opposite.

"Yes, yes, I wasn't chastising you," Clive said. "Just noting you'd been offered stunning opportunities." *And had ignored them all* went unsaid.

"We're glad you're here now," Janice said, with a glance around the table.

"Hear, hear," Spenser and the boys, listening from the other table, lifted their glasses.

My only consolation was that Sam hadn't been there to witness my humiliation.

It couldn't get much worse.

Don't ever challenge Fate on making things worse. Breakfast, after four frustrating hours in the becalmed estuary, started with a shriek.

"Someone took my earrings," Lettice cried.

Arabella looked concerned. "What kind of earrings?"

"Diamond studs," Lettice said. "They're worth ten thousand dollars."

I met Janice's gaze, wondered if we were both thinking, *What kind of woman brings ten thousand dollars' worth of earrings to bird watch in a cabin on the coast of Morocco?*

"It was that girl," Lettice said. "I saw her eyeing them. Get her in here right now!"

"What girl?" I asked.

"That Moroccan one. I want my earrings back!" Lettice wasn't big, but she was loud.

Four locals worked at the cabin. All, I guessed, were Moroccan. I hadn't seen a girl.

"I'm sure she didn't take them," Arabella said.

"I'm sure she did!" Lettice said. "She'd be able to feed her family for months on those earrings. All they want is money," she muttered. "The rowers, the boys on the beach. Money, money, money."

"I'm sure she'd rather keep her job," I said. "Are you sure you didn't just mislay them?"

Lettice narrowed her gaze at me. "I'm not some doddering old lady who loses her glasses on top of her head. My earrings are gone, and unless you took them, that Moroccan girl did!"

First I'm unambitious, then a failure, now I'm a thief?

I held my tongue. This couple were Sam's biggest funders. The top names on all his e-mails, the backbone of his program. Offending them might hurt Sam's career, his position.

Last night, I'd lost any possible prestige or job opportunity. "While Janice goes and gets the girl," I said, noticing she had already escaped, "why don't we just look through your stuff to be sure?" Lettice was an older lady, and I'd seen her misplace her bins twice in less than forty-eight hours.

"I'm not looking through my 'stuff,' as you put it. I know what I'm talking about. Don't you dare patronize me! I'm getting Sam!"

"Look," I snapped. "I'm just trying to keep you from embarrassing yourself and hurting some innocent girl who needs this job."

"She won't have it by the time I'm finished with her," Lettice said, and stormed past me. The wooden door inched shut.

"Shit," Arabella said.

"You know she just misplaced them," I said, eyeing Lettice's bed, her luggage at the end of it.

"Well, but—"

I took a step toward Lettice's bags.

"Don't," Arabella said. "I know what you are planning to do, and just don't."

"Stay put," I said as I opened the older woman's luggage and started looking through it, fast. "I don't want to be accused next."

"Sam is going to be furious," Arabella said.

"That's why I'm trying to find the damn things," I said, thinking. People oftentimes put things in safe places, to be lost for eternity. The toe of a sock? Maybe in the dirty clothes?

Neither option panned out.

Arabella was inching toward the door. I zipped the bag and moved on to Lettice's cosmetics case. Tubes and jars of expensive stuff. Where were those earrings?

"What are you doing?" Lettice shrieked.

I turned, busted, guilty. "Trying to save some poor girl," I said, feeling my face hot.

Sam walked in behind Lettice, his expression pained. "Lettice says her earrings are missing?"

"I was trying to find them, since she couldn't be bothered to look," I said, my expression not a glare, but not friendly, either.

He sighed. "Did you?"

"No," I muttered. "I can't think like her."

Lettice walked up to me, I thought she was going to slap my hand.

"There's nothing we can do now," Arabella said.

"Yes we can! We can call that girl, get her up here to answer some questions!" Lettice shouted.

"I doubt," I said, "that she has a phone." Or for that matter, what we would call a house. The older woman was so determined she was right, so certain no other possibility existed. I took a step back.

"The thieving lot of them," Lettice said, zipping her cosmetics bag. "You stay out of my things, lady!" she barked at me, and stomped out to the dining cabin.

Sam let out a sigh and Arabella half-shrugged as she walked out ahead of us. "Shall we?" he said to me.

"I don't want to be in the same room as that woman," I said. She reminded me of someone; so sure she was right, despite the facts.

"I'm sure she feels the same way about you," he said, leaving me alone.

❖

We sat down to breakfast. Lettice had filled everyone in on her version of the truth already.

"They're money-grubbers. All they want is cash and kif," Clive said, patting his wife's hand. She glared at me as I sat down between John and Spenser.

I drank some bottled water and said nothing.

I recalled the Marrakesh lunch, where the Moroccan men had all rejoiced in good friends and thoughtful conversation. Yeah, they were stoned on kif, but what else did they have to do? No land to farm, no jobs to be had other than as tour guides. Bribes were needed to do even that. You needed money to make money. I picked at my fish, and concentrated on being silent.

"Corruption has been the way in the east for millennia," Spenser said in his world-weary way. "Not too many years ago, one could buy and sell anything, tax-free, in Tangier. And I do mean anything."

A lewd chuckle.

"Our rower has been quite nice," Flamingo Hat said. "Said we only should pay him what it was worth."

"Code for giving him your whole wallet," John said.

I turned a surprised glance on him. I thought he was one of the rational ones.

"We're the only game in town right now," Sam said. "To them, we are impossibly wealthy."

"Poorer than before," Lettice said.

Clive patted her hand. "They were insured, dear."

"I don't care! That girl should be brought in here and made to explain herself!"

"Excuse me," I said, getting up with my glass. I walked out of the dining room and down the track to the beach. The wind blew at me, blew the words and the taint of "us" versus "them" away. Sam was right; to them we were impossibly wealthy. That didn't make them thieves. Even those who took advantage of a service—like my Berber henna artist from the mountains, I thought, touching my palm where the flower still bloomed—did something for it.

The old lady had *lost* her earrings.

Shake it off, I told myself, like a duck flicking water off its back. I found the blankets beside the dead fire and sat down. The roar of the sea, the tang of salt in the air, scented with orange blossom, enveloped me. I could just sleep out here tonight, avoid the group altogether. How could Sam stand those people, Clive and Lettice? Regardless of what they paid him, how they helped finance him!

Erik jumped into my brain, like he'd been hiding behind a mental curtain. For a moment, I allowed myself to wonder what he would have said to Lettice. He would have been calm, for starters. He would have soothed her in some way, then helped her rethink her movements. He wouldn't have attacked her, but would have somehow let her become the hero by finding her own damn earrings.

Well, Elize, if you know what to do, why can't you do it?

Because she's a mean old crow, I thought, and sipped my juice. *Judgmental and rude.*

And not so different from you.

Did everyone else hate their internal voice? Voices?

I sighed and stared up at the noon sky. Few bird species traveled during the day, most migrated at night. They knew the stars. They could somehow read the constellations and the poles and knew how to position themselves to get from their summer grounds to the winter grounds.

Like having an instinctive GPS.

Though birds did overshoot from time to time. Some would build new nesting grounds, or wintering grounds; some would just die.

The next generation, the ones who didn't overshoot, wouldn't. Genetically, they could learn from one another's mistakes.

An ability that human DNA didn't seem to have.

"Well, you've gone and done it," Sam said, sitting down beside me. "She's on a tear."

"If you're going to sit here, with me, we can't discuss her," I said.

"You're right," he said, putting his arm around me. "Too perfect a day to bring up ugly emotions." He placed a bottle of wine on the ground. "I rescued it," he said.

If that's what it took to avoid her. "What's been the best part so far?" I asked him, a question guaranteed to get a birder going and keep him going. Because the day's story led to the last birding trip's story and before you knew it, it was dark and the bottles were empty.

That was true, even on daily walks through the Dubya.

Walks that Frankie was leading now. Frankie, who couldn't tell the difference between a willet and a curlew . . . I sighed and let it go.

"The flamingoes. We don't get them in California, not in the wild. And you?"

"The European hoopoe. A first time for me." It had been mixed in with a group of bee-eaters, also new to me, who had all stopped for a snack on their way inland. "A definite rarity." The bird looked almost like a giant butterfly, all tawny top and black and white below, but then he'd landed and raised his crest, transforming into an '80s rock star with a black and white mohawk. I smiled, remembering.

"I missed that, I guess," he said. "I saw a hoopoe on my trip to Turkey, a few years ago. Spring migration over the Bosporus. A thousand birds at a time, coming home to breed."

"You're lucky to have traveled so much."

"Why haven't you?"

I shrugged. "Just a homebody, I guess."

"You've got such great wetlands there, you don't need to go see anyone else's."

I would love to travel the world, to see every different kind of ibis, to watch the cranes' mating dance in the snows of Asia, to see the nineteen kinds of hummingbirds in South America. To see the Northern Bald Ibis, two hundred miles from here.

"What does keep you in Texas?" he asked.

Not again. "You've never come to see me in Texas," I said. Best defense and all that.

"You've never invited me."

"Excuse me," a voice prompted. I looked toward the shore and saw Gull Jacket, with bins in hand. "Everyone else is going into Larache. Are you two going?"

I looked at the whitewashed village, just visible in the distance. However, between Tangier and Marrakesh I'd about had my fill of Moroccan cities.

"This might be the perfect chance for us to get to know each other better," Sam murmured to me, and I felt a small charge. Maybe we could work this out? Maybe my libido would come out and play? I smiled back.

He shouted back, "Is my mother going?"

"Lettice has gone to find the managers, to ask about her earrings."

His *mother*? That woman was his mother? No wonder she knew so much about me. No wonder she had an opinion.

So Clive was his dad? That's why he looked familiar.

I was already on my feet. "Your mother cannot be allowed to ruin that poor girl's life."

"Girl? Poor girl?"

"The Moroccan girl."

"Oh, her. What if she did take them?" he asked.

"Why would she?"

He shrugged. "They're pretty. Expensive."

"She'd have to sell them to make any money, which would require taking a bus to a major town. Then finding someone with that kind of money. Then, probably, she'd have to explain where she got them. And I don't know, maybe she couldn't even receive the money without a male protector's permission. Remember, this is a country where not too long ago they chopped people's hands off!"

"Saudi Arabia," Sam said. "Not Morocco."

"Whatever. You know what I mean."

"Are you coming?" Gull Jacket called.

"I am going to take a nap," I stated, as any trace of attraction vanished.

"Oh, all right," Sam called back. "Guess I'll go straighten out Lettice," he said to me. "You remind me of her. That's probably why you two don't get along. Yet."

"You think I'm like Lettice?"

"You have the same aura." He brushed his lips across mine, oblivious to my stone-like mouth. "Sleep well. I'll see you about four-thirty for Round Two."

I hoped he was referring to birding and not making out.

Charged from our conversation I found myself online instead of napping. I'd gotten no response from Zephyr. Weird. I typed so fast my fingers got tangled.

Sam thinks I'm like his mother. I hate his mother. She's pushy, hard to please, unbending and . . . mean.

I stared at the words, imagining Zephyr reading them, silently chastising me for being so harsh.

On the other hand, she looks amazing for a woman her age, she's a whiz with birds and her husband and son both adore her.

Not such a bad commentary.

Met another guy, just a . . .

I should have thought of Erik in terms of toy or pet or something equally dismissive, but I couldn't.

I erased the sentence, tried again.

The reason I was so delayed had ripped abs and . . .

Again my fingers ceased typing as I stared at the screen. Zephyr would tell me to go for Erik. I didn't need to hear that. I was already talking myself out of him on an hourly basis.

I canceled the message to Zephyr and just for fun, for distraction, I searched: "Bald ibis Morocco."

❖

Arabella woke me up. "Larache was cool! I'm sorry you didn't go. Look what I got!" I peeled open one dry eyeball as she unrolled a long gown embroidered in gold. "And these, too!" A pair of the backless shoes, babouches, in red. "I wanted to get them matching my dress, but the sales guy said women wear red shoes, and men wear yellow or white. Doesn't look too bad, does it?"

"My first surfboard was that color combo," I said. "A red and orange sunset with a silhouette of a palm tree." Arabella looked up from her orange dress and red shoes. "Looks fine," I said.

"I wanted to get my hands done, too," she said. "But Lettice advised against it. Said I might have a reaction to the dye."

"It's henna," I said. "All natural. Most people have no problem."

Janice came in, also burdened with bags. She pulled out Spanish sausages and wine, cheese and bread. "I'm starving," she said. "It's like a little port in Spain, except they still speak Moroccan." She opened the wine, fixed a plate, and we sat on the beds. "Try this tortilla," she said, slicing into a quiche of potatoes.

They told me how quaint Larache was, so Spanish it even had a Catholic church.

"Oh, a picnic!" Lettice sang as she joined us, also carrying bags. Sam thought I was like her?

"Arabella, that is just the prettiest djellaba I've seen!" Lettice said. "It's going to be lovely with your skin." Lettice displayed some new scarves, a pair of shoes. "And I found these," she said, pulling out a plastic vitamin box and popping it open. Diamonds winked inside. Both women gasped.

"I remember now," Lettice said. "I'd started having some reaction to the water or air and my ears were ringing. So I took my earrings off and put them here, where they'd be safe."

"You told the manager you found them, right?" I interjected into their congratulations.

"I'll mention it to him at dinner," she said, not even glancing in my direction.

"What about the girl? Surely you'll apologize?"

Lettice stood at the foot of her bed. "I have nothing to apologize for."

"You accused the girl of theft! She might get fired!" I looked at Janice, at Arabella, but neither of them backed me up. I looked back at who I could be in the future, who I could become. "Clearly," I said, "it was your mistake."

"Everyone makes them," Lettice said.

"Yes. Everyone does. But the consequences of your mistake, this time . . . "

"Do not lecture me, young lady," Lettice snapped, and turned her back on me.

"Someone should, because for all your money and manners, you are an inconsiderate bitch."

It was then I knew I had to leave.

A little while later I heard the group head out to the boats, but I didn't stand up, didn't grab my bins and water and hat and Oakleys. I just listened to them until there was nothing to hear except wind and waves and birdcalls.

They hovered, at all heights, about three hundred feet apart. The Eleonora's falcon was rare, protected. Though I knew that, I couldn't escape the inherent cruelty of it all, the mockery of its false tear markings.

The air was dense with migrants. They'd piled up in Spain, and as the winds shifted, they began pouring like a river down the coastline of Africa. No need for me to take a boat into the estuary, or do anything more than just look up.

I watched one Eleonora's falcon choose its prey, one of the five million willow warblers that would pass this way. Another falcon joined the first and they hassled the tired bird, chasing it, diving after it. I closed my eyes and when I opened them, the falcon had stripped the bird of its feathers and was on its way to the nest to feed its young.

Unlike most every other bird on the planet, Eleonora's falcons bred late, and by the time the European migrants were working their way to Africa, the falcon's young needed lots of food. It was drive-thru convenience. The twenty thousand or so falcons would consume between five and ten million songbirds in this season alone.

It was smart of the falcons to live here. They had no competition, no predators. But it was a little like watching a Hitchcock film. You knew disaster, well-dressed though it might be, was coming.

The pair of falcons had already snatched four birds out of the sky in less than twenty minutes. The passerines flew through the gauntlet to land exhausted in the trees and on the shore. Far above, I saw the graceful arcs and swoops of the large birds, riding thermals.

Ducks and waders, warblers and flycatchers, they settled into feeding on insects and seeds, fruits and fish. I cataloged them: Reed warbler, looking like a frumpy woman in the grocery line, with a pale, perpetual frown. Sounded grumpy, too.

Blackcaps, who looked like little kids with bright eyes and baseball caps.

Bonelli's warbler, the only one in the bunch with even a hint of color, a little green edge to its wings.

On the whole, New World warblers looked like Las Vegas showgirls —red! yellow! blue! necklaces! bars!—compared to the grays and beiges of Old World warblers.

Feeling like I was cheating, I turned to the ducks.

The pochard, still represented, made me grin as it upended in search of food. The male tufted ducks, with long feathers hanging over their heads, brought to mind pale-faced, black T-shirt-wearing youths with more attitude than bodyweight, who had shaved heads except for one long lock, usually dyed black. A knob of pochards.

The Shelduck looked like he'd been painted by a six-year-old with ADD. Gargeneys weren't in their breeding plumage, so were only distinguished by their raised foreheads.

No ibises, though. The bald ibis was miles away. My earlier research had delivered maps, guides, schedules on this endangered bird, from a family of birds I'd studied my whole life.

Friends don't let friends text when drunk. It was one of Zephyr's rules, one I was getting ready to break, in spirit if not in actuality.

I was drunk and had a list of e-mails to send. At 3 a.m., on a professional birding expedition. I crept down the hallway of my cabin, creaked open the door and closed it with a click.

Giddiness rose up and I dashed out of range before I giggled. When was the last time I'd sneaked into or out of anything? The computer center's door was locked, so I pushed open the window, set my half-full wine glass and empty bottle inside on the ledge, then hauled myself after them.

Legs out the window, another flood of giggles overtook me. I thudded onto the floor and waited for lights, shouts, reaction. Silence. I wasn't the only one enjoying the Spanish wine.

Green lights. Passwords.

The keyboard was the same mishmash as in M'kesh, but I figured it was clear enough. First, to Zephyr:

Taking two more weeks. Please relate that to Junior and the Witch Moth.

Then to Mama:

Hope you are enjoying your cruise. Should be some nice birds arriving.

Sam:

You're sleeping right now. On consideration, this isn't going to work. Thanks. I hope we can still be birding friends.

I had to resort to "friends," because I couldn't find a *g* on the keyboard for "colleagues."

My hands felt sticky as I began to type the last note, the one whose e-mail address I'd memorized on sight.

Going after the NBI in the Souss-Massa. Join me.
Attached: map, route, directions.
Love, Elize

I hit send before my brain caught up, before Zephyr shook her head at me, before logic or pride or fear awakened. I stored my empty wine glass and the bottle under the desk, and crawled back out the window.

Darkest before the dawn.

The Journey

"You can't go," Sam said, his gaze pleading with me, his voice quiet. I'd rejoined the group for the morning outing; I was already up and fighting a hangover. So far, an utter bust; too much wind through the Straits had kept the birds down on the Iberian side. We'd watched and waited, but even the residents had hidden from the stinging sand and cold wind. We'd gone back to lunch, a disgruntled crowd.

Lettice, I guessed, was angry because she'd found her earrings and thus had nothing about which to complain. The Moroccans were angry because of the accusations. The girl accused had been fired, a great disgrace, despite the earrings being found. Arabella was angry because Clive was unhappy and being vocal about it; Jackson and John sat stiffly beside each other, obviously in a tiff; Spenser was hung over; and Janice kept glaring at me, after asking where I'd been last night.

Lettice's answer, "To fornicate with Sam," hadn't been very soothing, but I kept both my tongue and temper in check.

"I study ibis," I explained to the group in general as we ate more chicken. "To not take this opportunity to see a species brought back from near-extinction, when it's only a half-day away, would be criminal."

"You don't speak the language, or know the customs," Spenser said.

"I got here, didn't I?"

"Three days late," Arabella muttered.

"We can all go, if you want," Sam said. I think it was his effort to apologize for yesterday. What had gotten into him?

"Thanks, but I'll be fine," I said. "I've already called for a taxi."

"Let her go if she wants," Lettice said, "less trouble for everyone."

"Mother . . . "

"This isn't your concern," I said to Lettice. More interaction than I wanted, but I hated being discussed as though I wasn't here.

"You're the gold-digger who can't hold a job and wants my boy, but you're not going to get him," Lettice said.

"No, Mother," Sam said. "That's Ellen, the dental hygienist. This is Elize."

Lettice sniffed and refused to look at me.

Sam looked a bit pink around his ears. So there was an Ellen, was there? While he was kissing me? "Thanks for your concern," I said, hoping the sarcasm wasn't lost. "But I'll be just fine."

"Are you coming back?" Jackson asked.

"Depends on what I see," I said, getting to my feet. "Y'all take care."

Arabella followed me to the cabins. "You can't just leave," she said. "Sam will go nuts, he's been so looking forward to seeing you."

I heard something in her voice that I'd missed before; a bit of jealousy. His assistant had the hots for him? If I had any advice to give her, I forgot it when one of the Moroccan servers told me the taxi had arrived.

"Please, let me take," the server said, rushing forward to grab my bag. I wondered if I had any small change to tip him.

"Nice to meet you, Arabella," I said. "Good luck."

"Wish I could go with you," she said.

"You'll do fine," I said, lying through my teeth. The taxi driver was all smiles. I got inside, found enough change to tip the server, and we were off, down the road.

Souss-Massa was less than two hundred miles south. I'd be there by dark.

Reason would suggest that since I hadn't gotten anywhere in this country on even the same day, why would I start now? Still, I believed. I was going forward and I'd be rewarded for my boldness.

I settled back for the ride.

❖

Six hours later, I still sat in the back seat, though of a different taxi. The directions were damp between my fingers, but at least I had directions. I also, at last, had the right kind of taxi, one authorized to drive from Agadir to Sidi Rabat.

Who could have guessed the color differentiation of the cabs meant something? It wasn't just company branding or personal preference, but worked like the plumage of birds. Breeding plumage meant a bird was ready to mate, a signal given to select potential partners. Different colors of taxis meant different things, indicating availability for different services.

City taxis could only travel inside the city, and each municipality had their own color. *Grande* taxis could, when carrying up to six people, make longer runs. Different colors meant different routes, and *only* those routes.

Just hopping in a taxi to go where you wanted wasn't possible. Or legal.

In order to save the difference of paying for five people, I'd gotten a specially authorized city taxi. Getting the dispensation for a city taxi to go into the countryside had taken another hour, and I'd lost that taxi driver in the mix, but here I was. At last. Penultimate leg of the journey.

"*Aqui!*" I shouted from the back seat as he approached the turn. Then, in case shouting Spanish to a French-speaking Arab wasn't enough, I shouted, "*Droite!*" Showing off all of my international vocabulary at once. I stifled an almost hysterical giggle. No sleep. Hangover. Sidi R'bat and the bald ibis ahead. Almost there.

The driver slowed down at a corner. Women on one side of the street, covered, including socks and gloves, walked from car to car selling tagines. My driver gave one some change, but it was not for food. He seemed a little fearful, like he was afraid to cross her. On the other corner camels walked alone, going from nowhere to nowhere, ambling.

Ambling . . . I sounded like Led Zeppelin. I giggled again, exhausted and a little high from all the sugar in the tea I'd had during the taxi haggling.

A small café, with a single card table surrounded by broken plastic chairs, sat alone in what looked like the parking lot of an empty strip mall.

Almost there. Where was I going?

Was all it took a little bit of effort, determination, and cash to get somewhere in this country? We drove through a town and I craned to see any other signs. On the other side of town, we turned onto a two-lane road. It was so rough it made the previous thoroughfare look like a highway.

Finally, at a T-junction, a sign proclaimed Sidi R'bat, to the left; Souss-Massa, to the right. Conundrum.

Souss-Massa was the park.

Sidi R'bat was the closest town.

The map didn't help. Forget comfort; I'd check out the park. I'd sleep in the park cabins the website had mentioned, if necessary. Glad I'd bought emergency rations of French pastry and soda. Tomorrow I'd get into town, either for supplies or to return to Larache.

Triumphant.

"*Allez tout droit*," I said. I'd picked it up somewhere. Not too much different than the Spanish *derecho*.

The road led up, out of town. The driver slowed.

"Souss-Massa, *s'il vous plait*," I said and pointed straight. A guess. I didn't see any flying birds or green belts to indicate where the park might be, and no one was around to ask. "*S'il vous plait*," I said again. Pointing straight.

He stepped on the gas and we drove out onto a rockier road. Sweat dripped down my back. Though the window was open, there wasn't much of a relieving breeze at five miles an hour. The landscape was nothing but rocks, scrub brush, and a thousand captured plastic bags whistling in the wind.

They crinkled and whispered as the car drove by, bags of red and blue and black and white, trying to break free.

Maybe something over this next hill? But I saw no indications of life. No goats. No houses. No shepherd with dark staring gaze. Nothing but the heat, the sun, and the rattling bags. The driver slowed.

"Souss-Massa," I said.

The aged Mercedes shook as we crept forward. The taxi driver hunched over his wheel, watching the temperature gauge, not the road.

I saw no green. No river. No flocks of flamingoes, purported residents of the park. The directions just said, "Go to Souss-Massa." Now I realized those directions might also apply to "Go to the moon." Great. Fine, but how do you *get* there? It was around here, it had to be.

We approached a sign saying Ksar Massa, written artfully, with an arrow indicating straight. *At least it said Massa*, I thought, telling the driver to continue straight. But what was a ksar? Or, for that matter, a Sous?

The car was overheating, even though he drove slower than I could walk. Every rock—now they were the size of duck eggs—rattled off the doors, the undercarriage. The driver slowed several times, like he was stopping. *You are not throwing me out*, I thought. *We will drive into the ocean if we have to, but you're not leaving me here.*

How ironic. As Clive had pointed out, I'd received the invitations. The Amazon, Turkey, the Parque de Nacionale in Spain. All expeditions with teams and experts. I hadn't gone on one. Well, I hadn't believed any of them were true.

Now, I had finally decided to *do* something, and ended up alone on a rock-strewn plateau with a nervous driver and not more than a clue of where to go.

The language barrier helped. I didn't have to admit we were going to be driving to the ocean.

roadway all but vanished, turning into a rising plain of rock. I guess he would just aim and drive? Like the Mercedes was a plow?

He's going to want a big tip. Would he take euros? A few dollars in change from my lunch back in Miami?

We'd been driving for a thousand years.

He stopped.

"*La!*" I cried, sitting forward. "Ksar Massa, *allez!*"

He spoke rapidly, gestured frantically. The car was redlining.

Keep him from shifting it into park, I thought. "Ksar Massa," I repeated a half dozen times. I pointed. I gestured that he drive.

Finally I sat back and crossed my arms. Unmovable. "Ksar Massa, *s'il vous plaît.*" I could be polite, but I wasn't going to change my mind.

At this point, I couldn't. *Too much at stake. Especially my pride.*

With a huff, the driver stepped on the gas. The Mercedes lurched forward and tore up the hill, rocks and stones pinging and dinging, until my head ached.

I could give him my earrings as a tip. He could give them to his wife. He's gotta have a wife; they all have wives. Where were those Hands of Fatima? In my suitcase, hostage in the trunk? They weren't valuable, but all I had.

The Mercedes screamed—all of 20 mph—around a bend and screeched to a halt.

Paradise lay before us.

Not the park, but the mysterious Ksar Massa. Pisé walls and towers stood against the turquoise of the North Atlantic.

I pointed and he drove into the parking lot, joining two Land Rovers and a van.

"*Un moment,*" I said, getting out with my duffel. He climbed out and walked to the trunk. Guarding it.

I ran through a gate. Those magical symbols were on the glass of an interior door: Visa. MasterCard. American Express. My heart pounded, and I felt on the verge of tears. Relief.

Who cared about the cost? Still, I should ask, make sure those signs were valid. Or that they would be, by the time I left. Which in my dreams, would be never.

I couldn't find anyone, but a delicious smell led me down a walkway that overlooked the beach. Low tables, set with festive linens and native pottery, clustered along a balcony.

I ducked into a bar. An older European man in a djellaba greeted me. "*Parlez-vous anglais?*" I asked.

"Yes."

The speed and surprise of his response left me almost at a loss. "Do you have room for one night?" I said.

"Full board or half board?"

No decisions to make about where to go or what to get. Just sum it up on plastic and forget about it. No pressure. "Full."

"You are alone?" he asked, looking around me, as though a gaggle of goslings might be trailing.

"Yes, and my taxi driver is very irritated and holding my bag hostage. I came for the Souss-Massa. Is it close?"

"Oh yes, the park is a ten minute walk. I'll come with you to talk to your driver, and then you can pick a room."

"Will I be able to get a taxi tomorrow, to leave?"

"Oh yes, no problem."

No problem. What exquisite words. I wanted to hug him, but instead I followed him into the parking lot. He answered all of my questions. He confirmed they took credit cards. We walked up through a garden-filled courtyard lined with doors. Each one was inscribed with a bird: flamingo, heron, stork. It was paradise.

"My name is Roald," he said. "Welcome to Ksar Massa."

With a minimum of fuss in conversing with the taxi driver, who I was certain would triple the fee, Roald told me a price below what I and the taxi driver had originally agreed on. With a tip it cleaned me out of cash, but it was reasonable.

The driver took off, whistling. After all his fussing, too.

Was that part of the game, like with the Berber girl, that I didn't understand?

A uniformed boy showed up to take my bags.

"Would you like to see the rooms?" Roald asked. "We have only a few guests at the moment. You can take your pick of accommodations."

I didn't even look at the room, just picked it because it was named after the bald ibis. The walls were ochre colored, with a low, silk-covered bed. The smoothed concrete floor, studded with tiles, glass and pottery pieces, was layered with rough-woven rugs. A table with two chairs faced a window that opened onto a small, private window seat that overlooked a private garden. Which in turn, overlooked the Atlantic.

Thick towels in the bathroom. A narrow, curtainless room for the shower. I checked: both water pressure and hot water!

Roald told me dinner would be at nine. I would have plenty of time to see the flamingoes and the ibis. "There are, I think," he said, pursing his lips, "maybe three hundred *flamant rose* and twenty, thirty ibis there now."

The directions were simple.

He pointed to a pisé stump on the dune by the beach. "The end of the Ksar Massa. The rest is national park. Go maybe a hundred meters and you will see the gate. If you go too far, there is a little valley where the Oued Massa used to run to the sea. The park is just in there."

Back in my room I rinsed my face, stashed my chocolate crois-sants for a park treat, packed bins, balm, bug spray, notepad and pen, camera and hat.

Bald ibis, here I come!

Steep dunes, but the sand was luscious. *Don't use that word*, I told myself. Don't make yourself miss him. Neither lunch in Marrakesh nor this sand could be considered luscious.

Had Erik received my e-mail? I tried to reason with myself: did it matter?

What did matter was that Zephyr hadn't responded. At all. I guess she wasn't my assistant any more. Assistants didn't have assistants, right? But . . . just a brief note? We'd been friends, too.

The familiar calls of the gulls drew me. This whole place welcomed me. It was like it was built for me. Of course, that was a ridiculous thought, but Zephyr would consider it all "a sign."

For that matter, Erik might too.

Stop thinking about him.

I forced myself to take a minute and watch the sunset. Tendrils of purple and pink touched the clouds and turned the sea an opaque shimmering rose. I didn't see flamingoes, or anything else besides gulls, in the sky. So different from home, where the sun rose over the water and set over land.

Roald had said a hundred meters, but I hadn't seen a gate. Maybe he meant a thousand? At the far end of the beach I saw a white dome and some nested buildings. Behind me, Ksar Massa. No gates or rivers or riverbeds in between.

It's right by the sea. I'd seen the map. I walked farther.

Some kids played soccer on the beach, and without interrupting their game called for cigarettes from me, I waved to them and kept walking.

Before me, the white dome began to glow in the twilight. The sky had darkened to deep blues and purples, glossy ibis colors.

I felt eyes on me, but took out my bins and watched the gulls and terns and plovers who fed against the color-soaked sky and opalescent waves. A congregation of plovers.

Someone was following me.

It would be too dark to find the park now. Somehow, I'd missed the gate. I would come back tomorrow at dawn, a better time anyway. Bird watching was best at dusk and dawn. I kept walking, now past the dome and the whitewashed houses clustered in the cliffside.

An outcropping fifty feet ahead effectively ended the beach. The steps behind me grew closer. Better to face it now, in the twilight, than in total darkness.

I had no cash, just expensive equipment.

I turned around to see a young man in a sweater and baggy Moroccan pants standing just a few steps behind me. "Hello," he said.

"Hi! Hello." I was already thrown off.

"Welcome to Morocco. Where are you from?"

One of Erik's replies came to me. "Everywhere."

"And your passport?" He stepped closer.

"Your country is very beautiful."

No one else was around, just empty fishing boats, a sinking sun and an incoming tide.

"You come to see the bald ibis?"

I angled my back to the sea, opposite him. He was in his mid-twenties, healthy looking. Would my scream be heard above the crash of the surf? "Yes, the bald ibis."

"He is here," the man said, pointing to the cliffs that overhung the shore line. "Maybe thirty, fifty birds."

I peered through the darkness. Excreta covered the cliff, but no birds roosted now. I took another sideways step. "I don't see any."

"No, not now. Maybe ten, ten-thirty in the morning. You come and I will be your guide."

Another sideways step. No longer trapped against the outcropping. "You will? That's very nice."

"You pay me what you think it's worth."

Not that again.

He stepped closer. "You are English? Australian? Kee-Wee?"

I smiled, tinged my voice like the Crocodile Hunter. "How'd you guess?"

"You need a place to stay? To sleep? My village—"

"No, thank you." It was almost dark now, the first stars pricking the sky.

"You stay at the ksar?"

"The park," I said.

"Ah, by the park," he said. He'd inched within grabbing room.

I felt a large rock at my Achilles tendon. I could kick him, and run. But the way was rocky and the tide was coming in. I'd have to be cautious. Were there others, waiting?

"Would you like to come for tea?"

"If I come to see the ibis tomorrow." Like that would happen.

"No. Take tea now. My family—"

Erik would know what to say, to do. I had no idea, but suddenly I felt ashamed. This guy wasn't accosting me. He was trying to be hospitable and maybe make some money on the side. The words from that lunch came back to me: Moroccan men suffer eighty-five percent unemployment. All the government did was allow them kif, as an opiate to silence their frustration.

I stepped up on the rock. "No, thank you. I must get back to my husband. But here, take these—" I riffled through my bag and found the pretty sack of French treats. "—for your family. For tea."

With his thanks ringing in my ears, I picked my way past the dome, up the beach. A flashlight would have been useful. But the night, the stars brighter than I saw them at home and the sky the color of a starling's wing, was too beautiful for me to be angry with myself for unpreparedness.

A shape emerged from the darkness, a uniformed worker striding through the sand in his black lace-up shoes. The wind shifted, cool now.

Just follow the waterline. Pay attention on the shore. Ksar Massa was above the beach. With lots of lights.

Yeah, and the so-called gate was impossible to miss. How many miles had I walked just watching the gulls and the waves? Sooner or later the moon would rise. At the worst I'd wait for its glow and use it to find my way back. Wait.

My stomach growled.

I should have just given him my dirham change and *not* my fabulous French croissants. What had I been thinking? I pulled the neck of my shirt closer in the chill and trudged on. The sand was softer and each step was an effort.

Then I saw the lights of Ksar Massa, a three-quarter moon rising behind it. I couldn't walk any faster in this mushy sand, at least not in sandals. As I approached the ksar I saw the gate off to my right: parallel white blocks set in from the beach about a hundred meters from the sea, a clear ten-foot path between them. Not a gate in a traditional sense, but a gateway. The park! No wonder I hadn't seen it. I'd be back at dawn.

I trudged through the sand, feeling the work of it in my quads and glutes, to the steps of the ksar.

"*Bonsoir*. We wondered what happened to you," Roald said, when I reached the top.

A thousand tiny cobalt lights illuminated the pathway and the outdoor seating. "Please, some champagne apéritif?" he said, handing me a goblet.

This *was* paradise. "Please," I said, sinking onto a banquette.

"Some mezze?"

I took a sip of the champagne. Like a photo developing with the light of the moon, the room came into focus. Tiny tagines filled with marinated vegetables and spicy dips appeared before me, with steaming bread in rounds the size of my palm. "This is such a beautiful place," I said.

Roald sipped from his own glass. He wore an elaborate robe, yards of fabric, and was clean-shaven.

"It is nice to call it home."

I closed my eyes and listened to the sea. Yes, it would be nice to call this home.

❖

Dawn was breaking as I walked down the path to the beach. The sound of the crashing waves and the cries of gulls accompanied the swish of my shoes on the steps. The gate was close to the ksar. I adjusted my pack and looked to the left.

Didn't see it.

I walked farther on, but still didn't see it.

Don't make the mistake of going too far, I thought, as I backtracked. It was here somewhere. I had seen it last night! The sky was broken lines of blue with white clouds; I had to get to the park. I didn't want to miss the ibis.

Inland, I started over the dunes, trying to pick a path someone else had taken, so at least I wasn't squashing plant life in a national park just because I'd lost the gate. Again.

I kept my eye on the sky, searching for the arriving birds. A body of freshwater stretched out in the distance, and I found a path. Narrow but deliberate, it ran alongside the water. Somehow I was in the park, though maybe not on the main thoroughfare.

The flamingoes were waking. I felt tears choke my throat as I raised my bins. There must have been two hundred of them, a sea of pink, studded with the white of juveniles. As the sun touched them, they woke, stretching and preening, before dipping their bills for breakfast.

Flamingoes seem the calmest, most complacent of birds. They were the tallest waterbirds, extremely sociable, and traveled in large flocks. The food they ate, tiny invertebrates that accounted for the birds' pink color, was almost exclusively theirs. They had no fear of someone else eating a place bare, because their diet was so specialized.

I'd been in South Beach, Miami, the first time I saw flamingoes, and to me, fashion models who preened and strutted, who flocked in groups and subsisted on a specialized diet of cigarettes and champagne, seemed very much like them. A stand of flamingoes; a stand of models.

Flamingoes overlook most of the birds that feed beside them. Models, from what I observed, only paid attention to those equally young and beautiful. Not in a cruel way, but in a rose-colored-glasses —or feathers, if the analogy held—way.

I grinned at myself. Things I would never confess to any one else. Anthropomorphism is fine for the birding masses, but as a professional ornithologist? Extremely unprofessional. Degrading, almost. Kiss of death, certainly. Though how much more dead could I be, professionally?

Birding is the best thing in the world: birds don't judge. You can't fail a bird, you can't disappoint, you can't lose with one.

Mixed in with the flamingoes were a few white ibis, hardworking as accountants. Awake, and already searching for food. I smiled. An accounting of ibis.

I knew that they preened and stared into birdy oblivion just like the others, but it seemed that whenever I had observed them, even when all the other birds rested, the ibis worked. When other birds enjoyed the sun on their wings, the ibis worked. When other birds were engrossed in communication or conflict, the ibis just kept working.

Here they were, on the edges of the lake of flamingoes, working. I laughed and moved on.

I moved my bins over ducks and other waterbirds, identifying them automatically in my head; many were the same or similar to what we had at the Dubya, or what I'd seen in Larache. I kept a steady scan of the sky.

By noon I was reaching for my Oakleys and swatting away midges, sweat dripping down my back. I'd wandered down the park path, stopped at a few blinds, and come back along the main road by the gateway. How could I have missed it? A small hut stood nearby, empty.

I walked down the packed dirt path, and saw the hill that led to the ksar. My feet were hot in closed shoes and midges were stuck in my eyes, my lashes, my nostrils.

Lunch was already laid out at the ksar, and I smiled greetings at the scarf-wrapped girls who were mopping and cleaning the rooms. As far as I could tell, these rooms had been empty, but maybe the people had just stayed inside and left early?

At about 2 P.M. I left for the beach. The girls were cleaning the tables now, and smiled greetings again, speaking to me in French, laughing good-naturedly at my ignorance and smile.

I'd always thought I was too old to learn another language.

I'd been around German for most of my life. As a child, church services were in German, but it never resonated with me. My practice had been limited, because I hated to be corrected. Especially by Pop.

While reading page sixteen of *Birds of Morocco*, I saw a group of people coming down the beach. Young Moroccan men and a handful of blonde girls.

One of the men detached from the group, came over and crouched down beside me. "Hi, and how are you?" he said. "Have you seen the bald ibis yet?" He looked about twenty, dressed in soccer shirt and sandals. I'd never seen him before in my life.

Who was he? How did he know? Did it matter? "Not yet."

"This evening, I will meet you here and take you, yes?"

"You know where the bald ibis are?" I asked.

"I am from here. I take you. My name is Achmed," he said, extending his hand. "Six o'clock?"

I shook his hand, feeling excitement. "Achmed, nice to meet you. Six o'clock."

"Six o'clock, we see the ibis. I have led many tours, for many people, from universities all over the world. For Japanese."

What did I have to lose? As a local, he might have an inside track. *You're Frankie in this situation*, I told myself. *You don't know all that you think you know. Accept some help.* "Wow. Well, I'll see you then," I said.

"I go now," he said, rejoining the group as they continued down the beach.

The bald ibis, I thought. Tonight.

The Search

Tonight couldn't come fast enough. I did what I promised myself I wouldn't do and checked my e-mail. Nothing. Not even from Erik. After signing it "love" and everything. Had I ever signed anything "love" before? Three A.M. writing was my excuse. But how can you miss someone you've never been with?

It seemed my body screamed at me. Especially when I had contemplated touching Sam. No touch but Erik's would do. Nothing else would satisfy.

It's just a craving because I wasn't sated. But that was bullshit. I was a grown woman and knew how to sate myself. As I stared unseeing at the waves, I knew what my problem was.

I was in love with Erik.

No! He was a vagabond. He didn't answer even *one* question directly. I had that sense that I was always on the verge of disappointing him. He wasn't that good looking, or that young, two things I staked as requirements. He wasn't birdy in the least.

But I knew he would be willing to learn.

He wants to know you, Crazy-Elize said. *He stops time for you. Being in his space is what heals and feeds you.*

There's no logic there, I told that crazy version of me. *Nothing to build a life on, and anyway, I'm too old for building a new life. I'm established, I'm—*

You're almost forty, with a Jeep, a surfboard, a set of Swarovski bins, a Lalique falcon, and enough anger and rage to form a storm system the size of Hurricane Rita. You've burned every bridge you've ever had; your grandmother only talks to you out of obligation. Zephyr, who lives to be misused, is ignoring you now. Your father is dead, gone forever.

The birds can't hear you.

"Fuck off," I muttered out loud and returned to the book. Nine *o*'s in the first sentence.

Erik didn't fit.

But he was It. That fictional It, that girls dream of from the time they play with dolls. White wedding It. House with picket fence It. "Fuck," I said again, willing the tears away. I'd missed that boat. I'd missed it in college. I swore that children and fences and the whole baby and bathtub would have nothing to do with me.

He didn't mean it.

I put the book down. Obviously, three glasses of wine at lunch was too much. That "he" wasn't Erik. That had been Alan. My best friend, my first great love, my heartbreak hotel.

"It is not possible that I am sitting on a beach in Morocco, thinking about my high school boyfriend because, twenty years later, I'm still not over him," I hissed.

Not him, Crazy-Elize said, *It. The dream. The glimpse you had of living in harmony, of being united with someone.* The tears started down my cheeks. I pushed my Oakleys up my nose and held the book in front of me. Five *o*'s in the second sentence. Not that anyone was around. A tear slid off my nose. Three *i*'s in the chapter head.

I'd known Alan my whole life; we'd grown up down the street from each other. We'd gone to school together. We'd competed in everything, and when it was time for college, we, with great maturity, had decided that we'd attend different schools.

Then, that day.

I ducked my head. Would I ever not feel sick thinking about it? How cold I'd been, how cool. Icy, perhaps? The reality of what had happened had taken another six months to settle in. But by that time, he'd married some girl he'd just met.

And I had barely taken off his class ring.

"No," I said, getting up and throwing my book and glasses on the chair. "No!"

I dove into the water and felt the thoughts wash away. Activity was the key. Move, so you don't think. Watch nature, so even in those moments of silence, your mind is moving, calculating, counting, observing. Be angry at other things, immovable things, unchangeable things, so you don't have to be angry at your own stupidity.

Why didn't you say, "No, that's not what I meant?"

Swimming, straight out against the waves. Arm, arm, breathe, arm, arm, breathe.

He was just protecting himself from your rejection. Why didn't you poke a hole in what you knew was only a defense mechanism?

Dolphin kick, breaststroke, hard, hard. I dove down, thinking I heard shouting, but the water was roiling and loud around me.

In an instant, I felt the surf dragging me, pulling me. Tangled in the riptide, I fought for a gasp upward, then tumbled, head over heels, feeling the icy current wrap around me. *Go with it,* I thought. *Surface, then break past it.* The ksar was a blur. I was being pulled along, fast.

I dove forward, out of the drag, away from the riptide. The water was deeper, but calmer. I came up gasping for breath. A man ran along the beach's edge, whistling and waving his arms. *Yeah, buddy, I'll get there when I can.* My heart pounded as I swam parallel to the beach, away from the riptide. I was about a half mile away now, past the gateway to the park, close to where the village began.

In a bikini, in a Muslim country.

I dove under the water, fighting through the current to the beach, coming up in the shallows.

The little man ran into the water. "No, no," he shouted. I was spitting up water. "Danger," he said, pointing to a sign, one I hadn't seen before, the international symbol for dangerous swimming. Had I just walked out past it, so absorbed in my own world that I didn't read a sign that warned me against potential death? Could I be that oblivious, that self-destructive? Was I that much like Fischer?

The man was drawing a map on the beach now, showing me the reefs, how the current moved. "Yes?" he said to me, nodding. "Danger, yes?"

I nodded back. Yeah, danger.

But less dangerous than the thoughts that had been swept away in the current. I staggered back to my chair, then wrapped up in my towel and cover-up. Enough water for the day.

❖

Six-thirty already.

Achmed was late.

I kept a watch on the sky, looking for the distinctive line of ibis flying. Nothing. The only other thing moving on the beach was an ant, determinedly marching straight out to sea alone. Suicidal?

I lifted my bins and scanned the sky again. Watch check. Where the hell was he? The ant was making great progress, speeding along his way.

I stepped in front of him. He didn't go over me, but detoured around, then righted his direction and headed toward the shore. No birds. I looked down at the ant again; proportionately, I think he'd covered about twenty miles already. I put a rock in front of him. He went right over it.

Why was he rushing to the sea? What did he hope to find?

"You're gonna die out there, buddy."

No Achmed, no birds. He'd made me too late to catch seeing anything else, either. I sighed and stared at the waves. Now I could tell how dark they were, indicating potential destruction. I thought I'd had a healthy respect for water, but the leeriness I felt now superseded anything that had gone before. The ant was almost to the waterline when I heard my name shouted.

Achmed came running down the beach. "We go, we go. We're late," he said. Then stopped. "No, no," he said, and took the scarf I was wearing and tied it around my hair and ears, knotting it in the front, at my hairline. "Now, you are like a Berber, like your hand," he said, pointing to the fading henna flower from Marrakesh, still visible on my palm. "Come, we go."

He took off over the sand.

Touching the scarf, the knot that made me about four inches taller, I chased after him. In four minutes of race walking we cut over the dunes in the fading light. My skepticism about him faded as he identified four birds by call in less than a minute. Maybe he did know about the Waldrapp. "Come," he said, running down the road, me on his tail.

He halted in the middle of the road. "See? Snake."

A glittery freshly shed snakeskin marked a line in the sand. "For you," he said, tying it around my wrist.

Moroccans have no concept of personal space, I thought, once again speechless as I was touched. With another "We go," we set off over the hill. Unless there was another pond, this wasn't the correct habitat. "Look, look," he said, pointing to a pale object.

The words, "It's not a bald ibis," were already on the tip of my tongue as I brought my bins up. *Athene noctua*, a Little Owl. Another Life List bird for me, since I'd never seen one. The light was almost gone, and the bird flew. Achmed took off after it, running.

"It roosts on the cabin," he said.

The bird before you in the twilight is worth ones who have already gone, I told myself, and followed Achmed. The owl was perched above a whitewashed shack. Achmed shifted from foot to foot as I watched the owl, its white eyebrow, its glowing, blinkless eyes.

"So, no ibis," I said.

"Too late tonight," he said. "Tomorrow, I will show you. Pay only what you think it's worth." With that one phrase, I heard a mental clang.

Sucker. They do just want money and kif. My shoulders stiffened, shooting pain into the base of my neck.

"Is too dark now, we go back to the ksar," he said. "Smoke?"

I shook my head while he lit up, suddenly chatty and still, as darkness surrounded us. Everything he said was an echo of that

Marrakesh lunch. Either every man in Morocco lied, convincingly and in agreement, or the situation of no jobs did force every person into this sort of knowledge-for-hire scenario.

"We go to tea, at my house," he said, stubbing out his cigarette. "You not eat at the ksar for another two hours? Nine o'clock? You take tea, with me, my family, now. Yes?"

Why not? Sounding a little more enthusiastic than I felt, I agreed, and we cut up a dune, arriving at the top of the hill that overlooked the ksar. Not a light flared anywhere, and the street was a mass of trash: cigarette butts, plastic bags, glass. I picked my way through as children raced in circles. "My cousins," he said, wending his way between squat, whitewashed buildings that looked new.

"Welcome are you, to my home," he said, opening a door into a narrow, yellow-painted hallway, barely discernible in the waning dusk. Not a thing adorned the walls, or covered the floor. We stepped into a kitchen the size of a closet, with a hot plate on a center island. One head-height shelf holding crockery lined the room.

We crossed into another hallway and he introduced me to his mother and father, two much older people, both smoking. They spared a glance before he took me into the living room.

I could only guess at its true size, now magnified by having nothing more than a few cushions and a low table in it. Achmed took a candle stub from beside the door, lit it, dripped the wax on a plate, then fixed the candle upright in the wax. "My mother will make tea," he said, then shouted at her.

She shouted back.

He shouted again, then got to his feet and walked into the foyer area. Company, I guess, hadn't been expected. Candles lit the table, and I saw small gaping holes in the walls—outlets that hadn't been installed. I asked Achmed about them when he came back. The builders had made space for electricity, but the village had none. He shrugged. They had candles.

He lit another cigarette and began the interrogation. Where was I from, did I like Morocco, where had I been? Did I think Moroccan men were sexy? Then he left and returned with a tray, mint tea already steaming in glasses and two cookies on a plate.

I took the tea, but declined the cookie. I would be at Ksar Massa in an hour, feasting on fish and poultry and salads and sweets. He needed his cookie. "So, you have a boyfriend?" he said, staring at me across the candlelit table with big brown eyes. He was a pretty boy, slight, with a wiry, tensile strength I'd seen in the men here.

"Yes," I lied. Or rather, told the truth my heart felt. "Yes, I do."

"He is Moroccan?"

I shook my head.

"He is English?"

I shook my head again.

"He is American, then?"

Damned if I knew, but I shrugged.

"Where is this boyfriend? Why does he let you travel by yourself? Is he not a man?"

The tea was perhaps the best I'd had, fresh mint, super sweet, but I was learning to like it sweet. "He is a man," I said. "He's going to join me." Maybe not a lie?

"I don't believe this boyfriend exist. Why do you stay at the ksar? Is much cheaper here. We let you have this whole room, for only twenty dirham. Fifty dirham."

Instead of feeling annoyed, I felt sad for him. How hard, how hideous to hustle strangers and be forced, by economics, to take them into your home.

His mother appeared in the doorway; her scarf was knotted on the top of her head. Were they Berbers, or was this just the way a woman wore her scarf? She coughed. It sounded, to my untrained ear, fairly severe. Achmed shouted at her, and she shouted back.

"My mother, she is sick," he said.

"I hope she gets better," I said, hoping she wasn't contagious.

"She will paint your hand," he said. "She is henna artist."

I put my right hand in my lap, protecting myself. "I don't want it painted."

"She is very good. She gives parties at the ksar, for her painting. For weddings."

"I'm not getting married."

"Maybe your boyfriend, he comes, you get married at the ksar? My mother will paint your hands, very cheap. For everyone, very cheap. Good, but cheap."

I finished my tea. "No, thank you," I said, but then his mother started talking directly to me in French. She was missing quite a few teeth, the gaps visible even in the flickering candlelight. She gestured, smiled, and I could see her eyes. Light colored, and intelligent.

For this moment, I wished I knew French. Wished I could talk to a woman in this country, ask her what life was like.

"You must go," Achmed said, interrupting my thoughts, his mother's speech. "I have a date." He was on his feet, the two cookies still on the plate.

"Of course," I said, getting up, feeling dismissed.

As I was leaving, saying my thank yous and goodbyes, his mother took my hand in hers, kissed it, then touched her heart and head. Her movement touched me with its grace.

"It is the Dutch girls," Achmed said as we walked from the dark village down to the tastefully designed and artistically lit ksar. "You see them on the beach, today, yes? I go to the Dutch girls tonight. Tomorrow, I take you to the bald ibis. Yes?" He stopped in the darkness, faced me. "Tomorrow?" he repeated. "Today I was a good guide, yes? Tomorrow I take you to the bald ibis. In the morning. Before it goes to the cliffs at ten-thirty, twelve-thirty, yes?"

"Before ten-thirty?" I said. If I saw the bald ibis tomorrow morning, I could still get out of the ksar by the noon checkout time. I needed to confirm that detail. "On the beach, in the morning."

"On the beach," he said. "Eight o'clock."

"Eight o'clock," I said, then just to be sure, "tomorrow morning."

Achmed nodded, then lit another cigarette. "I must go to my date."

"Have a nice time," I said, feeling constrained and awkward, but not certain why.

"I was a good guide, yes? Pay only what you think it's worth."

Dammit. Money. Guide. I swallowed my surprised "Oh," and fumbled in my bag for whatever I had. Maybe Roald would be able to give me cash against my credit card when I checked out, to tip all the workers at the ksar. I slipped Achmed whatever dirham note I had—the last one. He disappeared down the road and I walked toward the moon, rising now, shining with almost daytime brightness on the ksar.

Roald was out walking his dogs. "Dinner tonight is very special," he said. "Later than usual, but we have guests. You will join us, yes?"

"Sure," I said.

He smiled as one of the many female workers at the ksar vanished into a sauna building. "Have you done *gommage*?" he asked.

Was that like decoupage? I shook my head.

"My treat," he said. "It is a very healthful bath, clear the toxins from your body, your mind. Go," he said, indicating the door. "She is very good. I will tell her to expect you in, say, ten minutes?" His face was so mobile, so expressive. Gommage—a bath—sure. I nodded again, wondering what to do about a tip.

It wasn't a sauna; a sauna is dry heat.

I stepped into almost 90 percent humidity. The girl, whom I'd seen swathed in robe and head scarf before, now wore a leotard and Spandex shorts to very great advantage. Through a series of pantomimes, I learned I needed to undress down to my panties, then lie on a mat on the floor.

A fire burned in the corner of the room, and an oilcan held water so hot that I felt cold when it touched me.

She spread a black, oily paste on me, then took what seemed like a Brillo pad to my skin. I watched, repulsed, as long gray snakes of dead epidermis peeled off, helped by the not-quite-scalding water. She took a handful of the gray disgusting dirt-skin combo and showed it to me.

I wanted to protest that I bathed, I exfoliated, but as I watched her scrub at my skin like an old-style washerwoman on a marble floor, I began to doubt myself. Maybe I never had been clean before? I closed my eyes, and the scratch of the pad, the refreshing heat of the water, felt like it was scouring not only my skin, but me.

You. The woman who, even at eighteen was so terrified of being bested that when the man she loved, and had loved for years, said on that fateful day, "Do you think we'll ever get married?" had answered, "No."

He'd swallowed and said, "Yeah, you're right. We're just playing here. Just a game. Nothing real."

You were a coward. You should have taken his hand and said, "Of course. We've dreamed of that, talked of it, planned on it our whole lives. Why would it change now?" If he'd been about to break up or change his mind, he would have spoken. He likely just wanted confirmation from you before proposing. But you were so scared of rejection. I opened my eyes, She was scrubbing my thighs now. She took my hand and rubbed it across my own skin, letting me feel the difference. My skin was lighter where she'd cleaned it, so soft, so fragile. My sobs startled me, shook me. Took me over.

"You can't understand a word I'm saying," I said, "but I have to talk to someone. Someone in this world. Why didn't I let myself be fragile with Alan? Why was I so scared? Always fucking up, that's how I felt with everyone except him. Why didn't I let myself be safe?"

She didn't understand my words, but she hugged me, murmuring in French. I clung to this half-naked Moroccan woman. "I've ruined my life," I said. "I have nothing, I'm half dead, and I've nothing to show for it. I'm so scared," I whimpered, pulling back to wipe my nose. I looked into her eyes, dark eyes surrounded by black makeup that didn't run in this humidity, eyes that understood my pain. "Why am I so scared?"

She doused me with hot water, poured it over my head and down my back and shoulders, cooler as it touched my legs, my feet. Again and again, she poured, washing away the tears. She started scraping on my other thigh and I lay back on the mat. I couldn't stop the thoughts, I couldn't stop them coming, I couldn't control myself. *Just get it all out. It's an infection that needs to be lanced, and washed clean.*

Thoughts I'd fought back for years, I now summoned.

Men. Boys.

I'd kept them off balance, all of them, keeping myself in charge. Better to be exciting and sexy than to be naked and real. Kick them out by 3 A.M., because dawn is too intimate a time. Sleeping together, true sleep, with limbs intertwined and morning breath brewing and bad hair coiling. Too much information for *me* to reveal.

My tears felt cold on skin that was so hot from the water. The scrubbing moved down my legs. Was this what a snake felt like, once a year? Fresh start? All new?

I thought of the glittery snakeskin lying in the path. To be able to walk away once a year, start over. What a blessing, what a gift.

The girl stripped me like a carrot, peels of the dreck on my body washing down the drain in the middle of the room. She indicated for me to turn over, and her touch was steady and strict, cleaning, cleaning, cleaning. *Clean all of me*, I thought, I wept, I whispered. Could I make my heart as fresh as my skin? Could I rinse away all the grime and grit that corroded me, clogged me?

"Alan, forgive me," I whispered. We'd been so close; if my heart had been broken, his had, too. Never mind that he married in minutes. Never mind that we'd never even spoken again. Proof of what I'd done to him. What I'd done to us both.

Hot water, buckets of it, flushed across my back, my buttocks, and I heard myself laughing in between the rushes. Wash it away, wash it all away.

For those who had proclaimed they loved me, just to have me tell them lighten up, to get out. I'd been so callous. Whether the emotion was real or not, someone had risked saying it. Why hadn't I respected that risk? Why hadn't I recognized it as a risk? "I'm sorry," I whispered to those faces and bodies half-remembered, those names I maybe never knew. I'd not taken the time to learn, just to take.

Parasitically.

No more. Not again.

I sat up and she dumped bucket after bucket over me, the water running over my breasts, down my belly, between my legs. I closed my eyes and leaned back, letting her rinse through my hair, over my face, laughing for the lightness of it. She touched my hand to my arm. My skin felt like living glass, smooth, seamless. I just wanted to touch myself, not for the sexual charge, but for the innocent, awed pleasure of it. She smiled at me, nodding. "*C'est bien?*"

Bien. Good. "*Oui, c'est très bien*," I said.

"*Parlez-vous français?*" she said, looking shocked.

"No," I said, my momentary boldness to butcher one of her languages gone. "*Merci beaucoup.*" Surely I couldn't mess that up.

She stood up, washing the floor around me. It was over. The gommage was done. I'd always wanted to fly: I almost felt I could, now, so light and . . . free. I felt like I had the hollow bones; I just needed feathers.

The night air brought instant goosebumps to my new skin as I hurried to my room. I could get used to this.

❖

The table was already seated when I arrived in the dining room. Roald was in full Moroccan regalia, and the chic guests I pegged as French.

"*Bonsoir!*" Roald said, jumping to his feet. "Elize, *ma petite*," he said, kissing me on both cheeks, effusive in his greetings. "How was gommage?" He shrugged. "Your words I do not need, your eyes, you sparkle tonight. So fresh. She is good, yes?"

I hoped she would be able to change the twenty-dollar bill I'd given to her, all I'd had. It would be a nice tip in dirhams, but a pittance to pay for her kindness. I nodded and smiled, and was introduced around.

The woman with razor-short hair, narrow glasses, petite and fit, was Giselle. She shook my hand. Philippe was older, handsome in a salt-and-pepper sort of way. Clemson, the youngest, was a handsome young man with dreadlocks. Everyone had dressed for dinner, and I was glad, once more, for the belt from Zephyr.

Where was Zephyr? Why the e-mail silence? I touched the Hand of Fatima in my ear, just as Giselle expressed her admiration for it.

Roald opened some champagne and we sipped. They were interested to hear that I was there to see the bald ibis. Had I been successful, yet?

"I hear there are maybe seventy birds?" Giselle said. She pronounced her *h*'s with precision, so her accent wasn't very noticeable.

"So I've heard, too," I said. "Heard that they sleep in the caves down there, that they have afternoon tea up here, and that they fly over the park every time I'm not there, looking."

Everyone at the table chuckled, and a few French comments were thrown back and forth. What a beautiful language.

"Pardon me," Clemson said, "I do not know how to translate this into English, but I said, I think, that Nature is unpredictable."

"That's translated well," I said. "Furthermore, it's true." I should know that you couldn't count on birds to show or not show. "Tomorrow," I said.

Mezze arrived, a dozen small plates with bites of food. Olives, a variety of salads—grated carrot, sliced eggplant, mixed tomato, lemon and mint—hummus, a fiery red liquid, and bread with which to eat it all.

"So, please pardon my questions, but tell me about you, Elize," Giselle said. "Americans usually travel in groups, *non?*"

A herd of Americans. Or maybe we'd be a convocation. I thought of my "group" watching over the waters for the migrants. "I came here for the bald ibis," I said. "Stumbling on this place was a stroke of good fortune."

Giselle shrugged. "Sometimes, we must be made to be in a place at a certain time in order to complete our destiny. It is our karma, *non?*"

Zephyr with her omens, Erik with his signs, now Giselle with her karma. Was I the only person who saw what was there, tangible, and nothing else? Was—the thought occurred to me—my vision limited? "What brings you here?" I asked.

"Ah, well, we are contracted by the Moroccan government to observe the national parks, and places that should become national parks, to advise how to promote eco-tourism. Morocco wants to become a destination. With its unspoiled beaches, its reasonable currency, its beauty. All it needs is access."

I felt my heart growing still. "If you give everyone access to a place like this, places like this won't exist."

"We're observing that. Maybe if we advise for only so many people a day or—"

"No roads," Roald said.

"That track we drove in on is a deterrent," Clemson concurred.

"It's our guardian at the gate," Roald said.

"You have to want to be here," I said, sipping my wine, suddenly angry. "Why does Morocco—?" But my words died on my lips. Morocco needed an industry for that 85 percent of married, unemployed men. "How do you keep it from getting out of hand?"

"Out of hand? *Comment ça?*" Giselle asked Philippe, who translated.

"We are being very slow, very careful," she said. "Morocco is hesitant, which is good, and watches other countries who have changed so much when they welcomed the tourist euro. It's the euro here, it's not an American destination."

"Only for birders, I would guess," I said.

"When birders come to a place like this, what do they want?" she asked, then put her hand over her mouth. "Forgive me, discussing business at such a feast. Maybe tomorrow, say lunch, we could talk? I could ask you questions about the park?"

What did you talk about at dinner, if not work? "Sure," I said, feeling a bit shut out, because the conversation was growing more and more French.

The main course, a whole baked fish with lemons and olives and spices, two couscouses, and another range of salads, was served.

"It's beautiful!" Giselle said. "Couscous! We had the best couscous at this wedding in Tangier, what . . . a week ago?" she asked Clemson.

"The wedding at the Continental?" I asked.

"Yes, yes! You were there? No, I would have remembered such a girl."

From an American male, "girl'" would have insulted me, but from a chic French woman, it sounded complimentary.

"No, I heard it from my room."

"Why didn't you come? A wedding feast, and the dancing. The groom's father was a Berber," Giselle explained to Roald.

Roald began speaking in some non-English, non-French, non-Arabic tongue. "What is that?" I asked. It was the language that Erik had spoken.

"Berber," Roald said. "From the mountains."

"The Rif or the Atlas?" Clemson said, "Are they different dialects?"

Roald shrugged. "Yes, different. But when it becomes complicated, I turn to French."

❖

"Why didn't you come to the wedding?" Giselle asked me later, as we sipped demitasses of espresso, while another couscous, this one with sugar and raisins and covered in sweet milk, waited on our plates.

"It never occurred to me that I was invited," I said. "At home, weddings are private affairs."

"You have been to a Moroccan home, yes? They are a wonderfully gracious people."

"I have," I said, grateful for the experience of having lunch with Erik's friends. "They are very gracious." I turned toward her. She was around my age, with olive skin and dark eyes, her cropped hair showing off her cheekbones and the tiny earrings she wore. Her skin wasn't flawless, and her teeth weren't great, but she wore it all with such a smoky confidence that she looked perfect to me.

"How do you work in such a man's country? I went with a friend, to his friend's house. The wife of the host fixed this wonderful meal, but didn't join us. Our host, when I asked, said he would have to kill his friends if they saw his wife. Everyone laughed, but I'm not sure they were joking."

Giselle shrugged. "I am European, so the Moroccans we deal with don't expect me to behave like a Muslim woman. Granted, I don't wear revealing clothes and I talk about my husband and children—"

"You have husband and children?" I choked out.

She smiled. "Three little ones. My husband watches them."

"How old?"

"Ah, well, three years, one is fourteen months and one is four." She raised an eyebrow at me. "The little one, he was a surprise, but," she shrugged, so French, "children always are a surprise."

"Let me get this straight," I said, choking again, but this time on a combination of awe and jealousy. "You travel the world, visiting potential tourist sites for the benefit of various countries, consulting. You speak four, five languages?"

"Six," she said, smiling but puzzled.

"And you're married, with three small children."

"*Oui*. For ten years, married. The children, so new."

"How the hell do you do it?" The question blurted out of me; the table fell silent.

Giselle glanced at the men, then looked at me. "There is nothing that I do. Marriage, children, these are natural things. My work, I am good at it. I have, as you say, an eye for it. There is nothing extraordinary in my life. I just live."

"But you travel all the time?"

"A week out of the month, maybe two. Paris is close to everything and I am close to Paris."

"You have to be almost forty," I said.

"Forty-two," she murmured.

I looked away. To me, homes and children and families always came with big price tags: No more this. Can't afford that. Your freedom, your independence, your will, are gone. Stay in one place, for the schools. Disruption of a routine is bad. A child needs stability.

Hadn't those been the excuses I'd always heard? The reasons why I was from Mission, Texas, instead of living all over the world? The reasons why I had "folks" instead of parents, instead of a father in a condo in Chicago? That whole *I'm doing this for you, honeybunch* bullshit, which meant *I'm not willing to make these sacrifices to have you with me. You cost too much.*

"American women," Clemson said, "seem to think that you pick and choose what part of life you want to live."

"His girlfriend is American," Giselle whispered to me.

"But it's life, you live it all," he said. "When it happens, it happens."

"Aren't you worried, leaving your children in a world this broken, overpopulated . . . " I trailed off, aware of the awkward silence.

"France is dying out," Philippe said. "We need more Frenchmen. Our newer generations are being taught to protect the environment. To be responsible. Irresponsible overpopulation is a problem, but when a family exists and can provide . . . " he shrugged. "*C'est la vie.*"

I chuckled. They did say that.

"Shall we retire?" Roald said, rising. "Some liqueur? A smoke?"

"I tire," Giselle said. "My little one is still not sleeping through the night. I have to take my chance to rest when I can." She kissed everyone good night, confirmed that she and I were meeting for lunch tomorrow, and left. I excused myself, too. The men followed Roald back to his quarters for a nightcap.

I sat down by the pool in the shadows of a bougainvillea. The moon hung above. What a perfect evening; what a revelation. I thought of Giselle: She hiked and biked and swam and picnicked and cooked and worked and traveled and had even walked half of the Paris Marathon.

I hadn't asked how much in-home help she had, or how rich she was. Those things were part of the equation, but it seemed far more significant that she didn't compartmentalize her life. Yes, she had children, but how else did they learn to hike unless they went along with Maman and Papa, safe in a backpack? How else to appreciate beauty other than starting in a stroller on Sunday walks through the Louvre?

Giselle worked for one of the big greens, a for-profit company that was trying to be a good steward of the environment. She had a degree in business and a degree in botany. She . . . I sighed and stared up at the sky. It didn't matter. I wasn't her, I wasn't French and I wasn't that . . . secure? Sure? Aware? I wasn't sure which word it was, but I wasn't it. Never had been. Could I ever be?

You could, Crazy-Elize whispered.

Palm trees etched against the clouds, a view of the sea, a billion stars scattered across the sky, a bedroom made for sex, and birds to look forward to in the morning. I couldn't think of a more romantic setting. I didn't want to be alone. I didn't want to be alone here. One call, that's all it would take.

Sam, I could make my own. He'd be gorgeous lounging by the pool, fit and tanned. He'd be charming with Roald. He'd be triumphant in the park, as we found the ibis together.

But when the images flashed into my mind, it wasn't Sam's planed face and Hollywood smile I saw. It was Erik's time-stopping chipped incisor smile, his indigo eyes.

I'd substituted a dozen—or more, I'd never counted, and never would—men for Alan. I knew that now. Unfair to them, unfair to me. I wasn't going to substitute Sam for Erik. I didn't think I could. It was better to be alone than to be with someone other than Erik.

But if I got another chance with him, I'd take it.

If I didn't, well then, it was my karma, *non?*

The Gift

Though bleary-eyed, I was up before dawn. The skies seemed to be lighting slowly this morning, as I sat by the pool. I hadn't rested, either due to the rich food or my excitement about today.

See the ibis, have lunch, go back to Larache: today's goals. I still had a paper to write and a new job to find. The Institute wasn't it for me, not anymore. I couldn't go back to Wilkerson's smirks and Frankie's simpering, winning smile.

I needed to level with Sam about the Dubya, to ask his advice, as a colleague.

The thought rankled, and I pushed it away. Today, ibis. I scampered down the steps to the breakfast tables overlooking the water. Achmed wasn't on the beach, yet. I didn't see my waiter either.

When Ali finally arrived to set my place, I ordered coffee. This eyrie was the perfect place to watch for Achmed. My juice appeared first. Then Ali brought the tray: mini-tagines of salt and spice, warm bread, jams, cheeses, and a personal tagine of herb-spiked fried eggs and hummus.

Five minutes later he returned and poured my coffee. Today I waved away the sugar and milk.

"It's no problem," he said, milk pitcher in hand.

"No, that's okay," I said.

"Bald ibis today?" he said with a smile.

"Yes, yes. Bald ibis."

"*Bon appétit*," he said, and bowed.

I didn't want Achmed to show and me not be there. The eggs took two bites, some bread, a few figs, the juice in a long swallow and the coffee in a few shots.

It was just turning eight o'clock as I waved goodbye to Ali and bolted down the steps to meet Achmed, still swallowing.

No Achmed.

Maybe he'd gotten lucky with his date?

I walked toward the park myself, my steps slow. The park guardian was awake, a thin man in a uniform standing outside the little hut I passed the other day. He welcomed me in broken English, introduced himself as Tawfiq, and offered me tea.

"Here for bald ibis," I said, scanning the lake, and for some reason speaking Tarzan-English, thinking I'd be easier to understand.

"No ibis today," he said, going into his hut.

How did he know? I looked at my watch. Not even 9 A.M.

He brought out a battered tray with small glasses filled with mint leaves and a steaming squat, silver pot. Also a hunk of bread, and some amber gelatin.

"For you," he said, offering me the tea. I thought I'd refused his offer earlier, but it seemed rude to do so now. I took the tea, and he tore off a hunk of bread, dipped it in the gelatin and motioned for me to do the same. It tasted like honey.

He called out birds as they flew past, in English and in French. His knowledge was thorough: he could identify them by calls or flight patterns. By drawing in the sand, we discussed how thermals moved over the Sous, thermals that some birds used as power. The honey was delicious, and when I asked, he said it was argan honey. Berber.

"Are you Berber?" I said.

He tapped his chest and I looked at him properly for the first time. He was young, with huge dark eyes surrounded by ostrich-long eyelashes. His black hair was neatly clipped, his face smooth, his uniform clean, though too big. He smiled; he was beautiful. "Berber, from the mountains. Argan mountains. There, we also have the bald ibis."

Scientists had banded a few of the bald ibis, to track where the birds went when not in residence at the park, to ascertain who or what contributed to their mortality. Maybe that's what he was talking about.

He was the park guardian, and he knew his birds. Were the bald ibis also somewhere else? Was it possible there was an unbanded pair? Where were the Argan mountains? Rif and Atlas I'd heard of, but Argan?

The sun was almost overhead when I got back to the ksar. Giselle sat by the pool in a sleek one-piece bathing suit, working on papers and looking at maps. "Bald ibis?" she asked, after greeting me by kissing me on both cheeks.

"Not today, but there's still tonight," I said. My credit card would cover another day, even another month. Did I have to go back to Larache? To Texas? Staying here the rest of my life would be perfect.

"Poor you, to play for another day in paradise," she said with a smile. "I will order a wine and meet you at lunch, in, say, an hour?"

"Perfect," I said, going into the scented shadows of my room. The maids had cleaned, opened the curtains and windows, and the smell of the sea blew through. I stripped off my DEET-soaked clothing, and stepped into the shower space, a narrow curved corridor with a high window at the far end.

I used the black paste in the terracotta jar—*ghasoul*, the same stuff the girl had used on me during gommage. It felt as if every nerve ending was waking up. The smell was pungent: spices, things I didn't know, but would associate with this sense of clean, of liveliness. Awareness, without tension and timelines. Schedules.

Paradise. I *was* in paradise as Giselle had called it. I had another day to play in paradise.

Play.

The water coursed through my hair, down my back, and I wondered about play. A lot of the things I did would be considered play.

Things other people did on their weekends, or for relaxation. But for me it was work.

Kayaking to observe birds. Swimming and diving to observe and monitor marine life. Biking to get from point A to point B without burning gas. Sex was tension relief, to help me sleep better. What was play? Pedicures, I thought as I washed my feet, were an investment. Pamper your feet and they wouldn't fail you. Massages? Only if I injured something. Play . . . what was play?

I rinsed and stepped into the room. The light caught the metallic threads woven through the bedspread and the gold and copper of the lamps, turning the whole room iridescent red and purple and gold. The colors of the bald ibis. I picked up my birding clothes, but decided against them. Instead, I dug in my bag and put on the beaded cover-up, tied on Zephyr's scarf as a sarong and draped the belt over it. Lots of glittery things, but in the space of the room, in this place where even the maids wore armfuls of bangles and black around their eyes, it seemed appropriate.

And . . . I liked it.

❖

Giselle sat beneath the awning, framed by the blue of the sea. I took the banquette opposite and we exchanged greetings while Ali brought us a bottle of white wine, chilled. Wine at lunch, a business lunch at that. I smiled.

"Roald tells me you are an ornithologist," Giselle said. "You work for the state? The government?"

"A private institution," I said. "My specialty is waterbirds. Ibis." I found I wanted to talk, to share, to be known. "I study and monitor wading birds. I was in Larache for migration but decided I'd rather see the bald ibis." I took the wineglass. "I don't speak French, so that decision ended up being more challenging than I'd expected."

She smiled. "What did your American author say? 'Abroad is always closed.' *Henri* James, perhaps?"

"Perhaps." I had no idea. When *Loser* whispered through my mind, I told myself that I had focused on other things. Not everyone could know everything.

"So your job is the reason for your bald ibis watching?"

I shrugged. "Yes, partly."

"Tchin-tchin," she said, raising her glass. We touched glasses, and sipped. Giselle turned the bottle, looked at the label. It was written in French, and apparently passed muster.

"What is this 'partly,'" she said. "You travel alone, yes?" I hesitated and she laughed conspiratorially. "Business and pleasure, *pas de problème?*"

I shrugged again.

"You shrug like a Frenchwoman," she said. "We keep our secrets that way."

"I met a guy, a man."

"*Un homme Maroc?*"

"No, I don't think so."

She leaned forward, "You must tell me this story! I am an old married woman now, so I must enjoy through you." She winked as she spoke.

How easy to spill the details: how we'd met, the day in Marrakesh, the way he made me feel.

Ali appeared with our mezze: small fried fish, olives, tomatoes grilled with spices, and sliced boiled eggs. He refilled our glasses, brought another bottle of wine, and left us to the breeze and the blue sky and sea.

I'd finished by describing the 3 A.M. e-mail, my attempt at an invitation.

"You have heard nothing, then?" she said, hooked by the story.

"Nothing."

Giselle shook her head as the mezze was removed for fish, rubbed in *ras al hanout* and served on thinly sliced grilled vegetables.

"*Bon appétit,*" Giselle said.

"*Et vous*," I guessed.

"*Vous aussi*," she corrected me.

I bit into the fish, crushed. I knew I couldn't speak French, couldn't look chic, couldn't do any of it! Why had I even tried?

"Your inflection is quite good," she said. "You should learn French. With your knowledge of wading birds, you could work for us, liaise the Souss-Massa."

When I was silent, she glanced up to see me staring, dumbstruck, at her.

"Of course, it is very far from Texas. But I think, maybe, being far from Texas isn't a bad thing, *non*?" A knowing smile.

"What exactly do you do here?" I asked. That such a thing was possibly even possible?

Through a growing haze of envy and respect, I listened. The vision she had, the way her company was guiding not just the Moroccan government, but others they worked with. Encouraging them to protect their natural assets by growing in measured and sustainable stages, rather than expending those same resources in a short, income-producing rush.

I wanted to send them to Port Rockton, to Aransas and Corpus, to still the short-sighted greed leading those communities into environmental peril, and the birds to a drawn-out death, in the name of the Immediate Almighty Tax Base.

As we poured more wine, I blurted, "How did you meet your husband?"

Giselle looked surprised for only a moment. "I was a feminist. No man, no children, though of course, lovers."

"Of course."

"He was in South Africa. Though he is a *Pied-Noir*, do you know this phrase?"

I shook my head.

"His father was with the Legion, on the Cote d'Ivoire. His mother was Italian, from Milan. *Pied-Noir* is from the boots of war the legionnaires wore."

"Combat boots?"

"Ah, *oui*—black feet. *Les pieds noirs.* So," she said, pouring wine into our glasses, "he is touring *Afrique*, I am there in Johannesburg to speak to someone about . . . I forget. Something green. I am in a suit, very dressy. He is in a jumper. Suddenly, shots I am hearing, and everyone ducks. I try to run, but my heel sticks in the—" She pointed to the ground. "Between the pavements?"

"Crack?"

"*Oui*, the crack. I am halted. He jumps on me—*bouff*—we fall to the ground. The glass broken falls on him, because he protected me. After the hospital I take him to my hotel room." She grinned. "He is the bullet I did not, how do you say, dodge?"

I chuckled. "Is he an environmentalist, too?"

"*Non*. He only went to school so his parents would let him play football. He is good with his hands. To make things, to grow things. So I work, and he is *Maman et Papa*."

"Was it hard?" I asked, eating a crescent-shaped cookie. "To go from one life into another? Single, and suddenly double?"

"*Non*, but we didn't swear, at first, to love each other always. It was like an affair, but it kept . . . climbing? Going up?" She made a mountain with her cupped palm. "Growing, yes? So the decisions to live here, to do this thing, they were not big. No courage was necessary because we did not know there were . . . ah, when you gamble?"

"Stakes?"

"Yes. The stakes were *petites*, small. Just a day became a week, became a year."

"And became a marriage?"

"That . . . ah," she chuckled. "That was a moment of cold water. To realize we were marrying. But it was him, not just marriage, and that was not so scary. A day, a breakfast with friends, and life continued as it had, only now with rings and more government forms."

She put down her glass and looked at me. I knew I was beyond tipsy, but she appeared only a little flushed and her English seemed improved. "Things we are meant to be, to have, to happen, these things we are not escaping. Your bird, your man, they will happen. But you must breathe to get there."

For a moment her dark eyes looked like Zephyr's. Goosebumps rose on my arms and I couldn't look away. Fortunately, Roald interrupted us with after-lunch tea and the shesh besh board.

He and Giselle arranged the round markers and rolled dice in little cups. I leaned against the banquette, listening to the clatter of the pieces against the sides of the board. Someone sang in the kitchen, and the maids, cleaning the empty rooms, giggled as they worked. The sun warmed my feet and a breeze from the sea played with the fringe on the scarf around my hips.

Roald and Giselle spoke in French. I thought they spoke of me, "*elle*," but I didn't mind.

"Are you sleeping?" Giselle asked a little while later.

"No," I said, opening my eyes. "Dreaming what it would be like to live here."

"Roald said you could take this little house they are building," Giselle said, pointing to a laid-out rectangle of cinder blocks on the hill twenty steps away.

"I don't speak French," I said, rather than confess I was about to be broke. Yeah, I could charge up the card, but I had no way of paying it off.

"A simple thing to learn," Roald said, "especially living here." He moved his pieces, provoking a cry from Giselle.

I thanked Giselle for lunch, kissed each of them on both cheeks, and walked down to the beach. The local boys waved at me as they played soccer. They knew me on sight; I was becoming a fixture. How I wished I could be.

A house here, a job. How much of that was just an invitation, spur of the moment, to make me feel good? How much was real?

Clouds in a hundred changing formations drifted above. At some point, I stopped identifying them as cumulus and cirrus, and began to see that they were really pigs or dragons or strangely contorted trees.

Water that wasn't satisfying on a surfboard made for great body surfing. For hours I floated and swam, avoiding the rip zone, my body stiff to ride the waves, or limp as I watched the doings on the sea floor. I stayed within the boundaries and the guard waved at me with a smile on his march along the shore

I got out, my fingers shriveled, and sat down. Tourists had come and gone from the ksar. Scheduled lunchtime guests, here to see the birds, brought a steady income, Roald had said. I wrapped up in my towel and watched the sky begin its change as the sun descended.

Then they appeared to my left, necks outstretched, in the rising and falling line I knew so well. There were about thirty leaving the park, headed for their nests. From this distance there was little to distinguish them as bald, but they were undoubtedly ibis. My heart rose into my throat and my eyes watered.

Tomorrow I'd see the ibis, visit with them; suddenly I had no doubt. "Tomorrow," I whispered to their silhouettes against the blue and purple streaked sky.

"Tomorrow," they promised back.

The Birds

I swirled the cream in my coffee. "*Merci, Ali,*" I said, trying out the words I'd heard all around me for two weeks now. "*Je voudrais plus pain, s'il vous plait.*"

Ali blushed when he placed it before me.

Draping my bins around me, I took the path, watching the gulls in the surf, listening to the wind. The sand was sumptuous, soft as mousse as I sank with each step. No one ever needed a gym, just a sliding pit of sand to walk in. Maybe I should do that, return to Port Rockton and open a Sand Gym. Make it the new trend, make millions of dollars, and then buy the Dubya from Wilkerson.

Tawfiq was drinking his tea, and it took three refusals before I found myself sipping mint tea as well. We squatted in the dirt, drawing silhouettes of the various birds that came through seasonally. It became a game, and I realized he was quite talented, even drawing his finger in the sand.

He managed to catch the line of the bird in flight, capturing the sense of its movement, an art few could manage. Most illustrated field guides were static, offering a profile image to convey field marks. Sometimes confusing to beginners, because birds rarely held still. Audubon's images had been active, but then, in many cases, he'd wired the corpses and arranged them in dynamic poses, like puppets.

"*C'est très jolie,*" I said, smiling at Tawfiq.

He murmured *merci*, then gestured. "I must to go," he said. "*Je dois partir.*"

I thanked him and turned my bins to the sky, marveling at the calm I felt, the certainty.

At 9 A.M., the ibis appeared.

A line of them, about sixty, flew in over the Sous. I watched them, their airborne undulation moving above me. They flew directly overhead; I could see their red heads and feet. Would they land? Would I be able to observe them? But they flew past the park, out toward the sea.

To their morning roost up the beach, or their evening roost down the beach? I started over the dunes. My eye skimmed the sky, unable to discern their direction. Where had they gone? Birds don't just vanish! Then I dropped my gaze to the beach. Dozens of dark speckles clustered on the white sand. For a moment I tried to identify what kind of shore bird sat like that. Then I realized: the ibis were on the beach!

I ducked from dune to dune, moving as fast as I dared without disturbing them. About fifty feet away, I crouched, my bins to my eyes.

Sitting on the beach. In the morning. No freshwater ponds for them to eat from, no caves for them to roost in. They just sat, on the beach, for anyone to see. A few groomed themselves, a few others stretched their wings and let the sun heat them, and yet others stood on one foot, staring into the distance, a behavior I'd seen in other waterbirds, but rarely in an ibis.

They weren't working. They were standing there, just being.

I put my bins down. It was extraordinary. They were so unlike any ibis I'd ever seen. It was like they knew they were special, and thus had license to just sit and stare, or socialize.

I tightened my focus and saw the ruff that distinguished them, a standing collar of dark red feathers, like a vampire's cape, over an iridescent bronze, green, burgundy, and purple body. They were just like ibises, but ibises with confidence. Security.

They moved with majesty, seemingly self-aware. Aware of their importance.

All my life I'd admired ibis, the white, the white-faced, the glossy, for their industry, but these Waldrapps . . . I laughed quietly, settling myself in the sand, making notes at my side, counting the minutes in whispers. These I admired for their indolence.

It was enough that they were who they were. I felt awed, a little shut out and envious. To be enough, just by being? My vision of their bejeweled feathers blurred, and I blinked back tears.

I hadn't been enough for Fischer. I had been too much for Mama and Pop. I hadn't been "right" for the Institute. The birds—*and Erik*, Crazy-Elize whispered—seemed to be the only places where I was just right.

"My life is a fucking Goldilocks story," I whispered, careful not to disturb the birds. With long, aristocratic eyes, they looked at me and I felt their pity, seeing me as the lonely white ibis.

I dropped my bins as they approached.

"*Bonjour, Mademoiselle Elize. Vous avez vu les ibis?*" Ali asked as I sat down at the table hours later, my notebook filled with scribbles. "*Voulez-vous du café?*"

"I saw the ibis," I gushed. "They surrounded me! They were stunning in their ugliness. I mean, an ibis is not a beautiful bird, but these are exceptional, with bare skin heads and the ruff around their necks. So beautiful by being so . . . "

"*Joli-laid,*" a voice behind me said.

My heart didn't stop, or turn over, or anything. I knew he would come; I'd felt it when I saw the ibis. Certainty. Warmth pooled through me as I turned around and saw Erik seated in the shade of the awning. "Pretty-ugly," he said. "It's a French concept." He pushed his glasses up and I saw his eyes, and then my heart *did* flip over. "Coffee?"

Erik stood. He wore the same tunic as before, but over a pair of weathered jeans. His bag was at his feet and his hair gleamed like a raven's wing. I walked into his arms and he held me, my heart matching the beat of his, all of time slowing around us until we stood in a blue bubble of sky and water.

"I'm glad you're here," I said, feeling the heat, the hardness of him beneath the shirt.

"Thank you for inviting me," he said, his words warm against my face. "And for the map. It's not the easiest place to find."

I started laughing. He pulled back to look into my face. "You saw your ibis, did you?"

"They were fantastic," I said, humming with excitement.

"How many?"

"Fifty maybe, just sitting there."

"What do you call fifty ibis? I mean, there's a murder of crows—"

"—a muster of storks, a kettle of falcons—"

"So what's a group of ibis?"

I looked into his dark blue eyes. "A seduction of ibis."

He blinked. "Even the hardworking ones?"

"An accounting of white ibis, but a seduction of Waldrapps." Maybe not scientifically correct, but it felt true.

He tucked the hair behind my ear, brushed my chin with a silver-ringed finger. "I like how you think. Tell me more?"

"With pleasure," I said, asking Ali to send up champagne as I led Erik off the patio and up the stairs to my rooms. The serving girls waved and giggled as we passed. When we got inside, I pushed the door closed. We stood in the sudden darkness, the only tangible thing our linked hands.

"Elize," he murmured and grabbed me, pressing me against the wall, kissing me with open-mouthed passion, overwhelming desire. We tossed clothes to the floor, entangled limbs, but when I reached for him, I still felt cloth. Erik groaned within my grasp; I realized he was still half-dressed. I was the only one stark naked.

That was going to change. I reached for him.

❖

"You saw your ibis," he said, his finger tracing invisible tattoos on my shoulder.

"They were glorious!"

He kissed my forehead. "Are you forsaking your—white-faced, was it? glossy?—for the Waldrapp? A seduction of Waldrapps?"

"The colors are similar," I said. "In breeding plumage, the white-faced glimmers and glows. The skin on its face turns white and its feathers deepen into burgundy and violet iridescence." I chuckled. "The glossy, which is also dark, gets a bluish-purple eye ring that looks like . . . well, reminds me of—remember, I went to school in the eighties—"

"Me, too."

I broke off and looked at him. "How old are you?" I accused. But the little details my hands had appreciated, even if my eyes hadn't seen, told me. The limb-looseness of twenty-something had been replaced by knitted surety. His muscles had a density you didn't find in a boy, the skin around his waist tight and drawn, tapered from shoulders sculpted by life, not a gym.

He watched me, bemused. "Disappointed?"

A little intimidated. "Surprised, I guess."

He caught his fingers in my hair and pulled me toward him. "What do the glossy remind you of?"

"Friday night football games," I said, my words slipping in between our kisses. "Blue eye shadow on the girls. Metallic blue, you could see it across the field. You could almost tell which girls had gotten ready together, using the same Maybelline."

"Were you one of those girls?"

My image of me: tall and scrawny, but comfortable in my skin, thanks to sports. Me, seated with the string bean boys and Alan. I chuckled. "My eyes have never known blue eye shadow."

But Erik wasn't listening anymore, and I couldn't think. I tipped my head over the bed's edge, looking through the delicately embroidered curtains that dimmed the sun, but didn't hide the blue of the sky and water. Upside down palm trees burned themselves into my retinas as my fingers clenched in Erik's dark hair, my body tense beneath his expert fingers and mouth.

He took his time, tasting, savoring, leisurely driving me out of my mind. For hours we'd been lost in each other's skin, taste, smell and touch. "Let go, Elize," he whispered.

"I've already come a dozen times," I said. It was true, and then I'd lost count.

"No," he chuckled. "Let go of the idea that orgasm is a goal." I sat up and stared at him. My tan was so dark I looked like I had on a white bikini. His face was a stark contrast; seeing his hair against my skin made my toes curl. "What?" I said, when nothing more intelligent or insightful presented itself to the nine brain cells I had working.

He grinned at me. "Lady Impatience."

"I am not impatient! We've been fooling around for hours, and I haven't leaped on top of you! I'm being patient." For some reason, I was willing to follow his lead.

He kissed my inner thigh, nuzzled his bent nose against me. I was supposed to converse like this? "Do you like food?"

"Food?"

"To eat," he said.

"Nutrition is good," I said slowly, trying to guess where he was going with this.

"Do you like this?" he said, draping the silk-fringed edge of the coverlet along my leg.

"It feels nice," I said.

He set it aside and looked up at me. "What do you remember about the souk?"

"Erik—" But he put a finger over my lips and shook his head. I stared into his eyes, and he dropped his hand to my chest. Holding my gaze, he matched my breath, until we were in complete sync.

"What do you remember?"

"The souk? It was confusing, loud. Smelled—different. Like a Port-O-Let and Christmas baking at the same time."

He chuckled. "That's a helluva combination."

I laughed too, "I remember mint, everywhere. It was minty."

He nodded. "And you heard?"

"Chaos. Confusion. Those same five notes up and down and up and down the scale."

His hand rested between my legs, rested, didn't move, just . . . kept me warm. "Why?"

"Describe your ibis to me. As if I've never seen it."

"You probably haven't," I said.

"Anyway. Describe it. Not like you would write it for a journal or something, but how you see it."

"My ibis? The white-faced?"

"Glossy, whatever. Yeah, the one with eighties blue eye shadow."

"Okay, well . . . You want to see it in the sunshine, so you can appreciate its coloration. The body of the bird is about the size of chicken, but it has long, brilliant red legs, and a long neck. Its beak is decurved—"

"Too scientific."

"Its beak curves, like . . . " This was incredibly hard. "It curves like the side of a cello, a delicate downward slope. Around the bird's eyes, Maybelline-blue skin—" Erik grinned. "—meets purple feathers that cover its head, turning magenta as they grow down its neck. The body is like an iridescent . . . red velvet cake—"

"Cool," he said, smiling.

"Yet for every patch of reddish-purple, there's a section—" I tossed words like "flight feathers" and "secondaries" out of my mind. "—that is teal-black, but also gold and copper and bronze. The bird appears gilded. When it steps from the shadows, a rather small, almost homely creature, its beak too big for true beauty, and the light shines on it, it takes your breath away."

Erik applauded, his one hand patting my sex.

I turned the tables, pushing him back, straddling him. "What was that about?"

His hand moved over my leg. "What's this?"

"Tan line."

"I see that, but . . . " He squirmed up, looking at my legs closely. "How many tan lines do you have?"

I was, effectively, striped. "That one is from work shorts," I said, pointing to the line just above my knee. "That's board shorts," about an inch higher. "Tennis skirt; boy shorts, for surfing; and my bikini."

Erik kissed my bikini tan line. "You are so sexual," he said, then looked up at me. "Body confidence, awareness, sensitivity, but . . . " He shook his head, his expression puzzled. "I can't figure it out."

I slid to his side, looking at him as he struggled with something. I brushed the hair off his face, the pieces slipping right back into his eyes. Then he looked at me. "I don't want to offend you."

Instinctively, I tensed. This was what you got for trying something new, for being open with a stranger. I felt my forehead tighten.

"I noticed it when we ate breakfast."

That I was a mess with crumbs? That I took no sugar in my coffee? Had I had food in my teeth and just not known it? I crossed my arms over my legs, feeling vulnerable, trying to shut out the *Loser* refrain in my head.

"You're not sensual."

I sat back, insulted, staring at him, on the verge of tears.

"You're sexy, God, you're sexy. I wanted you from the beginning. But you, you don't take pleasure in things of the flesh."

"Because I don't pig out?" I did. "Because I don't wear jewelry or makeup?"

"No, because you don't actually taste what you eat, or feel what you touch, or hear, or smell." He kissed me; I was pretty resistant. "How is it that the way you see the natural world with its . . . " He sighed. "All the nuances and subtleties, and the way you regard everything else, how is it that those things are so separate?

"No, don't close up on me," he said, kissing my knees, my elbows, about the only parts he could get to. "I'm not attacking, Elize. I'm trying to understand."

"Why?" I snapped.

Erik lay back on the bed, his fingers on my feet, touching, caressing, his other hand on his belly, also caressing. Enjoying his skin, not gross but sensual. "Why do I want to understand you better?" he asked, looking at me, his eyes dark glitters in the dim light. "That's the question?"

I nodded.

"Because . . . I think I could love you." His fingers stilled on my feet; my body also stilled. My heart took up the slack.

"I'm not here because you're a holiday fling," he said. "I came because of the woman I thought you were, you proved yourself to be."

"Huh?"

"In Marrakesh, you were uncomfortable. It wasn't your first choice to be there, but you did want to see the bird, this bird."

"The bald ibis."

He nodded. "But you wouldn't come here. Legitimate reasons why, but still, not following your dream." He sat up, and I respectfully kept my eyes fixed on his earnest face instead of watching his stomach flex as he moved. "You stood at a juncture, and you took this path of discovery. That's when I knew I could maybe, possibly, love you."

My body felt hot, but from what? Pleasure? Irritation? "That's wildly unromantic, but still—"

"It's honesty, Elize. We're alone in this world. We're born alone, we die that way. It's an honor to choose someone to share your life, for however many days or years. Just like you discovered you could get here, you could make the thing you wanted most happen, and your life could be better for it."

"Definitely," I said, images of those arrogant, ruffed birds strolling on the beach like it was a piazza and they were Italian nobility, in my mind. "Most definitely."

"I think you'll discover the sensual world, and love life more because of it."

"You're trying to change me?"

"No, I think you want to change yourself. I'm trying to encourage you, aid you if I can." He kissed me. It should have been abrupt. This conversation had been libido-killing, illusion-destroying, and we both needed some time to digest.

I just wanted to be alone. Somewhere else. This room had become a cell.

But Erik—he kissed me. Slow and soft, his breath in my mouth calming me, soothing me. His hands roamed my body, but gently, tingling fingertips and the edge of a nail here and there. He used his hands to play my body like it was an instrument, using the heat and cool of his silver rings to bring awareness to me. "How did they lock you in a box, letting only your birding soul fly free?" he whispered against my ear.

He knew me.

I wrapped myself around him, and he held me tight. Visions of white ibis flying from the yard filled my mind. Visions seen through glass panes. The panes of my "box."

"Tell me a story," I said. We were curled up on the lounge outside our room. *Our room.* Wow, that thinking had happened fast. I still smelled the after-dinner licorice liqueur, "digestif," we'd had with Roald. The moon was fat above us, and the stars unfamiliar in some ways, but I could always find the uneven *w*-shape of Cassiopeia.

Sometimes she was all I could find, even on the island.

"Inspired by Scheherazade?" Erik said, his fingers playing with the ends of my hair.

Roald had told a few Arabian Nights stories over dinner, tales about djinns and camels and mysterious maidens. "Or you can just tell me about you."

"You'll learn," he said. "A story?"

"Your favorite story," I decided.

"Well, all life's questions can be answered by 'The Fisher King.'"

I jackknifed up at the word.

"What's wrong?"

His words made me feel cold. I shook my head. "Something, uh, crawled on me."

Erik brushed my hair down my shoulder. "You're shaking."

"Cold, I think," I said, clenching my hands together. I don't believe in signs. Coincidences.

"Come to bed," he said, and took my hand.

We hadn't discussed this; I'd kind of assumed he'd stay with me, but I didn't think we'd actually sleep. But he didn't pursue sex, just pleasure. I wasn't complaining, but I figured I needed to sleep tonight. "I don't sleep well with others," I said. Explained. Hinted.

"You never did," he muttered. "If it gets bad, I'll take the chaise."

But we crawled into bed, and I felt the warmth of him against my cold skin. I draped a thigh over his, my head on his chest and started to doze off.

Right before I slept, however, I wondered what he'd meant.

The Conversation

"What did you mean by last night, when you said, 'You never did'?"

"I wondered how long it would take you to ask me," he said, adding a ton of milk to his coffee. "We've been together before, Elize. In a past life."

"A past life," I repeated, buttering a flat, Moroccan-style biscuit as I stared at Erik.

"I knew you would freak out," he said.

"I'm not freaked. It's not scary. It's just odd." And that I wasn't freaked or scared was doubly odd.

Ali appeared with tagines of eggs and hummus, set them down, and disappeared.

"Can't you see the signs?" Erik said. He ticked them off his fingers, silver flashing in the sun. "Same wedding party."

"I wasn't there."

"You were, you just didn't attend."

He was like an astrologer, so vague that he couldn't be pinned down as wrong. "I wasn't there. But go on."

"Then the train. I had to bribe the steward to let me on board. Yours was the only berth available." He looked at me. "The taxi."

"You stole my taxi!"

"No, I was waiting in line. You walked in front of me, just as the taxi pulled up."

That could have been the case. I admit I wasn't so clear on the details.

"Then I saved your life and bought you breakfast."

The horn. The car. "I wouldn't have really been run over?"

"In the Place? Of course you would have. You had no more sense than a newborn for those first few hours." He saw my offended expression and sighed. "It's a common reaction. It's the Superbowl and Cirque de Soleil and Barnum and Bailey, all thrown together! It's crazy at first."

"Was it crazy for you?"

He shrugged. "Easier. I was ten when I saw it the first time."

"Ten?"

"Coincidence number three: you're a birder."

"You're not, so I fail to see the coincidence."

"I," he said, smiling and tapping his chest, "I'm a Raven."

Okay, so a chill did run up my spine. I'd thought of him in raveny terms on several occasions. "Is that a . . . "

"Surname."

"Your name is Erik Raven?"

He nodded.

I sighed, finished my eggs, and dabbed at my mouth. "Erik Raven, I don't see any great coincidences here. Not of—" I made quote marks in the air. "—'past lives quality.'"

I couldn't see behind his glasses, but I felt his gaze. It came to me in a rush: he wasn't kidding. This wasn't a joke to him. It was his religion, for the lack of a better word. He believed it. He thought he knew me. That he had loved me . . . in a past life. This was serious to him.

"No matter," he said, patting my hand. "You will."

❖

I learned how to play shesh besh that day, overlooking the rolling waves. By about four, I was yawning, and Erik said he wanted to talk to Roald. I went up to the room and lay down. The imprints of where I'd slept all night in Erik's arms had been cleaned away, but I lay down where he'd slept, holding me.

The silk coverlet beneath me wasn't smooth. It had nubs—slubs, I think they were called—and bands of contrasting embroidery. I ran my hand along the embroidery; it felt like bumps to me. I closed my eyes, imagined that I was blind, and it was Braille. Did the blind spell words in Braille, or did they use ideograms? Was Braille centralized? If you knew Braille, did you know all languages?

I touched the embroidery carefully, pouring all my focus through my fingertips. The bumps discerned themselves, not into anything specific, but no longer just a mass of embroidery. I felt the narrow thread that led to the next part of the design, then the few beads that provided emphasis.

While I felt the embroidery, though, my body felt everything else. Possibly every single thing in the room. My clothes, the way they lay on my body; the weight and movement of my hair; the temperature and texture of the coverlet, and the contrasts between the blanket I lay on, and the part on which I rested my feet. Behind my closed eyes, I felt the warmth of the painted walls, smelled the faint tinge of decay from the goatskin lamp. My forehead relaxed, and I sighed into the bed.

Erik woke me by sitting on the bed, though I had thought I'd smell him when he came in. I started to open my eyes, but he put his hand over them. "Ssh," he said, then drew my hand to his pants. He was hard; a shock ran through me to feel him, thick, heavy, ready. "Let me watch you," he said.

I fluttered my eyes open and saw him, looking down on me. His face was sharper, harder. Hungry, I realized. His mouth was red, wet and when he looked at my nipples and down my body, still clothed, I groaned.

Masturbation, for me, is energy management. It wakes me up, or sends me to sleep. There is little sensual about it, and everything mechanical. But as I slid up the headboard, giving Erik the view he wanted, I wanted to feel it, too. Not just the release, but feel it like I had felt the embroidery, how I'd come to sense the room. Feel the sensuality of it.

Erik turned me sideways, and put his head on my stomach, finding a spot where I could breathe and he wouldn't be stabbed in the head by bones. "I want to feel you, too," he said, then kissed my hipbone.

As many things as I've done as a sexually active adult woman, performing for a live audience wasn't one. I put my hand between my legs, feeling awkward and sexy and a little ashamed, all at the same time. A minute or two of stroking got me more and more out of the mood. I dropped my hand. "I feel like a bad porn star," I said, staring at the ceiling. I think I was blushing.

He turned to me and I noticed he was still hard. Dressed, too. I tugged at his shirt and he pulled it off, threw it over his head. "Have you ever had an energy orgasm?"

"I caught a vibrator on fire once, does that count?"

"I bet you've melted a couple, too," he said, with a chuckle. "No, I'm talking about energizing your entire body."

The hardest words in my personal vocabulary squeezed from between my teeth: "Teach me."

I was light, he explained. Different points of my body were chakras, energy centers, symbolized by different colors of light. My kundalini energy—"You don't have to tell me where that is. The name sounds like it."—was basically in my sex, my tailbone, my deepest core.

"The kundalini works as the detonator," he said. "You'll draw all the other colors down to your first chakra, and then the energy will explode outward in white light and well-being."

"I do this all with my mind?" I said, looking up at him, now crouched beside me like a coach on the field.

"Completely with your mind. It's not sexual. It's orgasmic, but . . . a different sensation."

"I'm not a yoga person," I said, closing my eyes, laying my hands, palm down, on my belly like he'd said. "Sitting and staring seems pretty boring to me."

"It's probably exactly what you need," he said, "to sit and stare."

I looked up at him again. "You promised me an orgasm."

He kissed me, hard, hot, deep, an orgasm in itself. "Think about colored light," he said. "I'll walk you through it."

The tunnels and doorways and, for that matter, windmills, of my mind were always vaguely threatening. They held a lot of unwelcome residents. I twitched as I remembered Erik saying 'Fisher King.'

"Are you okay?"

"How were you ten when you first saw the Place?"

"I told you, I'm from everywhere."

"I thought you were blowing me off."

He chuckled. "That, I would never do."

"You said I was potentially the woman you wanted, in Marrakesh. Not actually her."

"That has to do with walking similar paths. You'd never understand, much less love or appreciate me, if you hadn't taken this risk of coming here alone. Of pursuing your dream of the bald ibis."

I thought about that for a moment.

"Think of your kundalini," he said, dropping his voice. "You're in a passageway, walking toward the end . . . "

The games, apparently, had begun.

My kundalini wasn't at the end of a passageway. It was through a Spanish-moss covered walkway that looked suspiciously like a trail through the palm forest at the Dubya. But the imagined purple flowers melted into light and I did feel . . . something.

"Okay," he said softly. "Now think from the crown of your head, gather that energy."

I felt like I was scraping cobwebs from the ceiling, all shining with silvery gold light.

"Now from here," he said, touching between my brows, where Indian women in *National Geographic* have red dots.

We moved from my "third eye" into my throat—"creativity and communication"—to my chest, where the color was light yellow, like a Magnolia Warbler. Then to my navel, and down into the purple petunias (it's what I thought!) of my kundalini.

"Draw all those colors together," Erik said, "into a huge ball of energy."

I felt like I was fishing for seaweed with a net, gathering all the different balls together. But it did feel like something moved down through my body.

"Now breathe, Elize," he said. "Feed that energy into your kundalini and watch it explode throughout you, shooting through the top of your head, out your fingertips and toes, everywhere, sending light."

Breathing deeply, I gathered my net of seaweed balls and tossed them into the garden, the purple garden.

"Feel it build," he said.

It seemed the flowers grew to the size of plates, of tires, filling me up with every breath and burning hotter, to blue, to white.

Rocked with sensation, awareness and white light, I bucked up on heels and head. Screaming, laughing, I stayed upside down, as the world reintroduced itself.

My head echoed.

Erik propped himself so that he was upside down too. "I think you got it," he said with a flash of incisor.

I laughed, so light, so clear headed. "You could make a pupil out of me," I said, still laughing, catching my breath. "That was incredible."

"Ah, Elize," he groaned, and we slid down into each other's arms, into the reality of skin and sweat and smell. I forced myself to move slowly over his body, the contrast of silky skin and crisp chest hair, the dozen small nicks and indentations that mark a body. We compared scars—bikes, boards of all kinds, trees, fights, friends, and yes! hockey—and kissed and fondled and groped and writhed.

❖

Later, outside on the beach, I asked him. "Is there a reason we're not having sex?"

"We aren't having sex?" he said.

"Okay, but we haven't consummated anything," I amended.

"We've known each other for a week," he said.

"According to you, that's only in this life."

"It's the one we're living," he said.

"Okay." I wasn't being impatient, just curious. Maybe it was also the difference between a twenty-something male and a thirty-something? Or, and this thought struck me as more truthful, it's the difference between sex and making love.

That's what we had been doing: making love. The objective to be together, to communicate on another level, the most personal, private level, instead of just a hit of adrenaline. Or an escape. I sat up.

"Y'okay?" he said from behind his dark glasses.

"I don't use drugs," I said.

"Okay."

"But I just realized I've been addicted to the adrenaline of sex for, well . . . since I discovered it."

"Have you ever not had an orgasm?" he asked.

"No," I said. "That's the whole point."

"Get in, get out, get on with your life?"

I fell over laughing, embarrassed because it was true. Not a great reflection on me. I flopped to his side. "I've never had to wait."

"Ah, I see."

"I mean, not for sex."

"Are you complaining?"

"No." I took a deep breath and moved his glasses so I could see into his eyes. "We're making love."

He stared back with navy-black eyes. "We're making love."

I lay back down, my hand over my head as I watched the herons fly by. A siege of herons. "It's my first time," I said.

He squeezed my hand, then kissed the palm of it. "You're a natural."

The words "I love you" wanted to spout from my mouth, but they seemed so trite, so overdone. I loved Dos Amigos ice cream. I loved late-summer sunsets. I loved when the wave sets were medium-fast, so you had time to breathe on your board in between great rides. I loved vanilla candles, and the chatter of green parakeets in the trees by my folks. I'd overused the word "love." I needed some other vocabulary.

Maybe that was a reason to learn French. So that "I love you" would be new, with new meaning, to me.

❖

Stars above, blanket around us, another delicious meal still melting off our taste buds. "Do you want to make love another way?" Erik asked nonchalantly.

"Sure," I said, wondering if costumes or vegetables would be involved. Neither appealed to me, but I'd be open. With Erik.

"Let me take you to the mountains."

"Just . . . us?" I glanced around the ksar. I didn't want to leave, even for Erik, even for the mountains.

"Us. And the bald ibis."

I sat up as ice ran down my spine, and stared at him.

"I talked to some Berbers, got directions." He smiled. "A possible pair. Outliers." He winked.

I stared.

"Roald has equipment, since we'd be camping. You camp, right?"

I nodded.

"Elize?"

I stared into his eyes, now concerned, a small frown between his brows.

"Were you," I said, my voice soft, "this good to me in our past life?"

"No," he said, his voice quiet, sad in the night. "I wasn't. But you were this good to me."

The Mountains

The taxi driver downshifted as we creaked up an incline steeper than some ski slopes. To my left, the unshouldered road fell away into overgrown shrubbery hundreds of feet below. We screamed around a slight downhill corner and I gasped as the rear fishtailed.

"He's done this before," Erik said, patting my hand in comfort. He smiled at me, and I thought, *Taxi, what taxi?* But when I looked out again at the culvert we were crossing, I saw the rusted carcass of a taxi.

Hopefully *not* one of Erik's signs.

Just in case, I wrote down my full name, complete with phone number for Mama. Just in case. I passed it to Erik.

"We won't need it," he said, tucking it into his pocket without a glance.

The taxi fishtailed again. We headed toward the ledge. I swallowed a scream as the taxi skidded to a stop, seconds before we plunged over the side. For a moment, no one breathed. Then the driver laughed and said something that sounded a lot like, "Exciting, no?"

Erik chuckled. "We have a flat," he said, getting out. I opened the passenger side door and looked down. Bad idea. Down was a thousand feet. The mental image of the taxi bouncing down the curves of the road we'd just climbed played on an endless loop in my head. I crawled out on Erik's side.

The taxi driver pulled out his jack, and offered Erik something from what looked like a ring.

"Fig?" Erik said, offering me the ring. They'd been dried and strung together like a flexible wreath. I took one and listened to the cheerful whistle of the driver as he jacked the car up. Erik had disappeared into some bushes on the other side of the road. I scanned the sky with my bins. A falcon or two and several types of lark dotted the hillside in the heat of the afternoon. Crested larks, native to Morocco, so well camouflaged that I thought rocks were moving at first.

"What do you call them?" Erik asked.

"Two larks?"

"A group of larks."

"An ascension." They fluttered away as we watched. The taxi driver finished changing the flat, offered the figs around again, and announced, "Is fixed."

We all climbed back in, and the road continued upward.

An hour later, the road continued downward.

We passed a sprawl of trees, squat and enormous. I jerked my head as we passed, staring, focusing, identifying and then processing it all again. No. Impossible. We passed another orchard, same vision. "Are those . . . goats? In the trees?"

Erik laughed and said something to the driver, who also laughed. "Goats love argan trees," Erik said. "One of the most important laws in this part of the country is that only *your* goat can eat from *your* argan tree during the season."

"We stop?" the driver said.

"Sure," Erik said.

Again we swerved onto the side of the road. Still no shoulder, but nowhere to plummet, either. I rolled my window down, not wanting to disturb this crazy sight.

Full-grown goats stood on the branches of the tree, eating away. "There's, what, eight goats in that tree?" I said, marveling at them, scattered across the limbs like overgrown Christmas ornaments. "What is argan?"

"It's a berry," Erik said. "The Berbers use it for everything. The base of the local economy."

"I had some argan honey," I said. "Delicious."

"Only place in the world argan growing," the driver said clearly. "Only place for? with?" He looked at Erik in the rearview mirror for confirmation. Erik gave a quick nod. "*For* argan," the taxi driver said.

We drove on, and up. And up some more. I looked down behind us, where the road snaked through the rough hillside at impossible angles. Birds flew, raptors and songbirds, but I couldn't get identifications.

"Not much farther," Erik said, then leaned over and kissed me.

"It's a couple-hour hike," Erik said, later. "Not much farther."

I watched the taxi's tail lights disappear around the curve, leaving us alone on the Moroccan high plains. The road had just . . . ended here. Our gear lay scattered around us, and above I heard the low glide of a raptor. I looked at Erik, seeing him through bins for just a moment. A stranger, with no visible means of support. Well-spoken, hot as hell, but . . . a stranger.

I was in a foreign mountain desert, at the end of the road, with a stranger.

I swallowed, somehow okay with that. There was nowhere else I'd rather be. I was living. Not waiting. Zephyr would be proud.

We both buckled on backpacks loaded with borrowed camping gear, sleeping bags, and provisions from Agadir's souk, the biggest city by Ksar Massa. I followed Erik up a goat path, climbing toward the descending sun.

Hours later, we made camp in a rocky outpost. Green polka dots sprinkled the valleys—argan trees.

While I gathered wood for a fire, Erik set up the tent. All around us, the sky turned Scarlet Tanager colors, siren orange and fire truck red, and I kept slowing down to watch. The sky wasn't just up, from here, it was also down. We were high, and it was going to be cold, but we had food and fire and warm bags. *And each other,* Crazy-Elize whispered.

I'd gotten the fire going, when I felt Erik's hands on my waist. "Do you want to sleep in the tent, or outside?" he asked.

His touch, in any form, made me dizzy. His hands burned through my clothes and I leaned back against him, suddenly aware that he was aroused. My pulse hiccupped and quickened to double-time.

"Because . . . " he said, turning me in his arms, his indigo eyes all but black in the dusk, "I want to see the stars reflected in your eyes—" He pressed against me, and I felt like I melted at his imprint. "—when I come into you."

He was everything I'd dreamed *and* he was Erik, an unknown quantity that delighted and amazed me in every way. We came together like puzzle pieces, and when I saw him smile as he finally released, I knew that this world we'd entered was entirely different than anything I'd known before.

Yeah, it was sex, and the human body can only do so much, but with him, we weren't restricted to just our bodies. He made me feel like "Nights in White Satin" sounded, like dimensions I'd only dreamed of were now within my grasp. Our minds and bodies and spirits made love.

When we finally unclenched, the cool temperature was a relief. I felt like a banked fire. Erik felt like a working stove.

"We forgot to eat," he said, his arm beneath my head. I made no attempt to move, and neither did he.

"No room service here."

"Candy bars?" he said, then retrieved a couple after I nodded. We ate, staring at the stars, our limbs draped together. "Do you know this place?" I asked him, hushed in the night.

"Yeah. Found it hiking," he said. "I walked across Morocco, all along the ridge of the mountains, from the desert up to the high Atlas and into the Rif along the sea."

My hand, of its own accord, rubbed his skin, still hot. He was so lean, with clearly defined muscles under a thin layer of skin. Skin that felt like feathers when you stroke them soothingly, with the grain. Soft, almost fragile, but with incredible contained strength.

I heard the rhythm of his breathing slow. My lover had fallen asleep, in the tradition of postcoital men.

I chuckled to myself. I'd always been the one to fall asleep, and here I was wide awake. I kissed his hand and slipped away for water. When I came back, I fitted myself to his body. I'd try to sleep with him, for just a few minutes.

Must be true love.

Whether I felt it because I'd been on a sexual tension high-wire since I'd met Erik, or because of the setting, I didn't know. I just knew I felt some magic circle, some mojo, lingered in a physical sense around Erik. He contained a time zone, an air current, an electricity, and I wanted to be around it, in it. I snuggled closer to him. He was hot, in so many ways. I stuck my legs out of the bag to regulate my temperature, and fell asleep.

Birdsong woke us. Perfect. Erik fixed breakfast, a big camper's breakfast with eggs and coffee and bread made in the ashes of the fire, while I stalked a Houbara Bustard. A big, rare bird, even here. This place was amazing! Then it flew away, slow and resigned, but flaunting its striking black and white wings.

"How did you sleep?" Erik asked me when I came back.

"Splendidly. And you?"

He grinned over his coffee cup. "Intermittently."

"I wasn't the one who wanted seconds, or ninths, or whatever, at three A.M.," I teased. But just the memory of his hungry kiss jarring me from sleep into instant, intense arousal, of his erection already like a rock as I fumbled a condom on him, made me wet. Again. The teasing faded from my expression as I allowed the rawness of what I was feeling to show. Coffee was forgotten as we clung together again, finding quick release, more intense than before.

Which was saying something.

❖

A while later, we packed up camp and set off and up. As crowded as Marrakesh had been, our walk was that solitary now. "What's that?" Erik said, pointing to the sky.

"Some kind of raptor," I said. "Maybe a Peregrine or a Lanner."

"How can you tell?"

"See the beak for tearing the prey? And the talons?" I said. "See how it spirals upward, like steam from a kettle? It rides the thermals." The raptor's flight took it right beside us. We were so high that we were almost at its level. "We need to be careful, in case its nest is around somewhere. In the olden days, when birders took eggs and killed birds in order to study them, it was common for the men to climb giant trees and fight off the parent birds in order to complete their collections. There's lots of stories about people, crazy oologists who are now famous, getting attacked or wounded by an enraged bird. Especially raptors."

"They killed birds?" he said. "I thought Audubon and his group were about preserving birds."

"It is now. But John James Audubon was an artist, first. He drew pictures of the birds in the wild, but he also collected their skins." I paused, catching my breath. "A lot of times the bird's name is based on some detail that you would literally have to have the bird in hand in order to see. That's because the original group of men—"

"All men?"

"Until about the turn of the century, yes. Until then, bird fanatics worked for museums that had enormous collections of taxidermied birds, their skins, their eggs. It was all about acquisition. Some collectors, rich men like Max Peet and James Fleming, had tens of thousands of skins and eggs. The University of Michigan still has one of the largest collections in their bird museum." One of Frankie's great advantages, I realized.

"So museums are where endangerment began?"

I shook my head, and he looked back at my silence. "No. Probably not. For as many birds as they were taking to study, with the exception of things like the Carolina Parakeet, there was an abundance in the wild. No, the true blame lies in fashion."

Erik stopped and turned to me. He looked pale around the eyes, but maybe he didn't sweat much, didn't turn red with exertion. "Fashion?"

I nodded. "Think about the time. Ladies' hats were these huge contraptions with birds and fruits and flowers and all kinds of stuff. Get a thousand women, each with three hats they wear for a few months, each hat requiring half a bird's feathers—"

"Fashion killed the birds?"

I sighed deeply. "It started the downward cycle. In the twentieth century, it's been about birds losing natural habitat." I paused again for breath. How high were we? The raptor made circles over the valley below. "Shorebirds have to compete with beachfront property."

"Can't they just be shorebirds *on* the beachfront property?"

"Sometimes," I said, "but a lot of birds need space in order to feed, or nest. You can't put them in subdivision style nests. They need territory. And if they lay their eggs on the beach, well, it's all over. The other big cause is pesticides."

"That one I understand," he said, slowing a little. "Chemicals aren't good for anyone. But you'd think they'd learn to not eat certain things, within a few generations."

"That is a point. Except that birds have been around for millions of years. In all that time, most everything has been edible. If not nutritious, then at least not harmful. You're talking about a few generations, but that's the wink of an owl's eye in contrast to how long they've been a species."

"So they're killing themselves eating?" Erik asked.

"It's more than just an instant choking death from poison," I said. "A lot of the danger comes from things like decreasing shell thickness. An egg is more vulnerable before it hatches, and the young are weaker when they are hatched, because breaking through the shell isn't the battle for life and death, the epic Darwinian struggle, that it's supposed to be."

We walked in silence for a while, our steps in sync. My heart wanted to burst, I was so happy.

At an estimated thousand meters up, we stopped for lunch. Sitting side by side, looking across the Anti-Atlas range over to the Atlas, hidden in clouds, was perfect. "What about the eggs?" he asked as we unwrapped our lunches.

"Outlawing DDT was a start."

"A good start," he said.

"But now it's development. Something as small as cutting a stand of trees to make room for a park bench could be hazardous, even deadly, to a group of migrants who feed there. It's a battle for space now."

"Everywhere," he said, eating a pita sandwich and watching me.

"The greed for acquisition has turned from skins into acres. We're forcing populations to shrink, which upsets the ecosystem. Very few birds come back from the edge like the bald ibis."

"So what are you doing? Obviously you're informed and passionate, but what are you doing?"

My sandwich lost some of its flavor. "I belong to all the organizations. I drink shade-grown coffee to preserve the rainforest. I don't eat lobster or mahi-mahi or other overfished species. I recycle, I vote, I write letters to my congressman." I exhaled deeply. "And I watch the National Seashore get drilled. I see parks plow down swathes of trees that migrants use." I set down my sandwich, sick.

I looked out over the plain. It probably looked the same a thousand, ten thousand years ago. "I spend a lot of time being very, very angry." One of the reasons I didn't want to go to the fundraising dinners, where golfers refused to give up their greens, where homeowners refused to plant friendly foliage, yet swore they loved the birds.

"But you work for a conservation place, right?"

Oh, Mr. Woodrow, we tried, didn't we? "I did," I said, listening, with surprise, to the words coming out of my mouth. "I used to." I felt a rush of relief: I wouldn't have to work with that community, a community I didn't respect and I didn't trust and I didn't even like, again.

"You don't anymore?" Erik said, watching me with blue eyes.

I held his gaze. So much for the e-mail asking for more vacation. "I don't. I just forgot to tell them that I don't."

In my mind I heard Zephyr cheer. *Finally! You've stopped waiting!*

The Darkness

Dinner was roasted rabbit on skewers. Erik's competence was so sexy. He could hunt *and* he could cook. We sat by the fire, sipping wine, while we played shesh besh. After that we made slow love, since I finally beat him in one of six games, and fell asleep in each other's arms.

Then the nightmare began.

I pushed him off me at one point in the night. Erik was so hot. How could that be normal? I drank some water and fell back asleep, but even in my dreams, I felt the heat radiating off his body. Something made me open my eyes and listen. Was it an animal? A human? I prodded the fire to life, and peered into the darkness.

Silence.

Not creepy, not like "something's coming" silence, just general silence. A few underbrush twitterings and scrapings. What had awoken me with such a feeling of dread?

Erik's breathing was . . . strange. Labored, almost. I reached out to shake him awake, and my hand was burning even before I touched him. His skin was scalding hot. "Erik," I said, shaking him, fanning my hands before touching him again. "Wake up, honey." The endearment came so easily, like I'd always been wanting, waiting, to use it. "Erik?"

He didn't wake.

"Erik," I said, my voice firmer now, my grip on his scorching body determined. "Wake up, c'mon now." I shook him hard, moving him, but he didn't wake; his eyelashes didn't even flutter. He had a fever. How much of one, I didn't know, but I'd guess well over a hundred.

How did he get a fever? Did he get bitten? Stung?

Quickly I ran through the steps I'd learned: A—his airway seemed clear. B—his breathing was labored. C—for circulation. I took his pulse. Okay, but not great. With a deep breath I moved to D—disability.

"Erik!" I shouted. "Wake up! Talk to me!" He tossed his head—thank God—muttering, frowning. But he didn't wake up, just continued to burn.

E—for exposure. I started my inspection in the dark. What had bitten him? Stung him? How could he have gone from fine to this sick, so fast?

I got some of the water for tomorrow's coffee, and bathed his brow with it. The water didn't exactly sizzle on his skin, but it vanished quickly.

Fever. An infection. From what? I looked for swelling, for the center of the heat, for broken skin. He whimpered when I touched him, like every point of contact brought pain. I turned on the flashlight and shone it on my pinched-face lover. He was not resting comfortably.

I sorted through my first aid kit, pausing on the EpiPen. But it didn't seem like he was having a reaction. Was he allergic to something we'd eaten?

I ransacked his bag. His passport showed a photo of a man with short, business-length hair, wearing a suit and tie. Erik Raven. A storytelling of ravens; so much nicer than the other collective noun, an unkindness of ravens. I tapped the passport on my knee, thinking, then put it away. His phone was dead.

Whatever was wrong, I knew the first hour after a trauma was sustained was the most important. A scorpion sting? I knew the deadliest of them rarely left marks, but Erik didn't seem to be in anaphylactic reaction or shock. Just . . . something was off. By a lot. I turned off the light, to save it.

Dawn was close. I bathed him again, covered him up though he pushed the blankets away, and watched. An African flu? He'd seemed so healthy, but maybe. I took my own temperature. We'd made love, protected, but if he had the flu, I should be getting it too. I felt fine. I counted to a hundred backwards; my brain seemed okay. Not hallucinatory.

Was this a withdrawal? Except, if he had a drug habit he hadn't been using for the past few days. We hadn't been out of each other's sight. I would have noticed if he'd suddenly had a different energy, or been impaired.

Wouldn't I?

I lay my head by his shoulder. "Tell me what's wrong with you," I whispered, placing my hand over his heart.

His thrashing and teeth chattering woke me, though he had to be a hundred plus degrees. The sun peeked over the horizon. I called him again, tried to shake him awake. Inch by inch I surveyed his body for redness or bumps or bruising or blood, any way some infection could have gotten inside him in the past twelve hours and wreaked such havoc.

I broke a generic aspirin in half, and tried to feed it to him. He didn't swallow it, but he drank water eagerly. *He needs fluids*, I thought, and refilled the cup again and again. It would help him flush it out of his system. A raptor flew in lazy circles above, watching us. I wrapped Erik back in his bag and watched the sun rise.

Full sun didn't wake him. I set about building an awning over him with parts of the tent. At least he wouldn't get sunburned, too. I went through his bag again, looking carefully at each item. He traveled light, even for a guy: a bar of soap, a washcloth, a toothbrush that looked like he cleaned grills with it, too, a plastic bottle of something that smelled like flowers, a worn razor, a length of string and a handkerchief. No aspirin, no stomach meds, no nothing. Made me glad I'd had a few things.

He'd said he didn't get sick. I glanced at his sallow complexion— jaundice? Or was the light from the awning distorted, making him look yellowed?

Fevers had a cycle during the day. The afternoon was the worst, and it would get worse before it broke. I needed to watch, to pay attention. All I had was water, no ice. I was going to need more than his washcloth. A shadow passed over us, and I looked up to see the raptor hanging not far above.

I turned my back on the falcon, its ever-vigilant eye on me.

I poured some water on the cloth, dabbing it at Erik's brow, like a Civil War heroine. Even without corsets and petticoats, I was approximately that useless. Should I go back down the mountain? Hail someone on the road?

My stomach growled, so I dove into some of the easier food we'd brought: cookies. But sugar never really satisfies, and when I realized I had eaten half the package, I closed them up. Erik seemed to be sleeping more calmly at this point. I took his pulse and resisted the urge to pull back his eyelid. If he was sleeping peacefully, I was sure that doing so would segue his dreams into something from *A Clockwork Orange.*

Humming with sugar, I got up, stretched, splashed some water on my face and changed my shirt. The sun felt good on my bare skin and I stood, topless, to feel it. Then I recalled I wasn't wearing sunscreen, and proceeded to slather it on. Erik slept. I shaded my eyes and looked up at the raptor kettling, rising higher and higher on the thermals until it disappeared from sight. Smaller Lanner, or larger Peregrine? I still couldn't decide.

According to my watch it was only 9:17 A.M. What the hell was I going to do with my day? I was terrible at being still, at being silent. In that eerie way he had, almost as if he could read my mind, Erik began to thrash around, muttering. I ran back to his side, and dabbed the cloth on his head, soothing him as best I could.

This was what I was going to do with my day.

He calmed after a few minutes, not having woken at all, but seeming a little bit cooler. I pushed the hair off his face, massaging his forehead, smoothing the lines of—was that pain?—off his brow. Pain from a fever?

He stilled and returned to whatever dark place he was resting. I kept touching him; he was all but unconscious, but I couldn't stop. I traced the lines of his brows, the bent angle of his nose. With one careful finger I touched the end of his lashes, those spikes that looked like they must be fake eyelashes.

Some girl—had it been my babysitter?—had worn them, and I'd spent the whole time just watching her eyes move, how those long fluttery things emphasized her expressions, her gestures. Then I'd gone and looked into the mirror, my own unexceptional face staring back at me, sandy lashes that weren't long or curly framing plain blue eyes, and realized I'd never be the flirtatious, glamorous girl.

I touched my lashes. They'd darkened with age, so they framed my eyes nicely, which was good, because I was in the Gulf too often to worry with mascara. Had I thought of that girl, that moment, in the past twenty years?

Your father's girlfriend. Wonder how she's feeling about now.

Abruptly I turned back to Erik, relieved that his skin seemed cooler.

His sleeping bag had seventeen seams sewn on it.

Any minute he'd wake up. This would be fine. I glanced up at the raptor. We'd be fine.

Dusk was falling when he opened his eyes. I couldn't be sure in the light, but his whites looked a little yellow. "Freezing," he said, following his statement up with a shiver. I piled my sleeping bag and towel on him, hoping it would help.

"Are you feeling better?" I asked.

"Liars," he muttered, his voice raw.

"Who's a liar?" I asked, wondering if he was hallucinating.

"They said, they said . . . I'd be fine."

"Who said? Said about what?" But he was already lost to me again, shivering, teeth chattering. I pulled the blankets up to his neck, put a hat on him, and counted the teeth in his bag's zipper.

Several times.

"Elize?" his voice was weak, but it startled me awake. The moonlight was almost as bright as day, casting the shadow of the awning on the ground. "I'm hungry."

"Thank God," I said, rustling in the bag for food. I'd finished the bag of cookies at dark, and felt hungry too. "First, tell me what is wrong with you. Can you take aspirin?"

"Allergic," he said. "Wouldn't do good. It's a strain of malaria."

I stopped feeding the fire and turned to look at him. "Malaria? You're kidding, right?" But I had this feeling he wasn't.

"Malaria."

"I thought you didn't get sick."

"Not diarrhea sick," he said.

"Thanks for that clarification," I said, angry. "Where's your medicine? What do I do?"

He sighed, and for a moment breathed so softly that I thought he'd fallen back into sleep. I finished building the fire and made up the couscous we'd brought, pouring sweetened milk over it and adding raisins. He needed strength, right? Besides, the recipe was in English, right on the side of the bag.

Fifteen *o*'s in the directions.

Erik was too weak to hold the spoon, so I leaned him against my bent legs and fed him. "Nothing to do."

"Why are your eyes yellow?" I said. "I thought maybe it was jaundice."

He shook his head, chewing slowly. "A symptom. They told me mine was a once-in-a-lifetime strain. Not *falciparum*. Other one. Said I'd be fine. This must be a remnant."

"Do you need quinine? Isn't malaria a chronic illness?" Unless you got the kind that killed you immediately. Horribly.

"Bastards," he muttered under his breath, but without venom. He took the spoon to eat the last bit of couscous by himself. Good sign. "I'll be fine. Just a fever."

"Why didn't you tell me? When did you get it? Where did you get it?"

"My job," he said, his voice weak.

"You work?"

His glance was appraising, I'd say amused, but I think he was too tired to be amused. "Did. Petrodollars."

The passport picture. The suit. "How long ago?"

He shrugged. "It was a sign to quit," he said.

"Getting malaria?"

His eyes closed for a moment. I wondered if he'd fallen asleep. *Malaria.* "Anopheles mosquito," I muttered. Just like in any biology, there were different species. If he had one species, or strain, but had been told another . . . I swallowed my fear.

His lashed fluttered and he opened his eyes again. "It used to kill," he said.

"Still does," I said, though I couldn't recall the statistics exactly. Was it one person every minute in Africa? Fifteen seconds? "What can I do for you?" I said.

"My strain. I'll be 'kay. Sorry," he said, then fell asleep. I watched him, ran my fingers through his sticky hair. He seemed to be sleeping peacefully. Almost a normal temperature.

Malaria. Somehow the spleen would swell, sometimes rupture, which caused death. I ran my hands under the blankets and over Erik's belly and waist, feeling for any telltale bulge. Instead I felt skin valleys and bone ridges and skin that was heating up again. Involuntarily, he began to shiver and twitch.

"I was the silver-tongued devil who went into the community and pointed out the benefits of letting my company drill."

I was disoriented. It took me a second to realize I'd fallen asleep and Erik was talking. His voice was weak. Then I heard what he'd said.

"Malaria attacked! 'bout the time I was realizing what a bastard I was, and Thomas and Mary kept me for two weeks, despite my plans to plunder, safe in the village. Safe . . . fevered. I was fevered. Malaria attacked! and it wasn't my body anymore. Sharing it with Marylaria."

His eyes were closed. And his voice was singsongy, almost drunk. Delirious? Then I heard what he'd said: Two weeks. He'd been sick for two weeks? I glanced at the bag of couscous I'd used so liberally. He'd said he'd be fine. I'd thought this "spell" would be like the flu, that we'd be walking out of here in two or three days, max.

I had seven pieces of wood left for the fire. Erik had surrounded the pit with thirty-two rocks.

"I walked away from Marylaria, from Thomas and the village, walked away, one step two step, red step blue step." He frowned. "Doc said I was fine. Lying bastards! Just a little bed rest, then sign the papers and keep walking."

I kissed his brow. Two weeks?

Erik opened his eyes, but I couldn't tell how awake he was. His lashes patterned his cheeks as he glanced around. "That feels good," he whispered, almost sounding normal.

I'd been unconsciously rubbing his forehead, trying to wipe away the frown lines, the tightness around his jaw and brows that came from being so uncomfortable. "I know I'm sick, because for the first time, the thought of you doesn't make me . . . " Erik grinned, a glimmer of his usual self within the wan body.

I kissed his brow again, lingering next to his skin. "First time, hmm?"

"It was your perfume, originally," he said. "After smelling it all night I was rather embarrassed to wake up in a . . . state . . . on the train. I had to get out of there, splash a lot of cold water on my face."

"I don't wear perfume."

"I know that now, but the combination of stuff you do wear smelled like perfume to me. Tropical islands. Hammocks, with dancing girls."

"I guess Coppertone and Burt's Bees works for you," I said as I smoothed his hair back. His forehead was cool now, and he seemed lucid. "What should I do to help you?"

"I'll be fine," he said with a sigh. "Just need some rest. We'll have tomorrow to get out of here. It might be slow going, but we'll make it. All downhill from here."

Yeah, but three healthy days' worth of downhill. "So, you were a prospector for petroleum?"

"Geologist," he said, his words slurred. "Using my powers for evil."

"Are you still?"

"No, because if malaria wasn't punishment from God—and the way it feels, hell couldn't be much worse—then it was a Sign. A warning not to waste my life."

He said "sign" like it had a capital *S*. "Do you follow signs?" I asked.

"Have since then. Universe doesn't want people to screw up. Shows you what to do for the best." He was falling back into that stupor, that singsongyness. I didn't want him to, I didn't want to be alone out here again tonight.

"So you, what, sell drugs?"

"Drugs?" His eyes opened, didn't snap, but they were definitely more reactive.

"Kif, hash, whatever."

"You think that's what I do?" He almost sounded outraged. And amused.

"How else do you explain those plastic bags you handed to every other man we met in the souk?"

He closed his eyes. "That's why you were 'spicious, sssh, nothing about, Elize." He looked into my face. "You thought I was stupid enough to be a non-Moroccan selling kif?"

Well . . . yeah.

"I work with a vineyard," he said. "Grapes. Not of wrath. Samples for customers."

"In bags?" I challenged. Those weren't bottles he was passing around.

"Raisins," he said, glancing toward his backpack, "raisins for riads and restaurants that don't serve wine 'cause they're good Muslims." He smiled and opened his eyes, and for a moment the magic worked: time stopped, concerns faded, and it was a perfect world with just us. "We sell wine to the other kind of Muslim, too," he said. "But the raisins are an experiment. Trying to make the land profitable."

"Did you study this in school?" I asked.

"Geology undergrad. Thesis on volcanic regional viticulture. Can make wine, too, but I need more practice." His words were getting slushy again; I could feel his body temperature rising.

"Why didn't you tell me this before?" I said.

He shuddered, and his eyes snapped open. "It's starting again, Elize," he said. "I can feel it coming, my corpuscles being torn open so this parasite can reproduce." He was shaking. "I didn't tell you because I didn't want to make it safe for you. If you wanted me, it was going to have to be kinetic. Immediate." He clenched his teeth together. "Visceral. No suitability decisions, just desire and knowing we were right. That I was right for you."

"It was a test, not telling me about yourself?" I said.

But he was gone again, shivering and shaking. I piled on the blankets and mopped his face and then . . . sat. For agonizing hours, where the only sounds other than the jackals, or coyotes or whatever wild dogs Morocco had, howled at the moon. And Erik suffered before my eyes, with nothing I could do.

He had twenty-two freckles on his face.

❖

"Talk to me," he said when he woke up again, after he'd crawled over to relieve himself, after I'd poured more water down his throat. "Why did you want me to stay a stranger? I still don't know what caused your change of heart, what made you write to me." He grinned, but it was faded, and his face looked tighter, smaller, shrunken. "Who is Elize?"

"If this is the topic, then I need a drink," I said, crossing to the bottle of liqueur we'd brought. "I don't suppose it would help you?"

"I'm okay right now. I want to hear about you."

I poured a shot, downed it, and poured another. The stars danced above us, a slow rotation of constellations. Night seemed like it would last forever. I'd lost all sense of time with my catnapping while Erik rested. Or tossed and turned, rather.

Black licorice liqueur clung to my tongue, coated my teeth. "It's hard for me to talk," I said, taking the second shot and pouring a third.

"Yeah." Erik watched me from his pallet, his gaze focused, his words crisp, though his voice was tired.

I licked my lips. "Growing up, feelings, voiced feelings, were viewed as . . . unnecessary. Conversation was about tangible things, physical things, like what time the auction was tomorrow and what to get at the store, and how long until the green beans would be ready to pick."

"You grew up in an agricultural environment?" he said.

A flash of Chicago's "L" train moving through the city; but the vision was replaced by fields. "Yeah," I said. "Cows and plants." Though Pop was a pharmacist.

Erik was silent. Maybe asleep, but the licorice had melted into my body and I felt the tension leaving my neck, my shoulders. I sipped the next shot. "So I just don't talk."

"You'd rather do," he said, quiet.

My third shot still in hand, I walked back and sat beside him, holding his hand beneath the blanket. I felt his pulse as it moved through his fingers, felt the calluses of his palm, the edge of his fingernails, the shapes of the silver rings that covered every digit. "Life's a to-do list. Too much to do, and too little time in which to do it."

"He who dies with the most toys wins," Erik said.

"No, he who dies with the longest list wins," I said, suddenly aware of how similar that was to the Audubon Society's Life List concept. A practice I didn't strictly adhere to, though it matched my personal beliefs exactly.

Except I hated following the crowd. Even if we were all watching the same birds.

"Ah, Elize," he said, lacing his fingers with my own. His voice was sad, but he was almost smiling. "You are so caught."

"What's that mean?"

"Trapped in the world of your rules. You didn't pick them, and you're angry about them, but you haven't learned to make your own."

"At least I have rules," I said, but I reminded myself of the bossy kid on the playground, all bluster and no substance. Or worse, Lettice.

"Happy with 'em?"

I looked down at the inky shot in my cup. "Not happy at all." I felt embarrassed to admit something to him that I'd never even told myself, but I felt strangely disconnected from the emotion of it. Or was I just tipsy?

Erik's eyes closed.

"Are you going to be all right?" I said, worried again. "Do we need to airlift you out of here?"

"Ha," he said. "It just hurts."

"You sure you don't want a shot?" I asked, the only painkiller I could think of. He had to get healthy enough to walk out of the mountains. I couldn't carry him, even downhill.

"Please," he croaked.

Moments after I fed him my remaining liqueur, Erik fell asleep. His temperature seemed almost normal. I tucked in his blankets, banked the fire, ate the rest of the couscous, and fell asleep beside him.

My dreams were filled with Frankie and Zephyr standing as a barricade against a barrage of *o*'s and *i*'s.

❖

Dawn.

Erik was on fire, writhing and moaning, kicking off the blankets, pulling at his clothes. Instantly awake, I stripped him down and bathed him with cool water.

I poured half a liter of water down his throat, dribble by dribble until he realized what it was and guzzled heartily. *Flush the toxins faster. Get him healthy faster, and us out of here. How many days?* I hadn't kept track.

I hadn't kept track of a lot of things, because in the bags, where the two more bottles of water that I thought we had . . . was half a bottle.

I sat down, suddenly scared. We'd drunk the rest on the way up, since it had been a particularly warm day and Erik said we'd refill at the well. I hadn't seen a well.

He needed water. I was going to need water. I ran my fingers through my ponytail, tying it back again, changed my shirt, gathered my gear and covered Erik lightly.

We didn't, as far as I could find, have a map. I'd climb the hill for a better perspective on our position, see if I could spot the well he'd mentioned. How could we have wound up in this mountainous desert without a map? Had I completely lost my brain when I met Erik? Apparently so, because I was out here alone with him, no viable phone, no transport, and no known way out.

"You kidnapped me," I said to Erik's dozing form. "Actually, I kidnapped myself." I groaned. No one knew I was here. Everyone would think that I had been kidnapped. "I don't even know what my kidnapping talents are. Where did Zephyr come up with that stuff? Some movie she watched, about Morocco." I stared at Erik; he definitely looked hollowed out. Sallow. Yellow. "Why did I make myself powerless in this situation? Until you wake up, I don't even know where we are."

I cursed my own stupidity. *Just couldn't wait to have him all to yourself, to dazzle him by finding the Waldrapp ibis and writing, somehow, in a matter of days, a brilliant article that, what . . . allowed you a place to stay and work in Morocco?* I hiked up, out, continuing my expert self-flagellation. *You think you could live here, a place where you speak none of the languages? Or did you just want to appear brilliant to him, so that when he eventually walked away at least you would be a hard act to follow?*

What had possessed me? I continued climbing, my feet making dust clouds with every step. From higher ground, I'd be able to see something. We were in the middle of a populated country, after all.

I ducked as something flew at me. With crashing awareness I realized I was approaching the raptor's nest, and it wasn't too happy. The raptor—a peregrine—shrieked, and I realized I must be uncomfortably close, though the nest shouldn't have residents this late in the year.

"I just want to see if there's a well, or a village," I shouted to the bird. It waited above me, still screaming at my invasion. "I'm not hurting anything!" I shouted. "Leave me alone!"

But the bird wouldn't. I knew that one encounter with those talons, and I would never be the same. Not only would they slice through my exposed skin like the proverbial knife through butter, they were also dirty. Those filthy talons could fill me with a dozen or more illnesses, all of them dangerous and disgusting. Arms protecting my head, I walked around the curve, hoping the bird would let me be.

It screamed around the corner, and I dropped to the ground. That was the male, come to defend. Defend what? It was autumn. No eggs. No fledglings. In a half-crouch I jogged around to the other side of the hilltop, watching for an attack. Nothing flew at me, though I heard the sound of wind through wings, above.

From my position, I looked down the hillside, my bins moving from one dried-out streambed to another, from one lump of rocks to the next. Nothing on this side, no inhabited villages, no wells. Creeping like an oology freak, I sneaked around the other side, catching a glimpse of a greenish valley before I was dive-bombed again.

I jumped over the edge, judging the damage at being caught in the bushes on the lower trail the lesser of the evils, and landed hard, indeed, but safe, as the bird wheeled back into the sky. In the near distance I heard something falling over the side. Not until the glass shattered a moment later did I realize what I'd lost.

"My bins. Dammit!"

The bird sailed lazily in the sky. *Fraud. Pretending to care for a family, even though everyone knew it wasn't true, that he'd never cared before. He'd just left them—you—*

"Oh, God," I gulped, rubbing at my face, where dust and moisture had made mud. "Always watching!" I shouted to the bird, to that eye, that false tear mark. "Always pretending to care, but not enough to be inconvenienced, not enough to change, not enough to grow up!" I watched the raptor calmly circling and felt frustration well from the bottom of my feet.

"Grades weren't enough!" I shouted. "Just made you think I was siding with Pop! But I couldn't be rebellious like you, I couldn't . . . " I buried my face in my hands.

My father. My beautiful, young, hopelessly hip father, offering me a joint when I was just ten. The girl with the false lashes had been his girlfriend, not my babysitter, and she was one of his former students. Five, maybe six years older than me? But doe-eyed and adoring.

I'd responded with my grandfather's tone, disapproving on instinct.

"They've made you into one of them, the Frozen Chosen, honey-bunch," my father had said. "You need to get out of here, out of this no-name town and into somewhere real, exciting!"

"She should come with us to Chicago," the girlfriend—Miranda?—said.

I should have known he was stoned. All I had heard was that my father finally wanted me! Finally wanted me to be part of his glamorous lifestyle, full of cities and women in false-eyelashes, of important thinkers and—

I was crumpled in the shrubs, staring at the deep blue sky, bluer than the ocean, the color of the blue at Ksar Massa. An intense blue I'd never seen before Morocco, but realized I would never forget. Something crawled on me, multiple legs; an insect. I closed my eyes and felt the tears.

The bus had taken me to Dallas, where I'd caught another bus to Chicago.

I'd waited at the main station in Chicago for almost twenty-four hours. I called the number my father had given me. Eventually, I took a cab to the door. No one was around, so I'd sneaked into the apartment to wait. No recollection of how.

Inside, there was no sign of a little girl. None of the pictures the little girl had mailed, in the hopes that her famous artist daddy would send a note, or make a call, saying that he liked them. That he saw himself in her. That she belonged with him.

Pop had always shook his head at my art. Not Audubon, for certain. Mama was my term for grandmother, because I'd never known my mother. My father had returned from Canada one day, carrying a one-year-old, a child of sin, with no means to support her. Mama made cookies and attended the Lutheran Ladies' Guild meeting, and that was her version of love.

I watched the falcon wheeling in the sky.

Fischer, of one-name-only fame, just like Cher or Madonna, had eventually sent me a birthday present when I was thirteen. One for a girl aged two years younger. He never apologized, never acknowledged, probably never knew why I went from being his most devoted fan to shuddering when I saw his name. I shouted at the sky, at the impervious peregrine, who'd always reminded me of Fischer, always seemed to be the flashiest, most audience-pleasing of the raptors. My father, darling of everyone everywhere.

Except me.

I ran up the hill, jumping over the smaller bushes, skirting the holes in the earth. The falcon dropped like a rock, defending his territory. Keeping me out. Dirt clods flew from my hands, rocks, anything and everything I could throw. The bird dodged most of my missiles, fluttering its wings, puffing itself out. Staring.

"You don't intimidate me!" I shouted. "I don't care if I'm not cool enough to be your daughter!" I felt the weight of the rock in my hand. Some hidden voice cried *No!* in my brain. One fluttering wing cracked. The falcon squawked surprise. But I didn't hear it, didn't see it, just kept throwing rocks, crying. Then I realized my target wasn't avoiding me anymore.

I'd killed a bird.

I stared at the dust settling around the flight feathers, the moustachial stripe. I took a step forward, and the bird fluttered, but didn't move away. I saw blood on its false tear now, and tasted my own bile. I took another step and heard my groan in the terrible quiet of the day. The rock hadn't just broken its wing, it had pinned the bird in place, allowing all the other rocks—I looked at the handfuls of stones I'd thrown—to batter it. Its feathers were bloody and dirt stained. More than one of the rocks had drawn blood. Was it my imagination, or did its only eye look at me with wise sadness: *That which you hate you are doomed to emulate.*

My hand over my mouth, I backed away from the scene of my crime.

I killed a bird. Not for science, or research, or any of the other reasons that ornithologists will take birds in the field . . . but because . . .

I turned and ran.

My breath filled my ears, leaving no room for counting, no way of calming myself as I watched the ground beneath me. Trail running: never putting my whole foot down, never trusting my weight to any one step.

Dirt kicked up behind me, but I kept on, bursting onto the plateau of our campsite, out of breath and streaming with sweat.

I'd killed a bird. Killed it out of revenge, out of anger, out of madness. I bit my fist, grateful for the pain in my hand, which seemed to ease the wound in my heart, my mind. I'd killed a bird out of fury.

I'd murdered.

Erik didn't budge at my approach, but I could see he was shivering again. I piled the blankets on top of him. My head ached, from guilt, from shame. It seemed much hotter than yesterday. I retreated to the shade and fanned myself cool.

Heat would speed the decomposition process.

And the mate would arrive to find the corpse. Did birds grieve? Parrots did, notoriously. And geese. Did falcons? Did I just ruin the lives of two birds?

My hands were filthy, blood and dirt caking inside my nails like Lady Macbeth. I placed my head on Erik's chest, listening to the beat of his heart. He needed water. Had he gone to the bathroom yet? While I was in my rampage, had he needed me? Tears choked me again, but I didn't have time. Erik was sick. *Still* sick.

Water had to be my first priority.

What temperature did your brain start to fry at? I soaked the cloth and left it on his head. As I scarfed down the second half of the second bag of cookies, I gathered all our bottles. My note in the sand said: "Back soon." With one worried last glance, I set off, watching the crested larks, the redstarts, wondering if they could sense I was, in fact, a dangerous predator.

I counted my steps away and down from the camp.

I would never be the same.

I'd killed that which I'd spent my whole life researching and protecting.

Finally, I threw up.

The Descent

I hate the smell of vomit. Most people do, but I was that little kid who got sick just smelling someone else's sick. I was the first one the teacher ran for with the trashcan. Pop used to tease me, but apparently being sick was allowed in a girl, because the teasing was kindhearted, at least. Now I had the smell on my shirt, in my hair. My stomach still churned. I *had* to find water.

I watched the birds. Eventually, they would lead me there. It was late, almost five o'clock; how long had I spent railing at the falcon?

How long had it taken me to murder a bird?

No, I couldn't think like that. I had to see to Erik, to take care of him. Later—like for the rest of my life—I would have time to recall, reflect on the horror of what I'd done. The sun was moving toward the horizon, and I picked up my pace, pausing every few minutes to listen for bird calls. I tried to recall the method of collecting water at night: something about a tarp, a pail. The details just weren't there.

My specialty was waterbirds. Being without a water source wasn't something I thought I'd ever encounter.

At long last I found the patch of dirt the birds were flocking to, a low, muddy puddle. Just enough to scoop into the bottle, and dab at my shirt and my hair. And wash my Lady Macbeth hands. I'd ask Erik next time he woke; maybe he knew how to gather dew. It was our only shot, unless I stumbled across a faucet on the walk back.

Darkness was falling fast, and I concentrated on my steps, glancing up in time to see some movement across the last streaks of orange.

Necks outstretched. Flying in a row, three of them.

Ibis.

I went to lift my bins, but they were gone. Still, I knew that flying motion, knew it in my dreams and knew it on a daily basis. Ibis were here, but it was arid. Dry. I swallowed. All other ibis roost in trees; only the Waldrapp picks rocks and ledges.

I stood for a moment, waiting, knowing that night had come and they weren't going to fly back across the fading sky. But I waited anyway. The breeze was cool, lifting the clumps of my wet hair. I stank, and I couldn't bear to even look at myself, but the wind soothed me.

My eyes were tired. I felt my forehead stretched tight across my brow. My teeth ached and my shoulders tingled. What had I done?

When Cassiopeia, gleamed above, it dawned on me that I was going to be walking back in the dark. I picked my way carefully, stumbling into the camp.

"You're up!" I said.

Erik was dressed, sitting on top of his sleeping bag. "I was getting ready to go in search for you," he said. "It's almost midnight!"

"So much for Mister Zen," I snapped, marching over and handing him the water I'd managed to procure. "It's muddy," I said, as he held the bottle up to the firelight, "but it's liquid, at least."

"This looks like ditch water. Probably infected with Schistasoma parasites. You didn't get it on you, did you?" he asked. "Why didn't you just go to the well?"

I couldn't look at him, though I felt his gaze on me. "If I knew where a well was! This ditchwater took me hours to find!"

"The well on the other side," he said, but when his arm dropped after its half-gesture beyond our camp, I realized he was still sick. Weak.

I sank to my knees behind him. "I didn't know," I said, reaching out to touch him, aware that he might just pull away from me.

He leaned his head into my hand. "I'm sorry about this, Elize," he murmured. "I can barely think. Of course you don't know. It's just above the village . . . " His voice trailed off, and he sagged toward me. His temperature seemed normal, but he felt fragile in my arms, bones jutting up through his skin. I held him, caressing his spine with my fingertips, trying to soothe him.

"That feels nice," he murmured.

"Have you used the lavatory?"

"Yeah. I'm dehydrated."

"Then drink the ditchwater, it's better than nothing, and I'll go get some from the well," I said.

"The ditchwater is worse than anything. And it's too late," he said. "I'll drink the Coke, or Pepsi, or whatever we got."

"Orangina," I said.

"I'll drink that. The sugar should help me, too."

"Are you hungry?" I asked.

"No, but I should eat."

I brought the backpack to him, and he opened a tin of sardines and some crackers after swigging the Orangina. The fire was dying, and I was too tired to care. Erik was sitting out in his shirtsleeves and I hadn't cooled down from the day yet.

"I'm glad you're awake," I said, indicating the sardines. "I wouldn't have known what they were."

"From 'Saouira," he said, pointing to the Arabic writing on the can. "'S beautiful there."

"I think that's where the Eleonora's falcon is," I said, then froze, seized with nausea.

"Elize," he said, leaning forward. "Are you all right?"

"Oh fuck," I said. "Oh fuck fuckety fuck." I was on my hands and knees, one hand around my waist, staring at the ground, but seeing the afternoon. *It hadn't been a peregrine I'd killed.* "Oh fuck!"

"Elize?" Erik bent over me. "Elize?"

I started to laugh. Tears poured down my face, but I was laughing, howling. I sat back on my haunches, hearing the tinniness of my laughter, wiping the sandy tears across my face. "This is good," I said. "This is just great. I've gone and done it, fucked up royally, this time. Ah, hell . . . " I wiped my face and stared at the ashes where the fire used to be.

"What's wrong?"

"I killed an Eleonora's falcon today," I said. "Murdered it."

Erik was silent.

"It's ironic, when you look at it. Ornithologist. Just recently do I eat meat. I look down on those scientists who think the only way to discern one species from the next is to kill it and study the corpse." I wiped the tears away.

"Ask anyone and they'll say I'm in control. I'm the rock. I decide and I act and I don't let emotion cloud my vision." I choked back a sob. "I'm a scientist. I observe, and I don't do that if it's going to upset the natural balance. I believe that special birds should have special spaces, parks or whatever, be protected, whether the unwashed masses can view them or not. The birds' survival is the issue, not whether bird watching becomes the next theme park." My breath hitched.

"I'm a fucking liar!" I couldn't fight the tears anymore; they boiled up, choking me, fighting through the words in my mouth. "A hypocrite! A fraud!" I bent my head and felt it pour out of me, snot and tears and anger and sorrow and disillusionment.

"I was so angry today that I stoned a bird. Stoned it, like some Old Testament prophet. And not just any bird," I said, wiping my nose with the back of my hand. "No, no, a rare, special bird. Exotic. Protected."

I waited for Erik to withdraw in horror, to scream at me, but when I glanced at him I wasn't sure he was awake. He was reclined on one elbow, his eyes closed. But he opened them, alert.

"I killed an Eleonora's falcon," I said. "I'm a sociopath."

His gaze moved over my arms. "That's where those marks are from, then?"

I looked down at and saw blood-crusted gouges crisscrossing my forearms and the back of my hands. I stared, turning my arms this way and that. My mouth opened, but I didn't speak.

I hadn't seen them before. I . . . I hadn't known I'd been cut, caught. But now I saw there was blood all over my clothes, that what I'd thought to be water was blood. Dried blood.

"Do you have some antibiotic cream?" he said. "They might get infected. Did you wash them in the ditchwater?"

I sat down on the ground with a thud, still looking at my arms. "I don't know where these came from," I said, my voice shaking. "I don't know what happened." I cleared my throat. "I mean, I thought I knew what happened, but maybe not?" As I heard the question in my voice, I looked over at him.

"Killed a bird in self defense?" he said.

"I killed it in a rage. I thought it was my father."

"Ooh, boy."

"What do you mean?" Then, I felt a grin. "Yeah, I guess it does sound like a line from a soap opera."

Erik nodded. "More like a Freudian analysis. But I thought your parents were salt of the earth types. You've never seemed angry before when you mentioned them."

I almost smarted off, asking if he'd paid that much attention to what I'd said. Then I realized he probably had. "I wasn't being totally honest," I said. Now that I saw the cuts, they hurt.

Erik's shadow moved in front of the fire. My antibiotic cream fell into my lap. He dropped beside me, and I saw the sheen of sweat on his brow. Sweat was good, right? It indicated a break in fever? With gentle hands, he rubbed the cream on my arms. "Sins of omission?" he said.

"You sound like my Mama, which is what I call my grandmother." I swallowed. "I never knew my mother. Not even her name."

"That can't be easy."

I shrugged. "I was so tied up in knots over my father, it didn't much occur to me, I guess. Mama and Pop raised me. My father dumped me on their doorstep and visited once every five or so years." I chuckled, but felt the sting of tears in my throat. "We aren't what you'd call close." I glanced away, looking across the plateau, toward the valley. That should be past tense. I swallowed. "It wouldn't have been so bad, except he always hinted that he wanted me with him, that he was lonely without me, that everything he was doing was so I could join him. So I waited and waited and hoped . . . "

My voice trailed off as I recalled the year I lived out of a suitcase, so sure that he would call in the next ten minutes and need me to join him in Chicago, or New York, or whatever exotic port of call he was in.

"What made the love turn to anger?" Erik asked, drawing me back. He'd finished putting the cream on, but now I felt strips of fire on my forearms. I blew on them like a little kid, trying to make the sting go away.

"I realized he'd lied. That he liked the idea of me, or the image of himself as a father, more than the reality. I started to refuse his calls, ignore his invitations." I pressed my lips together. "I was going to be so great, such a cool kid, that he'd come begging for me to go home with him."

A beat of silence.

"However . . . " I said.

"That didn't happen?" Erik said.

I shook my head. "I didn't invite him to my high school graduation, or tell him where I was going to college. Pop had just been diagnosed with Alzheimer's, and my dad hadn't come home for that." I looked into Erik's dark eyes. "I finished with him, then. Realized he was a selfish boy who'd gotten lucky and won fame and fortune, but was nothing more than . . . a user. People served as props to him. My father, he . . . " I felt it again, that coppery taste in the back of my throat, the taste of fury, of anger. My body shook.

"Admit what you feel," Erik said, stroking the inside of my palm. "Just get it out."

"If I get it out, I'll never get it back in," I said, spitting the words. "If I admit what a shit he was, how inhumane, how self-centered, how repugnantly self-absorbed, then I accept that I'm part of him. I'm that shit, that—"

"No," Erik said. "If you spew the poison, you'll be free of it. A festering wound doesn't want the gunk back, remember? And as for what you might be part of, Elize . . . " He turned my face to his. I looked into his eyes. "Your father might have something to do with the beautiful blue of your eyes, or the way you simmer with energy, or maybe even why you can remember a thousand different details exactly. That might all be hereditary. But the rest of it, the traits you hate, or are scared of, those are formed through personal choice. Choose not to be a shit, and you won't be."

"You make it sound so easy," I groused.

"Elize, wouldn't it be easier than what you've done so far?"

His words stopped me cold.

"I killed a bird," I said, suddenly sobbing. "I love them, I've built my life around them, but I killed one because of this. Oh, God, I'm a monster!" Erik folded me into his arms, patting my head, swaying back and forth. I'd seen movies with mothers holding daughters this way, but Mama never had. My sobs grew harder now, so consuming that I didn't know why I was crying, I just was. I'd gasp for breath, have a moment of calm, and it would break over me again, waves of a storm raging across me.

"I felt like the falcon was watching me in the same judgmental way I'd always felt my father was, until I realized my father didn't even know how old I was. Then the, the falcon acted like it had a chick in its nest, angry and territorial, and I thought—" Another sob shook me. "I thought of how my father had made me think he loved me, wanted me. He always told me he was making a room for me, full of my favorite things. He told me he'd looked at schools for me, that we'd pick one together. That we'd go to the park and the zoo—

"But it was just a façade, so I would like him! He'd tell me anything to make me happy."

"What did you want, Elize?" Erik murmured.

"I just wanted my Daddy! I just wanted someone of my own! Someone who wanted just me!" I sobbed again. "I can't believe I said that, I—I—" I tried to pull away, horrified at my confession, embarrassed that anyone should know.

Erik held me tighter and rocked me until I felt the stiffness melt from my bones and I allowed myself to meld with him, hearts beating together, swaying to and fro in the coldness of the night air.

I swallowed, empty as an overturned nest in August. "Have you ever had your own person?"

Erik shook his head. "Just myself."

Silence was absolute; even nature was quiet.

"I don't even have myself," I whispered, overwhelmed. I was a no one who belonged to nothing and nowhere. Trembling seized me and Erik held me tighter, making calming noises. I clung to him while what felt like close-captioned fireworks exploded behind my eyes. Who was I? Where was I going? Why? "What's wrong with me?" I whimpered, my nose clogged, my throat sore.

"Nothing's wrong. Sometimes it just takes tears to make everything right," he said. "You gotta mourn so you can get free. You're wounded, you need to learn how to deal with your rage, but apparently your aim is perfect." He chuckled. "And shorts were made with you in mind."

I blushed into his neck, enjoying the scent of his skin, the rub of stubble against my cheek, the heat of his hands on my back. Hot, that heat. I pulled away and felt Erik's forehead. "Therapy session over," I said, suddenly calm and clear. "Your fever is back."

Erik shook his head. "Fuck," he said. "We should have been done with it. Now we're in trouble."

As Erik's mind began to wander in his fever, I extracted the directions to the well. I slid more Orangina down his throat. My own was parched because he'd explained schistosomiasis. After that, with visions of blindness and my intestines crawling with worms, I didn't dare drink the ditchwater. I set off for the well. A Berber well, Erik said, before breaking into another language.

To hear unknown words coming out of someone's mouth when they were ill and realize they know that language fluently, almost like a first tongue, was astonishing to me. He had depths.

I shuddered when I thought of my own depths, how far I'd plummeted. I resorted to counting the rocks as I walked, keeping track of how close, how far, I was.

As Erik had said, the well, a half-covered hole, sat in the center of a plateau just a few minutes below us. Somewhere in the dark, even lower, was a village. He'd had a plan before all this happened, I realized with wonder. Another way to make love to me, my mind and my spirit. I filled the bottles, as many as I could carry. I'd come back tomorrow for more.

❖

I sat at his side, dozing, waiting for him to wake for another application of fluids.

The falcon had scratched me twice on both arms: sixteen strips of shredded skin. I had no recollection of it whatsoever. A total blackout? I couldn't think about it.

"So you're accusing me of kidnapping?" His voice was raspy, but coherent and I grinned in response as I handed him a bottle of cool well water. Night again. How many nights had we been here?

"Didn't you?" I said.

"You were pretty willing. In fact, as soon as Roald mentioned he knew a taxi driver on his way to Tafraout who could drop us in the general region, you couldn't wait to get out of the ksar. Lady Impatience. How did I become your kidnapper?"

God, it was good to hear Erik laughing, teasing. Getting better? "It's a long story," I said.

"Oh, well, I have a dinner party tonight, then I was going to go to the discos, so I guess—"

I was laughing, and it sounded healthy in the crisp dusk. "Okay, okay. It is long, though, and you haven't had much of a tolerance recently. Are you better?"

"Yes. But if it means I have to pour water down my pants to stay awake, I will."

"You are definitely feeling better, then."

"Not well enough," he said, "or water wouldn't be what I'd want down my pants." He winked, and I felt a flurry of nerve endings switch from fear to flutter.

I was so relieved. He looked like himself, he sounded almost normal. I heaved a great sigh. We were through this. "Okay. I work—worked—with two other women."

"You three work for a guy named Charlie?"

I grinned. "One guy does call us 'Wilkerson's Angels.' He owns the local Mexican restaurant."

"Mexican food. It's been a long time since I thought of Mexican food."

Not so long for me, but the sudden image of ceviche and fish tacos and fajitas made my mouth water. "It's not important to the story," I said.

"Oh, well, forget that."

"So, Zephyr, girl number one, is my . . . assistant. She's, um . . . creative."

"You say that like you're not sure of it, or it's a bad thing."

"Neither, it's just that she's creative with life. Looks at things in ways I wouldn't." Though maybe Erik would?

"She's an ornithologist, too?"

"Yeah, and if she'd get off her ass and file her dissertation she'd be a PhD." Then both of them would outrank me, but that thought didn't sting so much now.

"So you and Zephyr walk into this bar—"

"Mexican restaurant, and Frankie's there. Girl number two. She's Miss Perfect."

"We're not fans of Frankie?"

"We are fans," I said, realizing that truth. "She's just sort of suspect sometimes."

Erik nodded. He still seemed conscious, interested. "So three ornithologists walk into a Mexican bar, and . . . ?"

"And Zephyr asks, 'What is your kidnapping talent?'"

"That's a helluva conversation starter."

"Well, that's Zephyr." I left off the part about her granny being an old-school New Orleans medium and her mom being a first-class wacko, who regularly got psychic messages. Correct ones. "Zephyr had seen some movie, set in Morocco, with Candice Bergen and James Bond, and she—what?"

He was laughing. He'd rolled over laughing. "James Bond?"

"Oh," I said, getting it. "One of the guys who played James Bond. The old handsome one."

Erik sat up, smiling. The sight of that incisor made me feel weak. "Sean Connery?"

"Maybe, but I think Zephyr actually did say James Bond. Anyway, he kidnaps Bergen and decides not to hurt her because she can play chess."

"Not because he's playing the role of an honorable Berber chieftain who would never harm a woman, he's just trying to get the attention of President Roosevelt, played by . . . " Erik tapped his fingers on his chin. "I don't remember who played him."

"You've seen this movie?"

He shrugged.

"So you know what a kidnapping talent is?"

"I'm guessing it's the reason a kidnapper would treat you well and then let you go peacefully?"

My turn to shrug. "I guess so. Zephyr said hers is étouffée. Or maybe gumbo. She can cook like a champ, if you have a thousand ingredients and all day."

"Ah, Lady Impatience."

"It's true! Cooking Cajun takes a lot of time. And it's messy."

"It's like making love. It takes a lot of time. And it's messy."

He was sick. Neither of us had showered in days. Yet one glint from those dark, laughing eyes, and I was ready to throw down here and now. "Takes energy, too," I said, reminding us both.

"Yeah," he said, with a half-hearted chuckle. "There's that. So what were your kidnapping talents?"

"Well, I asked a friend of mine what the dangers were, the possibility of being kidnapped, and she told me I was too tall, too skinny and too . . . old . . . to be worried."

We sat in silence for a moment.

"Hey, beautiful," Erik whispered. "I'll tell you what your kidnapping talents are. No one looks better to wake up to; I've never had tastier couscous, but don't tell any Moroccan I said that; and if a kidnapper ever tasted those lips, he'd tether you to him. Forever."

Erik kissed me, a soft, closed mouth kiss. He slid down to his side, held out his arms and embraced me until the sun rose.

Along with his fever. *Again.*

"You have got to be kidding me," I muttered to his body as I walked back down to the well. He'd faked me out last night. He wasn't getting better.

More water, to wash him down. We had a little bit of food left, and then . . . then?

I counted the rocks until I was at the right spot, but I didn't see the half-covered hole that had promised water and salvation. What I saw was a rock, wedged into the hole.

Someone had sealed the well overnight.

Despite pushing, shoving, prodding, and lying down and applying all my leg strength and glute power to it, the rock didn't budge. No sign of who'd come and why they'd done this. No sign of anyone.

Whoever had done this would return. He had to return. My mouth felt dry already as I settled in the shade, leaning against a scrubby tree. I hoped I wasn't sitting in ants; in Texas it's a concern any time you contemplate the ground, standing *or* sitting. Just ants can be annoying, but fire ants can make you want to die. Too many, and they can kill you.

That was a good thing about Africa, no fire ants. Anophele mosquitoes might get you, but not fire ants.

I would berate myself for so many things—arrogance, stupidity, ignorance—but I just didn't have the energy. We needed water.

Water. How many times had I not thought about water? Even in the farthest reaches of the Hill Country, there was always some form of water. And when you live on the water, the lack of it doesn't occur. Maybe in a hurricane, but I'd gotten lucky on that front.

The hurricane season was still on, and I wondered how Frankie was dealing with the uncertainty every time a storm built up in the Gulf. Prepping the Dubya was a pain, though Zephyr had been through it and would share her experience, because that's the kind of girl she was.

She was a great assistant. An even better friend. *She was my friend.* How had I not seen that before? How had I not treated her that way?

The palm trees and swoosh of the ocean seemed so far away, but if I wanted to I could summon the sensation of the sea. That internal swaying you felt after a day of playing in the water, riding the swells.

Dust blew into my face, reminding me I might as well be on Mars for as close as I was to the ocean. My eyes felt dry, itchy. And Erik—I wrapped my arms around my legs. I'd left him resting again, between bouts of thrashing and dreaming that moved between English, French, and Arabic.

If he didn't recover . . . I put my head on my crossed arms. Great, add another piece of guilt to the pile. What did it matter? Then again, had any part of my life mattered?

"Not the time to get maudlin," I said aloud.

But why not? I'd avoided thinking, I avoided myself all the rest of the time. My eyes ached as I looked around, counting automatically. Three trees on that ridge, two below it.

Giselle's life mattered; she made it matter. She was doing something for the next generation. As well she should, considering she was contributing to it.

A baby.

Part of the life I could never have. I put my head down again. I waited.

Waiting was something at which I was extremely proficient.

I'd waited for Alan to propose to me, or at least propose that we go to the same school.

I'd waited for schools to offer me scholarships, waited so long that the sole option left to me was local. Good, but lacking the international pedigree that the Institute wanted.

I'd waited for the invitations—join this expedition, come on this wetlands trip as an intern—to . . . what? For them to grow wings? They had; they'd flown away. The invitations had expired. The inviters had invited others. Given up.

Even then, I didn't know why I'd waited.

Even *now* I didn't know why. What had I been waiting for?

Then the Dubya. I'd waited for the promotion. Waited through Mr. Woodrow's death, waited through the will, waited through the grant process.

Waited to fall in love, waited to start a family, waited for more money before inviting my folks to live on the beach, waited . . . waited.

I sat up. I was waiting my life away.

Waiting for Daddy to come. The hateful words whispered in my mind.

I remembered the clock over the table, at that apartment in Chicago, the minutes clicking by as I'd waited. I'd counted the ceiling tiles, then I'd counted the lines in the ceiling tiles. I counted the cracks in the floor. I counted the tufts on the couch, I'd counted—that's when I'd started counting.

It hadn't been birds, it had been Fischer. Waiting for Fischer.

It replayed in my mind. Creeping out of my bedroom, pausing at the door. Hitchhiking to Corpus, then taking bus after bus after bus to Chicago. Waiting at the station, then realizing I had Fischer's address.

How had I gotten inside? No recollection, except the click as the door opened.

Had I noticed the windows were closed? The fridge was empty? The closets were stripped of clothes, and—I shook my head. I might have noticed, I was an observant child, but I hadn't realized *why* everything was so bare. Well-mannered, I'd sat by the door, not intruding on the rooms. Wanting Fischer to be the one to show me what he'd talked about, the space he said he'd made for me.

There had been ninety-nine *x*- and *o*-shaped pieces on the front of the box.

Ninety-five *o*'s in the ingredient list. Sixty-two *i*'s.

A tinkling sounded, but in my mind? Or actually here? Then another, and a baa. Sheep! I watched the flock spill over the edge of the ridge and down to the well. No little Bo Peep led them, it was just a group of roaming goats, with a few token sheep. They nosed around the well, then climbed up the side by me, looking into the valley.

A thump jolted me, and a goat leapt back from the ledge. It turned as I saw a little boy shuffle up the hill. He had a rock in his hand, and as I watched, he chucked it toward another goat, then whistled so shrilly it sounded like a bomb dropping. The rock landed an inch from the goat.

This kid had a future in baseball. His accuracy was dazzling. At the sound of the whistle, all the animals froze, obviously trained. When the rock landed, the goat it landed next to hustled back to the flock. The boy was shepherd and sheepdog, rolled into one. He'd taken competency to a new level.

I got up, startling the goats and getting the boy's attention. "English?" I said, stepping toward him. "Speak English?"

He said something, but not in English. Of course not in English. The boy stared at me with huge, dark eyes, surrounded with the same ostrich eyelashes that Tawfiq had. "*L'eau*," I said, pointing to the well, trying to get the French pronunciation of water right.

His gazed fixed on my arms, the gashes there, just now scabbing over, the skin still angry and puckered. "*Docteur?*" I said, stepping toward him. "Uh . . . *téléboutique? Téléphone?*"

The boy handed me his waterskin and I took a sip while he levered his shepherd's staff under the rock and popped it open. He poured water for the sheep as I drank from the skin. Then he refilled it and gestured with his head. To follow him? He whistled and the goats jumped to attention, wandering after him. I swatted them away from eating my pants and followed, too.

I tried to pay attention to the details, but the sun was bright and it was one dusty, rocky ledge after another. Down, I could see that much.

We meandered across rocks and ridges.

Once the boy stopped, turned, and threw a rock in such a single fluid motion that I almost applauded. The goat was shocked back to the proper direction and the others hustled past it. How had that child seen what the goat was doing? Shadows on the ground? Or was he like a parent and just knew how the goat was going to behave, so he knew how and when to intervene?

My grandparents hadn't known me, hadn't known how to intervene. They'd thought I'd run away, not that I'd gone to Fischer's. They'd known he was on vacation, so no one thought to look for me there. My face still burned—what, thirty years later?—when I recalled the sheriff escorting me from the Corpus airport, across multiple county lines, back home. Everyone watching. Like I'd run away for attention, not because I had a destination in mind. The newspapers, the reporters, all of it so humiliating.

Fischer had been furious. Miranda hadn't come home with him. They'd broken up on their trip. I felt sure she would have understood me. He'd been embarrassed to be on television, to be painted as an absent-minded father, "on vacation for two weeks, unaware that his estranged daughter was slowly dying at his home." I wasn't dying. I was counting, waiting. But that's not what the Chicago press had said.

The story had trailed him, like rotten eggs, every time he sold a piece for a million, every time he was featured on TV or in a magazine. Had the story trailed him to his deathbed?

Twelve goats with black faces; three with white.

The goats seemed to use a leapfrog system of locomotion, each in his turn. Like pelicans flying, one goat would be the lead while the others drafted, then it would drop back, letting another move in place. It made sense for birds, so that when one was facing the wind, everyone else conserved energy and remained fresh.

But here? Did the goats share authority? Were there such things as alpha males in the goat world? Zephyr probably knew. It sounded like it could have astrological implications.

Where are you, my friend? I thought in desperation. *Have I ruined our friendship? I'm sorry.* I shook my head. *I've been so blind.*

Zephyr's voice was so clear, so crisp in my head, that I jumped. *Wilkerson sent me away. I'm not at the Dubya. I haven't been.*

I halted. Now I was hallucinating? Had Zephyr just talked to me?

The boy waited for me on the ridge. He pointed.

I followed his direction: rocks.

I looked at him, he pointed again. I looked again. Rocks. He'd brought me to a rock pile?

My arms were covered with goose bumps. I didn't believe it, but still, somehow—that had been Zephyr.

The rocks gained dimension and I realized I was staring at a village, all the same color and texture as the surrounding rocks. The village Erik had mentioned? A place I wouldn't have found in a thousand years, it blended so completely into the valley. The boy nodded at me, smiling. I nodded and smiled back. Then he took off down the hill, calling "*Maman!*" at the top of his lungs.

I realized then that the closest house, shockingly well-camouflaged, was just a few yards away. A woman appeared in the doorway and the boy spoke in a rush. She looked up at me and beckoned with a wide smile, revealing a few gold teeth and a few missing ones. Behind her other women appeared. Short but solid, and dressed in layers of robes and dresses. No veils, but their hair was covered, scarves tied into a knot at their foreheads. Something familiar about that . . . Berbers!

The woman took my arm and pulled me into the house.

I ducked before I hit my head on the doorframe, and then realized I could barely stand up inside, the roof was so low. The women chattered at me, pulling, guiding me into an open room where they seated me on a banquette, then left.

The narrow room was lined with seating on three sides, and the fourth wall supported a shelf system with a variety of items: jars and a broken clock, a magnum of perfume in a spritzer bottle, and a few knickknacks like I'd seen for sale in Marrakesh.

An older woman, hair covered, with dark eyes and brows, entered the room. She greeted me, patting her chest and saying her name.

"Elize," I said, patting my chest. "*Mon marie c'est malade.*" I'd pieced the words together from reviewing all the conversations I'd heard during the last few weeks. "*S'il vous plaît, docteur? Téléphone? Auto?*"

She bowed, and I bowed. She lifted the giant bottle of eau de cologne and spritzed me with it. Another woman brought in a dish of water, and gestured for me to wash my hands. All the while they talked and motioned me to stay seated.

I pointed to one of the women's hands, to what looked like a wedding ring. "*Mon mari,*" I said, and pointed out of the house. "*C'est malade,*" I said, trying to show a sick face.

They patted my shoulders, sat me down again, and left the room. Again.

This felt strangely familiar; I'd never been here before, but it reminded me of something.

Six women came in next. They sat a tray on the table before me, and poured tea. The sweet mint smell seemed to me almost paradise, it was so heady, promising. "Take," one of the women said. "Take, take." Hospitality, Erik had said, was the most striking trait of the Berbers.

What could I do? If I accepted the glass of tea then according to the custom, wasn't I here for three of them? Hadn't Zephyr said that? *Then* would they help me? Could I just sit here and sip tea while Erik roasted beneath the awning?

"Take, take," they said, everyone watching me, waiting for me to sit back.

I'd left him the water. I hadn't had any since I used the rest on him during the night. A little refreshment would help me, in the long run. I sat back with my tea and they smiled.

They introduced themselves one by one. I repeated their names— two Fatimas, an Irka, Sharia and Elen—and immediately forgot them. They talked amongst themselves and stared at me, watching me drink the tea. One of them moved to sit beside me, taking my left hand in hers. She turned it over and exclaimed at the faded henna on my palm.

How long had I been here? No one had a watch, or a clock, and I couldn't see my watch with her holding my hand. Then I noticed that they all had hennaed hands, and feet.

"*Mon mari*," I started again.

But two more women came into the room and greeted the row of seated women, shaking their hands, then kissing their hands and pressing them against their heart and head. It was very formal, moving from the oldest woman to the youngest, greeting them with a set statement, whose rhythm I heard, but with words I couldn't identify. I was introduced as "Eeengleesssh" and my hand shaken and kissed. The new women sat down beside the five others, gossiping between themselves and watching me from the opposite couch.

Watching me among them, just like I'd been watched a few days ago. When was that? The bald ibis. I almost clapped my hand over my mouth to keep from shouting the realization. These women were like the Waldrapp!

After a life of watching ibis, sitting on the beach with the Waldrapps had been mind blowing. First of all, they made the weirdest noises. Chugs and huffs and squawks, beyond what other ibises used. I'd had to fight to keep from laughing out loud. They'd been slower moving, more majestic than other ibises, the royalty of the Threskiornithidae world. But the most striking observation had been the elaborate greeting ritual they'd gone through with each other.

A full bow, each and every bird, to each and every bird. Greetings held the hierarchy in place, kept birds—probably most animals— from attacking each other in a search for supremacy. But those glorious birds, with their tall collars and red heads, had bowed with such grace and majesty. No sewing machine motion; more like ballroom dancing.

And to interrupt would be . . . antagonistic.

Rude. Just like it would be here. Three cups of tea, then. Remembering names, if that's what it took. This wasn't just hurried hellos, this was some sort of ritual that kept order and respect—and beauty—in place.

The oldest woman poured me more tea, and pushed a plate of cookies closer to me. I took one, slowly inhaling the sugar sweetness of it, tasting the grainy texture on my tongue as I bit into it, nuts cracking between my teeth.

More exclamations, more women arriving. The same rituals, the same kissing and hand shaking, and the newcomers sat beside the others, forming the bottom of the *u* shape. Eleven women, and me. They watched me like the Waldrapps had, as they'd approached my still form in the sand. I'd stayed motionless, my bins in my lap, as they walked past me, preening, sunning and constantly chattering, talking, honking.

I sat as still, as quiet, and listened.

The woman seated next me, Sharia, took my left hand again and held it up, and the newcomers all exclaimed, just as everyone else had done before.

"Marrakesh?" one of them asked.

I nodded, grateful to understand a single word.

"*Maman*," a male voice said in the hallway.

The women scurried to pull veils over their heads and faces, then they turned their backs. A young man, maybe twenty years old, entered the room. He looked at me, surprised, then shook my hand like a westerner. He fired off a question to his mother. I guessed that he was the little shepherd's brother. He looked down the hallway, nodded and left, and the women unveiled again.

A quick glance at my watch; Erik was into the cooling afternoon. He'd be okay. He was possibly the most competent person I'd met. But he was sick! He'd be okay. *Take a breath, Lady Impatience. Enjoy this experience. Build these relationships, that's why you failed at the Dubya. No time for people. People are how things happen.*

Somewhere in that, Erik's voice had changed into Frankie's and then into my own.

I sat back with my third cup of tea. Regardless of whose voices I heard, the sugar rush felt great. I ate another cookie, savoring the crumbling in my mouth, the way the cookie seemed to skate like oil on water over my taste buds. The flavors didn't fade away. The women talked amongst themselves, they tried to talk to me.

Just pretend you want to be here, that you are not trying to get away. Just be.

The Waldrapps had surrounded me. I wouldn't have believed it, even if I'd seen it. Birds didn't mingle with humans. We were predators; they flew away. But those crazy birds had treated me like a rock, showing off their multihued feathers, eyeballing me.

These women were beautiful, with kohl-ringed eyes and gold jewelry, the patterns and colors of their dresses clashing and still matching, like the tiles that decorated most of Morocco. The oldest had a bone structure like Raquel Welch, her skin smooth, only her hands and the slight slump to her form indicating her age. Her daughter, the shepherd's mother, looked more careworn, her face wider, without the aristocratic lines.

The next four women appeared to be her daughters, the shepherd's sisters. Their faces were either wide like the mother's, or elegant like the oldest woman's. Everyone had the same eyes. Pale brown irises, circled with black and fringed with ostrich lashes. The tawniness of a Veery thrush's wings, but luminous.

More cried greetings, more women. My return smile was genuine now, because the anthropomorphism I always hid was suddenly reversed. They were the birds, not the other way around. The Berber women looked at me, smiling as they ran the reception line. Again, the exclamations over my hand; again, the introductions of the same few names. Again, no one spoke English.

What did one call a cluster of Berber women? A bevy, like partridges? Or an ostentation, like peacocks? No; a bazaar, like guillemots.

One of the new women nestled next to the mother and they held hands. She was young, and obviously not genetically part of the family, for her face, her coloring, was much lighter, and she was frailer than the others. She wore lots of jewelry, heavy silver pieces like I'd seen in the Marrakesh souk. The henna on her hands and feet was elaborate, and darkly distinctive against her pale skin.

Male's voice again, and now everyone except the new girl, the mother, and the grandmother hid their faces. The long-lashed young man poked his head in again, and when I saw the new girl blush I figured it out: she was the newly wed wife, the daughter-in-law.

Whatever he said generated motion, and the leave-taking began. Like the bald ibis, they had a different agenda than I did.

"Does anyone speak English?" I asked, again and again, as the women kissed my hand and theirs, bidding me farewell until only the family remained. The grandmother took my hand in hers, and sat with me on the banquette. I blinked away my tears; the sugar rush was fading, and I'd done nothing to help Erik.

The grandmother tugged at my hand, and when she saw I was trying not to cry, she took me in her arms and stroked my hair, leaning me against her chest, speaking a language I didn't know, but whose tone was soothing. She smelled of spices and the cheap cologne and the pungent aroma of ghasoul soap. Her jewelry clinked as she smoothed her hands over my hair, the rhythm regular and gentle, feminine.

❖

When I woke up, a little girl was standing in front of me; her amber eyes had lashes so long they beat at her glasses with every blink. She wore a robe, but the scarf over her hair was half off. Gold glinted in her ears. "Hello," she said. "My family is honored to have your visit of us."

"You speak English!" I almost shouted, sitting up, as she shrank back. "Oh, my God. I need a doctor. My boyfriend is sick, in the mountains. We're out of water, out of food. Do you have a telephone? Is there a teleboutique?"

The grandmother spoke, and the little girl spoke to her. I turned to the grandmother, pleading in my expression. "Whatever it costs, it doesn't matter. He's very sick. Sweating, unconscious." I was aware I was speaking too fast for the child to translate me, but I saw the flicker of understanding in the grandmother's eyes. "Thank your family for their generosity, for letting me visit with them," I said to the child. "But I must go, to see about my boyfriend. Do you have a phone?"

The grandmother shouted and conversation flowed between the daughters and the mother and grandmother. They seemed to be arguing with each other, but I couldn't tell. The new bride wandered in, and spoke softly. The sisters shot glances at each other, but no one said anything.

"My brother will takes you," the little girl said.

"Where's a phone? A doctor?" I asked my little translator, but she was in the midst of the conversation, just as loud and forceful as the others. The sound of seven women talking drew the brother, who walked in, and shouted at them. They shouted back. He left.

Not the picture of masculine domestic domination I'd imagined.

"Please," I said to the little girl. "I don't want to cause problems, but my boyfriend needs a doctor. He needs help. Where is a telephone? Is there a truck in the village?"

But even as I spoke, I wondered who I would call? Roald at Ksar Massa? Tawfiq, who was Berber, but unreachable in his hut at the park? The embassy? Did I know, for sure, Erik's nationality? I thought his passport was blue, with the reassuring gold stamp of the United States, but was I positive?

The brother barked orders and fled the room, his bride hurrying after him. The grandmother drew herself up and nodded at me, a smile on her lips. She kissed my hand and I turned and looked at the little girl.

"Inshallah," the girl said, and led me to the door. The mother handed me a plastic bottle full of water, and a little parcel that felt heavy, like food. "My brother take you," the girl said.

"I need a doctor," I said, my voice was breaking again.

The grandmother nodded and reached up to caress my hair, the gesture stilling me. "Will come," she said and smiled. "Inshallah."

As God wills it. The shepherd boy appeared in the doorway, and received orders from his grandmother, mother, and brother before disappearing down the hallway. I chased after him, shouting *merci* a dozen times. Was he leading me to the doctor? To the teleboutique?

❖

No.

He led me back to the plateau where Erik sweated and shivered in the shade of the awning. The shepherd whistled his goats away from our belongings and said bye as he left.

"*Docteur?*" I called after him. "*Téléboutique?*"

"Couscous," he said, before disappearing over the ridge.

I lifted Erik's head and dribbled the cool water down his throat. "Must piss," he muttered, struggling to get up. I helped him up and as he groused about my presence, I concluded maybe he was doing better. He collapsed back on his sleeping bag and accepted some of the bread I offered him, without asking where it was from, or how I got it.

After he fell asleep, with food and water in him, I gathered the rest of our bottles and went back to the well. The rock was in place, but I'd brought a stick, not unlike the one the shepherd boy had. Using it as a lever, I pushed the stone aside and the well exhaled a fresh, cool breeze on my face. I filled our jugs and bottles. I glanced up, but I didn't watch the shapes in the sky. I felt too guilty.

At the camp, I straightened things up, feeling a semblance of my normal self. Sweeping the area, moving our stuff, keeping our water in the shade, monitoring Erik. The sun was low, but the exhaustion that had been overtaking me wasn't there. Caffeine and sugar, as Erik had said, made the world go round. I hiked into the hills, walking aimlessly, but keeping count of how many turnings I'd made.

When the area looked familiar, I realized I was returning to the scene of my crime. I climbed up, watching for the mate. The remnant of the body was there, nature methodically taking care of the carcass. Everything that could be eaten had been; all that remained were battered, dirt-covered feathers, and a torn-apart skeleton.

The scream alerted me, and I rolled away, in that split second choosing brambles and rocks over talons and beak. The bird dove at me again. I knew it didn't know I was responsible for its mate's death—that was anthropomorphism to its most romantic extent—but it sure felt personal. I dashed away, keeping low to the ground. Those original ornithologists were insane. Then again, they went bird watching with guns.

The mate wheeled up into the sky, and I took an unsteady breath. Glancing across the valley, I saw them in silhouette: ibis. I blinked. Only one kind of ibis this far from water. Arid, mountain-dwelling ibis. Bald ibis, who needed cliffs for roosting. Could it be? Was this their outpost? Had that "outlier pair" become a family?

Tawfiq had said so. Erik had brought me here because rumor said so. Could it be?

It really was.

They disappeared into the horizon line.

The raptor called its warning, and I jumped farther down the path and out of range, thrumming with excitement. Were they indeed Waldrapps? Wild ones or banded? I needed binoculars, I needed a camera. A map. A GPS. Dammit!

I almost tripped over the black leather leash. My bins, which had shattered on the rocky ground, lay tangled in undergrowth. I pulled them free, ignoring the rattling sound of thousands of dollars of shattered Swarovision optics. Once back in civilization, I could send them for repairs.

My foot slid once as I took the path back to Erik too quickly, reminding me how easily this could become a disaster. I slowed my steps, forcing myself to calm, breathing *one two three*, stepping with each breath, slowing each breath, slowing each step. *One. Two. Three.* I'd still get there, but without a broken ankle. Without proving my incompetence. Not incompetence; just a hint of hope. Excitement.

"How am I?" he asked when I stepped to his side. I touched his brow.

"Hmm . . . more the temperature of hell instead of the surface of the sun," I said.

He blinked at me. He'd grown so thin. I knelt and got him water, holding his head as he drank it, feeling the knobs of his spine in my hand. I tore off some bread and fed it to him, brushing his hair back from his face as he dozed off. "How are you?" he asked, his eyes closed, his voice rough.

"It wasn't an Eleonora's falcon," I said. "Wrong habitat. My brain must have been addled to make that mistake. My crime isn't less, but at least it wasn't a rare species. It was a lanner." I swallowed hard. "Yet, despite my transgression . . . I think I saw the Waldrapp. Just a few miles over."

He didn't say anything, and I took note that we needed more wood to keep him warm through the night. "A sign," he muttered. I stood up, and his eyes flickered open. "So it's worth it, then?"

I looked down on him, his bones creating a topography inside the sleeping bag, his indigo eyes sunken, his raven dark hair dulled and dry.

"I mean, this could make your career couldn't it? Like discovering oil, this bird out here."

Yes. If I did something about it. Wrote a paper. Documented the location. Took photographs. Got colleagues in here to verify. If I didn't wait.

"Worth it?" I said, dropping down beside him, staring at him, his expression dazed and hazy with pain. "Nothing in the world is worth seeing you like this," I said, choking on the truth of my words. "No career, no achievement." I shook my head, looking away. "No ibis."

He took my hand, burning my skin with his. "I'll be okay," he said, then twisted in pain.

It was then I noticed what I'd seen, but not registered. All his rings were gone. I realized he hadn't had them on when he'd rubbed cream on my arms. He hadn't had them on when he held me. His hands, which were now crabbed as the malaria attacked, had gotten so thin his rings had slipped off. Or he had taken them off.

He'd never looked more defenseless. I pressed my lips together and brushed at his hair, smoothed his brow and sort of, maybe a little, began to pray.

❖

It was like that for the next uncountable hours. Erik writhed in agony while I watched, my expression of helplessness translated to tension in my brow and temples. I made him as comfortable as I could, helped him walk because he said it eased the pain. I rubbed his back when he vomited water and bread. By dusk, he'd fallen back asleep. I trusted it was sleep. If it was a coma, I didn't want to know.

I would return to the village, beg them for assistance. Bribe them, steal, kidnap or take a hostage. Screw courtesy and ritual. We needed a doctor. More accurately, we needed medicine. I curled up by Erik's side. I'd sleep until moonrise, then go back down there and get help. No more waiting. This wasn't just about my life.

The Berbers

The bell woke me, almost like the wind chimes that the Gulf breeze stirred on my balcony, but without the salt air.

I opened my eyes. It was still dark, though the stars lent brilliance to the sky. There again, the noise of goats approaching. Three of them, hung with bells. I sat up, drawing my feet beneath me, feeling the grime on my face, my hands. I hadn't wasted water on washing. I pushed my hair away from my face and looked at Erik. He seemed to be resting and I didn't want to disturb him by checking his temperature.

The moon peeked over the horizon, just the edge of it, glowing orange.

As I stood, I heard joyous singing in the distance. Shouts, laughter. I ran to the ledge and looked into the valley.

Shapes moved across the hillside, up the rocky paths. As the moon rose I made out men and women, glinting with jewelry, loaded with . . . stuff. Someone looked up, saw me and shouted, "Eeengleeesh!"

I waved back as tearless sobs shook me.

The Berbers arrived at the site, and the grandmother hugged me after kissing my hand. There was shouting and laughing, and I was seated while they went to work. It had to be . . . midnight? I watched the men set up a tent and the women build a fire. The goats gamboled and the children played tag while the women put pots on the fire, and the men played instruments and sang. A men's chorus. Not polished, but beautiful.

Another group appeared on the horizon, and everyone greeted the leader with great deference. My little translator appeared at my elbow, eyes gleaming, glasses gone. "Marabout is come to heal yours husband. Show him!"

A witch doctor, but I didn't care. Erik had faith in the men in Marrakesh who sold herbs and potions. He'd said they had greater wisdom than a lot of Western doctors. I pointed and the man knelt beside Erik. He spoke, and Erik's eyes fluttered open.

What happened was a question and answer session in, presumably, Berber. Erik's voice was weak, but his responses were firm. Fluent. He spoke Berber. Who was this man that I loved?

"He needs the couscous," the girl said, and taking my hand, tugged me away.

Inside the tent, the women had shed their robes and were preparing salads to serve alongside the enormous pot of couscous they'd brought. The grandmother took my hand and gave me a mound of mint to shred. It was good to work, to cover my hands in the green leaves and smell the freshness, the healing of them. Outside the music was louder, the laughter rowdier, and I thought I heard Erik's voice, ragged but audible.

The women talked, firing a thousand questions at me, which the translator struggled to keep up with.

How long had we been married?

Did we have children?

How did my hair get so white—it was like moonlight.

Did I want my other hand hennaed?

Every answer I gave suggested a thousand more questions. Aware that most cultures, even my own Lutheran synod, seriously disapproved of unwed couples traveling together, I let them believe we were married.

No children.

I was born of German and Swedish family, that's why my hair was blonde.

I would love to have my other hand hennaed.

When dinner was ready, the women veiled themselves and took the food out to the men seated by the fire. They shooed me out to eat with them. As a Western woman I guess I had some quasi-male standing. I sat beside the marabout.

"Your boyfriend is be well," the medicine man said to me in English.

"He has malaria," I said. "Do you know anything about it?"

"I live for a while in equator Africa," he said. "Sweating sickness very common among there." He nodded. "But I come back to the argan, because there is no place else like it in the world." He pushed a bowl of something toward me. "Argan honey. Eat, is best in the world."

I had to agree about the honey. "Doesn't he need quinine or something?"

"I have gave chloroquine. Fever is passed now. Couscous, he needs." Erik sat enthroned between two of the older men. I noticed the twenty-year-old, a few boys, and five old men. No one between the ages of twenty-five and fifty. I couldn't recall a war that would account for the lack, especially since there seemed to be a lot of preteens around. Well, just a lot of children in general. The girls worked with the women in the tent, but they also played with the boys, outside, running around, hair flying free, pants beneath their robes.

What was it like for a little girl to go from being a tomboy to becoming a creature of the kitchen, confined in clothes and behavior, having known freedom?

Yet no one I met seemed to be chafing at her role.

Abruptly, the men stopped eating. The mother appeared and removed the platters, leaving tea behind. I watched as, from pockets and parcels, the men brought out their kif and lit up. Erik's eyes glittered at me, but he didn't offer a smile. Did the meds make him feel bad? Or had the doctor gotten him stoned? Anything, I reminded myself, to ease the pain. Better yet, if it healed him.

I slipped into the women's tent.

Inside, they were eating the leftovers. Hierarchically. They were so like birds!

Mother, then the daughter-in-law, then the sisters. By the time the food got to the little girls, they'd poured buttermilk on it. No individual dishes, the same spoon. The youngest girl got the most milk and the least couscous. I turned down an offer to eat more and regretted that I'd had so much when I'd sat with the men.

Had it been the same way at Abdullah's? What we hadn't eaten at lunch, his invisible wife got to eat? Was that why the men ate so quickly, then pushed away so suddenly? Were they watching, taking a cue from Abdullah?

The dinner done, the women cleared everything away and I found myself grabbed.

"Henna for your hands and feet?" my little translator asked me, wiping milk from her mouth.

I'd do anything for these people; I'd let them do anything to me. They were my bald ibis people, my saviors. I nodded and smiled, weak with relief, exhausted. They seated me on cushions and one woman took my feet, another took my hands. The translator, bringing her cup of milk, sat down beside me. Around the tent, the other women combed each other's hair, talked, played with the babies, or sewed. I stifled a yawn. These were hardy people. And they'd carried all this up the hill to our camp.

The girl working my feet laughed away my apologies for their condition. Gommage, the last terrific bath I'd had, had been a week ago. Remnants of black and white polish clung to my toenails.

There were reasons I had a weekly pedicure. *We should have all gotten them*, I thought. *Frankie and Zephyr and me. Together. That would have been fun for the three of us: Wilkerson's Angels.*

Realizing I wasn't wounded or angry anymore at Frankie Stein shocked me silent. *Be honest.* I hadn't wanted the job, I'd put her in the perfect position to get it. I'd set myself up and hadn't even admitted it.

Irina covered my toes down to the first knuckle with a thick reddish paste, then rubbed it on my soles and heels, painting it around the rim of my foot. She squeezed some paste into what looked like a cake decorating tip, and drew a pattern of triangles and dots all along the sides of my foot. Then she pulled up a low stone brazier, still warm from cooking, and hung my foot over it, an inch above the ashes. "To dry," my translator explained.

Within a half hour I was sitting with each foot hanging over a brazier, and each hand on the edge of one. *Hot hot hot.* A flicker in the back of my head suggested it was a bet amongst them: let's see just how far we can push the western girl before she balks.

I was the only one sitting, baking.

The henna had certainly warmed on my skin, but it didn't sting like the stuff in Marrakesh.

They hadn't painted me in the elaborate patterns the Berber girl in Marrakesh used. When I told them that the artist had said she was "Berber from the mountains," my translator explained that the other girl was Berber from the Atlas. My current hosts were Berber from the Anti-Atlas. The two Berbers didn't even speak the same language.

"The Berber from the Rif speak Zenatiya. The Atlas Berber speak Tameerzight. We are argan people. Berber from the Anti-Atlas, and we speak Chleuh. The Spanish settled close—"

"*Habla español?*" I said.

"*Si. Un poco.*"

"*Toda su familia habla español también?*"

"*Sí. Por qué?*"

I laughed. Laughed at my stupidity and my assumptions, laughed at my arrogance. All this time I thought I was trapped in a vise of muteness, and they spoke Spanish?

"Mother," I called to the woman who'd been such a great hostess. "You speak Spanish?"

"You speak Spanish! We thought you were American, that you would speak only English!"

Suddenly it was a jumble, everyone speaking, though not everyone speaking Spanish. "I didn't know Spanish was spoken in Morocco!" I said. "I thought it was all French!"

"The French and the Spanish divided Morocco among themselves," one of the Fatimas said. "The French had Fez and Casablanca, and the Spanish received Larache and Ceuta. You haven't been to Ceuta?"

I shook my head. "So you speak Arabic and Berber and Spanish and French?"

"No," one of them said, looking shocked, "we don't speak Arabic. We are Berber."

I blundered on, confused, my Spanish fracturing. "Isn't Arabic the national language?"

"There are more Berber than Arab in Morocco. The Arab came in six hundred seventy, but the Berber, we are here from the time of God." She shrugged. "But we are not like Arab, not like French. We use land for all, not for one house here and no one can walk, one house there and no one can walk. For all to share."

I was embarrassed. Embarrassed because I'd assumed these women, these people, were ignorant. Never mind that they spoke more languages than I did. And I'd thought they were poor, badly spoken, scratching out a living because they had no choice.

They had community, pride, history. They were the Waldrapps.

"We are Argan Berber. Here from the time of God. My mother and her mother and her mother, all we work in the same fields. From the time of God."

"Where are your men? Your husbands?"

They were all answering now, beautifully spoken. I could see the intelligence gleaming in their eyes. "They go. To cities. To Spain. To France. To work."

"Eight-five percent unemployment," I recalled.

"Yes. Is very bad."

"My husband gone for eight months," one woman said, holding a baby in her arms.

"So you do all the work?" I asked. "The fields, the shepherding, the . . . I don't know what else you do with goats." They laughed.

"You are newly married," they said. "Your husband, he is so handsome! You must have been worried when he was so sick! What a good wife to walk to find help!"

Why hadn't I tried speaking in Spanish? The self-crucifying thought flashed across my mind, but I ignored it. I'd tried Spanish in the north and gotten nowhere. Now that I knew how the protectorates had been split, I saw why it didn't work. But I'd thought it was hopeless here, too. I'd made a mistake. It wasn't incompetency.

"How long have you been married?" I asked the newlywed girl. She blushed.

"Still on her honeymoon," my translator said, feeling a little left out now that she wasn't so useful. "One week."

"See! We all have wedding henna!" they said, showing me the patterns on feet and hands.

"That's so beautiful!"

"You have our everyday henna because Ikka, she is the artist who did all this, she is in bed."

"I'm sorry. Sick?"

"No, no, with baby about to come. Good luck for a pregnant woman to bless a new bride with henna."

I bit back my relief: glad she wasn't my artist. I didn't think I'd want that kind of blessing.

They'd all switched to Spanish, and now I understood a thousand little comments and questions. "You are all related?" I asked, and learned the way I'd pieced together the family had been correct. The other women, about twenty of them, were all either cousins, or daughters-in-law, from neighboring villages. All argan Berbers.

They knew these hills. They'd know if the bald ibis was here. I wanted to know, but I also didn't. Without confirmation, I would dream and stay in this place where I had a hundred cousins and aunts and sisters and mothers. A bazaar of Berbers. I'd never been around so many women before. Mama hadn't been much for socializing outside church, and her family had been spread through the U.S. Pop had had two brothers, no sisters.

Fischer was—*had been*, I corrected myself—an only child. My mother was still an unknown, and always would be, now.

"You look sad. Does the fire hurt?" Sharia asked.

"You're lucky," I said. "To have your family."

She looked around. Did she see the faces that resembled hers? Did she know all their stories so well that it drove her crazy with mundanity? Did she have memories she could use to make someone cry, or know how to make someone laugh until she begged for mercy? "Berber women are strong," she said. "We have each other, which makes us strong."

But the way she said it in Spanish, didn't translate into English exactly. The picture her words drew brought to mind the argan tree, with the trunk being the women, and each generation drawing on the strength of that trunk to grow. "He is not your husband, is he?"

I glanced at her. She was younger than me—hell, they all were, except the mother and grandmother—but she had several children and a knowing look. I shook my head. "It's not the way of, uh, my people."

"You don't marry?"

"Not easily. Not young." Not very successfully either, but I kept that to myself.

"He is your beau?" The French word amidst the Spanish was charming.

"My beau, yes."

"Would you like to Berber marry him?"

A Berber wedding? On this moonlit night, in this singing, generous, Spanish-speaking family? "Yes." I shocked myself.

"We will make a Berber wedding! My sister, she has her jewelry, her dress. You can make like a Berber wedding! And take a picture!"

Her excitement stirred everyone up, and the language reverted to Berber, with moments of Spanish to inform me what I was to do, which was to finish baking my henna. I asked how much longer and was told I had to sit still for two more hours.

Enough time to "make" a Berber wedding.

They all walked with me down to a lower plateau where camp had been relocated, including our gear, the couscous, and Erik.

I needed their help, because if I looked down to see where I was stepping, the coin-hung bridal headdress they'd brought from the village would slip. Flanked by Sharia and Irini, I walked down the hill in the communal brocade gown that the brides before me had worn, that those girls now playing would wear.

It smelled of ghasoul, cologne, and wedding nerves.

It had been a week since I'd bathed, and I hated to think what I was contributing to it, even though I was wearing it over my cleanest, but still not clean, clothes.

They hadn't judged or even commented as they'd unbraided my filthy hair—sweat, dirt, blood, who knows—and combed argan oil through it until shimmering waves fell over my shoulders. Hair which they immediately covered with scarves.

We turned, jingling like a volley of goats, and my eyes pricked with tears as I heard the men, grandfathers, boys, the marabout and even Erik, singing from below.

My life seemed unreal right now. Had I dreamed of getting married as a girl? I'm sure I did. Had I surrendered those thoughts as a woman? Probably not entirely, but I'd not dreamed of a dress or an event or even, really, a man.

But when the Berbers had slipped this dress over my head, and presented the museum-quality headdress they sat on the "Berber knot" of my scarf-tied head, I'd become speechless. All I could do was feel: the brocade, the heavy bracelets, the coins across my forehead draping down by my ears to my collarbone, the links and beads of the necklace that covered my throat and my chest.

I knew it wasn't a real wedding, just some kind of dress-up, with me and Erik as the dolls. But even knowing that, the grace, acceptance and charm of these women seemed true. They'd kissed me, blessed me.

Moving with them, advancing toward my groom inside this silver light, I couldn't think of an avian parallel. Maybe I hadn't seen enough birds to recognize this practice, maybe I was putting too much meaning on a dress and some jewelry. *Or maybe*, a voice in my head said with a snicker, *only humans embrace each other this way.*

I saw Erik seated on the plateau. He wasn't wearing jewelry, but his tunic shone white. I guessed he was in communal groom attire. His bones looked prominent, though his skin color had improved. He raised his glance to me.

For the first time, I intuited what he felt, for I knew what I looked like. I'd seen the image I presented in the mirror the women had brought.

Stunning. Shocking. Exotic.

The women paused, stepping away from me, allowing me the moment. I straightened my back to show off the headdress, the necklace, and all the woven glitter throughout my dress. With my suntanned skin and pale blue eyes, I looked beautiful, in a National Geographic sort of way. I felt beautiful.

All of this I saw reflected in his expression. But other emotions, too, feelings I'm not sure I'd ever seen before, or recognized on someone's face when they looked at me: Pride. Awe. Wonder. Gratitude. He just stared.

Then, with effort and assistance from the marabout, Erik rose to his feet. All around me the women ululated, and we stepped down the hill to the males' welcoming cheers.

The Berbers joined our hands and spoke. We fed each other argan honey, and they spoke. The singing started again.

Erik sank into his chair, and they brought me the second one. I sat next to him, my peripheral vision filled with coins, only my eyes mobile. The weight, the weave of everything I wore felt good. Right.

He squeezed my hand.

"It's not," I whispered, "legally binding, is it?"

"No. Not real."

My heart sank. Not that I wanted to just fall into marriage, but so much of my life had been pretend. A game. For show.

"But, Elize," he said, moving into my sight, touching my chin with his fingers. "It is—we are—true. Maybe not real, but we are true." His dark gaze held me, refusing to look away, forcing me to see the truth in his eyes. *True.* Deep within I felt some internal gash, a split I'd never realized existed, close up. Seal.

Heal.

"You are amazing," he said. Then he grinned and I saw his chipped incisor. "Wife."

When he kissed me, the Berbers cheered.

Then I was standing by his side, facing the red light of the camera through the coins in my headdress, arching my back to balance the wealth of the dowry laying on my chest, and surrounded by the scent of Erik, of henna, of goats and body odor and the dusty aroma of dawn in the argan mountains.

Erik kissed the back of my hand and the camera shot us, in the time-honored pose of daguerreotypes.

My wedding portrait.

The Dawn

We woke about afternoon o'clock. I'd given away my watch, along with all the stuff I'd bought in the souk, the earrings and scarves. But the prize had been my Nike watch, given to the grandmother. It was the one non-Moroccan thing I carried. I glanced at the coin-hung bangle I'd been given in exchange.

They had sung as they'd taken our picture. Erik's voice had been rusty, but rising into the mountain air under the setting moon, it had been perfect. A perfect wedding. And someone was going to e-mail us the pictures.

Erik looked like a live human instead of an animated skeleton. They'd left us tons of food. He had given away his pocket knife, cards, rings, and CK cologne.

"And I thought you smelled that way naturally," I said, curling into his side after we'd cleaned up our campsite and gotten dressed. Slowly.

"Just a guy. Stink like anyone else," he said. He glanced at me from the corner of his eye. "It was my secret weapon."

I lay on the ground, watching the sky. They wheeled in it, the raptors, eyes on the ground looking for movement. "Miss your rings?"

He sighed. "It was quite a collection."

"What were they?" I turned to look at him. "I know they couldn't have just been jewelry."

"A ring a month, for each month I'd been clean."

I blinked, letting my assumption rise, then fade, understanding him. "Clean of your company, I'm thinking."

He kissed the back of my hand. "You got it." We settled back, watching the raptors who watched us. I tried not to feel guilty.

"When will you be ready to walk out of here?" he said.

"When will you be?" I countered. "I'm not the one who's been down with malaria for five days."

"Sheesh. Five days. I'm so sorry, Elize. I had no idea. Those liars."

"Are you gonna sue?"

"You took good care of me!"

I chuckled. "Funny. Sue them. The ones who put you in position to get sick. The ones who lied about what kind of sick you are."

"I should, but . . . " he shrugged. "I'd have to go back to that world in order to do it. It might not be worth the taint."

"So you'll never know when an attack is going to hit?"

"I'll do what half of Africa does. Take quinine. Gin and tonics might save my life."

"Could be worse."

"Did you ask about your ibis?" I shook my head. "Not exactly."

"I thought once you knew you had a common language, you'd be all over those people for information. Isn't that what hotshot field researchers do?" His tone teased me, yet it was what I thought I'd wanted for so long, to be a field researcher.

"I know it's the bald ibis."

"I thought you broke your bins?"

"I did, but I've watched ibis all my life. It's the wrong environment for any other known ibis, but right for the bald."

He propped himself up on an elbow. "So what are you waiting for?"

I smiled. "A . . . sign."

"So you believe now?"

"Well, I don't disbelieve." I ran my hand over my forearm, where two applications of argan oil had mostly healed the skin, like some juiced-up Neosporin. Had it been less to do with the oil and more to do with how much I'd trusted the marabout, who'd said it would close up? "What did you mean about the magnification of money?" I asked.

"People think money solves problems, but it doesn't. It magnifies them."

"Still, it would be nice to have," I said. How many millions had Fischer wasted, money that could have been applied toward buying land through the Nature Conservancy, or buying politicians to vote green?

"Well," he said, "in these past few days, how would money have helped?"

"I would have been able to . . . " I trailed off. "Once I got to the village, I would have been able to buy our way free. To a hospital."

Erik chuckled. "Throw money at the problem."

"Of course," I admitted, "I would have missed out on everything." I thought for a minute. "I would have been able to sidestep personal interaction in favor of progress." People as props. Tools. Devices. Fischer's attitude. I felt sick. "How'd you learn so much?" I asked Erik, my voice soft.

"I had a lot of money. But it didn't make me happier, or more balanced, or less fearful, or kinder, or more disciplined. It just made me more efficient at getting my own way and avoiding my true self in the process."

"Money would be helpful right now!" I said.

"Why?" Erik asked, turning to look at me.

"Get a taxi up here, get us back to civilization—"

"A ride will come," he said.

I sat up and mimed watching a busy intersection. "Nope, don't see it."

"You make it true," he said.

"What's that mean?"

"You make it true with your thoughts."

"There's truth, and there's my thoughts. Sometimes they coexist."

"Remember the woman at the Place? Our bet? That woman?"

"Balancing the parcel? Yes."

"Did you expect her to fail?"

"Of course. What she was doing was almost impossible. That load on her head was bigger than she was. The square was too crowded, the movements of other people too unpredictable. No question. Though," I said, trying to listen, to live in my new skin, "'failure' might be an extreme term."

"And if I told you that I've seen her cross the Place, probably five hundred times, and never touch the parcel, would you believe me?"

"Have you?"

"Would you?"

I stared at the sky. I couldn't answer. "What's your point?"

"Your belief that she would fail made it happen."

"That is ridiculous!" I sat up. "My thoughts can't reach out and . . . touch someone." But Zephyr had spoken to me, across time and space. I didn't believe it . . . but it had happened. Still, not the same thing.

"You don't believe in prayer, that we can move the hands of God just by wanting? Wishing? Believing?"

I'd wanted, wished for Fischer to come home, to show me the room he'd made for me, the space in his life for a daughter. Had I believed it?

No.

"Just believing makes it so?"

"Active believing," Erik said.

In the distance we heard a motor.

"A taxi in the desert?" Erik said.

I ran to the ledge and looked down. A Land Rover, covered in bike tour ads, was working its way up the hill. The driver saw me, paused, and poked his head out of the truck. "*Bonjour,*" he shouted up.

"*Bonjour.*"

He shouted a lot of French, but around the word *Americaine*. I shouted, "*Oui!*" and ran back to Erik.

"This is why you packed up. You knew."

Erik shrugged. "I said a ride. I didn't say when, exactly."

"Wish he would have brought a GPS," I said.
"He did."

As we headed back to civilization, the dark shapes of the single bald ibis family moved across the sky. Borrowed bins confirmed they weren't banded. My heart pounded with the discovery. I held the GPS in my hand.

Orthnithology was all about numbers. Now I had their coordinates.

The Parting

We were safely buckled in, fingers interlaced as the Atlantic fell away beneath us. The green Souss-Massa spread out below us as we headed north, above the migrating birds going south. In hours we'd be in Paris.

It was the best choice. Erik needed to get to Chicago, see a real doctor, not a petrodollars yes man, and check in with his business partners and family. Parents and two sisters; weird to see him in that way.

I had a standby ticket to Dallas. Zephyr hadn't answered me at all—I knew I thought I'd heard from her spirit-self, saying she wasn't at the Dubya, but that couldn't be right. Where else would she be? *Unless they'd evacuated for a hurricane.* I dismissed the thought; hurricanes threatened, but they didn't deliver. Not on Port Rockton.

Erik had showed me how to shop for tickets online, and now we found ourselves flying toward the City of Lights.

Our last weekend together. No plans beyond that, which for the moment was okay.

Erik rested, his eyes closed. His skin still looked sallow, but better than the past week. His bare hands still made me sad. All those months of counting, gone. He glanced at me, then crooked a brow.

"You look strange with clothes on." My cheeks reddened as he chuckled. "I mean, adult clothes are a different plumage for you."

"It's not like I've been in short pants or a pinafore."

"How many stashes do you have?" When we'd arrived from the anti-Atlas back in Agadir, we'd gone straight to the souk. We cleaned up in the *hammam*, the community bathhouse—gommage again—and I'd bought a dress. Erik had removed a whole new suitcase, with clean, fresh, professional clothes, from a locker. Now he wore a collared shirt, dark jeans, boots, and a small silver earring. He was still scruffy, but no longer the beat-up backpacker I'd met in Marrakesh. "It's like you're a spy. A wine spy."

He shook his head with a smile, then looked out the window. "Should be passing over Larache soon."

I hadn't e-mailed Sam. As far as anyone knew, I *had* been kidnapped. I'd have to remedy that soon, but not in Paris. Paris was for us. Erik's fingers tightened, as though he heard my thoughts.

"Why didn't you just go to Larache in the first place?" he asked. "Karmically, I know you had to meet me and didn't deign to attend the wedding in Tangier—" Again, teasing. "—but you were hundreds of miles away in the wrong direction."

An idiot? Incompetent? I heard the whirring in my head. I'd trusted this man with my past. We'd shared a near-death experience and gotten married. Sort of. Still, I wondered how silly he'd think I was. Had been. *No. Just say it.* "In Tangier. In the souk. I was grabbed."

He snapped alert. "Grabbed?"

"It was nothing, I'm sure. But he, well—when we first met I thought it had been you—he pulled me into an alley."

His eyes had gone very dark, he bristled. "And?"

I looked over his shoulder, out at the sky, the water, all shades of indigo bunting-blue with a mist of clouds. "That was it. That's the whole story. I was tired, I had missed all my connections. I'm sure I made too much—"

Erik put his finger to my lips, shushing me. He had an edge I'd not seen before, but it suddenly seemed reasonable that he'd traveled the wilds of Morocco in complete safety. Gone was Zen. In its place was a focus I hadn't seen. "Listen to me," he said. "Someone laid hands on you, tried to remove you, physically, from a street in a foreign country. You not only eluded him, you didn't use it as an excuse, however legitimate, to give up on your dream. Not many people, men or women, would be okay after that. Some of them, not ever."

My eyes had filled with tears, but I couldn't look away.

"You're brave, Elize. Strong. Capable."

My tears reached his finger and he brushed them away. "You said he looked like me?"

"Except the rings. He didn't have any."

He shook his head. "You must have been terrified when I arrived in your berth, drunk."

"I didn't know that detail, but yes, I was."

He kissed me softly. "No wonder you were so cautious in the Place."

"That was just me being me, since I was still trying to figure you out."

"And you thought I dealt kif."

"Well, yes."

"That I was stupid, too," he said, teasing.

"'Raisin dealer' wasn't an occupation I'd heard of!"

He leaned back again, tension cut from his body. "We almost didn't meet." He looked at me. "I would have missed you."

"According to you, this is all karma." We moved over the Atlantic, beyond Morocco, and left Africa behind. My heart felt a tearing, and Crazy-Elize whispered that we'd be back.

Erik kissed my hand.

"I don't believe," I said. "In any of it."

"You don't have to."

As he spoke, I wondered why I refused to even contemplate it. *Live once and then you're before the Lord,* I heard some long-dead Lutheran Sunday school teacher say. "Then tell me, what past life? Who were we?"

He turned to me, taking measure with eyes that looked blue again. "We weren't anybody special. Not famous, or history-making, not politicians or celebrities."

"Not Cleopatra and Caesar, then?"

"Can you imagine the karmic consequences they have to face? The lessons to learn? No."

"So we were just folks?"

"Folks who loved each other."

Blood pounded in my forehead.

"You were the better of us," he said. "You loved me well."

Erik kissed my hand again. "In this life, I want to love you well."

Flip responses lined up in my head, some comment to break up this intensity. But the intensity didn't scare me anymore. He wasn't demanding what I couldn't or wouldn't give. He wasn't holding to some impossible standard. This wasn't black or white. Nothing but a gift.

Not like the white ibis, working, working, working, but like the Waldrapp, open and easy and accepting of good things. Deserving of them. Just receive the gift. No effort; allowance. Which was way harder, in some ways. "Thank you."

"I love you, Elize."

I couldn't use those words I'd devalued ever again. Not with Erik. I could say new ones, though. "*Je t'aime.*"

If it hadn't been a whole weekend of saying farewell, maybe it would have looked less like a montage from an in-flight movie. As it was, we held hands, kissed in the autumn rain and played tourist.

Eiffel Tower. Seine cruise. Luxembourg Gardens. The Louvre.

Every day was gray. Our *pension* was on the top floor of a Marais townhouse. We spent our euros on very good wine and standard bistro food, and one trip to the Agent Provocateur lingerie shop . . . after which we missed the ballet.

Most of migration season was past; I hadn't seen any nonresident birds in the occasional bursts of sunshine. But we had seen a lot of common pigeons, whose neck marks looked like the scarves both French men and women wore. A loft of pigeons.

Now, on Monday, the rain was intermittent. My trench coat had come in handy, but I felt the wind changing, cutting through the plain cotton. Fall was upon us. Was this what it felt like to migrating birds? Cues that it was time to go?

The trundling of our luggage sounded in symphony.

Erik glanced at his new watch. "*Voyons, à Roissy.* I'm afraid it's time for the airport."

I didn't want to go. I took a deep breath and looked around me, absorbing these last few minutes of Paris. He hailed a taxi, which stopped too soon. The cafés gleamed with warm light, beckoning. Maybe one more coffee? I looked across the street and froze.

"French for English Speakers," proclaimed the sign. I'd seen it, I'd read it when we'd passed by before. But seated on top of it, preening, was a flamboyantly-colored, far out of season, European Roller. I'd been prepared to see it in Larache, and now I couldn't look away.

"Your bag?" Erik said. The trunk of the taxi was open, the doors waited for me, the cab was ready.

I looked at the roller. "He's African," I said.

"He's probably second generation Parisian, though," Erik said. "*Pied-Noir.*"

I glanced at the taxi driver, then at Erik, then at the bird. "Not the cabbie. Him." I pointed to the roller, who thoughtfully ruffled his turquoise feathers for maximum effect in the gray day. His flight feathers were Moroccan blue, his back ochre. He was stunning as he hopped around on the sign.

What was he doing in Europe? In October?

My glance fell to the sign.

Sign. An African bird on a sign in Paris, advertising French for English speakers, minutes before I had to leave. Sign.

You asked for it, Crazy-Elize said . . .

A sudden rush of adrenaline. I turned to Erik and kissed him hard on the mouth. "E-mail me," I said, "Or better yet, I'll get a phone. Let me know what your doctor says."

Erik glanced at the bird, then back to me, the expression in his blue eyes confused. Then he looked back to the sign and read it. "You're staying." It was a statement.

"I'm staying." I didn't know what this meant for us. I didn't know if there *was* an us beyond this moment, but it was right that I stay. Like a floodlight on irrigation channels, the pathway was revealed. "Giselle needs someone at Souss-Massa. So I need to know French. Roald told me I could stay on the ksar's property. The mountain Waldrapps will need careful observation, and I can stay with the Berbers." I grinned. "Those are all invitations, and they are real. But I need French."

"*Oui, chérie*, you do." He reached in his pocket, pulled out a card, and handed it to me.

A business card with numbers written on the back, a local exchange for Paris. I flipped it over again and looked at the name. "You're kidding me."

"That was the first sign," he said, smiling rather triumphantly.

"Your last name actually is Raven?" Of course it was, I'd seen it on his passport. It had just seemed so . . . unlikely. Obvious. Hallucinatory, like most of our time in the mountains. My gaze fell on the talon marks that were nothing more than white lines on my brown skin. Some parts seemed more real than others. *A storytelling of ravens.*

"Erik Raven," he said. "Who better for me than an ornithologist?"

I stared at the card, the letters in black on white paper. "Please to meet you," I said, extending my hand formally, "I'm Elize Zeinrockensteinhaufstadt."

Erik blinked at me, but didn't move. "Say that again?"

I repeated my incomprehensible last name, with its tricky silent syllable so it didn't sound like it looked; a name that usually garnered comments like, "How did that get through Ellis Island?" A name that Fischer had, understandably, dropped in his quest to be the next Andy Warhol. I waited for Erik's response.

"That little girl," he said.

My heart stopped.

"The little girl who waited for her father. Who ate cat food to stay alive. That was you?"

My face was on fire, my head so tight I could have bowled with it. The Meow Mix box had sixty-two *o*'s in the ingredient list, forty-three *i*'s, and as I'd eaten each *o* and *x*, I'd counted them, again and again, dividing them in case Fischer didn't come home immediately, if it took another day . . . "You were in Chicago then?" I asked.

"Raised there."

My words poured out, but they weren't ashamed protestations anymore. "I thought he'd invited me," I said. "I'd come at his invitation." I didn't feel the shattering sense of humiliation that had always come with every recounting, every time he was interviewed: "*I did not invite her. She's needy. She just showed up.*"

The thing had happened; I'd survived. Part of my past. My history. Over. Done.

As of weeks ago, also buried.

Erik smiled, his wicked incisor revealed, the time-stopping expression in his eyes swirling us up into the clouds. "Another sign," he said. "I paid attention to that story, it might have been the first time I'd ever watched TV news, because that little girl was my same age. But they called you Elizabeth."

I shrugged. "After that, I couldn't stand to be called Elizabeth. The press. It was everywhere."

"So your Dad is . . . ?"

I nodded.

"He just died, didn't he? All those stars went to his funeral?"

I nodded again. "My Pop is deceased, two years ago. My grandmother, Mama, decided to go on a cruise before the publicity began. She didn't need reporters camped on the front lawn, with all their questions: 'Was it suicide?' 'Was it an overdose?'"

"You came to Morocco to escape the paparazzi?"

My glance rested on the roller. "I thought to escape a lot of things, but I realize now that I was searching." I just hadn't known for what.

Erik's navy gaze was steady.

"It sounds corny, unbelievable, but I was looking for . . . me." I squeezed his hand. "I'm ragged in places, but present. Alive. Excited." I glanced down, then back to his face. "Thanks for being on the voyage of discovery."

"It's just beginning," he said and leaned forward to kiss me. His soft lips and the scent of him surrounded me. I didn't want to let go. "We're only beginning. And it's a long journey."

My forehead felt tight, but then the tension eased away. I had to ask, I had to respond. I couldn't wait any more; I had to speak. "Might take years," I whispered against his cheek.

He held me tighter. "I'm counting on the rest of my life."

I still felt his kiss, even as he drove away.

The roller took flight too, coming toward me, reminding me to look both ways as I crossed the street toward the Sign, my henna-stained hands tight on my bags.

Through African eyes, the bird watched the ornithologist. Without a glance she passed the newspaper stand, headlines screaming in a dozen languages:

U.S. GULF COAST LAID WASTE

Port Rockton, TX—This sleepy fishing village on one of Texas's barrier islands has been flayed, flattened, and cut off by late-season Hurricane Gamma, the thirtieth named storm in this history-making hurricane season.

Many are feared dead.

A Glossary of Poetic Plurals

sedge/siege of bitterns

chain of bobolinks

wake of buzzards

brood of chickens

flock/peep of chickens

brood/chattering/clutch of chicks

chattering of choughs

bury of conies

cover of coots

gulp of cormorants

sedge/siege of cranes

murder of crows

herd of curlews

**bevy/cote/dole/dule/piteousness/
pitying** of doves

brace/raft/paddling/flush of ducks

aerie of eagles

stand of flamingos

gaggle of geese

skein of geese (in flight)

wedge of geese (flying in a "V")

charm of goldfinches

skein of goslings

covey of grouse

bazaar of guillemots

colony of gulls

aerie/cast/kettle of hawks

brood of hens

hedge/sedge/siege of herons

charm of hummingbirds

scold of jays

deceit of lapwings

ascension/exaltation of larks

tidings of magpies

sord of mallards

watch of nightingales

parliament of owls

pandemonium of parrots

covey of partridges

ostentation of peacocks

colony/parcel/rookery/huddle/ crèche of penguins

covey/nide/nye of pheasants (on the ground)

bouquet of pheasants (when flushed)

flight of pigeons

congregation of plovers

covey of ptarmigans

bevy/covey of quail

conspirancy/storytelling/ unkindness of ravens

building/clamor/parliament of rooks

wisp of snipes

host of sparrows

murmuration of starlings

a fifth of starlings

muster of storks

flight of swallows

lamentation of swans

wedge of swans (flying in a "V")

flock of swifts

spring of teals

rafter of turkeys

brood of turkeys (immature)

pitying of turtledoves

committee of vultures

plump of waterfowl

raft of wigeons

chime of wrens

fall of woodcocks

descent of woodpeckers